THEN SHE FELT HIS STRONG, FIRM HAND

I really am desperate, she thought, trying to open her eyes. *Two wild dreams in two nights. What a total loser.*

But she couldn't open her eyes. She kept trying, struggling to see if Sariel was really there, but her muscles wouldn't work, her lids heavy. A dream. Another flipping dream. It was so nice, though, feeling him next to her, touching her, and she stopped caring if this was a dream or not. He leaned over and kissed her forehead, her eyebrow, her nose, her cheek, her chin. She moved her face to where she thought his lips would be, and he kissed her softly, his mouth on hers. First it was lips, soft and dry, and then tongues, slow, smooth. She breathed in, pressed harder, wanting more.

Oh, she started to think.

"Be quiet," he said. "Stop thinking. Quiet."

His dark hair was thick and smooth against her face. She wanted to reach down and touch him, everywhere, but she was trapped by his arms, his body, this blanket, her eyes stuck shut.

"There's time for that," he said. "Be patient."

But you're not acting patient, she said, pressing into him, listening to his quick breaths. *You couldn't even wait one night?*

"You're magic," he said.

Also by Jessica Inclán

REASON TO BELIEVE

BELIEVE IN ME

Published by Zebra Books

When You Believe

JESSICA INCLÁN

ZEBRA BOOKS
KENSINGTON PUBLISHING CORP.
www.kensingtonbooks.com

ZEBRA BOOKS are published by

Kensington Publishing Corp.
850 Third Avenue
New York, NY 10022

ISBN-13: 978-0-8217-8081-7
ISBN-10: 0-8217-8081-6

First Zebra Trade Paperback Printing: June 2006
First Zebra Mass Market Paperback Printing: August 2007

10 9 8 7 6 5 4 3 2 1

Printed in the United States of America

PROLOGUE

She beckoned him forward, and he followed her command, feeling it like a slick silk rope around his neck, a comfortable, accustomed noose that he had worn for two years. Her call was warm, dark like brandy, sweet and addictive. He could never disobey her; he knew that in his blood and bones and mind.

As if in a dream, he was putting together his belongings, things he needed. He needed them all, didn't he? He wouldn't come back here, to this house he'd built on the hill overlooking the ocean. With her, he would change the world and make it better, cleaner, more whole, more purposeful.

That's right, *she thought, her robe spinning around her as she put it on, her hair a dark drape behind her shoulders. Her eyes glinted like wet obsidian, her lips like blood.*

Hurry, he's waiting for us, *she thought.*

He nodded, the silk cord yanking him back to his task.

Use magic to pack, *she thought.* Quain is waiting.

The noose yanked tighter, but he flinched, hearing that name. Quain. The thought of the man scratched against his mind. Not Quain. No.

Yes, *she thought.* Let's not go through this again, shall we?

The noose tightened, his breath harsh in his throat.

What he wanted to do now was to stop packing, to pull the woman to him and kiss her into quiet. All he wanted was to be with her, here, in this house, without the name of the other man, without Quain, in either of their thoughts.

He's the only one who matters, you fool. I thought you understood that by now. I thought I didn't have anything left to teach you.

She pulled back with her hand, and he jerked and then began to fall forward. Before he hit the ground, she stopped him up short, and then wound the cord around him, pressing tightly, pushing his breath and life out of him as she worked up his body.

As the feeling left his feet and legs and then torso, he woke up, saw the living room clearly. His house. His room. And her. She was doing this, all of it. He didn't want any part of her plan or her life.

Rufus! *he called out, barely getting the loud cry out of his mind before she yanked hard, and he passed out, nothing in his body but the empty spin of dead thoughts.*

Chapter One

The men had been after her for a good three blocks. At first, it seemed almost funny, the old catcalls and whistles—something Miranda Stead was used to. They must be boys, she'd thought, teenagers with nothing better to do on an Indian summer San Francisco night.

But as she clacked down the sidewalk, tilting in the black, strappy high heels she'd decided to wear at the last minute, she realized these guys weren't just ordinary catcallers. Men had been looking at her since she miraculously morphed from knobby knees and no breasts to decent looking at seventeen, and she knew how to turn, give whomever the finger, and walk on, her head held high. These guys, though, were persistent, matching and then slowly beginning to overtake her strides. She glanced back at them quickly; three large men coming closer, their shoulders rounded, hulking, and headed toward her.

In the time it had taken her to walk from Geary Street to Post, Miranda had gotten scared.

As she walked, her arms moving quickly at her sides, Miranda wondered where the hell everyone else was. When she'd left the bar and said good night to the group she'd been with, there'd been people strolling on the sidewalks, cars driving by, lights on in windows, music from clubs, flashing billboards, the clatter and clink of plates and glasses from nearby restaurants.

Now Post Street was deserted, as if someone had vacuumed up all the noise and people, except, of course, for the three awful men behind her.

"Hey, baby," one of them said, half a block away. "What's your hurry?"

"Little sweet thing," called another, "don't you like us? We won't bite unless you ask us to."

Clutching her purse, Miranda looked down each cross street she passed for the parking lot she'd raced into before the poetry reading. She'd been late, as usual. Roy Hempel, the owner of Mercurial Books, sighed with relief when she pushed open the door and almost ran to the podium. And after the poetry reading and book signing, Miranda had an apple martini with Roy, his wife, Clara, and Miranda's editor, Dan Negriete, at Zaps. Now she was lost, even though she'd lived in the city her entire life. She wished she'd listened to Dan when he asked if he could drive her to her car, but she'd been annoyed by his question, as usual.

"I'll be fine," she'd said, rolling her eyes as she turned away from him.

But clearly she wasn't fine. Not at all.

"Hey, baby," one of the men said, less than twenty feet behind her. "Can't find your car?"

"Lost, honey?" another one said. This man seemed closer, his voice just over her shoulder. She could almost smell him: car grease, sweat, days of tobacco.

She moved faster, knowing now was not the time to give anyone the finger. At the next intersection, Sutter and Van Ness, she looked for the parking lot, but everything seemed changed, off, as if she'd appeared in a movie-set replica of San Francisco made by someone who had studied the city but had never really been there. The lot should be there, right there, on the right-hand side of the street. A little shack in front of it, and an older Chinese man reading a newspaper inside. Where was the shack? Where was the Chinese man? Instead, there was a gas station on the corner, one she'd seen before but on Mission Street, blocks and blocks away. But no one was working at the station or pumping gas or buying lotto tickets.

What was going on? Where was her car? Where was the lot? Everything was gone. That's all she knew, so she ran faster, her lungs aching.

The men were right behind her now, and she raced across the street, swinging around the light post as she turned and ran up Fern Street. A bar she knew that had a poetry open mic every Friday night was just at the end of this block, or at least it used to be there, and it wasn't near closing time. Miranda hoped she could pound through the doors, lean against the wall, the sound of poetry saving her, as it always had. She knew she could make it, even as she heard the thud of heavy shoes just behind her.

"Don't go so fast," one of the men said, his voice full of exertion. "I want this to last a long time."

In a second, she knew they'd have her, pulling her into a basement stairwell, doing the dark things that usually happened during commercial breaks on television. She'd end up like a poor character in one of the many *Law & Order* shows, nothing left but clues.

She wasn't going to make it to the end of the block. Her shoes were slipping off her heels, and even all the adrenaline in her body couldn't make up for her lack of speed. Just ahead, six feet or so, there was a door—or what looked like a door—with a slim sliver of reddish light coming from underneath it. Maybe it was a bar or a restaurant. An illegal card room. A brothel. A crack house. It didn't matter now, though. Miranda ran as fast as she could, and as she passed the door, she stuck out her hand and slammed her body against the plaster and wood, falling through and then onto her side on a hallway floor. The men who were chasing her seemed to not even notice she had gone, their feet clomping by until the door slammed shut and everything went silent.

Breathing heavily on the floor, Miranda knew there were people around her. She could hear their surprised cries at her entrance and see chairs as well as legs and shoes, though everything seemed shadowy in the dim light—either that, or everyone was wearing black. Maybe she'd somehow stumbled into Manhattan.

But she was too exhausted and too embarrassed to look up right away. So for a second, she closed her eyes and listened to her body, feeling her fear and fatigue and pain, waiting to catch her breath. How was she going to explain this? she wondered, knowing that she had to say something. But what? Here she was on the floor like a klutz, her ribs aching, and her story of disappeared pedestrians and cars, missing parking lots, and transported gas stations along with three crazed hooligans seemed—even to her—made up. She knew she should call the police, though; the men would probably go after someone else now that she wasn't fair game. They were having too much fun to give up after only one failed attempt. She had to do something. Miranda owed the next woman that much.

Swallowing hard, she pushed herself up from the gritty wooden floor, but yelped as she tried to put weight on her ankle. She clutched at the legs of a wooden chair, breathing into the sharp pain that radiated up her leg.

"How did you get here?" a voice asked.

Miranda looked up and almost yelped again, but this time it wasn't because of her ankle but from the face looking down at her. Pushing her hair back, she leaned against what seemed to be a bar. The man bending over her moved closer, letting his black hood fall back to his thin shoulders. His eyes were dark, his face covered in a gray beard, and she could smell some kind of alcohol on him. A swirl of almost purple smoke hovered over his head and then twirled into the thick haze that hung in the room.

She relaxed and breathed in deeply. Thank God. It *was* a bar. And here was one of its drunken, pot-smoking patrons in costume. An early Halloween party or surprise birthday party in getup. That's all. She'd been in worse situations. Being on the floor with a broken ankle was a new twist, but she could handle herself.

"I just dropped in," she said. "Can't you tell?"

Maybe expecting some laughs, she looked around, but the room was silent, all the costumed people staring at her. Or at least they seemed to be staring at her, their hoods pointed her way. Miranda could almost make out their faces—men and women, both—but if this was a party, no one was having a very good time, all of them watching her grimly.

Between the people's billowing robes, she saw one man sitting at a table lit by a single candle, staring at her, his hood pulled back from his face. He was dark, tanned, and sipped something from a silver stein. Noticing her gaze, he looked up and smiled, his eyes, even in the gloom of the room, gold. For a second, Miranda thought she recognized him, almost imagining she'd remember his voice if he stood up, pushed away from the table, and shouted for everyone to back away. Had she met him before somewhere? But where? She didn't tend to meet robe wearers, even at the weirdest of poetry readings.

Just as he seemed to hear her thoughts, nodding at her, the crowd pushed in, murmuring, and as he'd appeared, he vanished in the swirl of robes.

"Who are you?" the man hovering over her asked, his voice low, deep, accusatory.

"My name's Miranda Stead."

"What are you?" the man asked, his voice louder, the suspicion even stronger.

Miranda blinked. What should she say? A woman? A human? Someone normal? Someone with some fashion sense? "A poet?" she said finally.

Someone laughed but was cut off; a flurry of whispers flew around the group and they pressed even closer.

"I'll ask you one more time," the man said, his breath now on her face. "How did you get here?"

"Look," Miranda said, pushing her hair off her face angrily. "Back off, will you? I've got a broken ankle here. And to be honest with you, I wouldn't have fallen in with you unless three degenerates hadn't been chasing me up the street. It was either here or the morgue, and I picked here, okay? So do you mind?"

She pushed up on the bar and grabbed onto a stool, slowly getting to standing position. "I'll just hobble on out of here, okay? Probably the guys wanting to kill me are long gone. Thanks so much for all your help."

No one said a word, and she took another deep breath, glad that it was so dark in the room. If there'd been any light, they would have seen her pulse beating in her temples, her face full of heat, her knees shaking. Turning slightly, she limped through a couple of steps, holding out her hand for the door. It should be right here, she thought, pressing on what seemed to be a wall. Okay, here. *Here!*

As she patted the wall, the terror she'd felt out on the street returned, but at least then, she'd been able to run. Now she was trapped, her ankle was broken, and she could feel the man with his deep distrust just at her shoulder.

Whirling around suddenly, Miranda sucked in air and then spat out, "Okay, cute joke. Can I go, please? Just show me where you put the door, and I'll just be on my merry way. No questions asked. I've never seen any of you or this place. What bar?" *What group of scary, insane, weird people on hallucinogenics?* she wanted to add. *Loser cult? Strung-out Dungeons and Dragons lunatics?*

Barely breathing, she stared at the man's angry face. As she would have done with an attacking dog or a child having a temper tantrum, she stood completely still and tried to show no fear.

The group stopped moving and was silent. Now that Miranda was standing, she could see the unhooded man in the corner, sipping his drink in the candlelight. He was still watching her, and she noticed his long dark hair tied at his neck, pulled away from his handsome face. Why more of this bunch couldn't be as friendly and good looking as he was, she couldn't figure.

"You want us to believe you just popped through the wall?" a woman's voice asked.

"Christ, no. I don't want you to believe I popped through the wall," Miranda said. "I pushed through the door, though. You know. A thing with hinges? A knob? Made of wood? It opened, I fell in."

There was some mumbling in the crowd, and then someone else said, "Oh, goodness, she's just *Moyenne.* Just ordinary."

"Right, Philomel. *Moyenne.* In here? Like that?" another voice said. "Through the vortex? Doesn't happen. Never happens."

"Don't believe it!" the man said, his voice full of anger now as well. "I've told you we have to be vigilant. This is exactly what Quain Dalzeil and his followers tried last week. Think of what they were almost able to do. We've got to do something to send them a message."

"Why don't we write it on her and send her back," said another male voice, this one, low, quiet, and full of hiss. "I'm just the person to do it."

Behind her back, Miranda tried to find a doorknob or handle. Her ankle throbbed, and she felt sweat trickle along her brow and dip under her jaw. She should have taken what the three guys outside would have given her. Maybe she would have lived through it. These people wanted to carve her up, and she couldn't find the doorknob, a handle, anything to get her out. *Out.*

"I'll take care of her," the man said, full of purpose now, his suspicions and the crowd's agreement giving him the answer he seemed to need. "Give me room."

"Stop it!" Miranda shouted, finding the voice that she'd learned how to use in the "Defense for Women" classes she'd taken years ago. "Leave me alone!"

The group was silent again until someone laughed, giggled, hiccupped, and then was quiet.

"Right," a voice whispered to her left. "Leave you alone."

The man took her arm, and she yelled, "Stop it!" again with all the voice she could find.

"She's *Moyenne*," the person named Philomel said again. "She's scared. Just let her go, Brennus. Even if she is a spy, she's not a very good one, thumping on the floor like that. Gave herself right away, for goodness' sake."

Miranda looked for Philomel, but the man was yanking on her, the group crowding in. Someone had her elbow, another her wrist, and she was being tugged and pulled toward the center of the room.

"Let her go," a new voice said, a smooth, strong man's voice.

Miranda thought she was imagining it, but everything really seemed to stop. Hands still grasped her tightly, but no one was moving anymore, as if they were scared of the man who was speaking. Even the haze that hovered over the room seemed to have cleared, and she could see who had spoken. It was the long-haired man from the corner of the room.

"Get out of the way, Sariel," said the dark man, still holding Miranda's upper arm tightly. "You've told us all that you don't want to be involved in anything related to Quain. It's none of your affair."

"But this is not your affair either, Brennus," Sariel said. "This woman is not who you imagine. She's no spy."

Brennus, the dark man, squeezed her arm harder, but Miranda felt others let go of her elbow, collar, waist.

"How would you know?" Brennus said, his voice angry. "You've chosen to ignore the signs. You don't want to even think about what Quain is trying to do to our world. You certainly haven't shown any interest in dealing with what you allowed to happen before. Things that were seemingly in your control."

Brennus leaned closer to Sariel, a conversation seeming to flow between them. Sariel frowned and crossed his arms.

"For instance, how *would* you even see a sign if it"—Brennus lifted up Miranda's arm and pushed her forward—"fell into our meeting?"

"This woman is not a messenger from Quain or even a poor *Moyenne* trapped by his magic." Sariel stared at Brennus, almost smiling, his gold eyes full of irritation. Miranda knew that if he looked at her like that during a fight, she'd want to kick his butt. But then, as he was trying to save her, she decided to try to like him. That, actually, wouldn't be too hard. He must be the bar stud, with his slow, smooth voice. Just look at the way he stood, straight and tall, his shoulders back. And then there was his black hair, a loose strand along his cheek, so sexy in his . . . his dark red robe? *Who are these people?* she thought, pulling at her arm, hoping this Brennus would take the hint and let her go.

"You said yourself that Quain has bigger plans," Sariel said. "How does it involve a fast-talking *Moyenne* tripping into a meeting? Don't you think he'd try another tack this time?"

"A spy," Brennus said, turning sarcastic. "Think beyond your ability, Sariel."

Miranda pulled, moving her good foot slightly, knowing that what happened tonight would be one hell of a poem. Or maybe a short story. Both. Dan wanted her to break into fiction; he'd said so earlier after the reading.

"Three successful books of poetry, and you're ready for a novel," he'd said earlier, raising his wineglass.

Dan didn't know how soon a story would come to her, Miranda thought, yanking her arm hard one last time. At the same time as she yanked up, Brennus let her go. She tried to find her balance, but screamed as she put weight on her ankle and then began to tip. *Back to the floor once more,* she thought, putting out her hands to break her fall. But then she was caught and lifted, pressed against Sariel, who held her to his side, his hand firm on her waist. She grabbed at his chest, balancing, feeling how tightly he was built, everything under her hands smooth and hard. She closed her eyes and breathed away the pain in her ankle, smelling him: oranges, musk, soap.

"This isn't about generosity of spirit now, is it," Brennus said. "You've always had a taste for bad meat."

Miranda breathed in and thought, *Screw you, jerk,* and was just about to say it aloud, when Sariel whispered in her ear, his voice soft and full of laughter, "Don't say it."

She looked at him, and thought, *Just like a man.* He nodded, winked, and said, "For now."

"For now, what?" Brennus said.

"For now, let me take her out of here. Back where she belongs," Sariel said. He held Miranda close to him, his shoulder pressed against the side of her face. "I'll do what needs to be done."

Brennus glowered, crossed his arms, stared at Sariel, but suddenly he didn't seem so frightening. More like an irritated grandfather. Miranda looked out at the crowd. Her eyes had adjusted to the dim light, and despite their dark kooky robes, most of the bar crowd looked like people she might meet at Safeway, pushing a cart and grabbing Campbell's soup off the shelves. Why they wanted to grab at her and carve her up was beyond her. Maybe it was a cult, some devil worshippers getting overexcited for some Halloween parade.

"You should see our jack-o'-lanterns," Sariel whispered, and he began to walk her toward the door.

The crowd moved aside as they passed, but Brennus yelled out as they reached the end of the bar.

"You know what to do with her after you've played the hero."

Her body buzzing with adrenaline, Miranda felt Sariel shrug. *What was he going to do with her?* she wondered, trying to keep her eyes focused in front of her.

"Don't worry. It won't be anything horrible," Sariel said. "Just keep moving."

Just before they were at the place where the door was or wasn't, a woman reached out a hand. "Sorry, dear." Turning, Miranda matched the voice to the face. It was Philomel, who turned out to be an older woman with wild springy gray hair so thick her hood couldn't tamp it down, the velvet seeming to levitate over her head. Philomel reached out, touching her arm, and Miranda smiled, knowing that Philomel was the only person in the room besides Sariel who'd not wanted to stomp her to death.

Miranda put her hand briefly on Philomel's and then let Sariel lead her to the door, which was there exactly as it had been when she fell through it. *Of course,* she thought. *Isn't that peachy.* Sariel clasped her shoulder, laughed low, and pushed out into the street.

Chapter Two

Outside, the street had burst back into normal life. There, finally, were all the people walking from bar to club to apartment. The lights shone from condo windows, the streets hummed with car and Muni life. A homeless man with a shopping cart walked by, his shoes scraping along the concrete, aluminum cans clinking as the cart hit bumps in the sidewalk. Three teenagers in huge pants and large puffy coats ran by, singing some kind of rap song.

But when she turned back to look at the door, it was gone, the stone wall smooth and seamless. She turned, put her hand on the wall, half expecting her fingers to disappear as she did. But instead, she touched only the cold wall, nothing more.

Miranda shook her head and sighed, almost afraid to look back at Sariel. For all she knew, he might have disappeared, leaving her here to hobble to the corner and try to hail a cab. She still felt him holding her around the waist, but she took a deep breath before looking at him. Of course, he'd changed. What else could she have expected in this ridiculous night? Now he was wearing a forest-green T-shirt and black jeans, his robe nowhere in sight. He looked like any guy she might have met in a bar, except better, his cotton shirt tight enough (but not too tight) to show his long, strong arms, his slim waist, his . . . *God,* she thought, shaking her head, blushing suddenly because she could almost feel him inside her head.

She said quickly, "I wish I had your quick-change talent. Might come in handy someday." Miranda held onto him tightly, her ankle throbbing.

"You're not surprised?" He looked at her, his eyes the color of cracked amber, dark flecked, intense.

"Oh, I'm now in perpetual surprise," she said. "But since this is just a crazy dream, I know anything can happen. Rooms and doors disappear. You can change your clothes without, well, changing your clothes. People can talk about carving other people up. I've given up on questions, though, because all you'll have to do is read my mind."

"I'm a telepath," Sariel said simply.

"I just hope you aren't a psychopath," Miranda said. "Look, I don't care what you are right now. I've given up. What I need is a hospital. My ankle is killing me."

Sariel brought his other hand to her shoulder and turned her toward him. Miranda blinked, her breath in her throat, blood rushing to her face. What was he going to do? Cave in and carve her up like the man in the bar suggested? Strangle her? Possess her mind? Or . . . or? Was he going to kiss her? *What nerve,* she thought, realizing she was tipping her suddenly heavy head back with her eyes half closed, as if she wanted nothing more than his mouth on hers. Already, she could imagine his lips, soft at first, insistent later with passion. *Yes,* she thought. *Well, no. Not now. Maybe later. Okay, now. Yes, oh yes.* He pressed her to him, and she smelled oranges again. She tried to say something, but her mouth wasn't working right, and she closed her eyes, rested against his chest, and fell asleep.

She awoke in a warm, dark room, in comfort, warm, happy, and soothed. But by what? Blinking, she raised herself up from the couch. A candle on the table burned red-orange, its light illuminating the walls of the room, which were lined with shelves, books stacked three deep and piling up on a smooth, dark wood floor. On a desk at the back of the room were scrolls and loose papers, some of which had fallen to the floor. A strange map was tacked onto the wall above the desk. The map looked like a normal world in some ways, but it was divided differently somehow, large red and gold and green sections that weren't the countries she was used to. On another wall hung an intricate Japanese robe, the silk flickering purple and gold in the light. A huge sheathed sword hung over a doorway that led to a hall where a brighter light shone. She lay back, breathing in. The room smelled like Sariel, orangey, spicy, and hot.

For a minute, she focused on the room, wondering what other bizarre things would happen before she woke up in her bed, twisted in sheets, and dripping with fever. Or maybe she would fly or transport to one of the weird countries on the map or turn into a toad before the doctor at General would say, "Miranda? Miranda? Snap out of it." But until then, what a dream! What a room!

I'm in Edgar Allan Poe's house, Miranda thought. *I hope he gives me some opium before he straps me under the pendulum or locks me in the cage.*

"No opium," Sariel said from somewhere down the hall. "But I have other palliatives."

"Since this is my bad dream or intense coma, I'd appreciate it if you'd turn off that mind-reading thing,"

Miranda said as he walked into the room carrying a silver tray. "It's very unnerving. And when I wake up from this quasi-nightmare, I want to pretend I kept a couple of secrets."

"I promise, you won't remember a thing," Sariel said, sitting down in a leather chair across from her and placing the tray on the table. As he arranged the contents of the tray, his hair hung down, framing his face. She could see the candle flickering in the dark, lamp-black strands as he worked, his eyes focused, his arm flexing as he stirred something in a bowl.

Miranda looked down at the tray—clay bowls full of what looked and smelled like sage and maybe lavender, one full of a liquid, a pyramid-kind of thing made of metal, and a cloth. There was nothing demented about these ingredients. No sharp knives or wicked pliers. No ropes or chains or long needles or saws. She looked up at him, watching him work with the fragrant plants, their tangy odors calming her further. He seemed so focused, so intent on helping her, that she truly felt her body soften, relax, fall back against the soft couch pillows.

"So why won't I remember a thing?" She crossed her arms. "I always remember my dreams, and they're always in color. Just like this."

"This isn't a dream. And I can't allow you to remember it." Sariel looked up at her, his amber eyes on fire in the candlelight.

Who made you the boss? she thought hard, but Sariel didn't look up, busy with the cloth and the herbs.

"Okay, why then?"

Sariel sighed and looked up. "May I have permission to heal your ankle?"

"Do you have to ask? Seems like you guys kind of do what you want. Transport people around without asking, make doors come and go, threaten to cut up injured women."

Sariel straightened, stared at her, the right corner of his mouth pulling into what might turn into a smile. "I have to ask permission. It's only polite. And your ankle needs healing."

"So not only are you a secret Dungeons and Dragons telepath, but you moonlight as a doctor?"

"I'm a homeopath," Sariel said, holding up a hand. "Not a psychopath. Or a sociopath."

Miranda leaned back and looked down at her ankle. It was swollen and throbbed still, the pain constant and heavy. If this were a dream, it was the most vivid she'd had. Probably she'd hit her head on a post somewhere and was in a coma at San Francisco General, Dan wringing his hands at her bedside. Clearly, she received a sharp blow and fell to the concrete with a severe concussion with epic delusions. Or maybe worse. So not only would she have the whole satanic cult trip to write about, she'd have a brain injury to focus on. If she could focus on anything once she woke up.

"Look," Sariel said. "I turned the telepathy off like you asked, so I don't know what's going through your head. I should tend to your ankle though. It's not going to heal quickly on its own."

"You can turn your mind off?" Miranda stared at him. "Like a TV or a radio?"

Sariel sighed again, and she could see that he was just barely controlling his irritation. Obviously, he'd never been in one of her dreams before, all of them full of twists and turns and ridiculous plot lines. He leaned back in his chair and pushed his hair off his forehead, breathing out. He watched her, and she felt blood pulse in her ears. In the flickering deep glow of the room, his eyes were full of light. Miranda remembered what it felt like to rest against his shoulder, his chest under her cheek, his smell of oranges and spice surrounding her. She remembered how light and floaty and wonderful she felt as he carried her off to wherever in the hell she was now.

"Okay, fine," she said quickly. "Yes, please, I mean. It'll be nice to regain consciousness with one less thing to worry about."

Sariel raised his eyebrows, a bit more of a smile on his lips, and then stood up and sat down on the couch next to her feet, bringing the cloth and herbs with him.

"Those shoes," he said, his dark eyebrows raised. "Unless you're a well-trained *penseur de mouvement*, I'd wear Nikes when running around the city."

Miranda stared at him as he took off her high heels and put them on the floor. "A thinker of movement? I do have some French, though I'd say it's stuck at sophomore year. And even then, I got a D."

He flicked a look at her, and then brought his hand to her ankle gently, sliding one palm underneath it. Holding the weight of her tender flesh in his hand, he lay the folded cloth full of herbs on the top of her ankle and wrapped it loosely. He lowered her leg to a pillow, but he didn't let go, his hand holding her firmly. She felt some warm energy move from his hand through the cloth and into her skin, under it, really, into muscle and bone.

"Lie back and relax," Sariel said. "This will take a little while."

She did as she was told, resting back on the pillow, closing her eyes, sinking into the darkness of the room around her.

She listened to his steady breathing and then focused on his hand on her ankle. She could feel his strong fingers hold her ankle softly, and she remembered what Brennus had said in the bar. "You have a taste for bad meat."

Bringing women to his house and seducing them with magic hands must be what Sariel did, she thought. Or what he did in desperate women's dreams. Or, well, whatever. Miranda didn't care, bad meat or not. She'd wake up eventually, but now she had his warm hand on her, and she wondered what would happen if he moved it up a little, touching her like this everywhere.

She held back a laugh, trying to stay serious so he wouldn't stop. How long had it been since she'd let a man touch her anywhere? Since Jack left, taking with him her computer, printer, and heart? Two years, almost exactly. No one since Jack and his brilliant words, his lean, poetic body, and his girlfriends on the side. Sure, Dan had been asking her out for six months now, but she couldn't get involved with her editor. Her poetry was all she had these days, and she couldn't even kiss a man without one or both of them wanting more, so she'd said no to it all, hugs, kisses, and comfort. By saying no to that, she was saying no to anxiety, betrayal, stolen goods, and sleepless nights where she relived her every wrong move. Sex had always messed up everything.

But this? Sariel's hands moving carefully on her ankle and shin? It was lovely. She felt so relaxed, so peaceful. Her ankle wasn't throbbing anymore and the energy from Sariel's touch was growing hotter, slowly radiating in bigger circles from the point of pain. His fingers were steady and firm. She could feel the color coming from him into her, something as hot and red as the candle on the table, something tangy and delicious. In a strange way, she could almost hear him thinking, sending all his thoughts into her very bone, knitting the fracture back together. But how could she hear that? She pushed the notion away, letting his motions take over. His energy moved up in bursts to her shin, her knee, her thigh, and then she gasped as the circle of heat pulsed up farther, tentacles of pleasure pulsing all the way to her center.

Miranda didn't think she made a sound, but she did, hearing it float around the room before it finally vanished. She'd moaned. Loudly. Opening her eyes, she sat up wide-eyed and blinking, leaning on her elbows.

Sariel looked at her, his yellow eyes steady. "Are you all right? Does it feel better?"

She breathed in, trying to ignore the heat heavily pooling in her belly, her heart beating out jungle drum rhythms in her chest. Miranda was sure that if the lights were on, she'd find herself with continents of blush on her face, throat, and chest, her pale skin aflame. "Yes. I'm fine now."

He began to lift his hand from her ankle, and she almost reached down to stop him. *Just a few seconds more,* she thought, but having an orgasm simply from a man's touch was too much for even a crazy dream.

"Are you sure? Does it still feel tender?"

Tender, she wanted to say, *you have no idea.* But Miranda shook her head. "Yes. I mean, no. I'm fine."

He took his hand away, and her body felt like someone had turned off her main switch. She swallowed and lay down on the pillow, holding back the urge to tell him that indeed she still felt a slight crick, a hitch in movement. But that would be a lie. Her ankle felt perfect, as if she could run a marathon in four-inch heels.

Sariel carefully folded up the cloth and watched her, unblinking, a tiny smile at the corner of his lips.

"Test the ankle. Make sure I did what I set out to."

If you only knew, she thought, lifting her foot off the pillow. "It feels great." She moved her foot slightly and smiled. "A miracle. You are magic after all."

"Let's give it a minute, and then I'll take you back where you belong." He stood up and looked down at her, smiling. His hair hung down below his shoulders, and she wished he'd put his robe back on, so she could have the full effect of her Prince of Darkness–crazed brain before she woke up. What would her old Jungian therapist say about this? She could never tell her mother, but what would her sister Viv think once she heard? Long-robed lunatics worried about a menacing threat and a sexy healer in a candlelit room? The potential for interpretation was limitless. Sariel was clearly her repressed sexuality. The group in the bar was what? Her most feared audience? The Holitzer application committee? A packed crowd at the Herbst Theatre waiting for her to deliver perfect poems? The editor at the *New York Times Book Review*? But what about the threat from . . . who was it? Quain?

"Who is Quain?" Miranda asked and then immediately wished she hadn't. His face shifted, closed, shut down, his warm energy gone, and he turned away from her, picking up the tray and taking it over to a larger table. There, he poured them each a glass of what looked like brandy and brought back the glasses, handing her one.

"You don't need to concern yourself with that." He swirled his glass and frowned, his eyes focused on his drink. "At least, for now your world doesn't have to worry."

"My world? What does that mean? Listen, since it's my dream and I'm going to forget it all anyway, why can't you tell me?" Miranda sat up straighter and took a sip of her brandy, which wasn't quite brandy but some kind of alcohol, thick and honey-flavored and smooth. "What can it hurt?"

Sariel stared down at her and then sat down in the chair. He pushed the loose strands of hair away from his face and crossed his arms. As he watched her, she wondered what she must look like. Not the well put together sight she'd been when she'd left her apartment for the poetry reading, stylish in her tight green dress and black heels. No. She'd run a half-dozen blocks, fallen on the dirty bar floor, struggled with robed loonies, and done some kind of transporting thing to this couch. Somewhere between Geary and Lombard, her hair had gone mad, and she could see it curling all around her head and down around her shoulders. It was her caged animal look, she knew, and it wasn't her best, her hair a bright cadmium aureole of tangle. But Sariel didn't seem to really be looking at her, but just beyond.

"Okay, fine," she said. "No Quain. Just give me the synopsis of what happened tonight. No, wait. First tell me what *Moyenne* means. What it is, I mean, beyond the French word."

Sariel sat back. "You are *Moyenne.* We use the meaning 'ordinary,' but it's to differentiate you from us."

"And you are?"

"*Croyant.*"

"Believer?"

He nodded and sipped his drink. She watched him press his lips together at the taste, and then she took another sip, too.

"Where do you come from?" She sank back into the pillow behind her.

"We come from where everyone comes from. It's just that somewhere along the line, *Croyant* learned how to do things differently. To manipulate the world in a way *Moyenne* can't. Or won't."

"So, well, how many of you believers are there?"

Sariel laughed. "You've been with me for about a minute and you already want someone else?"

"I like variety." Miranda smiled back, wishing he would laugh some more, loving the deep sound in the dark room. "Magic or not."

"Not surprising. You are a woman of infinite tastes," he said. "Well, let's see. We're maybe about one half of one percent of the total population, which is what? Six point five billion?"

"A baby born every half second."

"We humans are a fertile bunch." He looked at her, smiling again, and she sipped her drink, hoping to hide her ridiculous blush behind her glass. What was wrong with her? She was acting as if she'd never gone on stage and read poems about sex and very specific body parts. Something about the way she felt around him brought her back to junior high dances after school, her desperate hope that Matt Braccia would ask her to dance to "Stairway to Heaven," everyone's favorite oldie because it turned into a slow dance and lasted for twenty minutes.

Miranda put down her glass, forcing herself to concentrate. "Okay, so here I go, math major that I am not . . . That's three million? Three million! Where do you all hide?"

"In dark smoky rooms wearing robes. Where else?"

Miranda stared at him, thinking, watching the light reflect and flicker in his eyes. "Of course. How silly of me. Why *did* I ask? So, what about the language thing? All the French?"

"It's our history," Sariel said, swirling his drink. "In the fourteenth century, we formed a worldwide government that was first located in Paris, under the auspices of Louis XI. Times were different. *Moyenne* blamed us for an outbreak of plague. Well, I didn't do well in history classes, but creating our governing body—the Council—was a way to protect ourselves from . . ."

He trailed off, taking a deep breath. *Of course,* she thought. What happened to anyone in the past that seemed magic, different, strange? Salem, Spain, England. People thrown in water to see if they bobbed like corks, townsfolk tortured for the names of those who cast the evil eye, women who healed and midwifed thrown in prison.

"I know. To protect yourselves from us. The ignorant, torch bearing witch burners."

He nodded. Miranda watched as he took another sip and then brought the glass away from his mouth, his lower lip slightly wet, sticky with the aromatic sweetness. Embarrassed by her long gaze, she picked up her glass and took an awkward sip of her own.

"Doesn't sound like anything I ever learned in history," she said, licking the liquid off her lips. "But let's go back to tonight. What happened there?"

Sariel seemed to startle out of a thought and smiled. "You know more about it than I do. I was just there for the showdown."

"Well," Miranda said. "What about how I got in there? I mean, things were looking really strange. The parking lot was gone and a gas station from the Mission was there instead. No one was around. Then there was a door I pushed through and then there wasn't. Explain that."

Sariel laughed and shook his head. "Okay. But since this is a dream, you have to believe everything until I make you forget. Like in a dream, anything is possible."

Miranda smiled, a flick of nerves in her chest. "Agreed. But haven't I already gone along with quite a bit?"

He nodded and then took a sip of his brandy and then put down his glass. "We had arranged a meeting—"

"Who are *we*?" Miranda interrupted.

"A group of *Croyant*, brought together for a meeting."

"Believers of what?"

"Our full name is *Les Croyants de Trois*. But don't interrupt. It's my story."

She took another sip. The believers of three. Like in the trinity? Or was it even older than that, going back to the days of goddess worship, prehistoric belief centered on the maiden-mother-crone, three the number symbolizing the cycle of life?

Miranda licked her lips, put down her glass. At least they weren't Satanists. Then they would be believers of one. Satan was a real loner.

"Exactly," Sariel said. "And by the way, you don't look like a caged animal. Your hair is lovely, in fact." He leaned forward and touched a flyaway curl with his fingertips. "It's beautiful. Such an amazing color."

Once, again, Miranda was glad for the dark, her face burning. *Holy cow! What else had she thought?* "You cheater! You said you turned your mind off!"

"I did," Sariel said. "But then I turned it on. If I'm going to tell you secret stories, I need to see exactly what you need to forget."

"You really are going to make me forget?" Suddenly, her head felt woozy, as if he were trying already.

"I have no choice. Protocol."

Miranda touched the place where his hand had smoothed her curls. *Her lovely hair.* "Don't make a mess in there, okay? I'm a poet. My memory is my stock in trade."

"Of course. Now, can I tell the story? Or do you want to go home already?"

She knew she should feel irritated with him for listening to her thoughts, but the drink was making her feel warm and soft and slightly pliant. "All right. So you arranged a meeting."

"Right," he continued. "People were coming in from all over because we needed to talk about—well, we're having some issues. There's a faction that's trying to upset our balance. A power struggle. Problems with—"

"Problems with Quain—" She stopped speaking when she saw his forehead crease, his eyes flicking in quick anger. "Sorry. Go on."

Sariel swirled his drink, looking into his glass. "So in order to keep *Moyenne* away from the meeting, we created a vortex. It's like energy to push them away from us. Nothing was supposed to get through. Nothing ever has before that I know of."

"How—" Miranda began.

"Remember, you have to believe."

"You can tell me anything because I won't remember. Remember?"

"No, pro—"

"Protocol. Of course. How boring," she said, yawning. "Not even a hint?"

"Well," Sariel leaned back and watched her for a moment, rubbing a hand on his taut cheek. "Let's put it this way: thought is energy. That's how I got us here tonight. How I'll take you home. How a number of *Croyant* can think up a vortex together. But if we somehow moved a parking lot and brought in a gas station, we need a little refresher course. Someone wasn't focusing."

"Oh." Miranda blinked and tried to get her mind around that idea, but her head felt wobbly, and she could barely keep her eyes open. "Okay."

"So," he said, "somehow, you got through, dragging your three ghouls with you. And lucky for you, it seems that they didn't see the door or even you going into it. What I can't explain is how you walked right into the vortex. Very strange, indeed. They are usually one hundred percent *Moyenne* proof. But I suppose even with magic, nothing's perfect."

Miranda closed her eyes but laughed. "You are magic. My ankle . . ."

She heard Sariel sit up, the leather creaking. Then she felt him take the glass from her hand and set it on the table. She felt him touch her foot briefly, his fingers sliding over her heel, the tent of ankle bone, the top of her foot, and then he let his hand slide up her shin. *Thank God I shaved,* she thought, smiling, wondering if he'd heard her.

"Bad meat," she said softly, barely able to stay awake.

"That's another story for another time," he said, and then he was leaning up to her, kissing her gently on the lips.

"Smooth all over," he said, letting his mouth travel over her face, her jaw, the soft skin of her throat.

She could smell his warm skin against hers, and she tried to kiss him back, knowing she shouldn't. He'd turn out to be worse than Jack; Sariel would be a boyfriend who could literally bail out at will. But Miranda wanted to kiss him, though, wanted to feel his lips on her face, her throat, her . . . But, oh, she was so tired, her head too heavy to even move. And then later, when his arms went around her and he pressed her to him, just as he had done on the street, Miranda felt herself disappear into nothing, everything darkness.

Chapter Three

She was so soft, so smooth, so beautiful—so unconscious. Sariel brought his lips away from her face, laughed, and looked at Miranda's full upturned lips, a smile even as the potion finally took effect. He sat up and pushed his hair away from his face, wishing he didn't have to take her back to where she belonged.

He shook his head, breathing out in amazement. What was he doing? It had been a long while since he'd been this close to a *Moyenne*, no matter what rumors Brennus Broussard liked to spin across a meeting table. Sariel had kept his distance, but he wasn't the type of man to take advantage of any woman, *Moyenne* or *sorcière*, even if he wanted her. And he wanted Miranda Stead. From the minute she'd flung herself into the meeting. Or maybe even before, when he felt her energy as she pushed through the vortex. As he'd sat in the corner of the room, he'd listened to her mind, smiling as she made fun of them even as Brennus and his pals did their scary trip. Carving her up! Even though the threat from Quain was real, no one at the meeting would have hurt her once it was clear she wasn't a spy.

After all, wasn't the fight against Quain really a fight for the *Moyenne*, for them all? But Miranda hadn't known that, and she'd stood up on her fractured ankle and fought back.

Sariel smoothed a curl away from her forehead and sighed. But how had she gotten into the meeting? Sure, she'd told them all how she'd been running, terrified of the men close behind her, and pushed into the room; but it was unlikely that a *Moyenne* could find her way to them in the middle of a vortex. Amazing. Like her.

Miranda turned a bit, grabbing his hand in her sleep. Sariel watched her, feeling her dreams flit through his mind, random images—a shoe, a bar, a man. Words, unreadable, emerged on a page. Voices. Running. Pavement. And then darkness, velvet, candle wax, warmth, pleasure.

He shook his head, not wanting to know any more. What he wanted was to awaken her from her sleep and make love to her. Sariel knew she would be agreeable—he'd felt her thoughts when she first looked at him and had been reading them most of the evening. If she'd been able to read his—and actually at times he thought she was—she would have felt how much he appreciated her flushed bright face, her fetching red curls, her long full body. How wonderful it would be to slowly pull off her dress that clung to her curves, to put his hands on her lovely pale skin and breathe her in.

Afterward, he could put her back to sleep, peel away the memory of the past two hours, and take her home. End of story. She could go on with her poet life, unaware of the tension in the universe and the dark fight that Sariel and his people—*Les Croyants de Trois*—were embarking on, unaware of the threat to the most important objects in the world. Instead of staying here with Sariel, Miranda could hook up with the man—what was his name? Dan?—Sariel had felt in her thoughts.

There wasn't time for that or for any lovemaking right now, and he wouldn't take advantage of a woman, even if she were drugged and willing and beautiful. Brennus was probably fuming, the meeting had been interrupted, and Sariel, again, was probably blamed for it all, a rule-breaker to the end.

"You've got that right," said a familiar voice.

"Rufus," Sariel said. He extricated his hand from Miranda's grasp and stood up to face his brother. Rufus Valasay was a large man, tall—almost as tall as his younger brother Sariel—and heavy with muscle. Over his jeans and flannel shirt, he wore a burgundy robe and hood, his face reddened and his long brown hair tangled from the journey, his black eyes wide with concern.

"Exactly. I got the message from Brennus like a freight train," Rufus said, unbuttoning and taking off his robe and smoothing his hair with a large hand. "There I was eating a beautiful ham sandwich—I mean righteous beautiful—and wham. I'm on the floor! So I had to leave it all behind and get myself here before you do any more damage. You're lucky Brennus didn't get in touch with Felix first. He'd have your head."

Sariel walked over to Rufus and hugged him, glad to see his older brother, regardless of the situation. Rufus had lived in the U.K. for the past fifteen years, the last two in Edinburgh with his wife, a *sorcière* named Fabia. By day, he and Fabia worked at a local clinic as volunteers, a good cover for them both, but their real work was monitoring *Moyenne* thoughts in all of Britain to detect any sign of Quain influence in ordinary life, because that's where it would start first. Where it always had before. *Moyenne* would suddenly be fixated on staying away from a certain area, changing their daily patterns. One by one, *Moyenne* would be turned to Quain, and Quain and his followers could hide in plain sight, in the midst of the unconscious *Moyenne. Croyant* had to pay attention and listen carefully.

Sariel, Rufus, and their youngest brother Felix were all telepaths. Felix lived in Hilo, and only the most important news forced him off his Big Island tropical paradise.

"You're sounding more and more like Fabia." Sariel held his brother's shoulders, smiling. "I swear, that brogue is getting deeper by the month. In a year, I won't understand a damn thing you are saying."

Rufus laughed. "You'd be talking like her, too, if she were the only real voice you heard. Other than the folks I work with at the clinic, all I hear is drivel. I swear, Sariel, the thoughts! I'm sick to death of them. They're all daft! Day in and day out, nothing but money and commute and traffic and the bloody boss. Or it's the baby-sitter and who is sleeping with whom. I'm about ready to kidnap Fabia and whisk us away to Hawaii. I'm sure Felix won't mind us moving in and ruining his bachelor life. Not even a full Quain takeover is worth listening to *Moyenne* minutiae all day long!"

But Rufus punched Sariel gently on the shoulder. Rufus's telepathic gift had come later than either Sariel's or Felix's, and he was proud to be able to use it, no matter what he said. And under any circumstances, he'd never leave Fabia Fair. Not for all the Hilos in China.

"So tell me, brother." Rufus pointed over to the couch, raising his eyebrows. "Who's the lassie? And how did she get into the meeting?"

Sariel took Rufus by the arm, and they walked over to dark wooden chairs by the table. Sariel poured Rufus some red wine, and they both sat down.

"That's the question, Ru," Sariel said. "She's definitely *Moyenne*, but there she was flying through the portal. And something was off with the vortex. She claims that the geography was displaced. I know it was a clean vortex. It's as if she somehow—"

"That's impossible."

"I know it is," Sariel said.

Rufus looked over at Miranda and then back at Sariel, his dark eyebrow raised. "But is that the whole story? I think I know you a little better than that."

"Ru, you know I'm in no mood for women. After—"

"Don't mention her name." Rufus held up a hand. "Not that evil bitch or . . . or . . ." He stopped speaking, his language hooked on the name he, Sariel, and Felix couldn't say without a dark sad swallow.

A moment passed between them, Sariel reading the loss in his brother's thoughts. Finally, Rufus took a long sip of wine. "She'll get what's coming to her. They both will."

Sariel breathed out and rubbed his forehead. "Maybe Kallisto will get what she deserves, maybe she won't. That'll be up to Quain. Or us."

The brothers were silent, sipping their wine. Finally, Rufus put his goblet down and scratched his head, glancing at the bottle of amber liquid on the table.

"Is this a sleeping potion?" he asked. "Or did you knock her out with brandy and whip up a sleeping spell? Or did you make her swoon from your magnetic personality?"

Sariel looked over at Miranda, curled and warm on the couch. "She's a fighter, so my personality alone wouldn't have done it. I used a spell to get her here, but I knew I'd need her to sleep a while so I could take her home. And the *potion du sommeil* is healing, too."

"So do you think she's a spy? Brennus thought so. I think he's contacted Adalbert," Rufus said. "You'll probably get a message soon from the Council."

"A waste of time! Brennus is blinded by anger. He can't properly read anyone's thoughts anymore," Sariel said, snorting. "I've been in her head, Ru, and it was a fluke. She's a poet, worrying about her work and writing. Worrying about the men chasing her. She's not a highly trained operative, accustomed to shielding her mind. I actually think I picked up her thoughts before she burst into the meeting, when she was at the bottom of the street. I did almost feel like I recognized her in some way, but she's not working for—for him. She's as clear as a bell."

Rufus nodded. "I thought as much, but with what happened last week . . ." He trailed off, and both of them were silent. Sariel nodded, thinking about how Quain used *Moyenne* to attempt to steal one of three *Plaques de la Pensee*, the most sacred objects in the *Croyant* world. Who would have imagined bewitched *Moyenne* could walk into the Castle of Gaerwen and almost take it, just like that? It was such a simple plan no one was prepared for it. Only Quain had magic that strong. If Quain got his horrible hands on any one of the *plaques*, he would only grow stronger.

Now, belatedly, the *Croyant* were on high alert, listening and feeling for everything. The fact that Brennus managed to get the okay for Rufus to leave his post in Edinburgh showed how worried the Council was about any strange *Moyenne* behavior. With the *plaques*, Quain could harness their power and not only the *Croyant* but the *Moyenne* would pay—and pay for letting that happen. If Quain managed to convert more *Croyant*, to exert more influence on more *Moyenne*, life would change for everyone. He would first take land, resources, using his power to grip countries tightly and force everyone to work for him. And *Moyenne* thought bad presidents and prime ministers and dictators were awful. Wait until they got a load of Quain.

It didn't help that Quain had assistance from Kallisto, a *sorcière* once deep in the *Croyant*, and deep into Sariel.

Even now, sometimes Sariel would awaken at night from a deep, sound sleep and hear her repetitive, ugly thoughts: *power, need, steal, want.*

"So, you going to take her home or what?" Rufus winked and then drained his goblet. "Or did you have some wee plan that I interrupted?"

"You felt that, too, did you? You do know me too well."

"I felt you in the air, lad. I could hear you all the way in Edinburgh. She is very tempting. But you're right," Rufus said. "Best to put her back where she belongs."

"Would you mind taking care of her car while I take her home?" Sariel asked.

"Why not?" Rufus said, reaching out and putting a hand on Sariel's chest. "Give it to me."

Sariel closed his eyes and brought forth the image of the car he'd taken from Miranda's thoughts. An old, light green Volvo station wagon. Rusted through and through, paint chipped, but with brand-new tires, a present from her mother, June, on her last birthday.

"Got it, bro," Rufus said, taking his hand away. "I'll put it right back in her garage. Not a foot on the odometer."

"Thanks," Sariel said. "You can stay, right? This won't take much time." He stood and pushed in his chair.

"Of course." Rufus poured himself some more wine. "I'm not hitting the air again tonight. Fabia's on alert. I'll head back tomorrow morning."

Sariel put his hand on his brother's arm, and then walked over to Miranda. She was curled up on the couch, sleeping soundly, not one dream in her mind. Sitting down on the couch, he pulled her limp sleeping body to him, breathing in her soft skin and hair. For a moment, he wished Rufus was wrong. *What would it hurt to keep her here?*

Don't mind me, Rufus thought. *I can get a hotel room, you are quite clearly a desperate man. What would Mom say?*

Sariel laughed and shook his head. Their mother, Zosime, a telepath herself, had somehow managed not to go insane when the boys were teenagers. What she must have heard seeping through the bedroom walls. This simple business with Miranda would seem like a children's show.

Not looking back at his brother, Sariel held Miranda tightly against him, and thought them home.

Pressed against Miranda, Sariel sifted through her memories and found her home, an apartment on Lombard. Three rooms—no, four rooms—third floor. He waited until he was certain, even the dark pumpkin color of her dining room walls familiar, before he pushed them both from an embrace on his couch to an embrace on her bed. Sariel breathed out, looking around. Yes, this is what he'd seen. This window exactly, the view of the Bay Bridge and the East Bay, Oakland and Emeryville laid out in lights on the slowly graying horizon.

Gently, he laid her back on her bed, pulling a soft, loose blanket over her. He'd take the particular memories from her of the bar, his house, the healing of her ankle, and she'd wake up in the morning imagining she'd had one hell of a night. A rare, temporary blackout from one very strong, potent apple martini. For a few hours, confused and fuzzy, she'd expect a call from a friend, asking, "What was up with you last night?" or "Man, you were the life of the party." Or she'd wait for a strange man to call and say, "I can't wait to see you again." But those calls would never come, and she'd eventually forget about forgetting.

On the nightstand next to her bed, an answering machine blinked furiously, flashing *15, 15, 15* over and over again. Sariel closed his eyes and felt for them, his mind moving into the jumpy bumble of digital voices. Dan. Dan again. Roy—did she get home all right? June—Miranda's mother. Her sister, Viv, who wondered when Miranda was going to get her butt over to visit. Greta Smith from the Holitzer Grant Committee.

Suddenly, he opened his eyes and shook his head. What was he doing? He had no business listening to her messages and no business sitting by her on her bed. By now, he should have taken her memories and thought his way home to Rufus, who would read him the riot act and then drink him under the table.

Miranda moaned lightly and pulled the blanket tighter, turning onto her side. Sariel stood up and walked to her dresser. On top of the slightly dusty wood were pictures of an older woman—June, he thought as he picked up the frame—and a man he was certain he recognized. But how could he? It was impossible, but there was the memory of being in a room with other people, listening to someone talk, telling him a secret. And one of the people in the room was Miranda's father . . . Steve. Or did he just pick up an image of this man? But both notions were impossible. Sariel knew that Steve was dead. Could pick it up from the photo itself. Steve's dead. Miranda had lost her father, just as he had.

But he couldn't think about his father.

Sariel put down the photo, his fingers grazing jewelry, a brush, letters, a loose piece of paper, the handwriting faint in the darkness.

Picking up the paper, he walked to the window, dawn pushing at the eastern sky, busting open the gray. It was an untitled poem, written in longhand, lines scratched out, words scribbled in.

When I was four,
I flew in the backyard,
hovering over the patio

for minutes in my white Keds
and aqua shorts while
you admired me.

Later, as I ran inside to tell her,
our mother told me I had been
only dreaming under the hot sun,
but for years afterward, I used
to be able to see the truth of my first flight
in your black eyes, the yes of my magic
in your . . .

The poem seemed to trail off, and below it, Miranda had written: *Flying! Ha!*

Turning to look at her on the bed, he wondered if the poem were true. Writers always made up stories, but this story felt real. Had she flown? Sometimes, *Moyenne* had flares of ability that died away and disappeared by adolescence. They were wildly successful poltergeists, their bad energy heaving around plates and books until they grew up and learned to control their anger. They burst into other realities they later thought were dreams, trips to heaven and hell that they explained later as a terrible experience of acid reflux.

Maybe Miranda had truly been able to fly but believed what her mother had told her. It was only a dream. Just like Miranda had said earlier, "It's my dream and I'm going to forget it anyway."

That's why Sariel felt sad for *Moyenne*—all the magic in the world always cast as insanity, ghosts, hallucination, miracle, or dream. They couldn't let it in, for better or worse. And when magic finally did penetrate their ordinary world, it was something flukish, a one-time thing they imagined would happen over and over again, like Lourdes or the vision of the Virgin Guadalupe in Mexico City. Millions of desperate people wanting magic, pilgrimaging to a fixed place when all along, it was everywhere. All they had to do was look closely, carefully, stop talking.

Sariel put the poem back on the dresser and walked back to Miranda. He sat down in the warmth of her blankets and put his hand on her soft, curly hair, closing his eyes and feeling the heat of her memory. There was her run up the street, the meeting, Sariel's home, his story. Just below his fingertips was her surprise at seeing him in the corner of the room, her approval of his looks, smell, smile as he hugged her tightly and brought them to his house. The lush relaxed warmth of her resting on the couch, her body heavy with the potion. Everything about their one and only night together was right under his fingers, burning to be set free.

Chapter Four

Miranda woke up. And she remembered.

For the first moment of consciousness, Miranda stopped breathing, waiting for her next thought and then her next. She thought: daylight, bed, blanket, body. She felt her breath rising and falling, her steady pulse in her ear. She wasn't hungover. No headache, no nausea. But last night was still there. In the corner of her mind—a memory too bizarre to unfurl completely—was the strange spiral of the night before. That memory wasn't supposed to be there, lurking like a dark dog on a rug. Sariel had told her he'd take it away because she couldn't know, shouldn't know about his magic world. There was the protocol, the end of the world as she knew it, Quain, Brennus, and big trouble for Sariel.

Miranda flung her arm out and closed her eyes. *Great, I've gone insane,* she thought. *Maybe I am going to be a great poet after all, remembered for all time. A Poe, Plath, Stevens. Brilliant and nuts.*

Sitting upright, she stared at herself in the mirror over her dresser. She hadn't changed. She was still the same person who woke up in this bedroom every morning. Wild red hair, pale face. Alone.

Blinking, she looked at her reflection, hoping some little bubble would appear over her image, providing a telling caption: *After a bad night, Miranda Stead wonders who slipped her a mickey,* or, *Finally accepting her degraded mental health, Miranda Stead calls her therapist.*

Pushing away the blankets, Miranda saw she was still wearing her green dress, but her high heels were by the side of her bed, slightly scuffed, but neatly lined up. She leaned over and grabbed one, a memory (or hallucination) of how Sariel took them off flicking through her body. She could almost feel him touching her ankle, the warmth spreading up her calf, knee, thigh—her ankle! She reached down and touched the bone, almost wincing as she did, but it didn't hurt. Nothing hurt. Not one bit. She was fine.

"Shit," she said, picking up her phone and dialing Dan's number.

"Hello." Dan's voice was muffled.

"It's me. What happened last night? Did I drink too much?"

"Miranda?"

"Did I dance on the tables? Eat raw oysters? Pound back boilermakers? Did I talk to some guy? Did I leave with anyone? Did I go into an alley and buy drugs? What did I do?"

She heard Dan turning in his bed, the swish of sheets in the phone. He yawned, holding the phone away from his mouth.

"Sorry," he said. "God, I'm tired. I called you twice last night. Where were you?"

"That's what I'm asking you!" Miranda said impatiently, standing up and walking around her room, her ankle feeling better than ever. "I think I was abducted."

"By aliens? That's not your usual genre, but I'm sure someone would publish it."

"Dan, I'm serious. This isn't about writing. Something weird happened. Or I hit my head, stumbled home, and had the strangest dream of my life."

"So," Dan said. "Tell me about it."

Miranda paced, looking out the window toward the bay. She didn't know where to start. When she left the bar? With the guys chasing her? Those two things had been real. She knew it. But then things tilted, veered into abnormal. Like, where were all the people on the street? Where was her car, for one thing? The parking lot, for another. Oh, that's right. The vortex. She'd just tell Dan about the vortex and how the whatchamacallits, the Believers of Three made it, thinking intensely to scare away the ordinary people. Then she'd just sail into a long discussion of Sariel and his hot, healing touch. What about Quain and his evil plot? Sure, that's what she'd do. Then Dan would drop her books from his list and tell the poetry world she'd finally gone off the deep end in a rocket-powered barrel.

"It was crazy, that's all I can say. I must have walked into another bar or something and someone gave me that drug."

"The date-rape drug? You aren't supposed to remember anything after taking that."

"Okay, then. Something like LSD. Mushrooms. Mescaline. Pot brownies." Miranda sat back down on the bed and put her head in her free hand, rubbing her forehead. "I don't know. When did you call me?"

"About eleven-thirty. Then again at twelve. You didn't get the message?"

Miranda looked at her machine and the blinking red 15. "Which one?"

"Which one? The one from Greta Smith. From the

Holitzer. You got the grant. A Holitzer! Do you know what this will mean for your career?"

Miranda tried to feel happy, willing herself into a good feeling, needing to push away the memory of her wacked-out dream with Mr. Magic Hot Ass and his healing hands. She closed her eyes and tried to conjure forth the forty thousand dollars she'd get as well as the book sales Dan would eke out from the announcement. But all she could see were Sariel's cracked amber eyes.

"That's great," she said weakly. "Wow."

"Don't get too excited." Dan sounded disappointed. "You might have a stroke."

"No, really," she said with more energy. "I'm happy about it. I swear."

Dan paused. "I have to tell you, though, there's something kind of odd about it."

Miranda took the phone away from her mouth and sighed, wishing for once that he'd stick to the point. "What's odd?"

"Well, see, here's the thing. Jack won a Holitzer, too."

With all the crazy thoughts in her head, Miranda listened to Dan's words and then the silence in the phone without really understanding what he meant. "What do you mean Jack? My Jack? Jack Gellner?"

"Yeah, um, Jack," Dan said. "Your Jack."

"Oh." Miranda stared out the window, watching cars move slowly across the bridge. That would mean at the awards ceremony, she'd have to share a stage, a podium, a party with Jack, who probably won the award on bits of her poetry mixed into his now-award-winning verse. But as she sat, trying to feel something, anything, about the prize, Jack, or her stolen computer and poems, she couldn't muster much more than a sigh. What she really wanted was to find out about last night.

"I've ruined it for you, haven't I?" Dan asked. "I just thought you should know. I hope I didn't ruin it."

"No, it's great. Really. I just—well, I'm still confused about what happened after the reading. What did I drink?"

"Miranda, you had an apple martini, heavy on vermouth. Like always. One. You didn't dance on the tables or talk to guys with Harleys parked out front. Or smoke a spliff outside with punk rockers or runaway teenagers. We talked with Roy and Clara about books and music and then you left, alone," Dan said, adding, "like always."

She closed her eyes and waited until his last sentence died. "Then what?"

"We said good night and you walked up Geary toward your car, refusing to let me walk with you." He paused. "Anyway, there aren't too many bars that way."

Miranda pushed her hair off her forehead. "Maybe I have the flu. I always have crazy dreams when I'm sick. I feel hot and kind of jittery."

"Do you want me to come over? My mother always says *menudo* is the cure for hangovers and basically all illnesses. I can pick some up and be at your house in an hour."

In his offer was the seed in all his offers to her. He offered himself over and over again, and she wondered when he would give up. Or when she would give in out of pity or exhaustion.

"I think I'm going to take a cool shower and go back to bed. Take some Tylenol," she said, adding, "Thanks. I'll call you later. Sorry for waking you up."

Miranda hung up the phone and lay back on the bed, staring up at the ceiling, now lit with bright morning light. Everything that had happened last night had felt so real. It was more real than winning a Holitzer, which she couldn't even think about. Images pounded against her forehead. She could see the reddish light streaming from underneath the door that wasn't always a door, feel her ankle throbbing as she tried to escape the bar, taste the sweet drink Sariel had given her before he told her about the vortex. It wasn't dreamlike; she wasn't catching random glimpses of the scene. She remembered names: Brennus, Philomel, Quain. She could still smell the floor of the bar, feel the swish of velvet robes against her cheek as Brennus leaned over her. She knew she was *Moyenne*, ordinary, and Sariel and all the rest were members of *Les Croyants de Trois*, the believers of three.

No, she could recount the full narrative, except for the space of time between the street and Sariel's home and then the time from Sariel's couch to her bed. The rest, though, was all there, as quick to her mind as the poetry reading had been. Her night, from A to insane.

Shaking her head, she breathed in and looked up into the mirror. Okay, fine. So like she'd thought last night, this would be a poem. Or, if she was lucky, a short story. Whatever it was, she would use it. In fact, right after her shower, she was going to eat breakfast and then write for a couple hours. Maybe then she'd feel better. Maybe then some of this would make sense.

At her desk, Miranda stared at her computer keyboard, then at the wall above her computer, and then to her left, vaguely watching a tiny brown moth in the upper left of the windowpane. It fluttered, stopped, fluttered again, desperate for air. After a moment, Miranda looked back at the computer screen and typed a word, biting her lip. Could she tell it right? Did she have any language that would make sense? How could she wrap her words around Sariel's face, his hair, his smell, his arms carrying her places? How to say it, how to make it real, show the outstanding, original, outlandish weirdness of what she remembered?

She stopped typing, her hands still over the keys, her stare vacant. Just as she thought to type the letter *O*, the phone rang. Usually, Miranda didn't answer the phone when she was writing, but the past two hours at her desk had been so unsatisfying and difficult that she welcomed the annoying interruption.

"Yes," she said sullenly. "What is it?"

"Randa? It's me."

"Oh, hi."

"Well, why did you answer the phone, then?" her sister Vivian asked. "Christ, I'd rather talk to your machine than you in this state."

"How do you know I'm in a state?" Miranda asked, feeling the word *state* explode inside her, a low pulse of confusion, irritation, rage.

"How long have I known you? Thirty years? You started having states when you were sleeping in your crib. What's wrong? In the middle of a poem?"

Miranda leaned back in her chair. "No. Just in the middle of going crazy. Maybe going isn't the right verb. I *am* crazy. You won't believe the dream I had last night."

"I hope he was cute. It's about time you had some fun, even if it was in your unconscious," Viv said. "But aren't you going to go crazy about your award?"

"How did—"

"Dan called me," Viv said. "Don't be mad. He thought you weren't feeling so good, and he thought I might cheer you up. He doesn't know me very well, I guess."

Viv laughed, and Miranda smiled, despite her fatigue and the sense of confusion she'd awakened with. Viv usually cheered her up, especially when she took a night off from her three children and husband Seamus, took BART to the city and spent the night with Miranda.

Those visits had been fewer now that Viv was expecting her fourth baby, so even on this very strange morning, Miranda was glad to hear from her.

"It's great," Miranda said flatly. "Yeah, the money will be nice. I won't have to copyedit manuscripts for a while. I can give up teaching that class at the university extension."

"Go on gushing," Viv said. "Don't stop!"

"I really don't feel good." Miranda leaned back in her chair and closed her eyes.

"So what was the dream about?" Viv said, groaning. "Ugh. Sorry. Had to sit down. I am about to pop. Any moment."

"Really?" Miranda said, sitting up, wondering suddenly where her car was. She'd need it if she had to drive out to the East Bay. A good birth experience would take her mind off everything.

"No. I'm just fat. I weigh exactly one hundred and sixty point five pounds. All of it's baby, of course."

"Of course," Miranda said, knowing that Viv would lose all her baby weight in about two point five months, turning back into her long-limbed, smooth-stomached self without Pilates or yoga or step aerobics.

"Okay, so what was this dream about?"

"So I was running up a street," Miranda began. "Three guys were chasing me."

"Archetype total two. Street and the number three. A journey and completion. Go on."

"I was really scared and tired, and they almost had me. So I see what looks like a door—"

"Wait. A door. A change. A passage. A transition," Viv interrupted. "But was it a door or not?"

"Sometimes it was, and sometimes it wasn't."

"Very interesting. To change or not to change. Hmm. Go on."

"Then I escaped but ended up with these creepy people in robes."

"Could you see their faces?" Viv asked.

"Not at first."

"But you eventually did see them?"

"Yeah," said Miranda. "And they looked like Mom. Like people from her bridge group all decked out in Halloween outfits."

"That's enough to send anyone running. Then what? Were they all like that?"

"That's the best part. I was saved by a really amazing man with magic powers. God, was he good looking. Tall, dark, able to change clothes in an instant. He saved me from the group, healed my broken ankle, and told me an evil man named Quain was going to take over the entire world or something. His fingers were so amazing." Miranda knew she should be smiling or even laughing at the strange turns the story was taking, but nothing seemed funny, as if she believed in Quain. Or as if she believed in Sariel and the way she felt when he touched her.

Viv was silent for a moment, and then she said slowly in her big-sister voice, "Miranda. Don't you see?"

"What?"

"This is all about Jack."

"Jack!"

"Yes," Viv said. "Who else? You've never gotten over him. So you're dreaming up mysteries and magic guys."

"This is not about Jack. That is so over, Viv. You know it." Miranda shook her head. "Jeez. It's been two years."

"Well, if you are so over Jack, why won't you go out with Dan? You know how he feels about you."

Miranda sighed and closed her eyes. So that's what this phone call was about. Viv just couldn't let go of her protective routine, even though she had 3.9 children of her own to take care of. Viv wanted to see Miranda married, with her own house and children and pets that peed in the corners and ate all the socks.

"What did Dan say to you? Did he put you up to this?"

"No! He didn't say anything. I have no idea what you're talking about."

"Viv!"

"Oh, fine. But listen, he didn't say anything directly. He was just so worried about you and your weird dream and fever or whatever. And that whole thing about Jack and the prize. He's a nice man, Miranda. And after Jack, well, you deserve a nice man. Oh, hold on." Viv clunked down the phone, and Miranda heard her groan as she stood up and began talking to Hazel, her youngest.

Sitting back in her chair, Miranda knew Viv was right. She did deserve a nice man. A really nice man. But there was something too nice about Dan. He wanted her too, clearly. It was like what Groucho Marx used to say: "I'd never join a club that would have me as a member." Miranda had fought for Jack, earned him by ignoring the bottles of J&B in the kitchen, the sticky, redolent reefers in the bathroom drawer, and the giggling, late-night phone calls he said were "wrong numbers." Dan would never do drugs or drink too much or cheat on her, and she knew that was a good thing.

But could he do what Sariel had managed to do with one touch last night? Could Dan awaken all her flesh with one hot touch? Even if the whole thing was a dream, Miranda knew she wanted that feeling, that kind of man. Of course, she didn't even know what kind of man Sariel was—she didn't know if he was a man at all. But even if he were a wizard or magician or devil, she knew that he was beautiful, kind, and sexy. That was magic enough.

"God," Viv said, breathing hard into the phone. "I've got to go. Hazel has decided to take this very minute to potty-train herself. On the brand-new carpet, though. I'll call you later."

Viv hung up, and Miranda pressed the phone against her chest. All her life, she'd wanted to be just like Viv and had wondered why, with the same exact gene pool, she was her sister's complete opposite. Where Viv had been confident, popular, curvy, big breasted, and smooth skinned as a teenager, Miranda had been wacky, bouncing between her simultaneous girlhood art projects, all buckteeth and frizzy, enormous red hair and freckles. Viv had gotten all the dates, gone to every junior ball and senior prom throughout her high school career, while Miranda stayed at home and wrote dark, mournful poems into her journal, sure that she was destined to be dateless. Sure, a late puberty had darkened and tamed her hair, filled her out, and given her breasts, and years of braces had straightened her teeth, but she'd still felt like a washed-out, jerky beanpole, especially when next to Viv's blonde, dark-eyed lushness.

After high school, Miranda had gone to Wellesley and the University of Iowa, published her first book of poetry, taught when she felt like it, copyedited when she had to. Between her first and second book there had been disastrous Brad, even worse Vladimir, and horrible Jack in succession.

"You just don't have any luck with men," her mother, June, had said at least once or twice a month, more during the holiday season when Miranda was likely the only dateless woman at family and neighborhood gatherings. "Have you thought about using the Internet? Putting in an ad? Maybe an old-fashioned matchmaker? Your sister never had a problem."

That was true. Viv never really had problems. She graduated from Berkeley with her teaching credential and then married Seamus O'Keefe, who was gorgeous, smart, and loved Viv like crazy. All three of their kids were adorable and smart, and nothing had gone wrong for Viv, ever. It was like Miranda was the repository of bad karma, taking enough of it to keep her sister safe.

And since their father Steve had died ten years ago, Viv had taken charge of Miranda as well as June, consoling Miranda after breakups and writing rejections, showing up to every single poetry reading (unless a baby was due momentarily), and inviting her to every holiday, school, and social function Viv organized. Everything that their father had done—organizing Sunday afternoon barbecues and family trips to Playa del Carmen over Christmas and weeknight movie dates—Viv took over. Without her sister, Miranda would be an empty boat, paddling nowhere special.

Miranda reached over and hung up the phone. She closed her eyes, wishing she could stop seeing what wasn't really there: Sariel's house, the Japanese robe, the sword dangling on the wall, the tray, the herbs, his strong, beautiful hands. Everything about last night was bizarre and totally mad, but she knew the experience was built of more than the strangers in the room and travel through time and space. When she'd looked into Sariel's golden eyes, she'd felt connected. She'd felt safe. She'd felt as if she'd finally come home to someone she'd been waiting all her life to remember.

Ridiculous! she thought. How could anything overwhelm the weirdness of her adventure? How could any connection she felt redeem the craziness of flying around through time and place? But there it was—there he was. From the moment she'd seen him sitting at the corner table, she'd felt as though she'd recognized herself in him. It had seemed, despite her terrible vantage from the floor and all those musty robes, that he'd really seen who she was, unlike any man, even Jack.

Rubbing her eyes and then sighing, Miranda looked at the beginning of her poem hanging on the screen.

If you had told me
about your doors and handles,
I would have opened you up,
pulled you wide.
Walked right in.
O . . .

For a second, she thought about working on the poem some more in order to make her two hours of writing worth something. But she realized she didn't care what her *O* would do in the next line. She didn't care about the next line one bit. Now, in the early afternoon light, the voice of her too-real sister still in her ear, Miranda knew that Sariel and his magic touch had been nothing but a dream. A vivid, intense, amazing dream, but a dream nonetheless. What was real and true was here: her sister, Dan, the Holitzer, her own loneliness. She didn't need to waste one more second thinking about all that craziness last night. Traveling through thought. A terrible bad guy named Quain. Sariel's eyes.

Reaching her hands to the keyboard, she closed the file without saving it, turned off her computer, and left the room.

Miranda, he said into her ear.

Half in sleep, half awake, she reached out, felt her blankets, and didn't bother to open her eyes because all she grabbed was fabric.

Please, she thought. *No more dreams. I'm busy being miserable, all right?*

There was no answer, so she let herself slide back into sleep. But then she felt his strong, firm hand slide up her leg, slowly moving up the contours of her body through the blankets. Her knee, her hip, her waist, her shoulder, his hand leaving a long, lovely swath of heat.

Then he was stroking her hair, his touch as gentle as it had been the night before as he healed her ankle.

I really am desperate, she thought, trying to open her eyes. *Two wild dreams in two nights. What a total loser.*

But she couldn't open her eyes. She kept trying, struggling to see if Sariel was really there, but her muscles wouldn't work, her lids heavy, the way it felt to her when she tried to read something in a dream. A dream. Another flipping dream. It was so nice, though, feeling him next to her, touching her, and she stopped caring if this was a dream or not. He leaned over and kissed her forehead, her eyebrow, her nose, her cheek, her chin. She moved her face to where she thought his lips would be, and he kissed her softly, his mouth on hers. First it was lips, soft and dry, and then tongues, slow, smooth. He breathed in, pressed harder, wanting more.

Oh, she started to think.

"Enough," he said. "Stop thinking. Quiet."

Like before, he smelled like oranges. His dark hair was thick and smooth against her face. He lay his body down on hers, taking her face in his hands. She arched back with her hips and chest, knowing how much she wanted him, feeling how much he wanted her, so hard against her. She wanted to reach down and touch him, everywhere, but she was trapped by his arms, his body, this blanket, her eyes stuck shut.

"There's time for that," he said. "Be patient."

But you're not acting patient, she said, pressing into him, listening to his quick breaths. *You couldn't even wait one night?*

"You're magic," he said.

Nothing as magic as the body, she thought.

He laughed into her neck, and then kissed her again and again.

You're supposed to be a dream, she thought, kissing him back. *I wasn't supposed to remember.*

His hand slid under the blanket, his fingertips snaking up under her nightgown, his hand trailing down her throat, chest. Then he was touching her breast, breathing against her neck. Miranda tried to follow his instructions to not think, willing her brain to shut off. Her body was on, though, every vein pulsing to his touch. She felt her insides slick and shimmery with heat, and she pushed against him again, wanting to connect with his heat and hardness, irritated by the blankets and sheet.

"You aren't supposed to remember," he said, his voice quieter, and then he pulled his hand away, his body lifting off hers. "But I couldn't go through with it. Not yet. Not now."

Go through with what? she thought, trying to open her eyes again; but then there was darkness again and silence, his touch lifting slowly off her body and then evaporating away into the darkness.

Come back, she thought, her mind drifting, fading. *Don't go. Come back.* Then she felt the pillow, the blanket, and she turned on her side, already asleep.

Chapter Five

"Are you out of your mind?" Brennus Broussard slammed his hand on Sariel's table. "At any other time we could understand. Or at least tolerate your behavior. But now? With all that is going on?"

Sariel sighed and shook his head, trying not to yawn. He'd stayed up late pacing his wooden floors, until he couldn't help himself and went back to Miranda's for another look. One last touch. Another taste. *Merde!* She was beautiful. And there was something else, something he recognized in her, like an oldie on the radio that brings back a memory, fuzzy but compelling.

Come back, Miranda had thought, just as he'd left. *Come back.*

He hadn't wanted to leave. It had taken everything inside him to go before they were doing more than kissing.

"Listen, Brennus," Sariel said, irritated. "I haven't broken any laws. We've established that Miranda Stead is not, in fact, a spy. And anyway, I'm going East soon to . . . work."

"Yes." Brennus's mouth was grim and serious. "And

you should value how important your work is to all of us. You—of all people—close to Kallisto and connected to Quain."

Sariel crossed his arms, his jaw tight, and stared at his bookcase, his gardening books in green rows on the shelves. He knew what was coming, the lecture he'd gotten from everyone since he could remember.

Brennus slammed his hand again on the table, the sound a flesh crack in the air. "You owe it to your father. It's your duty. It's your legacy to do everything in your power to stop Quain."

Sariel uncrossed his arms and shook his head. "You don't have to tell me that. How could I possibly forget? He took everything from my family. And Kallisto tried to, as well. I don't want to see them succeed. I want to see them—"

"So why," Brennus said softly, his shoulders falling slightly, "would you put yourself at risk? Leave a vortex with a *Moyenne* woman? Manage to not take her memories? She's walking around San Francisco with our meeting in her mind, with faces and names. And you've left thoughts in her mind, thoughts Kallisto could extract to work on you."

Sariel opened his mouth to answer, but he couldn't find a reply. Why had he chosen to whisk Miranda from the meeting? Brennus would have found a way to get her home safely, if not scared out of her mind and hobbled by her broken ankle. And that was it. Sariel hadn't wanted her to be hurt or frightened. As the people had parted and he'd seen her looking at him from across the room, all he'd wanted to do was take away the fear she had so tried to hide under bluster. Her fear had pulled him away from his beer, across the room, and to her side.

"Look, no one will find Miranda or me," Sariel said. "I'll take her memories. All of them. Soon."

Brennus nodded, satisfied, buttoning his robe.

"But why would he want me?" Sariel asked. "He's done with us, my family."

Brennus looked up quickly and stared at Sariel, his eyes slits. Sariel tried to touch his mind, but Brennus had wrapped a veil around it.

"Just do as we ask," he said.

Fine, Sariel thought, standing up and walking to his window, which overlooked windblown Cyprus trees, brown coastal hills, and the Pacific Ocean. What he wouldn't do to be outside right now, tending to his rhododendrons or hiking Mount Tamalpais instead of being trapped inside with Brennus. For too many years now, the *Croyant* world had constricted, pulled tight, kept itself separate from the other worlds around them. Everything now was fear—who would attack them, steal from them, kill them—and Sariel had to slip into the world as an observer until he found those he needed to.

As his father, Hadrian, had done before him, Sariel found those practicing bad magic, abusing *Moyenne,* taking property or money or power that wasn't theirs. He did what he needed to do for the *Croyant* world and for the greater good of all, but there was something wrong in a world where trapping and sometimes killing others was necessary. He'd caught Quain followers, *sorcières* and *sorciers* who'd tried to undermine *Croyant* law, those who were dissatisfied with Adalbert and the Council, wanting a new leader, and new power. He'd found *Croyant* who wanted to rule over the *Moyenne,* to lead lives of kings and queens, saying that magic gave them that right.

There had been close calls. Just two years before, Rufus had nearly lost his life in battle against Quain, Kallisto, and a *sorcier* named Cadeyrn Macara, an important member of the *Croyant* community Quain had managed to enchant. At that point, Sariel realized that if Macara had been turned, so could anyone. Of course, Brennus's fears were legitimate, but the fight was weakening *Croyant* from the inside out, reducing life to good and bad, forcing everyone to be alert, suspicious, vigilant. And sometimes Sariel found himself hunting down *Croyant* who were once his friends or members of the Council, people who hadn't been able to say no to Quain.

But no matter who it was, Sariel could hunt thief or murderer or terrorist. That was his gift.

Through the many colored strands of thought in the universe, he could winnow out the pretenders, the decoys, until he could find the Quain follower in one crowded apartment in Prague or Bucharest or Tunis. In order to do so, he used the telepathic gift he was born with, and then he used the gift he learned, taking thoughts to bind his prisoner into silence, into motionlessness, into a light, persuasive, steadily more constrictive pain, until he could think them both to the *Croyant* Council at Rabley Heath.

Sometimes, though, things didn't go as planned. Sometimes things got . . . messy.

"I hope you understand this, young Valasay," Brennus said, standing up, his old bones creaking. "I don't want to have to come back here again before you head East. I'm warning you. Don't go back to the woman again. If your father knew—"

Sariel shook his head. "Don't talk about my father."

Brennus held up his hands, sighing, his eyes no longer filled with anger and reproach. Sariel's father, Hadrian, and Brennus had served on the Council together, and now Brennus's hands were stiff, spotted, lined with veins.

"Looks like you need a trip to the healer," Sariel said, struck suddenly by how old Brennus was. It wasn't just his rage at Quain making him forgetful and angry—it was his body.

"Mind your own concerns," Brennus said, flashing

the wild eyes he'd worn as a warrior in the battle against a rebellious troop of *Croyant* at Jacob's Well fifty years ago. "I can take care of myself and anything Quain throws at me. Now keep a low profile until you go. No good being spotted, especially when we can't trust anyone. Anyone!"

Sariel wanted to tell Brennus that not everyone was a spy or a thief, but in an instant, Brennus was gone, nothing blocking Sariel's view of the Pacific, the day outside warm and blue and full of salt.

He tried to stop himself. In fact, all day he worked in his garden, forcing himself to think of only soil, fertilizer, rootball, compost. Every time Miranda flickered into his mind, he shut down the thoughts. He wasn't always successful. One minute he was tamping down dirt around an azalea, and the next thing he knew, he was hovering in her bedroom, watching her try on a white blouse. She stood in front of her full-length mirror, wearing nothing but the blouse and her underwear, a postage-stamp piece of silk stretched tight across her lovely rear. The sun poured through the window, making her skin glow, the tender spot behind her knees too much for him to bear. He wanted to swoop down, kneel behind her, kiss those sweet spots, his lips tracing the pattern of her freckles, moving his hands up her thighs as he did.

Miranda stamped her left foot, pushed her hands through her curly hair. She was having a hard time matching button to buttonhole, each time making a mistake. "Crap," she said, sticking her tongue out at her own reflection. "Just focus! Stop being an idiot."

Then she tried again, her slim fingers flitting over the buttons.

"Crap," she said after the third attempt. She took off

the blouse, threw it on the bed and pulled a T-shirt out of a drawer. As she was closing the drawer, she turned, looked around, as if she'd felt his heart beating. At that moment, Sariel realized what he was doing and thought himself back to his yard, his hands on the earth, azalea leaves brushing his hair.

He'd made it back. But she'd almost seen him. She'd known he was there.

Later in the day, the sun just setting behind the flat pan of the Pacific, Sariel stood in front of his refrigerator, his hands on his hips, looking at food that seemed completely unacceptable. He didn't feel like eating, much less cooking, and he thought it might be easier to think himself to a restaurant in Sausalito. That seemed like too much effort, though, and he was motionless, blinking against the fridge light. He began to drift. One second he was looking at a lump of Swiss cheese, and then he was standing in her office watching her work at her computer. She'd pinned her hair up with a silver clip, the slim column of her neck just feet away from him. A few wild curls had escaped from the clip and spiraled down to her shoulder. He could just reach out, pull one gently and then move his hand along the curve of her neck and shoulder.

Sariel reached out, and he saw her stop typing, sit up straight. He saw her skin prick with goose bumps, and she very slowly began to turn toward him.

Go, he thought, and he was back in the kitchen, standing in front of the fridge, looking at cheese. Ketchup. A jar of pickles.

Everything got worse after one beer and then two. Sariel tried to contact Rufus, but his brother and Fabia were working, brought to London to listen to a particular apartment building. Rufus only had time to shoot back a quick, *Take a long run. Or a cold shower. Or both* before he needed to get back to work.

Felix was floating somewhere over Hana, reports of a curious group of tourists checking into a private house keeping him busy. These tourists never seemed to drive anywhere for food or supplies, but had been quite happily vacationing for weeks.

I'm just seeing who's having a good time, Felix thought. *If they're foes, we'll have some work on our hands. If they're friends, I'm ready to have some fun.*

Sariel paced, knowing there were spells he could cast on himself. Or he could actually go to a healer to have these Miranda memories lifted from his mind. That would do it. He knew the healer he'd visit, too, Justus, one of his teachers at school, a man known for extracting only what was requested, not a thought more. It was the perfect solution. Sariel could stay away from Miranda if he didn't have to keep breathing in her hair and her skin, the soft floral taste of her body. How easy to follow Brennus's orders if he didn't have to think about the way her breast felt in his hand, the hardness of her nipple against his tongue. He'd be just perfect if he didn't hear her laugh in his head, her funny comebacks, her throaty whisper.

Sariel stopped walking, looked out his window, the sky flush with stars. He knew what he had to do.

"It's me again," Sariel said, kissing her temple, his breath in her ear, his hands on her body. He let her consciousness rise higher, and Miranda opened her eyes, smiling.

"Not you again. Are you a recurring dream? Or is it nightmare?" She spoke aloud, not just thinking to him this time. "Or a ghost? I think you were haunting me all day."

He lay down beside her, letting his hands run the length of her long, smooth body. "What is it for you?" He could hear her nerves, the electricity inside her spiking at his touch, a thin layer of fear in her mind. When he felt her fear, Sariel wanted to erase it, needing her—for some reason—to trust him. To believe in him, even though he knew she must forget everything.

"Mostly a nightmare." She pulled him to her, her arms around his neck, shoulders. "Not the visiting part, but the awake part. I spend all my time convincing myself I'm not crazy. I can't write. I basically can't think. I can't even seem to put my clothes on right. And then you show up and it all makes sense."

"You're not crazy," Sariel said. "I'm the crazy one. I can't stop coming here. And I've been warned in the strictest terms not to."

Miranda pulled away, blinking, her eyes wide, looking at him, touching his hair, his face, her finger lingering on his lip. "That man? Brennus?"

He nodded. "And he's right. More than right."

"Why?" She looked at him, confused, and then laughed. "I don't get any of this. But the least of anyone's worries would be . . ." Miranda leaned over and kissed him. "Us."

Sariel didn't want to talk anymore, or think, letting her thoughts disappear from his mind. He pushed her back, holding her arms tightly, not letting her move. He kissed her face, her soft throat, feeling her pulse under his lips. Moving down, he found her lush breast, the nipple hard and firm and ready for his tongue.

"Oh," she moaned, struggling a little to free her arms, but he held tightly, his tongue circling her nipple, then sliding over to the other, just as eager.

She tasted like lavender, like something new, like

nothing he'd ever breathed in and swallowed before. He kissed his way down her ribs, stomach, all the way to her thighs. He let her hands go and slid his own under her smooth rear, taking her round, lovely flesh in his palms, and circled her heat with his tongue, pressing his lips against her wetness.

Miranda moaned lightly, trying to move her body to his wet strokes, but he held her still, whispering, "Don't move. Let me do this."

Her thoughts rushed through him—her confusion about who he was and her desire for him and his body. *No. Yes. No. Yes. Oh, God,* she thought, her mind blurring as Sariel moved his mouth and tongue against her. Wanting to enjoy this, he heard her tell herself, *Oh, Miranda! Just shut up!*

Sariel felt her relax, and he closed his eyes, letting himself savor her taste, her willingness to trust him even though she knew nothing about him or his life. Even though being with him made her think she was crazy. All he wanted to do was stay there, drinking her in, not thinking, just feeling, but his body wanted hers, in a way he hadn't wanted anyone since . . . Sariel couldn't think about the past, about her, so he focused on Miranda, the way she opened to him, her tiny thrusts against his mouth, her hands in his hair, her little moans as he moved faster, his name on her lips as she cried out and her body slowly quieted, relaxed, fell back onto the mattress.

He lifted his mouth and looked up. Miranda opened her eyes and smiled.

"Magic," she whispered, touching his hair, twirling a strand between her fingers.

Sariel stood up, whipped off his shirt, took off his pants, and knelt next to her, letting her feel his body, his chest, his stomach. He caught his breath, unable to stand how hard he was, how good her soft hands felt wrapped around him, how needful.

Leaning over her, he kissed her, letting her taste flow between them. She kissed him back, holding him tightly, and then she broke away.

"Don't tell me there's such a thing as a magical condom?" Miranda said, twining her legs around him, her hands on his shoulders. "An antipregnancy potion? A conception curse?"

"That's not my area of expertise," he said lightly, trying to keep himself from just taking her now without any protection. "I rely on *Moyenne* technology."

Sariel slowly pulled himself out of her embrace and grabbed his pants from the chair and pulled out a condom from a pocket. He fumbled with the wrapper, his fingers jittery.

"Let me," she said, moving his hands away, sliding the latex over him so smoothly, so firmly, he wasn't sure he'd make it until she was done.

"There," she said, letting him sink on top of her, kissing his neck, his mouth, lifting up her hips to him.

He couldn't speak, wanting only to feel her skin, her sleek shimmer as he pushed into her. Slowly, wanting to hold the sensation for as long as he could, he pressed himself as deep as he could. His mind became his feelings, his body, knowing only how warm and wet and good Miranda felt.

And they moved together. To Sariel, their back-and-forth rocking reminded him of how it felt to slip through time and matter, his body flowing, touching nothing, touching everything. Miranda moved with him, her breath against his lips, face, neck, her hands tight on his back.

"Are you real?" she said at one point, and Sariel didn't really know if he was, this lovemaking with her more magic than he'd seen in his life.

"I don't know," he said, lifting her hips to him, sliding in and out of her long and deep, and then they were slipping through everything, all at once, together.

They lay together on her bed, his arm around her, her head on his chest. With her fingertips, she drew light lines on his skin, her slightest touch waking him with feeling.

Outside, the sky was lightening, the Bay Bridge lights flittering in the gray near dawn, and soon he'd have to leave Miranda. Soon he'd have to leave the country. He had work to do, and she couldn't know about it or be a part of it. Miranda could never be a part of his life.

Sariel closed his eyes, ran a hand along the curve of hip. Miranda sighed, pulled him closer.

"So, how do you do it? The moving thing."

"Are you talking about this?" Sariel pulled her up on top of him, kissing her mouth, his hands on her breasts. "I want to move you all night."

Pushing herself up, she looked down, her sumptuous hair curling around her face, her eyes lapis in the dark. "I think we've moved this bed around the whole room. Larry downstairs probably thinks I'm redecorating. Or that I'm having my first ever orgy."

Sariel ran his finger on her cheek, closed his eyes, and breathed in her lavender scent. He was sure he'd never tire of her mouth on his or her skin under his hands. Probably she'd figured that out after the third time he'd hardened and pressed against her, wanting her again. He knew he'd have to make her forget him and everything about this night, but felt a deep, hollow pain at the idea that he'd be the only one who'd remember the way she held him against her heart after he'd come, her arms holding him tightly.

Sariel was silent, his hand smoothing her hair.

Miranda leaned into his touch. "But I really meant this thing." She lay on top of him, putting her arms around his neck. "When you hold me and we end up somewhere ridiculous. Like your house when we'd been on a street."

"Oh, that." He tried to sound light, but this was exactly what Brennus had warned him about. If he told her how he thought himself places, she'd just want to know more, the conduit between *Croyant* and *Moyenne* growing thicker and clearer. It wasn't likely, but it was possible that one of Sariel's enemies could track her down, find out information that would lead to Sariel. Miranda was soaking him in, learning more about him the longer they were together. By making love, Sariel was putting her at risk.

It would be so much easier if the *Croyant* and *Moyenne* worlds were fused. Sariel, Rufus, and Felix had debated pulling the two worlds together, for once and for all.

"Why keep it to ourselves?" Rufus had said over three too many steins of beer one late night. "It's not like they could use the information. Remember what Reynaldo always said, 'It's all one world.'"

Reynaldo De Bautista was a man they'd all met two years ago, a new magic voice in the world, one that Adalbert listened to closely. Reynaldo wasn't *Croyant*, but his magic, once brought into the *Croyant* world, would only bring people together.

"But you know what *Moyenne* can do, Ru. They could use us," Felix said. "They could make us do what they wanted."

When Felix had said that, Sariel remembered what had happened to their kind periodically through the ages: *Croyant* burned and drowned and stoned by hysterical *Moyenne* townsfolk. Whenever *Croyant* thought it would be safe to unveil one or two little bits of magic, *Moyenne* blamed them for the crops failing, for a sudden tornado, for the plague. Long ago, *Croyant* learned to keep their lives hidden or find a tribe or village somewhere that prized magic, understood it, and left *Croyant* folk to themselves. And now, with Quain using *Moyenne* to attack them, it was even more dangerous to trust anyone. But with Miranda, Sariel felt safe, as if she already knew and accepted his secrets. As if he'd met her before and knew hers. But that was ridiculous. He didn't know her. She couldn't possibly know him. She was just a woman. A lovely, beautiful, amazing woman, but *Moyenne* all the same.

"It's just a little something I picked up in India," Sariel said.

"Yeah, just like a Ganisha statue. You can buy anything on the street corners there. A healing spell, a little ability to travel through air. In fact, it doesn't have to be India. The other day I think I saw a book titled *Mind Reading for Dummies.*" She took her arms from around his neck and lay back on the pillow. "If I'm going to believe in you, I have to know you, Sariel. Otherwise, it *is* just a dream."

He sighed. How to explain? And should he? The risks were so great, but he could feel her need to know, her want to know. She was the first Moyenne woman he'd ever wanted to tell the truth to, most thinking he was just some sorry-ass jerk who disappeared after a couple of good dates. She was different, but the times were different, too. Brennus told him that giving her any information was dangerous, both to *Croyant* and to Miranda. Even though Sariel had scanned the area and found it empty of Quain influence or *Croyant* snooping, someone could be listening in. But that was unlikely. After all, wasn't it Sariel's gift to find those who tried to hide? He'd been focusing, hadn't he? He'd been paying attention. Aside from finding himself in Miranda's house twice in one day quite by accident, he was on top of everything.

"I don't know," he said.

"Come on," she said, tracing circles on his chest. "I promise to keep it all secret. It's in my best interest to do so. Otherwise, I'll be carted off to the loony bin in a white van. Straitjacket and everything."

Sariel pulled her close, kissed her hair, breathing in her scent. It really couldn't hurt. He was going to take Miranda's memories. Tomorrow. Just before he left. He had no choice. None at all.

"Well? I'm waiting?" she said, her voice filled with a stubborn, pretend pout.

Sariel smiled, trying to remember how Zosime taught them the basics of traveling by thought.

"Not everyone can do it," she had said. "But most of us can. You have to start imagining it when you're young."

Sariel turned onto his side to look at Miranda.

"If I tell you, you can't write poems about it. Some odd secrets you have to keep secret. Not like you did about flying."

Turning to him, she smiled. "You read that? It's a terrible poem. I'm not done working on it."

"You can't even write a terrible poem about what I'm going to tell you."

Her eyes sharpened. "Wait a minute. You're supposed to say it's not a terrible poem."

"You don't sound very interested in travel. Why don't we talk about flying instead?"

She punched him lightly on the arm. "Okay. I promise."

He kissed her forehead. "It wasn't a terrible poem."

"Tell me."

He cleared his throat, wondering how to explain something that he did automatically now. It was like trying to explain how to swallow or breathe or cry. But he remembered his mother, Zosime, and how she explained it to him and his brothers.

"So," he started, running a hand through her hair, looping curls on his fingers, "here it is. Energy is everything, everywhere. The human body has about enough energy inside it that if we released it all at once, it would be like twenty or thirty hydrogen bombs."

Miranda snorted. "So why haven't we all burst open and exploded?"

"Because," Sariel said, "most of us aren't very good at releasing it. The energy is trapped."

"That's good news," she said. "Otherwise, what a mess."

"Miranda, you have to be serious. I'm not kidding."

"Okay, okay. I think I might still be with you," she said.

"Good. So energy doesn't necessarily always flow but is made up in individual packets. You're a packet. I'm a packet. These packets are called quanta. But even though we're individual, we're all part of the same field of energy. Energy is liberated by matter—matter is energy waiting to happen."

He looked at Miranda, who was biting her lip, her forehead creased. "Quanta?" she queried.

"Look, we're all together. We're all the same. The same energy. The whole universe. The whole world. People, animals, stone, air, water. We look separate, but we're not. Atoms and molecules are in continual movement, dense or not dense. In quantum mechanics, there's a theory called—"

"Wait," she said, leaning up on an elbow. "This is too much for me. I can barely understand how a television set can pick up a show from the air," Miranda said.

"Well, that's easy to exp—"

"Don't bother. I got D's in science. It's a miracle I got into college."

"You're too smart. It can't have been that bad." He pulled gently on a curl, letting it go and watching it swirl back into shape.

"Indeed it was. I still think osmosis is a metaphor." She pressed closer to him.

He laughed, remembering how he'd doodled while Zosime talked. Felix was the only one who really knew how a *penseur de mouvement* worked the atomic universe, though he rarely chose to use his talent.

"Just tell me how you start," she said, leaning over him again. "Tell me how it feels in the body. Tell me what you have to think about."

Sariel closed his eyes and tried to find the words. "Well, I have to hold you when I travel with you. I'm thinking for us both. So I put my arms around you, and I imagine the world like an infinity of atoms. Everything between me and my destination had been rendered into a large, moving wall of energy that I think of as the *gray*. All I have to do is think myself—and you—into the part of the energy I want to go as. And then I open my eyes, and we're there. Because in a way, I was already there. It's all one same big space. One giant pie of energy."

Miranda was silent. He could feel her heart beating against his chest. For a second, he wished he could do exactly what he just explained and take her to his house in Marin, keeping her out of this world, her world. He wanted her to be with him, but even as he imagined Miranda working in his garden, traveling with him to Council meetings in England or to other countries for work, Sariel saw that it could never happen. Relationships with *Moyenne* weren't impossible, but the *Croyant* member of the couple usually slipped away from the *Croyant* world, magic too confusing and too difficult for the *Moyenne* partner to accept. Then there were children to consider. It was always easier to slip into an ordinary life, stay under the radar, let the kids grow up ignoring the magic of one parent. But it was harder to stay under the radar now due to the threat from Quain. As Quain loosed his power on the world, such a relationship was dangerous on top of everything else.

"Can you hang out in that energy wall? Can you live in there?" she asked. "I mean, can you get stuck? It must be pretty big."

Sariel caught his breath, and then exhaled, slowly. There it was. His dream, his nightmare, the one he'd had since childhood. In the dream, he is always running through the gray waves, matter streaming all around, through him. He can't find, he can't find . . . whoever it is he's looking for. He's calling out but makes no sound. He needs to find this person. He's trapped. Alone. Something evil is coming for him, is next to him, is upon him. *No,* he cries. But then he's awake and sweating.

He shook his head and then pulled Miranda closer. "Not that I know of. But it probably wouldn't be fun."

"Doesn't sound like it. I'd much rather be here with you." She kissed his shoulder, his ear, his cheek.

"So you believe all this? My weird stories?"

Without saying anything, she ran a hand along his side, down his thigh, and then back up, kissing his eyelid. "You're here, aren't you? I didn't see a taxi drop you off. I never see you leave. If I'm crazy, you're the best hallucination ever. If this is crazy, I want to stay this way."

"And you won't write about it? Not even for another Holitzer?"

She lifted her head and stared at him. "How do you—oh, I know. I must have been thinking about it."

"No, I saw the letter on your dresser."

Miranda laughed into his shoulder and then stopped, her mind filling with an idea. And that was when he heard her thought, her desire, felt it loud and clear. But before he answered her, he turned to look out the window. Early light was glinting on the bay, the morning dove gray and quiet.

"Let's go for a walk," he said.

"What?"

"Take me to that coffee place you were thinking about a minute ago. The one that opens before five. Serves the best coffee, makes the huge croissants."

"You are the spy, Sariel. Please don't let anyone ever say different. Don't let them say I was the spy."

Sariel pulled away the blankets and sat up, lifting her to his lap. "I won't ever let anyone say a thing about you, Miranda. Not one thing."

They were the only two people out on the street. Periodically, a car would race by, the driver loving the feel of driving in the city unfettered, no traffic, long lights, or traffic cops cramping style or speed. The coffee shop had just opened, and they were the first customers, ordering lattes and croissants to go. On their way back to her apartment, Miranda carried the bag of croissants and her coffee, looking at him as they walked.

"What?" he said, turning to her, smiling. "What is it? What are you thinking?"

"About you."

"Me, what?"

"You out in the real world. Drinking your coffee. Eating your pastry. Looking like a regular Joe just before dawn."

"What else am I supposed to do?" he asked. "How did you want to go to get coffee?"

"I don't know. Move us there by magic. Can't you materialize food or something? Or is that too *Star Trek*?"

"That's too *Star Trek*."

"There's no spell for food?" Miranda stopped walking. "What if you were trapped on an island or lost somewhere? Couldn't you make something to eat?"

He stopped, turning back to her. "Fine. Yes. We can do that. But we like to cook, too. You know. Enjoy the experience. Slice onions. Mince shallots. Taste the sauce."

"Are you enjoying this experience?"

Sariel shook his head, watched her in the earliest of morning light, the sky opening into a slight pale blue above them. "I love this experience."

"Good." She walked up to him, and as she did, he heard what she was thinking, the same thought she'd had in bed. She stared at him unblinking.

"No, I can't do that," he said.

"Please," she said. "Oh, come on! Take me somewhere. Take me somewhere I can't go because the flights are too expensive, even with the prize money from the Holitzer. Paris or something. Berlin. The Arctic. Cleveland, even."

And then, as he looked at her standing on the sidewalk, her hair wild, her face so beautiful, he knew he wanted to take her everywhere. How they would travel! If only she were someone else. If only she were *Croyant*. They could be like he'd imagined he and Kallisto should have been, together always, moving around the planet, twined in each other's thoughts, paired in a way *Moyenne* could never be.

Miranda walked up to him, put her hand on his cheek, looking into his eyes.

Sariel shook his head. This was intolerable. Why make it worse by pretending? Just as he was about to stop Miranda from asking him again, kissing her into forgetting her request, he felt the first tentative request in his mind—someone wanted to speak to him.

Sariel closed his eyes, feeling for recognition. Who was it? Who was calling him now? Then he recognized the tone, the laughter, could almost see the raised eyebrow without seeing the face. It was his younger brother Felix.

What now? Sariel thought. *I thought you were going to be busy with that wild bunch from Hana.*

Turned out to be drug dealers. Moyenne *drug dealers. They had some pals who were helicoptering in their supplies. I didn't stick around once I called the authorities.*

So why are you bothering me?

Bring her here. I heard what she wants. Just for an hour. I'll make piña coladas.

Don't you need your beauty sleep? Sariel thought back.

Not necessary. You know I'm the best-looking of the whole lot. So bring her. I'm juicing a pineapple as we think. Hurry up.

I shouldn't.

Always the shoulds. Look how far that's gotten you. Lighten up, bro.

"You ready?" Sariel turned to look at Miranda, who was smoothing her white sundress and adjusting the slim straps on her shoulders. He brought a hand to her arm, whisking it up to her shoulder, cupping her smooth flesh under his palm.

Miranda smiled. "I guess I'm ready. I've never been to Hawaii at night or ever, so my dressing options are limited. Is this okay?" She smiled at him, looking shy. She brought a hand to her hair and tried to press it smooth. The moment she took her hand away, the curls bounded back to life. Sariel wondered if Felix would mind if they didn't show up—he'd rather spend what remained of his time with Miranda in bed, no dress, no piña colada. He'd rather spend the time alone with her because there was so little left.

But she was so excited, her thoughts racing: *trip, hug*

him tight, don't let go, don't get stuck in the gray. His brother. You're meeting his brother. Don't let go.

Don't let go, Sariel wanted to say. *Ever.* But instead he smiled and nodded. "Perfect. Just the right dress for a two A.M. visit to Hawaii."

Sariel walked up to her, breathed in her sweet toothpaste breath and the flowers in her face lotion. He put his arms around her, feeling her body against him. "Don't be scared."

"I'm not scared," she said, but she was lying. And it wasn't just her thoughts of being stuck in the gray or lost that betrayed her. She trembled, her arms and legs shaking.

He pressed her tighter and brought them into the gray, imagining Felix's house in Hilo, seeing his brother sitting on his *lanai,* a drink in his hand, and then they were there.

"Finally," Felix said. "I'm already on my second."

Sariel let go of Miranda, but took her hand, squeezing it. She was dazed, her eyes wide, her thoughts almost electric. She blinked and then shook her head, looking at Felix.

"Oh. Hello."

Felix smiled, put down his drink, and stuck out a hand. "Felix Valasay. Sariel's younger, much better-looking brother."

Sariel rolled his eyes, knowing that it was true. When they were younger, people often mistook them for twins, both with the same shade of hair and light, almost golden brown eyes. But there was something about Felix—maybe it was that his eyes were just a shade lighter, verging on green in the sun. Or his hair was a bit longer, hanging down to the middle of his back. But Sariel knew it wasn't what Felix looked like on the outside. Really, the three brothers were cut from a similar cloth, but Felix was just a shade different. It was his confidence, the way he could do what he was doing now: shake Miranda's hand, smile at her as if she were the most interesting woman in the world. Of course, Sariel had to admit, she *was* the most interesting woman in the world. But he was acting with Miranda the way he acted with all women. Felix had always been able to bring home women whenever he pleased, but remained . . .

Free, Felix thought, winking. *Shut up. And let me focus on your lady love here.*

Sariel turned to Miranda, taking her hand. At his touch, she softened, relaxed, her body uncoiling, her thoughts turning lighter: *the air is so warm; is that the ocean? Am I here?* She looked at Sariel and then back at Felix.

"Well, I'm not sure about *better*-looking," Miranda said. "It might be a tie. But I am a bit partial to him, especially because he's going to really save me a bundle on airfare."

Sariel smiled but felt the feeling fake on his face. Felix heard his thought and thought back, *Enjoy the moment.* Sariel shrugged.

"Wait a minute," Miranda said, taking her hand from Sariel's. "Are you two talking? That's not fair. Turn it off, okay? I can barely handle a conversation with Sariel through regular channels."

"Okay," said Felix. "Will do. Bro?"

Nodding, Sariel turned off his thoughts, the world going from omnidimensional to almost flat, sound becoming a one- note tune. It always took him time to adjust to the plainness of the world without telepathy. And it made him sad that Miranda would never know what it felt like to hear and feel it all.

"Shut down," Sariel said. "So where are these drinks?"

Felix asked them to sit down, and he poured them

each a large glass of a frosty concoction. "Here you go. My specialty. Cheers."

They raised their glasses, and Sariel sipped, watching Miranda, who was smiling even as she sipped.

"So," Sariel said. "What are you doing up at three in the morning? Not tired after checking out the tourists? Don't you have better things to do than send your feelers out to me?"

Felix put down his drink. "Just a little restless from work." He shot Sariel a glance. "A little follow-up to do. So I thought to myself, what is my big bro doing? What could that sad sack possibly have going tonight? And to my surprise, well, sorry to interrupt!"

Miranda flushed, but she was still smiling.

"So how long have you two known each other?" Felix asked.

Miranda looked up from her drink. "Just a few days. But your brother saved me from a gang of your pals. And fixed my broken ankle. But it took me a while to realize he wasn't a dream or a ghost. I'm still not totally convinced. I have this feeling that any moment I'll wake up in the insane asylum with a nurse standing over me, yelling, 'Doctor, Doctor, she's come to.'"

Felix laughed. "Stay with Sariel long enough and that will happen no matter what."

"Very funny," Sariel said. And then he really heard Felix's words: *Stay with Sariel long enough.* There would be no long enough. He took another sip of the too-sweet drink and tried not to cough.

"So what do you do, Miranda?" Felix asked.

"Oh, I'm a poet." Miranda flushed and shrugged.

"Hey," said Felix. "You said that in the same tone you might use to say 'axe murderer' or 'sex offender.' As far as I know, a poet is a good thing."

"I hate saying it out loud. Some people think it's pretentious. Like I live in a garret wearing a beret, smoking

Gauloises, drinking absinthe, and talking about Nietzsche. Mostly I say I'm a writer, and people assume I've got steady work at a newspaper or something."

"What does a poet do, then?" Felix asked, smiling. "I mean, I always assumed smoking and drinking and writing about death was an industry standard."

Miranda smiled at Felix, and Sariel realized he'd never asked her how a poet lived. But then again, he'd watched her, seen her thinking and typing in front of her computer just yesterday. He'd first seen her after she'd read her poetry. Poets lived, well, like Miranda.

"I spend a lot of time reading. And I sit in front of my computer staring at the screen trying to figure out how to turn ideas into words. How to describe the heart with language. How to take a moment of indescribable beauty and not weaken it as I write it down. Mostly, I sit around writing drivel, waiting for the miracle."

"Don't listen to her. She's a wonderful poet," Sariel said, suddenly feeling so heavy and stuck in his own thoughts that he wanted to get up, wrap his arms around Miranda and leave. How could he just watch her, her skin pale in the Hawaiian moonlight, her eyes dark with excitement? How could he listen to one more minute of this when he knew it had to end?

He had no choice. So as she and Felix continued talking about poetry, he watched her move her hands as she explained her work, asked questions about where Felix and Sariel grew up and went to school. He tried to memorize everything.

She smiled at Sariel as Felix told her in detail about the plain tract home in Walnut Creek where Zosime raised them and gave her more roundabout information on the boarding school in Bampton, England.

"A boarding school? You have got to be kidding. Not a school like in those books with the wizard kid?"

Felix laughed, topped off her drink. "Probably not

much different from your school. We had to do calculus and research papers, the whole deal. Dangling modifiers and dissected frogs. Where did you go?"

Sariel watched her as she talked about Lowell High School and then college, her face flushed, her hair now wet tendrils in the Hawaiian humidity, her laughter a bell in the still-warm night. This couldn't go on any longer. It was torture to be around her quick mind, ready laugh, and beautiful body, when he knew that for her safety and his, he needed to clear her mind of everything. He couldn't drag this out for himself, knowing that it would be impossible to forget her. At least she would forget him, all of this a fuzzy blip in her memory, like *déjà vu*.

After another drink and more talk, the Hawaiian sun was on the horizon. San Francisco was already well into morning.

"We've got to go," Sariel said, standing up and holding out a hand to Miranda.

"All good things must end," Felix said, laughing, and then he stopped, shooting a quick look at Sariel. "I'm just glad I got a chance to meet you, Miranda."

Pushing Sariel away from Miranda, Felix gave her a quick hug, and Sariel closed his eyes. Felix had never really approved of any of the women Sariel had been with.

"Too needy," he'd say. "Wants to settle you down. Can't light a fire in her own fireplace much less do magic."

When Sariel brought Kallisto home for the first time, Felix hadn't wanted to get within one mile of her, even during the brief time when Zosime and Rufus thought she was the most wonderful *sorcière* on the planet.

"I don't like her," Felix told him once over too many beers, an evening that ended with Sariel setting down his beer stein and nailing Felix in the jaw. Sure, he'd healed his brother after the scuffle was over. But he heard Felix's words in his mind, heard his judgment.

Of course, Felix had been right about Kallisto. Completely. But here Felix was, totally smitten with the woman Sariel couldn't have. If Felix could hear his thoughts, Sariel would beat him down with a choice word or two.

"Okay, enough. We're off." Sariel hugged Felix. "I'll talk with you later."

"Safe journey," Felix said, waving.

Sariel put his arms around Miranda, thought them back into the gray, and then they were home, the light streaming into Miranda's bedroom. They were back. Back into the day Sariel would have to take her memories away and would have to learn to live with his own.

Chapter Six

Miranda held onto Sariel, knowing they weren't anywhere. She pressed her hands into his strong back, forced her cheek onto his chest. She felt his heart, a steady *thump, thump, thump,* and she wished hers was beating in such a calm rhythm. If she let go, what would happen? Would she stay stuck in nothingness? Would she be left behind in a place she could never escape from? A place where she would never see Sariel again? She gripped harder, pressed in closer, clenched her eyes closed tighter. Her back molars started to ache.

Then Sariel started to laugh, the lovely sound pulsing into her.

"Miranda, relax. We've been here for a couple of minutes. I think we're safe."

Slowly, she opened her eyes, the light from her bedroom window making her blink. Lightening her grip, she inched away from Sariel and then smiled back at him.

"That was unbelievable."

"Not really." Sariel sighed, put his hands in his pockets, and turned to look out the window.

"Yes, really," she said, looking up at him. She pushed a stand of hair away from his cheek, wishing she could read his mind. What was he thinking? Why did he look so sad?

He bit his lip and looked toward her bed. For a second, she hoped he would want to crawl back under the covers and stay there for the rest of the day. But instead, he pointed at her answering machine on the bedside table.

"Seems like someone's being trying to get ahold of you."

Miranda let go of him and walked to the bedside table and saw the machine blinking its always-urgent red. Five calls. When they'd left, there'd been none.

"Let me check," she said, sitting down on the bed. "I wonder. Oh, my God! I bet it's about Viv! The baby!"

Sariel sighed and sat by her. Miranda quickly pressed the buttons on the machine, and as she had thought, all the calls were from Seamus.

"Randa, where are you? Viv's gone into labor. We aren't going to the hospital yet, but soon. Call my cell."

The next call was a little more urgent, Seamus's voice a bit higher, until the fifth call, where he was positively shrill.

"It's happening so fast. We'll be at Mt. Diablo hospital. Get here quick."

Miranda slammed down the phone and looked over at Sariel.

"My sister's having her baby. I've got to get out there. But Christ, it's the tail end of the commute." Miranda walked over to the window and saw the usual morning parking lot on the bottom deck of the Bay Bridge, the top deck moving only slightly faster. "It'll take me over an hour to get there. I'll probably be too late."

Miranda turned away from the window, her breath high in her chest, her heart beating as fast as it had when Sariel thought them home from Hawaii. She had an idea, but she didn't know how to say it. A couple of days ago, she'd have thought she was nuts if she thought to ask Sariel to "materialize" her anywhere, much less Viv's birthing room. Last night in bed, though, or even an hour ago as they sat with Felix on his lanai drinking piña coladas, she'd have asked Sariel to take her to Concord and Viv's bedside in a second. But he seemed different now, cold, faraway, distant, as if he'd left part of himself in the gray. The part that liked her.

Miranda didn't have time to worry about him now, though. She had to think about Viv, Seamus, and the new baby. With Jack, she'd finally learned to not keep putting a man's needs in front of her own or her family's. Viv needed her, so with or without Sariel, she was going to Concord to help out. Miranda took a deep breath and walked to the closet, taking off her dress, trying not to imagine Sariel behind her watching. She'd jump on BART and then come home after the evening commute. Or she could spend the night at Viv's. So what did she need? Just a change of clothes, toothpaste. Did June know? She needed to call her mother.

"I'll take you," Sariel said, standing up and walking over to her. "But then I have to go."

His *go* sounded so heavy, Miranda had to breathe deeply to fight off her tears. Swallowing, she turned to face him.

"Thanks. I can't tell you how much I appreciate it. I need to get to my sister."

He nodded, not smiling back, not touching her, looking like the same isolated man she'd seen at the bar that first night, separated from everyone else and just fine with that. Drinking his beer while everyone else flipped out around him.

Where was the man who had healed her ankle? Who

had held her body all last night? Who had walked with her on the deserted city street this morning? Wrapped his arms around her tightly as he took her to Hawaii? Hawaii!

Miranda shook her head and turned back to the closet. As she grabbed clothes to wear, she closed her eyes and breathed in through her nose, trying to calm herself. Sariel could act like a total jerk, but she had important things to do. She pulled on her T-shirt and jeans, thinking about Viv in labor. Her sister. Someone who did need her.

Sariel obviously hadn't ever been to Mt. Diablo Hospital in Concord because rather than placing them somewhere inconspicuous, suddenly he and Miranda were in a rotunda in the main lobby, an older woman with a shopping bag at her feet blinking at them.

"My," she said, her eyes rheumy, her husband asleep and resting against her. "Oh, my. Did you . . . I mean, my goodness."

Sariel almost growled, pulling Miranda away from the woman, swearing under his breath. Stealing a glance at him, she slowed down, her feet frozen beneath her. His face was set, his brow furrowed, his eyes amber slits. His expression reminded her of countless teachers and several boyfriends, their irritation with her after she'd said something wrong, misbehaved, or laughed too loudly.

"Where are we going?" she asked, almost yanking her shoulder away from his grip, tears biting at the corners of her eyes. "I need to find Viv's room."

"Just over here. I need to say something first." He pointed to a hallway past the bank of elevators, and for a second, Miranda hoped he wanted to say good-bye to her properly. A hug. A kiss. A huge, all-encompassing apology. But from the look on his face, he didn't seem in the mood for tenderness.

"I better get up to Viv's room," she said. "Seamus sounded frantic on the message."

She refused to move, ignoring the pressure from his hand on her arm. Sariel turned to face her, and put both his hands on her shoulders. His face was still hard, but something was going on. If only he would tell her.

"Please." His eyes widened, and she could see his sadness again. "Come with me."

"My sister," she said, pointing to the elevators. "I've got to go."

"Now, Miranda."

For a second she would think about later, she knew his hand slid down and gripped her upper arm a bit too hard, and she felt the beginning of a tug. But then an elevator door opened, and June rushed out, clutching her purse. Miranda's mother looked as though she hadn't slept the night before, her short, dyed blonde hair a wild pinprick of style. The whites of her brown eyes were slightly red, her mascara flecked on her lower lids, though June had managed to smooth on a bow of lipstick, only slightly smudged.

Miranda knew that if things weren't somehow terribly wrong, June would never leave the house like this, always conscious of how she looked. Usually, she was always carefully coiffed, her hair a smooth, tidy helmet, her face made up in Lancôme grace, her clothes matching perfectly with her stylish shoes. But now, even June's pants were wrinkled, the buttons on her blouse askew. As she stared at her mother in surprise, Miranda saw for maybe only the third time in her life that she was related to her mother, both of them quite capable of style infractions.

"Mom!" Miranda yanked herself free of Sariel. "What's wrong?"

June looked at Miranda, tried to smile, and then burst into tears, mascara now starting to bleed down her face. "Where have you been!" she snuffled, almost barking out, "Operation."

"What?" Miranda walked to her mother and put her arm around her. "What do you mean?"

June pressed her head against Miranda's shoulder for a second and then stood back. "An emergency C-section. The labor's gone on too long and the baby's heartbeat is down . . . in distress. Your Aunt Bell just called me from her cell phone, and she's parking her car. We're going to go up to wait together. But I'm glad you're finally here, Miranda. Where on earth have you been?"

Giving Miranda a wobbly, worried smile, June looked over to Sariel, who'd stepped back, his hands behind his back.

"Mom, this is Sariel. He brought me here. Sariel, this is my mother, June."

Distracted, June shook her head and then looked up, confused. Finally, she put out a hand. "Sariel's an angel."

Sariel reached over and shook June's hand quickly and then stepped back to where he'd been, his hands quickly behind his back. "Yes," he said. "An archangel."

June tried to say something else, but Sariel interrupted. "Nice to meet you. I've got to be going."

He started to walk away and Miranda ran after him, following him as he turned a corner. When she caught up to him, she grabbed his shoulder. "Sariel, what's wrong? I—I wish you would stay. It would be nice to have . . ."

Miranda heard him sigh deeply, and he stopped moving and turned to her. But then his body went rigid. She gasped when he was flung against the wall, not looking at her. His face went from honey to sheet-white, and he was forced flat against the wall, his eyes flicking as if he were reading a cue card. He whispered, "No. It can't be true," and closed his eyes for a second, nodding.

"What is it?" Miranda leaned over him, breathing in his orange smell. "Are you all right?"

She stroked his hair, wondering if she should run out to the lobby and scream that she needed a doctor, and then he jerked his head toward her, found his breath, and stood up straight. His eyes were wide and full of thought, and he adjusted his hair behind him, keeping his gaze from her as he did.

When Sariel turned to her, his face was steady and revealing nothing. "I've got to go. It's important."

Miranda looked at him, hoping to find something in his expression to hold on to. He seemed to want to say something, his lips moving to words she couldn't hear, to thoughts she had no ability to read. She tried to concentrate, finding a way into his mind as he had into hers. What was going on? What couldn't he tell her? There was something. She thought she felt something. Fear. Anger. Something bad. Really awful. Or was she making up a horrible disaster because that would be the only justification for him treating her like this?

"What? Tell me. What's going on?"

"I can't." He moved toward her as if to kiss her, but then he shrugged, turned, and walked out the glass doors into the morning light.

Miranda watched him leave, and then she heard June come up behind her. Her mother put a hand on Miranda's shoulder, her fingers light.

"He had to go?" June asked. "Just like that?"

Miranda nodded, holding back her tears, and she and her mother watched him stride right by Aunt Bell, who turned to stare at him.

All at once, everything seemed gone. His saving her from the group at the bar, his healing, his touch, his love, the trip. Everything that they had talked about, learned about from each other, laughed over. All of their time together was riding away on his angry back.

His voice had been so hard, curt, sharp, his body so rigid, Miranda wanted nothing more than to wish him gone, to think loudly, *Leave. Let me be with my family.*

But she wouldn't mean it, despite everything.

Nervously, June fiddled with her purse and began to ramble. "Not only is Sariel an archangel, but a fallen one," June said.

"Fallen," Miranda repeated, not moving until Sariel disappeared behind a green slash of shrubs. "How do you know that, Mom?"

"Oh." June waved a hand. "Being Catholic has its perks."

She and Miranda walked toward the door, both of them with their eyes on Aunt Bell, who was lugging two large bags which were undoubtedly filled with snickerdoodles and chocolate oatmeal cookies, her knitting, and the sports page. "You're about as Catholic as I am these days."

June took a tissue from her dress pocket and wiped her lipstick off. "Okay. It was that angel class Bell took me to. After your dad died. We made those angel masks. Bell knitted the hair! So cute. Anyway, we had a list of all the angels. I remember Sariel because he wasn't always a good angel. Holy and fallen at the same time. That was Bell's favorite. 'More realistic,' she said."

"What?" Miranda grabbed her mother's arm. "What do you mean not always good?"

"I'm just full of silly knowledge, aren't I?" June said. "Sariel was the angel responsible for the fates of angels who disobey God's commands."

"Really?" Miranda said, wanting to know more, but then Aunt Bell was through the door, was in June's arms, and in a moment, all three of them rushed into the elevator and up to Viv.

* * *

There wasn't much any of them could do in the waiting room except eat cookies and try to discuss baseball with Bell, who read to them from the sports page. Seamus was in with Viv as the doctors delivered the baby, and Viv's best friend, Robin, was taking care of Summer, Jordie, and Hazel. So Miranda sat in between her mother and aunt on the white vinyl couch and watched television, the bad news of the day flickering on the screen for what seemed like hours. A two-year-old *Smithsonian* on her lap, Miranda wished she could read the article about the antebellum house in Savannah, but the minute she would flip a page, June would start up a conversation about her neighbors Doris DeLucca and Tom Biondi or the proper way to purchase a bare-root pear tree or how Viv's daughter, Summer, was just a bit out of control.

Finally, Miranda put down the magazine. She couldn't read or even respond to her mother, her head seeming to be full of the gray matter she'd traveled through earlier. She'd try to listen to her mother and then she'd think about Sariel's taut, tight skin; or she'd think about Sariel's smile and find herself worrying about Viv and anesthesia and sharp scalpels. Her stomach gurgled from too much sugar, her hands sweated, and she wondered when it was, exactly, that she'd stand up, scream, and be taken away to the fifth-floor psychiatric lock-up.

But finally, Seamus came into the waiting room, teary-eyed, pushing the mask off his mouth. He stood there, big and blue in his scrubs, and looked at all three of them, searching for words. His almost-white hair was flattened to his head, his blue eyes bloodshot but full of happiness.

June stood up, putting a hand on Miranda's shoulder for support. "Well?"

Seamus nodded, his smile wide. "She's beautiful!"

"It's a girl!" Aunt Bell said, pulling Miranda up with her. "How lovely."

"No," Seamus said, waving his hands. "Viv's beautiful. Amazing. Oh, you should have seen her in there. But we have another son. Fat little guy. Ten pounds! No wonder he didn't want to come out."

Miranda moved to Seamus, holding out her arms and pulling him tight. Viv was so lucky. Who else but a man totally in love would think anyone flat on her back, gut open, surgical cap on, babbling from anesthesia, was beautiful?

"Congratulations, Daddy. I'm so happy." She clung on, crying without meaning to. She was happy about the baby and relieved for Viv, but there was so much else—flying through time and space, Hawaii, Sariel, his terrible face as he left—going through her mind. And then she knew she was feeling sorry for herself and hating herself for doing so right now when she should be thinking of Viv and the baby.

"Oh, Auntie Randa. Don't be sad." Seamus hugged her back, seeming to know what she was feeling. *Great,* she thought, *my mind is an open book these days. Pretty soon, no one will have to talk to me at all.* "Your sis will be fine."

Miranda nodded and pulled away, letting June and Bell have their turns, hugging him, patting his arms, *oohing* and *ahhing* at his details. Finally, Seamus, with promises to let them know the minute Viv was awake, headed to the recovery room to be with his wife and child.

"Well," June said. She opened her purse, took out a gold compact and clicked it open. Methodically, she reapplied her lipstick and combed her hair, pinching her cheeks a couple of times and then looking at her teeth before closing the compact and stuffing it back in her purse. "There."

Miranda rolled her eyes. To June, the emergency had been avoided and everything needed to go right back to normal.

"Now," June said, putting her purse strap over her shoulder, "I'm glad that's over with. I hope she doesn't have any more children. I don't know if I could go through that kind of stress again. No more grandchildren."

Bell gave a look at June. "Heavens. You have another daughter with many years of childbearing ahead of her," she said, frowning and patting Miranda's hand. "Many years."

"Oh, Bell. Miranda knows what I mean. And Miranda's too busy with her writing to make any time for kids. She won a Holitzer Prize, did we tell you that?"

Aunt Bell clapped her hands together. "That's—"

"Well, too much excitement. Enough about that." June started walking toward the door, ending the conversation. "Let's go get some breakfast, and by then, Viv should be awake and we can see the baby. Come on."

Aunt Bell shrugged and put a hand on Miranda's arm, as if to say, *Never you mind her. She's a pain in the neck.* But Bell's warmth was unable to take away the old sting, the pain of June's uncaring that Miranda had grown up with, the sense that somehow, June really didn't like her at all.

Enough about that.

Miranda and Bell both followed June out of the door and down the hall, past the window of reddened newborns, all swaddled tight in hospital blankets. *Too busy for kids,* Miranda thought. *Great.* And then when someone finally came into her life who—though not normal—was wonderful, he wanted to leave it. And, of course, he was probably unreal, even though June had met him. Seen him. Talked about his name.

Miranda knew she'd have to go back to her post-Jack

behavior. No more men. Not real ones who drank and stole her poems; not fake ones who flew her to Hawaii and back in their arms.

June pressed the elevator button and began talking about Viv's amazing capacity for mothering, her endless patience, her ample compassion. Miranda closed her eyes, waiting, listening to the giant gears of the elevator rumble. From the minute she'd met Sariel, he wanted her to forget him. All along from the very beginning, he'd threatened her with amnesia, wanting to substitute a huge blank hole for the lush, warm space in which she held her new, strong feelings for him. If he could be this cold, this unfeeling when she really needed him, then maybe it was better he left before her heart would truly break.

I need to forget him, she thought. *Let him go back to his world. Go on with my own.*

Miranda got home around seven, taking BART home, and then Muni, finally walking up the steps to her apartment, her legs heavy, her head pounding, terrible hospital food and Bell's sweet cookies whirling in her stomach.

"There you are! The new auntie!"

Miranda looked up the stairwell and saw Dan looking over the rail, clutching a bouquet of irises, his face full of his wide smile.

"Dan," she said, trying to keep the sigh out of her voice. "Hi."

Breathing in, she clomped her way to her door. Dan held out the flowers, and she knew that if she were anyone else on the planet, he'd be the perfect suitor. Without having a date planned with her, he'd shown up to give his support for her role as a new aunt. He'd put on a tie (though maybe it was a little too loud with its wild red paisleys), a pair of dress pants, and a jacket. His shoes were shined, his shirt pressed, his face shaved. He brought flowers. He smelled good. And Dan could read and talk poetry, and he was always, *always*, glad to see her.

"That's so nice. Thank you." She took the flowers and pretended to smell them, too tired to breathe deeply. "How did you know?"

Dan took her purse and dug for her keys, opening the door and letting her in. "I couldn't get ahold of you, so I guessed what was going on. When I called Viv's, her friend Robin answered. Told me the whole story. We talked for a while. Anyway, a baby boy, huh? Did they name him yet?"

Miranda shook her head, and they walked into the dark apartment. She flicked on some lights, realizing that she hadn't cleaned up after her night with Sariel. She hoped Dan wouldn't go into the bedroom, notice the messy bed, the burned-down candles, the condom wrappers. "No name yet. Still Baby Boy O'Keefe. Have a seat. I'll put these in some water."

Dan sat down, and as she walked toward the kitchen, she skirted past her bedroom, pulling the door shut, turning back to Dan, saying, "God-awful mess."

"You writers," he said. "Too busy to clean."

"Right," she said. "We're horrible."

In the kitchen, she grabbed a coffee mug, filled it with water, crammed the flowers in it, and leaned the bouquet against a cabinet. If she could have wished on herself a worse evening, she didn't know whom she'd invite over. Maybe her mother. But no, Dan would have been her pick to end the day that though full of joy and Baby Boy O'Keefe, was full of sadness. For most of the day, she half expected Sariel to peek around a corner, see her, and say, "I'm so sorry about this morning. Please forgive me." Three times during her visit with

Viv, she thought she saw him. No, that wasn't it. Miranda thought she felt him, standing right behind her. She thought she could smell him. But when she whirled around, nothing. Just her desperate imagination.

So now here she was with Dan, his eagerness, and his flowers. She wished he would look at the dark circles hanging under her eyes like funeral boats, take a hint, and make a gracious exit.

But she could tell Dan wasn't in the mood to leave. His hair was combed too perfectly, his pants ironed on an exact crease, his skin tender and smelling of cologne. He wanted this to be a date.

Miranda patted her face with her wet hands. She wasn't going to be a victim here, she thought, giving herself a little slap. Just because her imaginary boyfriend turned out to be a shit didn't mean she had to take it out on Dan. She had to be nice. He was her editor, and she liked him, most of the time, at least. He was, as Viv said, a very nice man. And anyway, he was real. He didn't show up at night, unannounced. Dan used the telephone. He brought flowers. And unlike Sariel, he was sitting in her living room, waiting, wanting to be with her. If Miranda had brought him with her this morning, Dan would have stayed at the hospital, checking with the doctors every fifteen minutes on Viv's and the baby's condition. He would have cared.

"Do you want some wine?" she called out, opening a cupboard and taking down two glasses.

"Sounds wonderful," Dan said.

Almost wincing at the happiness in his reply, she yanked open the fridge, took out a bottle of Kendall Jackson chardonnay, and grabbed the corkscrew.

Picking up the glasses, she closed her eyes, sending Sariel a message. *I don't need you if you don't need me. So good-bye, okay? Don't come back.* She opened her eyes, trying to ignore the sad, heavy feeling in her throat, chest, stomach.

"Coming," Miranda said, and she walked into the living room, into the real world.

"I had to come back," he said. "And I had to leave earlier. Bad things have happened."

Miranda turned onto her side, trying to get away from her imagination, which was playing tricks on her again, even in her dreams. Sariel wasn't here, didn't want her, didn't need her. And the bad thing that had happened was that Sariel didn't want her.

"I do want you. I do need you. I can't have you," he said in her ear, his lips warm, his hands on her body, as warm as they had been that first night when he healed her ankle. "I have to let you go. You can't remember me."

Miranda tried to open her eyes, feeling his tight, strong body on top of her, his hand on her hair. *Let me see,* she thought. *Let me open my eyes.*

"It's better this way. And then I'll be a ghost of a memory."

Don't do it, she thought. *Please. Don't go without letting me say good-bye.*

Then she was twirling up into consciousness, staring into the darkness, feeling him, and then seeing him as her eyes adjusted to the light. He was looking down at her, his hair hanging on either side of his face, his eyes warm now, not cold, not distant, not the evil Sariel from at the hospital

"Why are you here?" she asked, pulling away from his touch. "You couldn't get away fast enough this morning."

He didn't say anything, bringing his hand back to

her hair, smoothing it with his palm. She felt something, or was it saw something? An object, something important, something that was now missing. She was just about to ask him what the object was when he asked, "How's your sister? Your nephew?"

She remembered his stern, cold face as he walked away from her at the hospital, his back tight as he passed Aunt Bell. "My nephew? How do you know?" she said.

"I—I looked in on you later on." He bent down and kissed her throat. "I couldn't stay away."

"I know," she said. "I thought so. I felt you there. But why? Why not just be there? Why pretend like you want to know about my life?" And then before he could answer, she went on. "Like you really care."

"But I do. Too much. Listen, please, just go back to sleep. Let me put you back to sleep." His voice was soft, comforting—manipulative, overbearing, bossy.

Miranda pushed herself out of his arms, turned to the bedside table, and yanked on the light and blinked, her eyes pained by the sudden brightness. She wanted to be furious at him, give him up and move on. The whole business was ridiculous—madness, insanity, pathetic fantasy. She looked up, ready to tell him to get lost, but she couldn't. He was so soft on her eyes, his long hair loose tonight, black swirls on the pillow and blankets. His skin reminded her of almonds and honey, something she wanted to taste. Something she had tasted. And his eyes. It wasn't just the flecks of deep yellow and gold in them, but the way he looked at her, like he was doing right now, taking all of her in and holding her steady in his gaze. No one had ever looked at her like that before. Not Jack. Certainly not Dan.

Sariel seemed to understand her under her skin, hearing who she was from her deepest parts, knowing exactly who she was. Of course, he could read her mind, which was a lot more than anyone else could do. So he had an unfair advantage, but even if he didn't, he knew her.

Miranda reached out and put her hand on his shoulder, not knowing what to say or how to act, when she noticed that he was wearing a robe, not the one she'd seen him in the night at the bar, a sturdier-looking one, one for cold, one for travel.

"You're going somewhere," she said. "Where?"

"I have business in the East," he said simply. "But I came to say good-bye."

Again, his emphasis on a word, this time *good-bye,* made her feel heavy, filled with sadness.

"I wanted to talk with you at the hospital, but it wasn't right. And Miranda," he said, taking her hand and kissing her palm, "I can't—I have to. Look, I don't want to do this, but I told you the first night we met—"

Miranda stopped breathing, her throat thick with feeling. "No. No, you can't. I won't let you. Not my memories. No, Sariel. You said you couldn't do it! You can't take us away from me! It's all I'll have. I want to remember Hawaii. I want to remember getting coffee with you this morning. I want to remember last night how you . . . how you . . ."

Looking up at her, his eyes were full of what? Tears? He shook his head, looking down, running a hand along the thin fabric of her nightgown, his fingers running small circles around her nipple. *Stop,* she thought. *Don't.*

Sariel absently moved his hand to her other breast, and she tried to focus as he spoke. "I was fooling myself. It's dangerous for you to know anything. About me. I've put you at a tremendous risk. Brennus was right about that. And I promise, it won't hurt. You won't remember a thing. Just let me—"

Then, like today at the hospital, he seemed to go

rigid. His skin paled, his hands clenched. His eyes moved back and forth, and he nodded, saying, "Yes. Of course. Right away." And then, as if a fist had released him from a terrible grip, he relaxed, brought his arm to her shoulder, pushing her down on the bed.

"I've got to go. Good-bye, Miranda. I—I'll . . ." and then his hand was sweeping under her hair, his palm on her neck. She looked up into his sunflower eyes, his pupils large and slick with feeling.

"No," she said. "Please don't go," but then she felt herself float off and away even as the words left her mouth. All she could feel were his fingertips on her forehead and then his voice, whispering, "Good-bye," the word hard and cold and heavy.

She thought to reach out to him, pull him close, but everything went dark, her consciousness vanishing like smoke.

Maybe it was minutes. Maybe hours. Miranda struggled with something in her mind, feeling as though she were holding onto ropes with all her strength. Somehow, she knew that if she let go of one rope, all would be lost, so she gripped tightly, the thick fibers ripping and burning into her hands.

Hold on, she urged herself, not wanting the ship to sink, or the kite to fly away, or the bucket to fall to the bottom of the well. *You can do it. It doesn't have to be like this. Hold on. Hold on!*

So she gritted her teeth, feeling the sweat on her face, under her arms. Her biceps and sides ached, and she pulled air into her lungs. For a while, she imagined herself climbing the face of a huge mountain, her crampons slowly slipping, her grip loosening, her cinches uncinching. But slowly, so slowly, Miranda realized she didn't have to clench so hard, and she relaxed, the ropes loose in her hand, her body stilled, the sweat dried on her forehead, her breathing quieting. Finally, she fell asleep, whatever she feared losing still with her, right there in her palms.

When Miranda woke up hours later—the sky a dull slate—the first thing she remembered was Sariel's good-bye, and then she felt his fingertips on her forehead, pressing into her thoughts. What had he been doing? Why had he put her to sleep? What had he tried to take?

"No!" she moaned, leaning back on the pillow, her mind a backward flurry of memory. What did he steal? What had he ripped from her? The way he held her ankle? Hilo? Their nights in this very bed, his skin against hers? The feel of his silky hair in her hands, his smooth, orange scented neck, his voice in the nighttime bedroom? Their walk down the dawn-dark street? No. Her memories were still there, pulsing like a migraine at the back of her head.

The hours and days with Sariel were all there, each and every memory they'd made together. Ankle, kisses, matter, laughter, the hospital, tonight as he was pushed back on the bed. Everything just as it should be.

Miranda sat up, her palm against her chest, and flicked on the light, searching the bed and floor for clues of where he'd gone. The only evidence that he'd been here was a slight ripple of blanket on the other side of the bed, a dip in the pillow, and one long ebony hair. She picked it up carefully with her fingers, bringing it to her lips.

Pathetic, she thought, opening her eyes. But she held onto the hair and laid it carefully in her bedside table drawer before she turned out the light.

For an hour, Miranda tried to sleep, but finally, she threw back the blankets and got out of bed. She paced the room, wishing she had a cigarette, a pack of them.

She had never smoked, but she craved the idea of having something dangerous and numbing to do while she tried to think. If it weren't three in the morning and Viv hadn't just had a baby by emergency C-section, Miranda knew she'd call her sister and tell her everything about Sariel. But she wouldn't be able to talk with Viv about this for weeks, not until Viv's milk came in and the baby was sleeping a bit through the night. And she knew that her sister shouldn't have to pick Miranda up, dust her off, and counsel her through yet another wacky relationship only hours after childbirth.

Relationship, she thought. *Right. More like sex. But it was magic. The whole thing, the sex included.*

She stood still in the room and thought about Sariel, the way he took her face in his hands, kissing her, bringing his lips down her throat, his skin smooth against hers. Closing her eyes, Miranda imagined bringing her hands down his chest, her fingers running over his stomach muscles, anticipating his quick, harsh inhale as her hands went farther, taking him in her hands, feeling how much he wanted her, so hard. And then he knew how much she wanted him back. God, she'd never felt so ready for a man, and when he put himself inside her—no matter whether he did it roughly or gently, teasing her—she was wet. It was almost embarrassing.

Miranda opened her eyes, shaking her head. The whole thing was embarrassing and wonderful and exhausting and crazy. Worse was that she'd felt that her reaction to his body was really a metaphor for her deeper feelings for him, a connection her body and mind responded to. She could, however, explain away her body. It had been a very long time since she'd slept with a man, and Sariel was sexy and beautiful and knew his way around the female form. Every single cell in her body jumped when his hand touched her. Every nerve jerked to full alert when his mouth kissed her shoulder, neck, breast, stomach. Anywhere.

But there was something else, a knowingness that went beyond the time they'd spent together. Miranda felt him even when he wasn't there. She could almost read into his thoughts. And she'd thought she meant something to him, enough that he wouldn't try to take back everything. Why had he left her all her memories? Or had he? Maybe that weird struggle of trying to hold on so tightly was really a story about her strength, her desire to keep part of him, no matter what. After all, if Sariel had had his way, she shouldn't be able to remember a thing. She wanted to weep and laugh and call Sariel names she thought she'd saved for Jack, if and when he ever returned.

What had she imagined? That suddenly her luck with men had changed? Hadn't Jack and Brad and Vladimir taught her that she wasn't worth the effort? No one had left her this quickly, though, and no one had ever vanished into thin air. Usually there were weeks of phone calls and visits to her apartment to pick up shirts and ties and shoes—and then there were months for Miranda to realize, again, that she was too quirky, too odd, too "creative" to have a true love.

"All your goddamn words," Brad had said the last time he'd left. "You're not really living anything unless you know you can write about it."

But at least she had words. They never left.

Walking into her office and sitting down at her desk, Miranda put her head in her hands, staring at the light coming in through the slits of her fingers. What exactly had happened tonight? He came to take her memories and then seemed to have a fit of some kind, the same kind he'd had that morning at the hospital. But he'd recovered too quickly for a fit. Was it a message? Maybe from that man, Brennus? Or from Felix? Whatever it was, it seemed to galvanize him, and he'd put her to sleep, ready to suck out the very best parts of their entire time together. He hadn't, though, and she remembered. Now he was gone. Did that mean he was going to come back? And from where? Sariel said he'd been going East, but which East? East as in the Sierras? East Coast? East as in Asia? Eastern Europe? In his magic world, did East mean something different? Another planet? Another universe?

Miranda sat up and turned on her computer, the hum of the motor echoing in the night room. Looking at the screen, she opened her word processing program and stared at the blank white page, her fingers on the keyboard, her eyes full of tears.

I like you better because you are
fallen, too much the lover
of God, cast out from everything
and everyone, just in time
to find me, fallen as well.

Miranda sighed, took her hands off the keyboard, and sat back. If the night had ended as she'd intended, she'd have awakened in the morning still angry at Sariel, Dan's irises fresh in the coffee mug in the kitchen. A few days would pass, and then weeks, and maybe Sariel would begin to fade away. Maybe, just maybe, she would find a way to be able to be with Dan in the way he wanted. How could she arrange the metaphorical lobotomy that would keep her expectations and desires low? Writing, a mediocre but reliable relationship, a flat happiness. Life, as she didn't know it, could go on.

Right, she thought. *I'll trade Sariel for the perfect crease in Dan's pants and his talent with a comma. I'll somehow for-*

get about Sariel's eyes and laugh and body and magic. Just like that.

Saving her document and then turning off her computer, Miranda hoped that maybe, as he had before, Sariel would come back, haunting her secretly. She was getting good at feeling him, though, and she'd be able to turn quickly, grab him tightly, force him to stay and stay and stay. Maybe that *good-bye* fell heavy only on her ear. Maybe he went to visit his other brother, Rufus. Maybe she'd totally imagined tonight's visit, this being the only one that wasn't true.

She stood and turned off the light, walked out of the office, praying she'd be able to fall asleep, lulled into unconsciousness. After all she'd been through that day—Hawaii, Viv's operation and the baby's birth, Dan's surprise date, Sariel's more surprising visit—she thought she'd fall to the bed, asleep before she even managed to close her eyes. All she wanted was to figure out how to see him again; all she hoped for was one more chance to find out why they couldn't be together. But she was clutching that hope so tightly, she knew she might kill it by morning.

Chapter Seven

Sariel pushed through the thick wooden doors of the pub, his robe billowing behind him, his face grim. Because of the power Quain's thefts of the first and now the second *plaque* would give him, the meeting had been changed from the usual Council Hall to this pub, the locals suddenly sure The Bishop's Finger was closed for the night, the vortex pushing them down the road to the warmth of The Quaggy Duck instead.

The meeting was already in progress, but at Sariel's entrance, the Armiger of the *Croyant* Council, Adalbert Baird, struck his gavel, and the talking stopped. Adalbert nodded, paused, and stared at Sariel, thinking straight at him, *We couldn't really begin until you were here. Sit, listen.*

"It's true then," Sariel said, pushing his hood back, staring at Adalbert, who sat with the other Council members at a long wooden table. Sariel glanced at the man sitting next to him, Cadeyrn Macara, giving him a terse nod. Like Sariel, Macara had once fallen under Kallisto's and Quain's mesmerizing spells, and between the two men was an understanding of how bad the situation could become if Quain were to obtain complete power.

Adalbert nodded at Sariel, his long gray hair gleaming in the candlelight. The other Council members nodded as well, silent, waiting for Adalbert to say something.

Finally, Adalbert put a hand to his chest, his wizened hand startlingly white against the rich hue of his purple silk robe. He cleared his throat, looking out toward the full room of *sorciers* and *sorcières* in front of him.

"Yes, what you've heard is true," Adalbert said. "We're sorry to have to message you so abruptly. Join us, Sariel."

Sariel nodded and sat down, turning to look at Rufus and then beyond him at Fabia, blonde and glittering in her midnight blue robe. Her quick smile and the concern in her face made Sariel suck in his breath and think of Miranda leaning over him, her eyes filled with worry as he took in the message about the second *plaque.* How he'd wanted to stay with Miranda, hold her close, promise her he'd be back soon. Holding her, touching her, feeling her, Sariel wanted to forget about the *plaques,* forget the urgent messages he'd received that day from the Council. How much easier to stay in the *Moyenne* world and live a *Moyenne* life. He could whisk her back home to Marin, put her on his bed, and make love to her. If he could forget who he was and what he had to do, they could just live together. They could just be.

Instead, he'd put her to sleep and taken away the very memories he himself held tightly, the memories that had swirled around him from the first moment he met her. Now only Sariel would be able to remember what they'd done together, and that fact made it all pretend, fantasy, a wonderful dream, too soon over.

But these protective measures were for her own

good, her safety, as well as the safety of *Moyenne* and *Croyant* alike. Sariel sighed and, turning to look at the row behind him, he saw Fabia's twin brother, Niall Fair, and next to him, Brennus, who nodded curtly. Rufus put a big hand on Sariel's knee, squeezed tight, and then they all faced the Council.

"His powers are almost total with the two *plaques*," Lutalo Olona was saying. Sariel knew Lutalo from school. He had gone on to be an alchemical master, able to change any matter into something else with the fastest of magic. Unfortunately, he'd often practiced on schoolmates as he was developing his skills. Once he turned Sariel's right toe into a frog. Lutalo had a wonderful laugh, and now as Sariel watched him speak, he could hear the laughter from all those years ago. "Frog!" Lutalo had said before falling to the floor. "It's a toe frog!"

But now Lutalo's round, broad face was serious. His hair seemed serious, slicked back and neat. Even his black robe seemed serious. All of this *was* serious. This meeting wasn't about Sariel losing Miranda. This was about the end of their world. About Quain taking over. Sariel breathed in. He had to focus. He had to stop drifting off, thinking about Miranda, thinking about frogs. Rufus put his hand on Sariel's knee again, thinking, *It's all right. Whatever you miss, I'll take in.*

Thanks, bro, Sariel thought back. He blinked, stared at Lutalo, Adalbert, the Council. He had to get it together. He couldn't think about Miranda.

"Already, we've lost touch with two dozen *Croyant*, maybe more," said Baris Fraser, another of Sariel's old schoolmates. Baris stood up from the Council table, walking around it as he spoke, his orange robe matching the orange streaks in his hair. Orange streaks?

Bro, thought Rufus.

Sariel rubbed his forehead.

Baris continued talking. "No one has heard from Phaedrus Mather for a couple of days. And he was in charge of the force protecting the second *plaque*."

"Yes," Adalbert said, nodding. "It's true. But we have people searching for him. It will be only a matter of time before he can give us a report."

"Quain is swallowing up their power, atom by atom," Brennus said, standing up from his chair in the row behind Sariel. "We need to do something this time. We can't let him get away again. Just two years ago he was in our grasp, and we couldn't figure out how to keep him tied down. We could have had him. If it weren't for Macara—"

"Let's not live in the past. We have had our opportunities, and this is no different. We have a chance now. His power is not complete," Adalbert said. "Without the third *plaque*, he is strong, but not invincible. Yes, we've lost many good people. Sadly, this is what we expect each time one of us rises up, wants what he cannot have."

The room was silent. While there had been skirmishes over the years with Quain and before him with other *sorciers* and *sorcières* who wanted to wrest power from the Council, most in this room were likely thinking back to the Battle of Jacob's Well. There, a *sorcier* named Cathal led an army of followers against Council troops, all of them fighting for the *plaques*. Adalbert had fought there, as had Brennus. These tired warriors knew what the *Croyant* world was up against. But this time, unlike the last, the betrayer already had two *plaques*, so most of the power was his.

Because the *Plaques de la Pensee* were never kept together, kept far apart for safety reasons, Sariel had only seen the first. It had been twenty-four years ago, but he could still feel the vibrant energy in the purple stone, the ancient writing on it making sense to him, even though he'd only been ten years old. He had tugged on Zosime's arm, asking her to explain what the *plaque* could do.

"The stone is condensed thought. Forged energy," she had said, holding his hand as they stood with a group of *Croyant* at a special viewing of the *plaque* in the Cave of Cruzado. Next to him, Rufus held Felix still as Zosime explained more. "Many people believe if the *plaques* are put together, each arranged in a perfect balance with its sister, that all their combined energy and thought can create."

Sariel had been young, so he ignored the main question in his mind, pushing past his mother's strange declaration that *Many people believe.* But not all.

"What do they create?" he'd asked instead.

Zosime stroked his hair, sighing. "Life. The materials that our lives are built from. Earth, air, fire."

"Who put them here?" Sariel had gone on, hearing his own voice echo in the cave. "Who made them? If they made life, where did they come from? And if there wasn't life before the *plaques,* how could they have been made? Who was alive before life? I don't get it."

Zosime turned to him, smiling, and said, "Clearly, it runs in the family. You are just like your father. An agnostic to your very core."

"Tell me, Mom," Sariel had said, but then the tour guide pressed them on, a surge of *Croyant* behind them wanting a turn to see. As they walked out of the cave, Zosime held his hand, turning to him, her eyes wide. "You might not believe, Sariel. But don't forget. In the right hands, energy is balanced and even. In the wrong, the *plaques* can destroy."

Now, Sariel closed his eyes. He believed now. He wasn't ten anymore. Two *plaques.* Two in Quain's control. Everything he'd been afraid to tell Miranda was coming true. They were all in danger, *Croyant* and *Moyenne.* Miranda was in danger. Miranda. He could still taste her, feel her under his hands, hear her laughter.

Rufus nudged him, thinking, *I know you are trying, but think about her later, lad. After this is all over, you can work it out. We need you here. Even with all of us here, the vortex around the building won't last for more than six hours.*

I'm sorry, Sariel thought back, trying to keep track of what people were saying.

"What will he do if he gets the third *plaque*?" said someone in the audience. "What's his plan?"

Adalbert paused, a hand on his beard. He cleared his throat. "I imagine that Quain will recreate our society as he wants to see it. Certainly there will be no Council, no governing body. I imagine he will not want to live the way we have with *Moyenne*. He won't want to keep magic in the background. He won't allow *Moyenne* politics to create cities, states, countries. He will want their resources, their power, their infrastructure. He will create a two-tiered world, slave and master. But he will pick those to be masters of the *Moyenne*. If he does obtain the third *plaque*, those who survive the ensuing battle will have to accept his way of life. Our spies have picked up that much at least. If he's successful a third time, he'll have the power to eliminate whatever he sees fit to. And he and his consort can begin anew."

"We have to get to him before he gets to the third *plaque*," Berk said loudly.

"For goodness' sake! Smart thinking. Wish I'd come up with it," Nala Nagode, a Council member, said, even as other Council members banged their gavels for silence. "Get Quain. Good idea."

There were startled murmurs at her harsh sarcasm, a laugh, quickly silenced, and Adalbert struck his gavel again.

"She's out of line," whispered Rufus.

"Someone needs to be," Sariel said, approving of

Nala's dark glare at Berk and then Adalbert, the anger in her eyes. He hoped Nala would be involved in whatever Adalbert had in mind for him. She was smart and strong, and she had the best ability to ward off spells that Sariel had ever seen. Once, with a thought and the tiniest flick of her finger, he'd seen her push away a *sortilège du emprisonnement* just like that when everyone else around her, including Sariel, was stopped, trapped by invisible manacles, and thrown to the ground.

"Of course, we must get Quain in our control," Akasma Saintonge said. She was a tall, imposing *sorcière*, who had sat on the Council for forty years. "*How* is the obvious question."

Adalbert shook his head. "Even with all the protection we've given the third *plaque*, I fear Quain will find a way. After what happened with the first, we thought the other two were safe. So you are right, Berk, we need to get to him first. But we have to work his ultimate weakness. We've banished him, taken his lands, his rights, but now we need to take the thing he loves almost as much as he loves power."

As the Council argued, Sariel felt as if he'd been hit with a hundred messages, his chest flattened, empty of air. Kallisto. Did Quain love Kallisto? Or did he just need her? In all the times he'd felt Kallisto's thoughts since she'd betrayed him, he'd never felt anything close to love flit through her mind. Sariel didn't think she could love, really. So if there was love in this equation, it would have to be Quain for her, but it seemed improbable somehow. Both of them wanted power and had found each other in order to get it. He thought he should stand up and say something, tell them that Kallisto wasn't the way in, but Sariel could hear and feel and almost taste the Council's need to find Kallisto, steal her away from Quain, taking his mind off his mission long enough to capture him. Long enough to kill him.

A sickening, sweaty memory of Kallisto and her long brown hair and black eyes came to him. There she was, beautiful, naked, on top of him, working her magic, elevating them over the bed, chanting in his ear as they moved together in the air. Every night seemed like this, long, languid, full of spices. She wrapped her perfect, sleek body not only around his body but his mind. When Sariel did magic, he tasted her, smelled her, touched her. When he moved through the gray, she was by his side. When he listened into the world for voices, hers was the only one he could find. She told him stories, using her voice like a body part to excite him, rouse him, taunt him. After a while, he didn't want or need anyone but her. Kallisto was all he thought, felt, touched. Kallisto was everything.

Sariel would have done anything for her, to her, with her. If Rufus hadn't intervened, almost killing himself in the process, Sariel would have gone with her to Quain despite his hatred of the man, cutting himself off from everything he loved and believed in.

Rufus clamped his hand back on his knee, and Sariel closed his eyes.

She was bad. She was horrible. But she's not part of you anymore, Rufus thought.

Yes, thought Sariel. *You're right.*

You know what's going to happen.

I do.

Rufus kept his hand on his leg, and Sariel tried to breathe, watching the Council talk. He knew exactly what they were going to do. Adalbert would send him to find her because Sariel knew her best and because that was his job. There was no other choice.

Rufus kept his own feelings about Kallisto blocked from Sariel, protecting him even now. Just as he had two years ago. Sariel breathed out, glad his brother was here. Rufus was the only one who knew the entire story, the only other person who'd been in the room that night with Kallisto. Not even Zosime or Felix knew exactly how Rufus had saved him.

Sariel quieted his heart and felt his brother's strong hand. Minutes passed, and for the first time since Sariel arrived at the meeting, he was able to focus. He was here because these were his people, and searching for those who would harm them was his job. He was here because at one time he was close to Kallisto. At one time. Not now. Not anymore. Never again. Rufus took his hand away, and Sariel nodded, finally able to listen to the back-and-forth between the Council members. Nala stood up, gesturing; Adalbert agreed. Baris and Lutalo made motions; Akasma warned against acting too rashly, too quickly. Brennus argued for swift, total retaliation. It went on and on, though Sariel knew that at any moment they would turn to him, tell him what he should do. And he would say yes. Like the Council, he had no choice.

"My boy," Adalbert said, putting a hand on Sariel's shoulder, looking him in the eye. "This mission will be arduous. And painful. But you won't be alone. We have gathered a group of the best. Some of whom are on the Council. All over the world, *Croyant* are gearing up for the worst, working on spells to keep Quain at bay if he should be able to harness the power of the three *plaques.* And from what our sources tell us, Quain followers have been 'disappearing,' either of their own volition or due to 'disciplinary' problems. But, well, more of that tomorrow when we discuss what we must do."

Sariel nodded, and Adalbert leaned back into his chair. They were sitting in Adalbert's comfortable living room by a fire, the room dark behind them. By Adalbert's feet, Zeno, his elderly Hungarian Kuvasz, slept, his thick white hair long and so shaggy, the dog looked like a rough-cut sheep. When Sariel had first entered the room, Zeno had gotten slowly to his feet and padded forward, his ears pressed back. But instead of a growl, he'd simply sniffed Sariel's hand and then given up any pretense of being the guardian he'd been bred to be, turning to walk back to the fire and falling into a still, silent sleep.

"There's no other way," Sariel said. "Kallisto has wound herself so tightly around Quain that if we peeled her away, he might crumble this time. It's a good plan. The only plan. I just wish—"

"You didn't have to be the one to do it. I know." Adalbert waved a hand. "It's a terrible thing to ask you to do, given your past history with Quain and Kallisto. But you're our best. You know her better than anyone."

They sipped the brandy Adalbert had poured, the liquid reflecting yellow, orange, amber, crimson in the firelight. Sariel thought of the first night he'd met Miranda, the way the candlelight flickered in her red hair as she slept, the way she tasted like the honey-flavored potion when he kissed her.

"Now that you bring her up, Sariel," Adalbert said, "I have to ask. Did you take her memories of you and all that you imparted about our world? At this point, we don't want Kallisto to have more to use against you."

Sariel nodded. "Before I left, I took all of them. Like that."

He snapped his fingers, the sound a dull flick in the dark room. How easy it had been to snuff out the relationship. At first he'd felt some resistance from her, as if she were trying to cling on, hold tight, not let him go. But then her mind was pliant under his fingertips, and he plucked every single thought of himself out of the narrative of her memory. Gone. He was entirely gone. Of course, it was a relationship he shouldn't have been in at all, even in the best of times, and this was certainly not the best of times.

Sighing, Sariel shook his head. "It was foolish of me to get involved with Miranda. I didn't pay attention to Brennus's warnings. I know. But she's different. It was as if—as if she wasn't really *Moyenne*. She could sense me at times. There was something . . . Anyway, she's amazing. In a way, I felt like I'd known her for a long time."

Adalbert held up a hand. "You don't need to explain to me, my boy. I don't begrudge you love. And at first I also thought Brennus was overly cautious, and, at that point, Quain had not stolen the first *plaque*. But it seems Brennus was correct about our need for caution after all. However, my boy, I have come to the conclusion that it is *her* memories that might put the mission in danger."

Sariel put down his drink and looked at Adalbert, finding meaning in the old man's mind.

"No. Not that."

"How would it be different than what you want to do with Kallisto?" Adalbert asked. "We want you to use your experiences with Kallisto in the past to lead us to her in the present. What you know of her and her character and her desires is what will hurt her. Then we are going to take what she knows and use it against Quain. If you are the one attacking her, why wouldn't Kallisto find a way to use whatever would hurt you the most?" Adalbert's voice was soft and kind, but it felt to Sariel as though he were yelling.

"But Miranda doesn't know anything now. I made sure of it," he said, thinking back to the moments as he leaned over on her bed, his hand on her forehead, the past slipping into his own body and then evaporating in the room. He'd taken them all, each and every one. Of course, he'd been nervous, sad, hurried, confused.

There was that feeling he had on having to fight her. Maybe he'd left something behind. Had he?

"It's quite possible," Adalbert said. "And if Kallisto were to get ahold of her, she could use Miranda to bring you closer, to keep you from getting to Quain, to trap you. But more realistically, she and Quain might get to you first and find out about Miranda that way. And when she was done with you, she would move on to Miranda—"

Sariel held up a hand, shaking his head. He couldn't bear to think of anything happening to Miranda. He hadn't liked seeing her on the floor of the bar or on his couch with her painful, swollen ankle. Worse was the look on her face as he tried to contain himself at the hospital, keeping everything inside. All he'd wanted to do was pull her toward him and kiss her. Instead, he'd hurt her. He'd seen it in her eyes, in the way her lips quivered, in the sudden flare of anger in her face.

"Stop. I know." Sariel looked into the fire, watching the flames hiss along the underside of the logs. Zeno growled in his sleep, ran after imaginary rabbits. Adalbert nudged the dog with his foot.

"Yes, but I need to say this," Adalbert spoke slowly. "You understand Kallisto, Sariel. She wouldn't mind killing, especially a *Moyenne* woman you loved. You who betrayed her."

"I didn't betray Kallisto," Sariel said, his face hot, knowing that if he'd betrayed anyone it was Miranda. "She betrayed me in the worst way. She used me, my family, everyone to get what she wanted. She hurt us all. She left me for him. For power."

"Yes, of course, though that's not how Kallisto sees it," Adalbert said sadly. "But now that's the power you have over her. She has deep, long-lasting feelings for you that will lead you directly to her."

Standing, Sariel paced in front of the fireplace, picking up the poker and moving two hot embers with the tip. "There's got to be another way, Adalbert."

The old man put down his drink and folded his hands. "I've thought of nothing else since the Council began talking of this plan. If you want to protect Miranda, and if I want to protect you, the choice is clear. Even now, though, it might be too late. Kallisto may already know about Miranda, but we have to try."

Sariel poked at the embers again, splitting the white-hot chunks with the iron. Of all the memories in his head, these were the ones he had to willingly give up? There were so many he wished he could give up instead, times he could barely think about without a searing jab of pain in his ribs. His father's death; the sound of Zosime crying in her room at night; the day he realized Kallisto had betrayed him. The afternoon he woke up at the healer's and realized that Kallisto had erased Rufus's memory and thrown him to the far corners half dead. But until now, Sariel had never let anyone take anything from him, even though Rufus, Felix, and Zosime had offered to do so many times. All that pain was his; he'd earned it, and he used it. It made him who he was.

And there were people who took advantage of such mind magic, walking around as clear and happy as a new bell, empty and full of only the present. Whenever something odd or different or irritating happened, within minutes, they had it sucked out. Some *Croyant* made a business of this, professionals at prying pain from weak minds. But Sariel wanted his pain even as he wished it were gone. All his pain made him who he was right now.

But this decision was intolerable. Finally, from the vastness of this huge world, he'd found a woman, a *Moyenne*, he couldn't stand to be away from. He loved her thoughts, her voice, her body, her smells. And now his memory of all of that was what he was left with. And what Adalbert was suggesting . . . what he wanted . . .

"I have to take them, my boy," Adalbert said softly. "All your memories of Miranda. I'll take Rufus's and Felix's, too. Anyone who has any idea about how much she means to you. Brennus and everyone at the meeting she managed to get into. And I have to do it tonight."

"What about Miranda?" Sariel asked. "Will you have to check to see if I took all her memories? And her mother. I met her mother. What will happen . . ." He couldn't go on. He put the poker in its stand and sat down in his chair heavily, shaking his head. There, in his mind, in his memories, he saw Miranda in her bed tonight, leaning over him, worried, her light eyes full of concern. Right in front of him was her lovely face, her red curls, her smooth hand on his forehead. In a moment, he wouldn't even remember to be sad about forgetting her. Adalbert would take even his regret.

"I won't bother Miranda or her mother. I have faith that you did your job tonight. If there is a residual feeling, a glimpse into a memory, it will feel like no more than *déjà vu. Moyenne* so rarely think twice about their glimpses into magic." Adalbert took a deep breath and rubbed his beard. "And if you and your family forget her, she as well as you will be protected from Kallisto."

The fire flicked and licked orange tongues against the wood, which spit and cracked into the silence. After being stupid enough to fall for Kallisto, Sariel had probably earned this as a just punishment. For a tiny drop of time, he'd been given Miranda, been able to hold her, take her places, listen to her voice in the night, be a part of her world, if only for a short time. But because he'd fueled Kallisto's slip into darkness, he deserved to be alone and without a woman, any woman, especially one he knew he loved.

No, thought Adalbert. *No*.

"Can you leave me with something, then?" Sariel asked. "Something small. Something so innocuous Kallisto won't know what to make of it. If I survive this mission and somehow these memories are lost, I can use what you leave to recognize Miranda and find her again."

Adalbert watched him, his brown eyes steady. Very softly, Sariel could feel the older man search his mind, turning over memories for something to leave behind, even though it was dangerous to leave any trace. Even though Kallisto could pick the clue from his thoughts and toss it up, letting it fall and smash and ruin everything.

Zeno barked in his sleep, running on his side for two small strides, and then rolled over. Outside, the wind whipped poplar branches against the thick windows. A quick hard rain began to fall, tapping out sound against the glass. In only hours, it would be morning, and Sariel would be on his way to find Kallisto and then Quain before they could find the third *plaque*.

Adalbert blinked, rubbed his eyes, and then nodded. "I can leave something. It might not be what you expect. But if you find need of it later, it will be there."

Pushing himself up off the chair, Adalbert stood slowly. "Let's start, Sariel. I have a few other people to work on, as you know. And you need to ready yourself for your journey."

Sariel stood up and moved close to Adalbert, letting the armiger touch his head.

Adalbert looked into Sariel's eyes, his gaze steady. "If you've known someone in the deepest ways, as you have Miranda, you won't forget. You can't. Memory is in your mind and body."

Confused, Sariel wanted to ask Adalbert what he meant. But then he forgot what he wanted to ask him. He couldn't find his last thought or remember why he was confused. Adalbert stared at him, his blue eyes slightly watery, and Sariel relaxed, his shoulders dropping a bit.

Close your eyes, Adalbert thought, and Sariel did. His thoughts began to swirl on the edge of his mind. Focusing on the warmth of the old man's fingers on his scalp, and before she was gone entirely, Sariel thought, *Miranda. I'm sorry. Miranda!* And then everything was heat.

An hour later, Sariel sat on the bed in Adalbert's guest bedroom, trying to figure out what he was doing. He felt slightly dizzy, numb from something, maybe the trip here or the incredibly long Council meeting. Usually he felt fine speeding through gray, but tonight's journey had been bumpy, the time and space full of rolls and waves, as if Quain's theft of the second *plaque* had caused a distortion in the field, a rare flume or eddy that sometimes pulled people out of not only space but time. Sariel looked at the clock, counting backward to California time. No, he was in the right time and the right place. So why did he feel loopy, as if he and Rufus had left the meeting and tipped back a few?

Sariel unbuttoned his robe, shaking his head. He felt as though there were something he had forgotten, needed to do, needed to remember, but even when he closed his eyes and pressed hard into his own thoughts, all he could find were Kallisto and Quain and the mission he was to embark on tomorrow.

Sighing, he shook his head and then stood up, walking to the closet to hang up his robe, when someone knocked on the door.

"Sariel," said his mother. "Are you awake?"

Walking to the door and opening it, Sariel realized he'd keenly wanted to see his mother, like long ago when she would comfort him about a fight with his brothers or when she would find him crying in his bed about his father, Hadrian. After his father died, Sariel would sneak a photo of him into his room at night, stare at his father's face. It wasn't that his father had the kindest of faces, either, soft and comforting. In fact, he was rather a scary *sorcier* with his stern look, black eyes, and firmly set lips. But Sariel and his two brothers knew better. They knew that they could throw themselves on him when Hadrian thought himself home after a long day, that he would play with them for hours, teaching them tiny magic before bedtime: how to levitate a circle of pennies and make it spin, how to fluff the pillows with a thought, how to turn off the lights with a nod.

After Hadrian died, Sariel would talk to the photo, thinking that maybe there was some magic left, enough to give his father's image words. And what was Sariel hoping to hear? Something like, "It's all right. I'll be back soon. I love you." But Hadrian hadn't left that kind of surprise. Zosime would hear Sariel and sweep into the room, open her arms and pull him close, her thoughts in his mind, promising him that things would be all right. Just fine.

Now, of course, he knew that things were often not fine, but he still needed her arms, even if he didn't like to admit that to himself or even think it enough so that Rufus or Felix would hear.

"Mom," he said, smiling, looking at his tiny mother in front of him, swathed in her deep blue robes, her face ruddy from travel. She smiled, her light brown eyes bright.

She walked into the room and hugged him, her arms open, as if she were going to fly—Fly? Flying? For a second, Sariel saw an image in his mind, a girl. A little girl flying? Sariel stopped up short and breathed in.

Zosime pulled back, looking at Sariel with her serious eyes. "What is it? A message from someone?"

"I don't know," he said, laughing. "Something I thought. Anyway." He hugged her again, tightly. "What are you doing here?"

"How could I not come and see two of my boys off on this fools' mission?" Zosime unbuttoned the top of her robe and sat down in a chair by the small fire in the grate. "I don't know what Adalbert is thinking, sending you two into that lion's den. That twisted lion and his she-beast."

Sitting in the chair opposite her, Sariel held her hand, patting it, trying to move her thoughts away from fear and Quain and, even worse, Hadrian. "It's the only way. I'll be able to find her. You know I can still pick up some of her thoughts, even from the Bay Area. They are only words or random images, but they come in loud and clear. If I'm in London, where they think she and Quain are, I won't have any trouble."

"You won't have any trouble? What about what happened last time with Rufus? She sure gave us trouble that time."

"I was being healed for most of that," Sariel said. "And Rufus and Felix did okay. They captured Cadeyrn Macara. Look how well that turned out."

"Maybe so," Zosime said, snorting. "Maybe you can sniff her out. Maybe you will be able to capture her. But then what? Quain has two *plaques.* I say we should put all our powers into protecting the third. We know he'll come for it sometime soon, so why not attack him there?"

Zosime, as usual, had a point. She hadn't sat on the Council since Sariel's father had been killed, but she knew their arguments, their points, their discussion, as if she'd never left.

"I don't even know where the third *plaque* is," he said. "Adalbert is keeping that from everyone at this point. But Quain would assume that's our plan. We need to catch him unaware. We need to find the other *plaque*, Mom. If we wait until he comes to us, we might not get them back. We might not get Kallisto." Sariel held her hand, squeezing tightly, and then let go, watching her think. She never seemed to age, her round face smooth, but now her long dark hair—so much like his and his brothers'—was gray, pulled back in a long thick braid.

"But Rufus. Must he go, too?" Zosime said. "He's barely recovered from what happened with Kallisto before. And this time, what if Fabia can't save him? What if both of you . . ."

Sariel took his mother's warm hands. "Mom, it's because of what happened before that he's here now," he said. "He knows how she works. And he's been recovered for two years."

Zosime shook her head. "Well, yes, of course. But it wasn't easy for him, losing his memories." Her voice was kind, holding off the blame Sariel knew she must direct toward him for what happened to Rufus. "But he and Fabia have important work in Edinburgh."

Sariel shrugged. "We need him here. He is so strong. And Fabia can take care of the work in Edinburgh. Her brother Niall's there with her, and—"

"I know. I know," Zosime interrupted. "Well . . . at least they've left Felix in Hilo. I don't know if I could bear it if all three of you were on this mission. If anything happens to either of you by Quain's hand . . ."

They were silent, both trying to tamp down their thoughts about Quain. Sariel breathed in, listening to the world outside the window. The rain outside had stopped, but the wind still blew leaves and twigs against the windows, the intermittent *pat pat* sound accompanying the satisfying hiss of the fire. For a second, he caught himself casting his mind out, listening for something, feeling his body want to sail into the gray to stand by someone. What was he trying to uncover? A message? Someone's thoughts? Was he already trying to find Kallisto?

He rubbed his forehead, focusing on the bright color of his mother's robes. He'd been having a hard time focusing since he arrived here. He needed to sleep. He needed to get ready for what was ahead of him. Battle.

Zosime sighed and looked at him, her eyes resuming their usual lightness. "How are you? I haven't heard too much from your neck of the woods lately. No girlfriends? Intrigues? Mysteries? There hasn't been a scrap of juicy gossip floating my way. Neither of your brothers has interrupted my day with Sariel updates of any kind. I actually think they are hiding things from me. And hiding what, I ask?"

Sariel opened his mouth as if to say something, feeling a story dissolve even before he could breathe it out. There was something he wanted to tell her, something wonderful. But what was it? He shrugged.

"Not much," he said.

"Okay, keep your secrets," Zosime said, standing up and smoothing her robe. "But I'll think it out of you somehow."

Sariel stood up with her, taking her arm as they walked to the door. "I'm glad you came, Mom."

"How could I not? That Brennus is such a chatterbox. I couldn't sleep for the life of me with his messages. Kallisto this, and Kallisto that. Disaster, retribution, revenge. My goodness! It was tiresome, but then when the *plaques* were stolen . . ." Zosime paused, the light tone falling from her voice. "Then I knew it was serious."

Sariel felt his mother's thought before he actually

saw it, Hadrian as a young man, turning toward her, his robes swirling around him, his eyes on her and only her.

"Mom," Sariel said.

Zosime waved him off. "Never mind that. So, Adalbert is such a dear friend, he invited me to spend the night so I could be here when you and Rufus left. Of course, if he were really such a dear friend, he would have asked two other *sorciers* to take your places."

"He has no choice, Mom." Sariel looked at his mother and reached out a hand to pat her shoulder. Without wanting to, he picked up her sadness that verged on despair. *Not another*, she thought. *Not another.*

But before her feeling overtook her, she closed her eyes, and Sariel saw her sadness whisk out of her mind, nothing but love and kindness replacing it.

Zosime stroked his cheek, her hand moving to his hair. "Anyway, get some sleep and I'll see you in the morning. Then, I'm sure, we will all hear the plan."

Sariel hugged Zosime again, and then he closed the door behind her, feeling like he wanted to call her back and tell her the truth, the real story, but even as he let go of the door handle, he knew there wasn't anything to say.

Chapter Eight

Miranda jolted awake, Sariel's call clear in her head. *Miranda. I'm sorry. Miranda!* He was upset, hurt, angry, maybe even scared, and she spun to the side of the bed where he'd been the night before, but he wasn't there. He wasn't there because he wanted her to forget him, to erase their entire relationship. She could still feel his fingertips on her forehead. But if he really wanted her to forget, why had he called out to her just now? He *had* called. It was his voice, in pain, suffering. She knew that. He'd needed her.

Or did he? Probably just another dream, she thought, looking at the sunlight on her walls. Not only was she inventing an entire relationship with a man who could disappear at will, but she was hearing voices, too. Paddy wagon material.

At least hearing voices was a symptom the doctors would believe. There were drugs for that.

Rubbing her eyes and throwing off the blankets, Miranda walked out of her room, desperately needing coffee. Dan was going to pick her up at ten and take her to an all day conference entitled, *Does Poetry Matter?*, held at the auditorium of the Palace of Fine Arts. The main question of the conference was moot because every attendee—poets and writers all—would, of course, think poetry mattered, and Miranda herself was on a panel to talk about why poetry was important to everyone and everything. Someone from the conference titled her panel, *Real Poets Speak to the Real World.* But somehow, words didn't seem that important to her at all right now. And which real world, she wondered? Hers or Sariel's or all the others that could be out there? If the theoretical physics Sariel talked about were true, there could be hundreds, thousands, millions of worlds, all incrementally or radically different from the one she was in.

Math could barely explain that idea. How could words?

All she knew was that poetry didn't matter at all right now. The truth of that matter was that it would be torture to think about anything other than Sariel's face as he lay pressed to the mattress, his eyes flicking back and forth. He'd received some kind of message, but what kind? And why did he choose then to try to take her memories? All she wanted to focus on was what he'd been trying to do with her mind. What had happened? She'd been trying to hang on to something, and it seemed that she had. Had she made that happen or had Sariel made a mistake?

Miranda opened her apartment door and picked up her copy of the *San Francisco Chronicle.* She stared at the front page, which showed another terrible thing that had happened in the world somewhere, some kind of fire or explosion, people running. No wonder she only read the arts section.

She closed the door, walking toward the kitchen. She just needed to know where Sariel went. And most importantly, she needed to know if she would see him again.

In the kitchen, Dan's flowers—slightly wilted—were still in the coffee mug. Despite her lazy arrangement of them, they were beautiful, white and deep yellow irises surrounded by delicate green eucalyptus leaves and baby's breath. Her hands on her hips, Miranda stared at Dan's gift. Two nights ago, he'd sat so close to her on the couch that she could feel the heat from his leg and smell his Altoid breath, his Irish Spring deodorant soap, his cologne that reeked of the Macy's men's department. If she could have, she would have scooted over on the couch and taken a deep, free breath. But Miranda didn't want to make him feel bad, and she knew she had nothing to be nervous about. Dan was nothing if not polite.

As they'd sat there together on her couch, she'd wished for Sariel's magical gift, needing to go into Dan's head and see what was really going on in there. Or better yet, she'd wished she could think her way out of the living room and into the gray, to wherever Sariel was. But instead, she'd had to sit through a bottle of wine and a long conversation before Dan stood up, smiling shyly, waiting for Miranda to say something more than, "Well, that was fun."

He'd stood in front of her for a while, his hands balled in his pockets, a smile on his face. Miranda had crossed her arms, and then stood up, moving toward the front door, yawning loudly. Finally, he'd gotten the message.

She turned on the tap, filled the coffeepot with water, and then poured it into the machine. As the coffee began to drip, she took the bouquet out of the coffee mug and brought it over to the sink, where she snipped the stem ends. Taking down a vase, she arranged the flowers, doing them justice, and brought the vase out to the dining room table. Just as she was doing a last bit of arranging, the doorbell rang. Panicked, she glanced up at the clock, but it was only nine A.M. Then, her heart jumping as if to a starting gun, she thought, *Sariel!* But he wouldn't use a door or the bell. No, he'd show up in secret and then wrap his arms around her, finding her from memory in the great expanse of energy and matter.

Blowing air out of her mouth, she walked to the front door and looked through the peephole. She looked down, shaking her head. It was Dan, of course, smiling into the tiny round glass window, his hair combed, his face smooth. He was early. Ready. Wanting to go and wanting her.

"So what I'm saying is that readers in America today are lazy," Archie Cornis-Piper said, leaning back in his chair. He was a small round man in a tweed jacket, his stomach like a tidy basketball under his button-down shirt. If he weren't so well published, few of the women staring at him from the rows of chairs would give him a second glance. But because he'd won prizes, he was sexy, even with his tufts of reddish hair and receding chin. "They want Stephen King, Tom Clancy. Not something that would actually make them think."

Pompous ass, Miranda thought, wishing that instead of speaking at this conference, she was in her nightgown on her couch reading a thick novel of indeterminate importance. Whatever the story was, she wanted it to be long and juicy and full of predictable but happy plot points. Girl finds boy, girl loses boy but only for three days, girl gets boy back in a huge, happy denouement. Boy loves girl forever and ever and all her problems are solved.

"Think!" Archie said, raising his hand. "Enlighten!" The women in front of him nodded, their eyes wide and glassy.

Miranda watched Archie speak, only able to think of the comic-book character Archie, and then, in succession, the character's friends Jughead, Veronica, Reggie, Moose, and Betty. Now *there* was some literature that could make you think.

"It's the image we should crave," Archie went on. "Not sensation. Not the hype. We need to focus on words that bring forth memory, idea, thought, and then feeling. Not the reverse."

Miranda stifled a yawn and looked out to the crowd, where fifty people sat, furiously taking notes, some on laptop computer, the keys clicking furiously. What were they writing? That the image was all-important? All Miranda wanted was sensation, the kind she'd had more of in the last week than she'd had in her entire life. She wished she could interrupt Archie and say, "Listen, that's all very well and good and sounds quite impressive, but have any of you ever slid through time and space? Do you know that our bodies are actually energy packets? Have you ever had something think through your flesh into the bone? Have you ever made love with a man who could later take you to Hawaii in minutes? Talk about sensation!"

But of course, she couldn't. She'd promised Sariel she wouldn't talk or write about it, and as she glanced at Dan sitting in the front row, she knew she didn't want to embarrass him, either, even if he could not, would not, understand that she would never date him. Not in a million years.

"Ms. Stead," a man in the audience asked. "Your poetry is really focused on the body. Do you agree with this idea about sensation?"

Channeling her pseudo-intellectual self, Miranda breathed in. "I think Mr. Cornis-Piper has some important thoughts, but I feel that since we are bodies and our experiences and thoughts are interpreted by our bodies, we should pay attention to our sensations. We sense an image before we understand it. Our eyes and brain and whole body see and feel and taste and smell a tree before we are able to understand it literally as *tree*. What does that process feel like? Whatever it feels like, it comes from within our bones and blood. Our bodies know things our mind has long forgotten. In our cells, we understand things we would often try to forget with our heads."

As she talked, she kept her eyes away from Archie. She started to remember what it felt like in her body to cling to Sariel and move through the gray, how her bones felt light and hollow, her skin almost transparent. She could feel the muscles in his shoulders, breathe in his warmth, feel the way they were moving, together, away from San Francisco toward Hilo. Time and space had moved through her, touched every part of her insides, as if the atoms in her body moved aside to let space through.

"And the body—" she was saying, and then, as something flickered at the back of the room, she almost gasped. What was that? She stopped talking, focusing on a pulse of gray at the back of the room. Was it? Could it be? And yes, there it was, hovering at the back of the auditorium. Miranda blinked, her mouth open as she squinted, focusing on the wave of matter that hung just beyond her.

She hadn't opened her eyes when she traveled with Sariel because she was so afraid and because she knew that he was taking care of their travel arrangements. But this—this matter—appeared for her, and she watched it, saw it spread wide and long at the back of the room, knew that if she closed her eyes and thought of, well, Hilo or New York or Paris, there she'd be. She had pulled it forth, all by herself. But how?

Miranda shook her head, her mouth open slightly.

"The body . . ." she repeated, zombielike. Archie Cornis-Piper coughed, and then Miranda shook her head.

There was no way she was responsible for that. Only *Croyant* could be. She was *Moyenne.* Everyone at the meeting had agreed, and as she had been on the floor and they had all been standing above her, how could she argue? Sariel had taken them everywhere. All she'd done was clutch on tightly.

The audience was silent, waiting. Miranda looked down at her hands in her lap and then peeked up, surprised that the gray now appeared to be rolling toward her, matter condensed and ready for her to step into and travel through. And what was that she could almost see? A building? A house? A dark room? Was she seeing it or feeling it?

"And the . . ." She stopped speaking, closed her eyes, tried to find the weight of her bones again, the heaviness of her flesh. How had she seen that? Had she actually conjured it herself? No. She wasn't magic. She was ordinary, average, *Moyenne,* blind to vortexes, unable to mind-read, clueless about space and time travel, and just generally a boring human.

All of this must be posttraumatic shock brought on from her insane fantasies of the perfect, magic man.

Breathing in, Miranda looked up again. The gray had vanished, nothing at the back of the auditorium but doors and people leaning against the walls, looking at her raptly. Even the women in the first rows were staring at her, mouths open, ready for wisdom.

Archie hissed, "And the body? Are you in yours? For Christ's sake, Miranda."

Miranda smiled at the audience. "Sorry, I think I started to write a poem just then."

Everyone laughed, and she sat back in her chair. Glancing down at the first row, she saw Dan was beaming at her, his face full of the exact glow she felt throughout her entire body when looking at Sariel.

After her panel ended, Miranda sat at a table in the lobby and signed books. She knew she was looking at people, smiling, talking to them about imagery and sensation and the current publication climate, but she was somewhere else altogether. Sometimes as she wrote her name, she realized that she was almost writing Sariel's name on the front page. Once, she had to stop in mid-S and reconfigure her written remarks. Luckily for Miranda, the woman who bought the book was named Sally.

"Sorry," Miranda said, turning Sariel's S into Sally and then writing her name below. At least she hadn't written something truly ridiculous, as she had one time at a signing that involved cocktails. Instead of writing *Happy Reading*, which she often did, she wrote *Happy Birthday*. The slightly tipsy man who'd bought the book hadn't noticed, and Miranda only realized her mistake in the cab on her way home.

But she had to get a grip. Even if she was obsessed with Sariel and hallucinating the gray, she had to get ahold of herself.

Finally, the poets and writers began to leave. Janitors came in, ready to fold up the tables and chairs. As Miranda was standing up from the table, saying good-bye to Archie Cornis-Piper, she saw a wisp of gray again, undulating at the far corner of the room, almost as if it were calling her. She stared at it, wanting to run toward it, throw herself into its wavery softness so that she could go wherever Sariel had disappeared to.

"Really," Archie said, putting a meaty hand on her arm. "You need to stop writing so much. You are completely spacey these days. You're not even here at all."

"You have no idea," said Miranda.

"Well, then, you must be ready to have a breakthrough. The perfect poem!" Archie clapped his hands. "Then we can argue about it next year at the conference."

Another year, thought Miranda as she walked toward Dan who was waiting for her by the door. How could she make it through another year when she didn't know how she would survive losing Sariel? Or making him up and then losing him. Or was it that she was making up what she didn't have? How could she live without having what she finally knew she needed?

On the way home from the conference, Miranda managed to convince Dan that she couldn't go out for a drink because she had to go see Viv and the new baby. Now, they sat in his car parked on Lombard below her apartment, Dan just about to unbuckle his seat belt and get out of the car.

"Oh, Dan. I told you. I've got to go see Viv. She's—you know, postpartum and all. A C-section is major surgery, and Seamus has the other three kids to take care of."

He turned to her, the glow diffused now, his eyes narrowed. "I can drive you. That's it. Let me drive you out there. We can pick up take-out and feed the whole family. Give them a break."

Miranda swallowed, shaking her head. "I think she's really tired. Wiped out. I'm going to go and sit with Viv, clean the house. Get the other kids into the bath. That kind of thing. It's going to be very quiet. As if I'm really not there. Just a member of the family."

Dan shrugged, irritable suddenly, and she didn't blame him. Ever since the first time he'd met her two years ago, Dan had been patient and kind, calling her, bringing her flowers, taking her out to dinners, insisting on picking up the bill, even though Salt Point Press had a very small entertainment budget. And what had she been? First she'd used Jack as her excuse. "Oh, it's too soon after my breakup. I don't want to do anything on the rebound."

But then, as the months went by, she found herself being evasive, detached, distant, and placating, anything to keep him at bay. She'd made up white lies, exaggerated her continuing feelings for Jack, told Dan that she was so deep into her poetry that she didn't dare interrupt her writing with other emotional concerns. She's screened calls, pretended to be gone for the weekend, and even made up relatives who were suddenly in town and wanted to see Coit Tower, Chinatown, Stinson Beach, Napa and every single winery there. Miranda knew she'd been horrible to Dan. She'd done nothing that deserved his glowing feelings.

"All right," he said quietly.

"Thanks so much for the ride," she said quickly. "It was a great conference. We sold a lot of books, didn't we? I think almost all of them."

He smiled, his color returning. "After that body talk, I sold your whole lot. Plus some of your backlist."

Miranda felt awash with gratitude, wishing she felt differently, wishing she could feel for Dan what she felt for someone who wasn't really even there, someone who didn't even want her to remember him. "That's great. Look, I'll call you later in the week, okay?"

She stepped out of the car and leaned down to look in the window. "Thanks for everything, Dan. You've been so great to me. I don't deserve it," she said, hoping he understood what she was saying.

But he didn't. His sappy smile slipped back onto his face, his desire blinding him to what she meant.

"It's my pleasure, Miranda," he said. "Always is."

* * *

Viv sat up in her bed, weeping.

"She's been like this since we got home from the hospital," Seamus said, whispering to Miranda as they stood just outside the open bedroom door. He held the just-nursed, newly named baby Colin in his arms. Seamus was exhausted, bags under his eyes, his hair uncombed, a single, slightly wet Corn Chex stuck on a back strand just behind his ear. Miranda pulled it gently from his hair and handed it to him. He looked at it, turned it in his fingers, said, "Hazel," and then ate it.

"So what is going on?" Miranda whispered.

"She was totally normal after the birth. You were there. She was fine. And then afterward in the room, she was laughing with the nurses. Everything was just fine. But on the way home, she sort of sat there, wouldn't look at me. Then when we got to the house, she just lost it. Her friend Robin was here for a while, but that visit didn't go well. Viv cried the entire time and kept asking for you."

Seamus rocked back and forth in a practiced father move. "It was never like this with the other three. But then, this was her first C-section. It's major surgery, you know."

Miranda patted his shoulder, thinking about how she'd just told Dan the same thing. She took her hand away from Seamus and lightly rubbed her hand over Colin's soft head. Major surgery was worth this baby, she thought. Worth anything.

"I'll talk with her. Put Colin down to sleep if you can. That should give me some time to find out what's going on before he's hungry again."

"Thanks, Randa," he said. "I'm really worried. This isn't like Viv at all. She's so—"

"In charge?" Miranda said, smiling. "Don't worry. She'll be back to her bossy self in no time. This is just anesthesia or postpartum blues or gas."

"Okay," he said. "All right. Just yell if you need me."

Somehow still rocking the baby, Seamus walked down the hall toward the nursery. Miranda went into the bedroom and closed the door behind herself, walking over to Viv and sitting down on the bed. Her sister barely looked like the confident, collected woman she usually was. Her hair was combed but dirty, the blonde almost brown in the dim bedroom light, and her face seemed swollen, flushed, her eyes puffy red slits. Miranda didn't expect anyone who'd just given birth to put on mascara, but Viv had an addiction to it, never leaving the house without a careful application or two. But Viv hadn't even cried her makeup off, no telltale raccoon eyes, no streaks. Just her sad face.

"Vivie," she said softly, taking her sister's hand. "What is it? What's wrong?"

Viv shook her head, the tears a slick wet shine on her face. "I can't."

"You can't what? Take care of a baby? Give me a break. You've been taking care of babies for years."

Viv didn't say anything. She just shook her head again.

"You are the best mother I've ever met," Miranda said. "Including and far surpassing our own."

At those words, Viv sobbed, wiping her eyes, leaning back against her pillows.

"Sweetie!" Miranda leaned closer to Viv, rubbing her sister's arm. "All you need is a little sleep, and then you'll feel great. This was major surgery. Everyone says so. It's takes a lot out of you. You'll be just as wonderful a mother with Colin as you were with the other three. Look at them. They're all fabulous. Maybe Hazel had a strange idea about potty-training, but that's nothing. They're great kids."

Now Viv was almost wailing, so Miranda pulled Viv to her, hugging her tightly, sympathetic tears pricking her eyes. What was wrong? She'd never seen Viv this upset, ever. Maybe her sister was having that reaction, that depression that makes mothers go crazy. Not just depression. Postpartum whatever. As she hugged her sister, Miranda decided she would stay for as long as it took, keeping an eye on Viv, Colin, Seamus, the kids. She'd move in if she had to.

"That's not . . ." Viv began, her voice muffled and full of tears.

"That's not what? What?"

"I'm not upset about the baby," Viv finally got out, clutching Miranda as she spoke. "Maybe it's because of the baby, but I'm thinking about something else."

Viv began to cry again, and Miranda plucked two tissues from the box by the bed and wiped her sister's cheeks and nose. "What, Vivie? What are you thinking about?"

"I can't."

"Yes, yes, you can," Miranda said softly. "Of course you can. You can tell me anything."

Viv snuffled, took the tissue from Miranda, blew her nose. She looked up, her eyes full of tears, red, so sad.

"Tell me," Miranda said, handing Viv a fresh tissue.

"Okay." Viv took a deep breath. "I didn't want to think about it. I didn't plan on it. But when I woke up from the surgery, I saw so clearly what I had to do. I felt it, and the thought kept getting bigger and bigger until I just couldn't hold it inside anymore. Like I finally had to pay attention."

"What is it?" Miranda pulled away, still holding onto Viv's shoulders. "Is it Seamus? Did he do something? What did he do?"

"No. No." Viv hiccupped, wiped her eyes on her nightgown sleeve, moaning slightly. Now her breasts were leaking, large, round wet patches on flannel.

"Wait. Just hold on." Miranda stood up and went to

the dresser, digging around until she found a clean nursing bra and nightgown.

Returning to Viv, she helped her sister change, noticing how slowly her sister moved, careful of the bandaged incision on her belly.

"Does it hurt?" Miranda asked, smoothing down the nightgown and adjusting the collar. "Do you need some pain pills? Should I call Mom?"

"No!" Viv said loudly. "Don't call Mom."

Viv started to cry again but quietly this time. She grabbed onto Miranda's hand.

"What is it?" Miranda stared into Viv's bloodshot eyes. "What is going on?"

"I feel—I feel . . ."

Miranda nodded. "I know. You feel tired. You feel like you need a shower. Let me wash your hair. I'll get a basin. You'll feel so much better."

"It's not my hair," Viv wailed. "It's you."

Breathing in, Miranda sat back. "It's me?"

Viv nodded. "When I came out of the anesthesia, I realized something. I have to tell you. I can't keep it a secret anymore. I've kept it in way too long."

Miranda relaxed, her body sinking down in relief. Thank God. Nothing had happened with Seamus and Vivian wasn't following Miranda's lead and going completely nuts. All this weeping was simply hormones and anesthesia and the stress of the surgery. She'd heard about people grabbing nurses when they awoke from surgery, telling them they were related to Queen Elizabeth or had been reincarnated from a prior life as a Nubian princess. Clara Hempell told her that when Roy went in for his hernia operation, he regaled the entire surgical team with lewd jokes and limericks before he went under and gave them more as soon as he woke up. Viv's experience had obviously not been that gleeful, but whatever had happened, it was just like a bad dream that would pass as soon as she calmed down and had a good sleep.

"Listen," Miranda began, ignoring her sudden thought that she'd initially believed Sariel was a dream. "Anesthesia does terrible things to your brain. It really messes—"

"No." She sniffed, pushing her hair back. "It's about knowing where you came from. Knowing who you are. Even though I was drugged, I felt them tug Colin out of me, and I kept wondering who felt you being born. When they brought Colin to me, I felt the grief for that mother and for you. Maybe I should have felt that way when I had the other three, but I didn't until now. I kept thinking, *Did you get to see her face? Did anyone hold you?* And why didn't anyone tell you? It's not fair. You need to know."

Her mouth open, Miranda stared at Viv, suddenly scared about what was going on in her sister's head. This wasn't just the surgery. She needed to go get Seamus. June, too. Robin. Maybe they should call the doctor. Call 911. Go back to the hospital right now.

"Calm down, Viv," Miranda said. "It's going to be—"

"You're adopted, Randa," Viv said quickly. "I knew I had to tell you. You had to know."

Miranda felt like her ears weren't working, Viv's words irritating noise she needed to shut out. She almost put her hands over her ears, thinking maybe she could drown out the sound. Viv stopped talking, watching her, wiping her nose on her sleeve.

"Viv?" Miranda said slowly, trying to stay composed. "What on earth are you talking about?"

"Randa. It was time you knew. You're adopted. Mom couldn't tell you, ever. Dad wanted to, but then he was gone."

With her secret out in the universe, Viv seemed calmer, sitting up straighter against the headboard, her eyes more focused. Miranda stared at her sister, trying to find the real world where Viv's words could be made sensical.

"Viv, I'm not adopted. If Mom wouldn't have told me, Dad would have. We talked about everything. You're just not feeling well. Let me go get—"

Vivian grabbed Miranda's arm, keeping her still. "I know I sound crazy, but I remember when you came home. I was almost four, Randa. Dad was gone again on one of his trips and then he came home. A trip somewhere. Far away. And then he walked into our room and put you in the crib. A couple of days before, Mom had had some handyman come and assemble it. I remember wanting to sleep in it because it'd been mine. Then he shows up with you and they both tell me that you are my new sister and said, 'Isn't your new baby the prettiest thing?' "

Through her tears, Viv smiled. "You weren't, though. I wanted to tell them that. You were ugly, a little pale ghost baby with a giant shock of flame-colored hair. Now I'd guess you were about three months old or so. Maybe four."

Miranda couldn't speak, so she closed her eyes. Somewhere, in a vision, in a dream, in a deep memory, she could remember the taut cradle of her father's arms, the clean smell of his cotton shirt. He was carrying her, taking her somewhere, carrying her away from another smell, another person. Then there was June, leaning close, but Miranda wanted her father's face, and more than his face, she wanted the other face. But that was it.

Viv grabbed her hands. "Don't be upset. I love you. Ever since that first day, I've loved you. I used to watch you sleep in your crib, and I really thought you were mine. I still do. I always will."

Shaking her head, Miranda couldn't look up. She

wanted to argue all of this away, but her memory and her body told her Viv was telling the truth. Viv had never lied to her, not once, not ever. But why did Viv have to tell her now? Every world Miranda had known was gone. No parents, no ordinary universe where people took airplanes to Hawaii, no Sariel.

"Randa, look at me," Viv said. "I'm sorry. I just couldn't keep it in. When he was sick, near the end, Dad made me promise I'd tell you, but the time never seemed right. I didn't know how to just say it. And I didn't want to upset Mom even more. But it's time. I always thought that if I told you, it would answer questions you seem to have about yourself. I know you feel different. Alone. Unable to find someone like you. I thought knowing you were adopted would help you find someone to be with. To love. It's stupid, but that's what I thought."

Viv began to cry again, and Miranda breathed out and looked up. Viv tried to smile, but she couldn't, hormones and sadness coursing through her body.

"Don't," Miranda said quietly. "It's okay. We'll be okay."

"Oh, Randa. Oh."

"Shhh. Stop."

"There's one more thing. In my garage. In grandpa's old army trunk. There's a box labeled *Dad's Stuff*. It's for you. I never looked in it, not once."

Viv fell back against the pillows, pressing a hand to her belly. Miranda sat there, watching Viv quietly. After a moment, Viv opened her mouth as if to say something, but in a few seconds, Miranda realized her sister had fallen asleep, mid-thought, exhausted by the birth of her baby and the huge truth she'd just delivered to Miranda.

Numb after leaving the bedroom, Miranda found herself walking straight into the kitchen, a fake smile on her face.

"Oh, she's going to be fine," she said to Seamus and Robin. "She's just exhausted. Let her sleep for as long as possible."

Seamus tried to get her to stay for dinner, but she made an excuse about needing to meet Dan for an early meeting in the morning. Saying her good-byes, she left through the kitchen door, the door that led into the garage.

Miranda flicked on the overhead light and looked at the shelving that held tidy rows of plastic storage boxes full of Christmas tree ornaments, Halloween costumes, records from prior tax years, and old computer cords and wires and keyboards and mouse pads. On the bottom row, she found her grandfather's trunk, and she opened it, holding the lid with one hand. Right on the top—as if waiting for her—was a box that was, as Viv had said, labeled *Dad's Stuff.* For a second, she thought of sitting right down on the cold cement floor and opening it, discovering the truth right there and then. If she had to, she could go back into Viv's room and shake her sister awake, demand answers to the questions that the box would provide.

But Miranda didn't want to wake Viv; she didn't really want to see Viv again tonight or even for a while. So she left through the garage door and got in her car. Miranda drove down the darkened freeways, through the Caldecott Tunnel, past Oakland and Berkeley, and over the Bay Bridge. She didn't feel at all a part of her body. Her hands gripped the steering wheel and managed to keep her clear of other cars, but she felt her mind floating somewhere in the car, bouncing between doors, the headliner, and the floor. Sometimes, she swore she saw the flicker of gray in her peripheral vision, but when she turned to look, it was gone.

How could this be true? she thought. Why didn't June and Viv tell her earlier? Why didn't her dad tell her before he died? Most people her age who had been adopted had been told before entering school, armed with the information other kids might tease them about. Some had pictures of birth mothers and stories about adoptive parents flying across the world to pick them specially. And if they hadn't known their birth mothers then, they met them later, arranging meetings at local restaurants or in living rooms with generations of relatives desperate to meet the missing family member. Eventually, they all reached some kind of agreement or shared tidbits of health information. But they knew. They all knew. The entire extended family knew. No one had kept the secret for thirty years. This entire tale was so Victorian, Miranda couldn't believe it was a modern story. Her modern story.

How could they have done this to me? How could they all have lied?

Back at her apartment, Miranda flicked on the living room light and stared into the room. There were all her things, but whose things were they? Miranda Stead's? Or Miranda Who's? Who was the poet? The Miranda who grew up with June and Steve? Or the Miranda who was torn from her real parents? Or given up gladly by her real parents? Who made the decisions that led her to this point? And why did her father seem to be the one with all the answers? What about her mother? From this minute on, Miranda would walk into this very living room as two people, the pretend Miranda and the real Miranda, and she didn't know who was who.

Walking into the bedroom, she put down her dad's box on the bed and stared at it for a moment. The desire she'd had in Viv's garage had died inside her, and she had no interest in opening the box. She wasn't ready to deal with what was inside, probably just more bad news, more information she didn't want. She sighed, throwing her coat on top of it, covering Viv's written *Dad's Stuff,* and then noticed the message machine blinking four. Probably all Dan. Dan making sure she got home. Dan hoping she was home safely and, *oh, how's the baby?* Dan wishing she would call with an update. Dan pretending to call about business. Some galleys she had to proof or a reading for next month. Dan, Dan, Dan, Dan.

Sariel wouldn't call, wondering if she'd made it home safely. If he'd wanted to find out about her, he would have just shown up in her apartment or at the conference or at Viv's house. Or he would have just read her mind from afar. But she hadn't felt a thing since the morning, when she heard him call, *Miranda. I'm sorry. Miranda!*

And anyway, he didn't want her to remember him at all. Now, she knew that the ropes she'd clung to in her sweaty dream that night had been her thoughts, her memories, her images of Sariel. She fought him. She wanted him more than he wanted her, fighting to keep what she'd earned. He'd left her, but she'd fought for him, keeping the only thing she could—her thoughts.

She stood still in her dark room, not noticing she was standing still in her dark room until the phone rang again. Leaning over the bed, she yanked the phone cord out of the wall. Probably it was Viv or Seamus. *Are you okay? Are you upset to find out we've all been lying to you? Are you upset to find out that you haven't known who you are for the past thirty years? Oh, and did you make it home safely?*

Wasn't it like Viv, the older sister, to make the executive decision that now was a perfect time for a life-changing revelation? Oh, sure, Viv had just had a baby, but she'd had three before. The same thing had happened—baby in, baby out. Three times before, someone had laid a baby on her chest, and three times before she could have decided to tell Miranda she was, in fact, an orphan. A changeling. Not who Miranda thought she was at all.

Viv could have thought about it between Summer and Jordie, finding a careful, concise way to bring up the matter, deciding on a quiet family meeting, Seamus and the kids away from home. June could have come over, armed with important, relevant information. There could have been space for Miranda to cry, to react, to get angry. Then the three of them could have looked through the *Dad's Stuff* box, discussing, organizing, planning.

But no. Viv had to go all Grand Guignol and make it a wretched Hallmark moment, orchestrating everything. She's the one who got to cry and moan and cathart all over the place. She hadn't thought of anyone but herself and her feelings, her guilt, her need to spew the ugly story.

Walking out of the bedroom and into her office, Miranda turned on the light and then the computer, sitting down hard in her chair. She would write about everything: Her family, her adoption, Sariel, his betrayal. She would write a poem that explained it all, from the time she began running away from the men on the street and plunged into the *Croyant* meeting to now. She didn't care anymore what she'd promised Sariel. After all, where was he? He wasn't here to help her with her terrible news. He just up and disappeared. Miranda laughed, tears just behind the sound, seeing how for once the word *disappeared* wasn't simply a metaphor.

Clicking on her word processing program, she put her fingers on the keyboard.

If I found myself
running from you, I'd stop.

I'd turn around, open my arms,
fly back to where we started.

Closing her eyes, she sat back in her chair. She couldn't write a thing. She wanted him so much, needed him now to help her figure out how to feel. Miranda had never felt like this about a man, not even trying to find Jack after he left, despite Viv's urging that she make a police report or hire a private detective to help search out her computer and the stolen poems. But not even now, now with Jack sharing a prize with her based on her words, would she try to find him. There was no one before Sariel worth seeking out.

Miranda breathed in, trying to stop her tears. *Enough,* she thought. There was no way to write about any of this and there was no way to think about it. Where would she start? If she did uncork her mind, she'd probably uncork a bottle of wine and keep trying to think until the bottle was empty. That wouldn't help. She needed to sleep. To forget for a few hours. And then maybe she'd know what to do.

Miranda Stead stood up, realizing that she didn't know who actually was standing up from her desk. Her name was Miranda, but what had her real mother called her? What name had her real mother given her in the womb? Or her real father? Had he decided on a name for her? Maybe it was Olivia who was turning off her computer or Dagmar who pushed in her chair. It could be Katie who walked to the door, turning to look back at her office. Or maybe it was really Sarah who sighed, found the light switch with her fingers, flicked off the light, and walked away in darkness.

The daylight streamed into her room, and Miranda pulled the blankets over her head. Her eyes felt gritty, as if each vein were a speed bump her lids were riding over. She'd been up almost the entire night, thinking, imagining, obsessing. She conjured forth her birth parents, this real mother and father who had given her away. She felt their hands passing her small body to her father, Steve. She watched them fade away from where they stood or sat, the picture fading as the car she was in took her away, to an airport or bus terminal or ferry landing.

After she played out that melodramatic scene about sixty times, she switched to Sariel. She saw him leaving, over and over again. One minute he was flat on her bed, the next, poof! Gone. After she made him disappear, she decided to relive every single one of their moments together, lingering especially on the pleasurable moments. His smile, his body, his kiss. In one taunting scene after the next, Sariel flashed through her mind: handsome magic guy in robe, handsome magic guy naked, handsome magic guy in Hawaii with drink. Her handsome magic guy. Once her handsome magic guy.

Then, for fun, she decided to think about Viv and Dan and June, saving Jack, the most torturous, for last. How he stole her computer and poems. How smug he would be on the Holitzer Prize stand. In her vision, she put them right next to each other, both dressed to the nines. Jack's date would be at a front table, clapping loudly, her breasts jiggling with each smack. Jack would wave, clutch his prize money. As he spoke to the crowd, Miranda would feel his arm loop up and rest on her shoulder, as if they were the best of friends, close, intimate writing partners. "Aren't we lucky," he would whisper.

"Jerk!" Miranda said from under the covers, finally flinging them off. "Total jerk!"

She turned her alarm clock toward her, squinting at the red numbers. Eleven in the morning. Then she glanced at her phone machine. Nothing was blinking. No one had called. No one loved her anymore. She shook her head, feeling the tears coming again, when she saw the phone cord. *Oh, yeah,* she thought. *Right.* She'd unplugged it.

Leaning over, Miranda stuck the cord back in the wall, and immediately the phone began to ring. She watched the phone for a while, again wishing that Sariel would call. All he needed to say was one word, and she'd forgive him anything.

"Yeah, because you're a wimp!" she said aloud.

The phone kept ringing, and finally Miranda grabbed it, pressing the receiver to her ear but not saying a word, waiting for the miracle. Then she realized that if Sariel were going to call, it would be through his mind and into hers.

"Miranda!" Viv said. "I know you're there."

"I'm here."

Viv started to cry again, soft snorting sounds on the other end of the line. Miranda shook her head. "Look, I can't talk about this now. I have to think."

"When can you talk about it?" Viv asked.

"I don't know." Miranda looked out her window, the sunlight and warmth outside. Below her window, traffic moved on the street, and she could hear the drifting sounds of people talking coming up from the sidewalk below.

"Tomorrow? If you don't talk to me tomorrow, I'm coming out there."

What would Miranda know by tomorrow that she didn't know now? Would she have gone through her father's box? Would she have figured out who she was? Would giant answers fling themselves down from the heavens for her to pick up and examine? No. This would take years—maybe her whole life—to understand.

"Tomorrow," Miranda said softly.

"Oh, Randa," Viv said. "I'm sorry."

In the background, Miranda could hear baby Colin cooing, and with that sound, she realized that what was bothering her the most was not being connected by blood to Viv. All her life, Viv had been her stability, her touchstone. How could Viv not really be her sister? How did that make any sense?

"How's the baby?" Miranda asked.

"Good," Viv said.

"How are you?"

"I'm—I'm better. But I need to see you."

"Tomorrow," Miranda said. "I'll call, okay? I've got to go."

"Miranda," Viv said. "Don't."

"Bye."

She hung up the phone and looked out the window again, hearing Viv's sadness in her head. But she was sad, too, and the only thing Miranda knew was that she didn't want to sit inside today. She didn't, under any circumstances, want to write. She wanted air, and sun, and absolutely a triple espresso. Looking back at the bed, she knew there was something else she wanted, someone else she wanted, but she needed to stay with what was possible right now. What was real. And she knew that she could get an espresso on any corner. She didn't need any magic for that.

The white ceramic cup was warm in her palm, and Miranda closed her eyes, looking up toward the sun. She sat at an outside table, the light, cool wind in her hair, her sweater buttoned. She breathed in, trying to find a calm place in her body. Ignoring the people all around her, the hiss of the espresso machine inside the coffee shop, the smell of the bakery a few doors down, the cigarette smoke swirling toward her from a nearby table, she forced herself to relax. There had to be a spot somewhere inside her that wasn't worried about something. She thought of the meditation class she'd taken with Clara Hempel the year before.

"Clear your mind. Let the thoughts come in, flow out," crooned the teacher. "Name them and let them go."

Miranda had counted her thoughts, one after the other. There'd been about 112, most of them named judgment, anger, fear, resentment, ambition, and Jack. Of course, lust and happiness and desire had shown up, but after the class, she realized that the only place she wanted to examine her thoughts was when she was writing.

But she kept her eyes closed, loosening her grip on her cup. What was in there now? She focused, and then she saw it. Her heart rate leapt, her nerves firing. There it was again, the rolling gray, the house, a dark room. My God, she was close enough to touch it.

"Miranda!"

With the sound of his voice, the gray, the house, the room were sucked out of her view, and Miranda opened her eyes, thinking, *I'll call this thought irritation.*

"Dan," she said.

Dan was standing over her, his hands in his tweed jacket pockets. "I've been looking for you. I called a couple times. Went to your apartment."

"I guess you figured I wasn't home," she said, trying to keep the sarcasm out of her voice. She sipped her espresso, and then put down her cup. "Have a seat."

Dan pulled out the bistro chair and sat at the table. "Viv called me."

Miranda shook her head, looking into her cup. "And?"

"She said you and she had some words. She was worried."

"Doesn't anyone think I can take care of myself around here?" She put the cup down hard onto its saucer, the little lemon rind and chocolate bouncing off and onto the table. Dan picked up the chocolate, peeled away the foil and ate it, chewing carefully.

I hate the way he chews, she thought, knowing that she also hated the way he would carefully fold the square of foil.

Dan began to carefully fold the square of foil, sucking on the chocolate as he did. Miranda tried not to shiver.

"Of course you can take care of yourself." Dan put the folded foil on her saucer.

"Then why are you always checking up on me? You're like Viv's search-and-rescue squad."

"We care about you." He watched her carefully as he said this, and Miranda forced herself to match his gaze. The breeze picked up locks of his brown hair, the early-afternoon sun made his skin glow bronze. Dan was a good-looking man. He was a nice man. A very nice man. She could hear Viv say, "He's great. You deserve him. He won't hurt you, ever."

Maybe this was true. After Jack, Miranda knew she deserved something better. But after being with Sariel for only a few days, she didn't just want great. She wanted wonderful.

Miranda rubbed her forehead. What was she supposed to do? And how could she expect to have anyone when she didn't even know who she was herself?

"Look," she said, pushing her chair back. "I'm fine. Viv and I have things to work out. But you don't have to worry. I promise."

She stood up, Dan staring at her. "I've got to go," she said. "I'll talk to you later."

Turning away, Miranda walked up the street, ignoring the surprised sound Dan made as she left, ignoring his intense, relentless stare that she could feel even when she turned the corner.

As always, books saved her. She spent the day at the Ferry Building, riffling through the self-help section at Book Passage. She found some of the following: *I'm Adopted, Now What?*, *Adopted Daughters*, *Birth Mothers*, *The Separated Family*, *Finding Your Family*. Sitting on a chair that looked out toward the Bay Bridge and Treasure Island, she read about people who discovered that they'd been adopted and then managed to find their birth parents, everything in their lives suddenly coming together like a miraculously completed Rubik's Cube.

As she walked home, Miranda knew that she had to open the box her father had left for her and look through the contents. She shouldn't be afraid of what she would find. Finally, she would know why she'd always felt different, left out, unable to catch up. She'd finally know why June never really liked her.

When she got home, the phone was ringing. She picked it up in the kitchen, breathing hard from having unlocked the door quickly and run to answer it before the machine did. As she picked up the phone, she realized that she was concerned about Viv. Sure, Miranda was angry, but Viv had just undergone surgery and delivered a baby. Miranda should have checked in during the day.

"Viv?"

"No, it's not Viv," said June. "It's your mother."

Miranda leaned against the wall, thinking for a second about the word *mother*. "Hi. What's wrong? Is it Viv?"

"Yes, it most certainly is Viv," June said, her voice sharp and stinging. "I can't believe you aren't over there. Seamus said something about you leaving after only being with Viv for half an hour last night. A half hour when she had surgery. You know it's major surgery, don't you?"

"I've heard. I—"

"I. That's right. I. Miranda, when are you going to start thinking about other people?"

"What are you talking about, Mom? I was with you all at the hospital. I went back to visit. She and I—"

"There you go again. You are so absorbed in your writing that you don't go much farther than your own nose."

Miranda blinked, her mouth open, searching for words she couldn't find.

"So, I want you to go back there this instant. I know Viv called you earlier. She's your sister. She needs you."

Sister. Mother. Miranda saw the words in her mind and knew they didn't make as much sense as they used to. They never would. "Look, Mom. Why don't you go over there? Ask Aunt Bell to go. I—I'll go tomorrow. I told Viv I'd call her tomorrow."

"That's just fine," June said stiffly.

"Mom," Miranda started.

"No. Don't say any more. I can see how you feel. Just like when you were a little girl. Selfish to the core. I won't mention to Viv that I talked to you. She couldn't bear to know that you were free but couldn't quite manage to get out to visit."

June hung up abruptly, but Miranda pressed the phone against her ear, thinking that if she waited just a bit longer, June would come back on the line, sigh, apologize, and say, "You know, I'm just anxious about Viv. Don't worry. I'll take care of it."

But June didn't come back on, and the phone stayed dead.

Selfish to the core. Can't go farther than her own nose.

Miranda hung up, tears pricking her eyes. As she

stood in her kitchen, she began to realize that she couldn't stand being in the city for one more second. She wanted to jump in her car and drive to—to where? Anywhere. Even LA. She'd check into a hotel under an assumed name and eat Hostess cupcakes in bed and watch HBO for a week. No. She'd drive to Napa and check into a spa. Have a massage every day until her money ran out. She'd be scrubbed with apricot pits, massaged with warmed stones, drenched in soothing oils. No. No. That wouldn't do. Driving would only give her more time to think about all the things she wished she could forget. She began to pace, crying. She wanted to just go. Now. She wanted Sariel.

Miranda knew she had to find Sariel, if just for a moment, even if he'd wished she'd go away for good. She just wanted to feel his arms go around her and hold her close and make her feel better. If only she could fly, even if it were for a tiny amount of time, like she did when she was little. If only she could just do what Sariel did, moving through all those waves and particles into space and time. If she could, she would be able to escape everything.

She breathed in, suddenly remembering what had happened at the auditorium and then later at the book signing and even today at the coffee shop. Opening her eyes, she stared out the window, reliving the moments when the gray appeared, hung there, open and inviting. How had she done that? Or had she? But if she had, she could find Sariel. What had he said before? *All I have to do is think myself—and you—into the part of the energy I want to go.*

But didn't you have to be *Croyant* to do that? This gray just didn't appear to ordinary, average people like Miranda. Nothing magic happened to *Moyenne.* But it had. Three times. And she'd seen a house and a dark room. Maybe that's where Sariel was right now. Maybe he was calling to her through his thoughts.

The least she could do was try.

Miranda took a glass from the cupboard and filled it at the sink, drinking it down. Then she left the kitchen and went into her bathroom and quickly brushed her teeth, washed her face, and combed her hair. In the bedroom, she grabbed her coat and her purse, making sure she had money and what? A passport? She didn't need it for this kind of flight, but if she found herself stuck in Istanbul or Tibet or Micronesia, she might need it to get home. What else? Searching through her bedside drawer, she grabbed her Swiss Army knife, mints, a pen, and some paper, stuffing them into her purse.

Miranda was almost laughing, giddy, feeling like someone who actually believed in Santa Claus or the Tooth Fairy. But she didn't stop, gathering essentials, putting on a sturdier pair of shoes, and then she went to the living room, turned off the lights, and stood still.

How to do it? Sariel hadn't seemed to perform any rituals. Basically, he'd asked her if she were ready and then they'd gone. Pressing a hand to her chest, Miranda took a deep breath and then exhaled. She folded her arms and then relaxed. She took her purse off her shoulder and then put it back. Shifting back and forth on her feet, Miranda wanted to laugh or cry or just go to bed. Her thoughts kept coming, and they were named *thrill, excitement, fear, sorrow,* and *hope.* But finally, after a few minutes, her body went still and then so did her mind, her thoughts shrinking, falling away, her mind full of nothing but a hum. From memory then, she pulled forth the gray as it had appeared to her the three times. She pictured it as it had been at the back of the large room, in the lobby as she signed books, today as she was trying to relax at the coffee shop. Slowly, like a bank of incredibly thick fog, it came to her, rolling, roiling, full of nothing, full of everything. It pressed around her, her body seeming to expand into it.

Taking in a breath, Miranda knew it was here, for real, right in front of her. This was it, and she opened her eyes, seeing the gray, the quick flicks of matter, and she thought about where she needed to go. But there was no *where.* There was only a *who. Sariel,* she thought. *Sariel. Tell me where you are.*

Somewhere, in the far recesses of the moving, living gray matter, she thought she saw something, felt him, heard him say, "I'm here. Come to me." And without another thought, she closed her eyes and moved in, felt herself pass through matter, felt matter pass through her. She was close now, almost with him. Sariel.

Chapter Nine

Early in the morning, Sariel, Rufus, and the rest of the recently assembled team sat at Adalbert's long wooden kitchen table. The room was filled with early, pinkish sunrise, a fire crackling in the corner fireplace. Adalbert stood over the hob, murmuring encouraging words to a large pot of oatmeal.

"Have you heard of a microwave?" Rufus said finally. "It's a wee miracle."

Adalbert held up a finger, stirred for a moment longer, and then stopped, bringing the pot to the table and serving up bowls for the group. Next to Sariel sat Nala, swathed in yellow robes, her face stern, no wisecracks this morning, and next to her was Sayblee Safipour, a *sorcière* Sariel had known well in school, though she wasn't in his class but in Felix's. Back then, she was fun to be around because no one ever knew what would burst into flame. When she was angry about a test score or at what the cooks had served up in the cafeteria for breakfast, things had a tendency to ignite: desks, cooks' hats, teacher's grade books. She could even create fire in the middle of the hardest, densest stone, evidenced by the bursting into flame of a toilet in the girl's bathroom. Apparently, Amanda Browne had teased Sayblee about her dress and Amanda was sitting on the toilet when the fire commenced. Sayblee was the toast of the school because everyone was evacuated during final exams as teachers rushed to put out the fire that kept springing back to life despite the charms and magic they threw at it.

Sayblee smiled up at him, her blue eyes serious. "Don't worry," she said, having read his thoughts. "I'm in a good mood. And I have better control now."

"I'm sure Amanda would be glad to hear of that," Sariel said.

Sayblee tucked her blonde hair behind her ear. "She loved it. Boys told her she had a hot ass after that."

"She had a hot ass," Rufus said. "And it wasn't because of your fire."

Sariel laughed, eating his oatmeal, smiling until he felt something pull at him, something he couldn't quite understand. Sayblee reminded him of a person or a conversation, maybe, or a thought, but then whatever she reminded him of vanished.

"We will likely need your skill, Sayblee. Who knows what Quain has in mind?" said Mazi Kakkilya, who'd just come in from Tanzania that morning. He was an older man, but his dark skin was unlined, smooth, as if he'd spent most of his life in the gray, traveling between times rather than being in one. His hair, while abundant, was mostly gray, the curls slightly wild, a pale halo around his face.

Across from Sariel sat Baris Fraser and Lutalo Olano, both of whom had spent the night at Adalbert's after the Council meeting as well. They were chatting about Lutalo's pet project, a bridge that changed from stone to wood to metal and back again.

"My wife hates it," Lutalo admitted. "She wanted a

nice wooden bridge over the pond in our backyard. But I was inspired."

"Sounds awesome," Baris said, running his hand through his orange hair. "Bet the kids love it." Baris had the ability to hold more thoughts in his head than most, a crowded stadium not overwhelming to him. On any mission, he was an asset, especially when things were in chaos.

Rufus joined in the conversation, telling everyone at the table about the house he and Fabia wanted to buy just outside of Edinburgh. Sariel rubbed his forehead. He needed to get himself together. All of these people had strong magic, were good people, had amazing skills. He was lucky to be working with them. And they hadn't even left yet, so all this unease was ridiculous. *For God's sake,* he thought, *how much more comfortable could I be? My mother is here.* Hearing his thought, Zosime touched him lightly with her hand as she finished saying something to Adalbert. She squeezed his arm gently, and he put a hand on top of hers.

I'm okay, he thought.

You are and you will be, she thought back. *That's always been the case with you.*

I keep on ticking, he thought.

She quickly turned to smile at him. "That's what I count on."

"Zosime," Mazi said. "Tell me what you make of Brennus. I do think he has gotten a bit, shall I say, intense? The messages he sent me!"

Zosime squeezed his arm one more time, and then she turned to talk with Mazi. Sariel shook his head, sat up straight, shifting in his seat, glancing at Rufus, who had always calmed him, and taking deep breaths. But nothing seemed to remedy his jumpiness.

Periodically, he had a flash of something, a woman with her arms outspread, ready for flight. For some reason, the flight seemed dangerous to him, as if the woman in his mind was stepping into something tenuous, air not buoyant enough to keep her aloft.

Then there was another thought, something darker, smaller, quieter, like a snail in the depths of its shell. But each time he reached out with his mind for explanation, the thought curled up and disappeared.

Sariel breathed out, shaking his head. Perhaps he was picking up someone's dreams or strong thoughts. Maybe the image of flight belonged to the milkman jangling by in his white truck, a thought the man had when dawn broke in the east, white and translucent. Or the image was simply his recollection of his mother's entrance last night combined with nerves about the mission. Nothing more.

Or he was just nervous, inventing images instead of focusing on the fact that he was afraid of what he might actually do when he saw Kallisto. Or when he saw Quain. He wanted nothing more than to give back the pain he and his family had suffered at both their hands, push all his hate and anger and desire for revenge into their minds and bodies until the story was finally over. Sariel had kept those feelings tamped down for so long, he wasn't sure what they would do when they erupted, red, jagged, full of spikes.

There was nothing he could do about the future now; he knew that. The only time he could work with was now, the present. And in the present, things were fine. He was with most of his family, trusted *sorciers* and *sorcières*. Everything was all right. Slowly, he felt himself relax, and soon, he was talking with everyone, laughing, almost happy.

When the oatmeal was gone and the last of the coffee poured into the thick mugs, Adalbert pushed his bowl aside, wiped his mouth, and looked at them all.

"I know this seems an informal way to set off on your

mission," he said, motioning to the breakfast table. "A casual meal like this. But we are trying to keep activity to a minimum. We've held no meetings at the Council buildings at Rabley Heath, just at the pub or in private homes. All Council members are going about routine business. We have protection spells around every sensitive site, including this house. I need you to keep your abilities tamped down, especially when you are traveling. It's important to contain your thoughts, keep them to yourselves until you need to join each other's. Use your skills only as needed. Only when required. As you know, we have Kallisto and Quain's current location, but until you arrive there, maintain protocol."

Adalbert looked at them all, but kept his gaze on Sariel a second longer, as if Sariel had done something against the code. As if he were the one to lose control and do something unexpected. *But what?* Sariel thought, searching for an answer. *All I've been doing,* he thought, *for years, since Kallisto, is my job.*

He flushed, pushing his hair away from his face. Rufus kicked him gently on the foot, and Sariel breathed in, controlling his confusion. Adalbert's gaze moved on, and then the old man folded his hands on the table.

"This mission is the most important one we've had to embark on for years, well over fifty," Adalbert continued. "And the battle at Jacob's Well cost us many good people and disrupted so much in our world. It was a time when we questioned our very way of life, our abilities, the choices we've made for generations. In order to keep what we have—to maintain the delicate balance between *Moyenne* and *Croyant*—we had to sacrifice so many of our best people. I don't want to see that kind of bloodshed again in my lifetime, though Quain's ability to get what he wants could give us just that. He has no compunction about killing, and he will continue unless we can stop him."

The kitchen was silent, the only noise the dying crackle of the fire. Sariel looked at Rufus and then Zosime, knowing that Adalbert's words were reminding them all of Hadrian.

"You have," Adalbert said, "my undying gratitude for your service to our community and all the communities on this planet. Most of the world doesn't know the reasons for all the disruption, can't understand the power outages, the market crashes, the wars breaking out like plagues. We are not in the days when *Croyant* were blamed for everything, but worse yet is that they blame each other. City-states and countries lash out at others that are not in the least to blame, causing the pain and suffering to be multiplied tenscore. The *Moyenne* may not know what is happening, but they would surely feel the absence of the *plaques* when things would only become worse."

Adalbert paused, pulled gently on his beard, turned again to look at Sariel, who swallowed. For a second, Adalbert's mind skimmed his, offering a thoughtful *Good luck, my boy.* But at the same time, he knew that the older man was looking for something, dipping into Sariel's thoughts with gentle, plucking probes. But almost as soon as Sariel noticed, Adalbert pulled his mind away from Sariel's, stood up, holding out his hands almost in supplication.

"May this mission be successful. May I have you all here at my table again soon." He pressed his hands together and bowed slightly.

Stern-faced, Nala Nagode nodded, stood up from the table, and then buttoned her robe and adjusted her hood. "Let's go, then," she said. "Let's start this so we can finish it."

Putting all their minds into a collective seam, the members of the group brought together their images and ideas about Quain and Kallisto, so all would know what each thought. This way, there would be no chance for mistakes, no way for Quain to trap one in the lie of another, no one left without a key piece of information, all able to use what was clearly hard won.

They stood together in a circle, clasped hands and closed their eyes. In a rush of electric current, Sariel felt the six other minds push into his with a jolt. He knew Rufus's thoughts almost as much as he knew his own, but it was always a shock to come into contact with so many others' minds. He calmed his breath, stilled his body, opened his mind.

Sariel concentrated, letting the others' feelings and images filter in: There was Nala's first meeting with Quain, fifteen years ago, his face a leer as he taunted the Council. Sariel almost gasped, hating Quain even in memory, wanting to fling a curse at his thin, wiry body, yank back his head with his lank, dark hair. Sariel wanted to hurt Quain, but not with magic. He wanted to use his hands, his own flesh, to try to take back what Quain had taken from the Valasay family: life.

In the memory, Quain couldn't feel Sariel's gaze, and as Sariel listened to the man's harsh, punctuated lecture to the Council, he knew the fight for the last *plaque* would be beyond anything he'd experienced. What they would face shortly was here, fifteen years earlier, in the mind of Nala Nagode. The power, the need, the desire. All of it was in Quain's eyes. Even in Nala's thoughts, Quain's eyes were the deepest black, almost without pupils, hard and full of hatred.

"You think that you can control me? You think that you can contain what I have become?"

"Sit down." Adalbert—red-faced and uncharacteristically discomposed—smacked the gavel on the Council table.

"No, I think I prefer not to." Quain sneered and he

raised his arms and vanished before the Council could deliver judgment or punishment, despite the charms and spells quickly thrown out to keep him in place. What had he done to be in front of the Council? Nala let the memory continue, showing the uproar in the meeting, the shouts and yells from the crowd, the *Croyant* vanishing in order to try to follow Quain.

"He must be found before he does worse," a younger Mazi was saying.

Now Sariel could see how Quain used *Moyenne* minds to get property, money, power, control. Wars in the Middle East, a blockade of Africa, warlords at each other's throats. Sariel took in a sharp breath, floored by the anger in Quain's strangely charismatic face. And then, creeping in through the outrage and anger and fear of that night, was a slim line of new thought, a shamed, quaking thought, but Nala gave it up, held it out for them to see so that she would have nothing to hide. She had appreciated Quain's looks, despite herself, wished he weren't the man he was, knew, though, exactly who he was. Once again, Nala brought Quain forth, let him move in front of the Council audience, passion in his face, in his movements. She turned her view to the crowd, and Sariel looked closely and saw how there were a few who were caught in his words, pulled forward with his energy. Without wanting to, Sariel could see why Kallisto went to him. How could she not?

Rufus's thoughts charged out, blasted through the circle. *She chose, dammit. And she chose wrong.*

The current between all of them bumped, pulsed, and Nala's thought shimmered briefly and then faded, the energy in the circle moving to Rufus.

I have to, Rufus thought, taking Sariel and the others away from the blank space that had just recently held Quain in front of the Council. Slowly, Rufus built his own memory, without sparing Sariel. First, windswept Marin hills, the Pacific to the right, San Francisco lights to the left. Rufus moving toward the house, fear in his throat, fear so deep Sariel could barely swallow. Rufus let them hear Sariel's strangled pleas for help that had brought him to Marin years ago, interrupting his plans to go to London: *Rufus!* Sariel had cried out in his mind. *Rufus, come!*

In the darkness, Rufus appeared in front of the house, his robes swirling around him. He had stood in Sariel's garden, his eyes closed, trying to determine how to enter the house. But even from outside, Rufus heard Kallisto's mocking taunts, Sariel's moans of pain and confusion. Rufus didn't wait, appearing in Sariel's living room, ready to do anything to save his brother.

The fight—Sariel couldn't look again—but he felt Rufus nudge him back to the thought. There, in his own house, Sariel hung in the middle of the room, suspended, naked, held still with a *sortilège du nature morte*, all but dead.

Sariel wanted to blink away this image, but he knew he had to watch, seeing this very scene as his most vulnerable moment, a place that Kallisto and Quain could pick and pull at to weaken him. Sariel hung in the room, enchanted, weak and useless, unable to move while Rufus and Kallisto fought with their bodies and their minds. Rufus used all his magic, throwing out spells and *charmes du protection*, but even in memory, Sariel could feel his brother growing weak, confused, empty. As she battled Rufus, Kallisto was smiling, laughing periodically, unafraid, unconcerned, completely in command.

She stood in the middle of the room, beautiful in her full red robe, her long hair whirling around her body as she and Rufus battled for Sariel's soul. Even in memory, even completely enchanted, he could feel how he was pulled to her power, her body, her ideas. *Watch!* he said to himself. *Watch how you hang there, filled only with her magic.*

Sariel wanted to fade back from the scene, but the group had to see what she could do, and Sariel's memory bled into Rufus's without a segue, giving the group another scene a month before Rufus arrived to do battle. Kallisto and Sariel were in bed, naked, touching, Kallisto waiting for Sariel to promise he would be with her always, share in all her power.

"We don't have to live by these rules. Their rules! These prohibitions and strictures were made when we were afraid of *Moyenne*! And why should we be afraid now? Why should we hide what we can do? We are now so powerful, we could destroy them all the moment they thought to hurt us. Maybe we should destroy them before they have the chance."

Kallisto pulled Sariel to her, kissing him hard, stroking his body as they lay together, the Pacific moon full in the bedroom window behind them. "Quain thinks as I do, and we will join him, Sariel. We will join him and his followers and leave this insipid existence. Quain has powerful people working for him now. Who needs the *Croyant* restrictions now? Who cares about the *Moyenne*! With the *plaques*, we could be everyone without their ordinary little lives!"

The image flickered, ripped apart, and another replaced it: Sariel agreeing to Kallisto's plan, making arrangements to leave the Bay Area, without telling Zosime or Rufus or Felix. As he decided how to close up his house and disappear from his job without a trace, he completely believed Kallisto. In the memory, he's bent over his desk, Kallisto standing behind him, thinking to him, cajoling him, *It will be wonderful working with Quain. We will always be together.*

Sariel reached out a hand to her, brought her close. What did he really care for the *Moyenne* world, after all? And he thought he could live without the ordinary beauty of the *Moyenne* world. Certainly, *Croyant* participated in the world, helped make roads and aided governments and created art. But they'd grown lazy, magic making art somehow unnecessary. *Moyenne* never stopped, turning paint into art and clay into relics and ideas into words and words into songs and novels and . . . and poetry. Poetry.

Confused, Sariel felt the image slip away, his mind go grainy, his head empty; but then another vision filled his and the others' minds.

Kallisto leaned over him, her black eyes full of lust, but not for him. Sariel could see that now. But not then. Not one bit. That night, every move of her body, every glimmering glance, every soft, lush kiss made the Sariel in the memory want to go with her more. Made him want to do whatever she asked of him. He let them all see what he thought then, all his yes's. All his desire. In the memory, Kallisto opened up like a red-winged blackbird, sleek and beautiful and ready for flight.

Then, like an incantation, Kallisto's thoughts pulsed into the memory, the same ones Nala heard from Quain: *property, money, power, control.*

With effort, Sariel forced one last image out, an image he did not see himself but was told about often: his father, Hadrian, who trusted Quain. Quain, who did nothing but laugh as he let energy stream from his body and push Hadrian up and fling him over and over . . .

As Hadrian fell, Sariel flashed another image of his father, one he did remember. It was late afternoon, over twenty years ago. The sun was out, Sariel and his brothers were playing in the backyard, and Hadrian appeared suddenly in the yard, back from a job. He turned, saw his boys, held out his arms, and laughed, his face wide with happiness.

Sariel couldn't hold it, the scene fading, everything falling into blackness. In the circle, the group rested for a moment, the current flat. But then Mazi, whose gift was prophecy, opened up his thoughts, a world where *Moyenne* lived in fear. Because Mazi's thoughts were only possibilities, unformed images flicked past quickly: whole cities darkened and shut down out of fear, *Moyenne* forced out of entire areas and placed in work camps, and executions, both *Croyant* and *Moyenne.*

Headlines from *Moyenne* newspapers flashed in front of their eyes: *Lower Part of State Evacuated to Designated Camps; New Croyant Authority to Take Over; Final Edition Today.*

All wealth was funneled to Quain, who ruled as world king, his eyes burning bright with avarice, the three *plaques* his. Mazi showed them a terrible tableaux, Quain on a throne, Kallisto standing next to him, a new Council in a wide circle in front of him, members from all *Croyant* groups.

Next, Mazi moved away from Quain and to the *plaques,* which were fitted together into the pyramid they could become if a *sorcier* or *sorcière* were magic enough to make them do so. Wafts of golden power streamed from the pointed top, filling the room with brilliant light, twirling around Quain, making him stronger and stronger and stronger, while outside, away from him, everything fell apart.

Mazi let the image dim and disappear. And then, quickly and horribly, there was Sayblee's brother Rasheed, turning away from Sayblee and her family, disappearing in a flurry of robes and wind.

"Please," a woman said as she grabbed onto Sayblee. "Follow him. Bring him back to us."

"He's lost to Quain, Mom," Sayblee said. "There's nothing I can do. We'll never see him again."

"Oh, you can find him. You can!" Sayblee's mother cried out. "Why won't you?"

Sayblee shook her head and simply stared at her mother in complete sadness.

Bringing her hands to her face, Sayblee's mother pushed herself away from her daughter and walked out of the room. Sayblee paced back and forth, throwing out hot, angry thoughts. In the corner of the room, a table and chairs burst into flame.

Lutalo's memory slipped in just as Sayblee's faded. It was a late night in July, a bar on the *Rive Gauche*, close enough to the Seine to see the many lighted *Bateaux-Mouches* power down the river. From his table on the sidewalk outside, Lutalo could hear the voices of the tourists echo up the street. He sipped his beer, and then turned to look for the waiter. Instead, his gaze landed on a man who sat at the bar, Quain, who was staring at him over the rim of a glass. Quain must have recognized Lutalo, known something about him because at that instant, Lutalo was unable to move his mind. If he'd been able, he would have turned Quain's bar stool to air, the bar to cellophane, giving himself enough time to disappear. But Quain held him tightly, staring at him, picking through his mind as if Lutalo were a filing cabinet. Lutalo was filled with a bone-shaking fear, knowing that he knew enough to give Quain an answer to some question. He tried to hold on, but his mind poured itself out. Quain's search seemed to go on for hours, but the next thing Lutalo knew, he was on the sidewalk, two men speaking hushed French above him.

The memory broke apart, spun into gray. Baris opened up his incredible mind and let loose a raft of *Croyant* news, all the latest Quain sightings, the fissures and cracks in *Moyenne* governments, the specifics of the *plaque* thefts. Hundreds of images came at them. Maps. Details. Known accomplices. Adalbert's and the Council's declarations, ideas, plans.

Suddenly, it was over, all of them hanging together in the gray, drained and resting. Sariel felt as though he'd already battled Quain and lost. He felt a collective exhaustion and worry, the circle drained dry of energy. *What is the use?* someone thought. *Why bother?*

They all must have thought too long about the futility of the mission because Mazi let loose a wild burst of hope, images of what could be: the Council orderly, *Moyenne* cities and governments concerned only with their business, the *plaques* separated to keep power equal and measured. There were problems and issues and work to be done connecting *Croyant* and *Moyenne* life, to be sure, but no one was trying to rule universally. Life was just as it had been before Quain.

Now, thought Nala. *London.*

Lightened, they thought together of London, brought their energy together, united, and slipped into time and space and the gray. In seconds, they opened their eyes into the courtyard of a Georgian house in Kensington, loaned to them by a *sorcier* who'd been following Quain and who'd disappeared without a trace. Breathing hard, they stared at each other, knowing more than ever what they had to do. They'd seen it all, and they could never let the horrible visions Mazi had shown them of Quain's takeover come to pass.

"That was a breeze," Rufus said, his hair standing on end, as it did whenever he traveled. He smiled, but his eyes were stunned, full of the images they'd all shared.

"You look as though you've been through one," Nala said archly, glancing at his hair. "Let's get to it. Rufus and Sariel, you and I will go to meet the contacts at The Fox and Pelican. The rest of you, work on collecting more information about Quain's location. We'll meet back here in the evening. And as a precaution, guard your minds. Keep your thoughts to yourself. We all know what we need to for now. Remember what Adalbert told us."

"Great," Rufus whispered to Sariel. "We're stuck with Nala as tour guide."

"You'd better watch it, bro," Sariel said, feeling rather than seeing the thoughts that Nala had often harbored about Rufus. "Fabia would not be pleased about what I'm sensing. That Nala has been after you for years."

Rufus rolled his eyes. "You are just jealous because your . . . because you don't have . . . because you . . ." He stopped talking and looked at Sariel, blinking and smoothing his hair with a hand. And then he shrugged. "Lost the rest of my riff."

"Just as well. Wouldn't want you to think something that might offend someone." Nala walked toward them. "Let's go."

She put a hand on Sariel's and Rufus's shoulders, and the three of them whirled back into the gray.

Like all vortexes, this one was hard to see, the only sign a shimmery quaver in the air, like a film gone slightly bad at the edges. They were standing in front of a pub on a quiet street, the vortex pushing away foot and automobile traffic. Sariel turned and saw a main road a few blocks down, just where the vortex ended. There was only limited movement: a car, a black cab, a bicycle passing. No one turned down the street or even seemed to glance at it, so the vortex was strong. For some reason, the idea of the vortex collapsing, breaking down, dissolving was pinging in his brain. What would happen if someone got in, heard the talk, and . . . and . . .

"Lovely weather," Nala said.

Sariel glanced upward. The sky was dark with clouds, flecks of rain hitting them.

"English weather," Rufus said. "You get used to it."

"I doubt it," Sariel said. "I'd be in the Bahamas every other day. A tropical island no one else knows about."

"Please don't talk to me about tropical islands. And you aren't seriously trying to tell me there isn't fog in the Bay Area? Constant summer dreariness in the Sunset District?"

"Enough." Nala shook her head. "Can't say a thing without you two embarking on a brotherly chat. Come on."

She pointed to the pub door, and the three of them walked through the intense vortex energy guarding the door and then pushed through, closing the door behind them. At their entrance, the group at the bar stood up, silent, one man finally walking up to them, pushing his hood back.

To Sariel, the man looked as though he'd been beaten. Maybe not by another person but by life. His eyes were full of fatigue and grief, his face pale, almost gray. His shoulders were held proudly, but it was as if he carried a heavy load regardless, gravity pulling him to ground, beckoning him to rest.

Nala held up a hand, ready to speak, but the man interrupted, his tired eyes suddenly sharp, focused, wary.

"I can't read you. Identify yourselves." The man crossed his arms, and Sariel could feel him try to slide into his thoughts, his energy skimming Sariel's mind. But the man couldn't find passage and pulled his mind away in irritation. Behind him, Sariel could sense the group's growing unease with the visit, and he readied himself for a short skirmish. Beside him, Rufus put his hands on his head, centered himself on his feet. Sariel wished he could think a few things to Rufus, but it wasn't safe. Quain had turned the best of *Croyant* to himself over the years. With two *plaques* in his control, he could turn even a group of the most talented *Croyant*, those completely loyal to Adalbert. It was entirely possible that this group could be a Quain trap.

"We were sent by Adalbert Baird," Nala said, seeming to grow a foot as she spoke, her yellow robes almost billowing. "On Council business that you are more than familiar with. Unless, of course, you aren't here on Council business at all."

Grimly, her gaze dark and firm, Nala handed the man an envelope that she pulled from a pocket in her robe, and they waited as he opened it and read Adalbert's words. As he read, the man looked up at them periodically, his face slowly changing, relief spreading through his expression, and then his body. His shoulders fell, and he sighed, shaking his head.

At the man's seeming acceptance of them, Sariel breathed in deeply, looking around at the twelve other bar patrons, *sorcières* and *sorciers*. The group was slumped over steins and glasses, some leaning on their elbows, one man almost asleep. Their robes were dirty, scorched, their eyes like the eyes of the man who still read Adalbert's letter, full of exhaustion and, Sariel had to admit, fear.

Strangely, he didn't know who any of them were. *They must exclusively work in Europe,* he thought. Or maybe this was a secret team, kept secret from most of *Croyant,* used only for emergencies. And this was how they looked? What had happened to them? What had Quain done?

Again, Sariel wished he could reach Nala. She should know these contacts; after all, she was a Council member, had been for years. But without the ability to go into her mind, Sariel couldn't determine her feelings beyond nerves. Nala looked blank, the muscles in her face trying to cover her anxiety.

The man folded the letter, and Sariel tensed again. The room felt dark, heavy, sodden with Quain thoughts he couldn't trace. The hair at the back of his neck prickled, and looking quickly at Rufus, he could see his brother felt just as uneasy.

The man put the paper back into the envelope, laying it on a table, where it burst into red flames that touched only the paper and disappeared when the letter was nothing more than smoke. For an instant, Sariel wished that Sayblee were here to see it.

After the letter and the fire were gone, the man looked up at them and nodded. "You were right to be tentative. Nothing and no one can be trusted right now. Adalbert was wise to have you shut your minds and your magic. This—this . . ." The man trailed off, using a hand to indicate his group. "This is what can happen if you face Quain without total preparation."

Nala nodded, dropping her heightened aspect, her fierce gaze. Her robes settled around her body. "I can only imagine. Nala Nagode. This is Sariel Valasay and Rufus Valasay."

The man's eyes grew sharp. "Hadrian's sons?"

"Two of them," Rufus said, extending his hand.

The man took it, shook hands firmly with Rufus and then with Sariel and Nala. "I knew Hadrian well. And I've heard about you both. I'm Phaedrus Mather. These good people"—he motioned to the group at the bar—"are what remain of my team. We were once fifty."

"What in the bloody hell happened, man?" Rufus asked. "What have you been up to?"

Phaedrus shook his head, breathing out deeply, his sigh full of too much past and even more sorrow. "Setting spells and casting protection around the *plaques*. Searching out Quain's location, rounding up his followers. We've managed to capture twoscore. We've been doing what all *Croyant* should have been doing. And sooner. But we need to talk about what is at hand. Sit."

He led them to a large round table, they and Phaedrus's group fitting easily around it. Sariel noticed that the group seemed to perk up, gather strength from the knowledge that Sariel, Rufus, and Nala were there to help, to take over. Even the man who'd been half asleep and slumped over the bar managed to say hello.

The barkeep brought over a tray of wine and goblets, and Sariel was glad to have something to do other than think about almost forty people dead. With only seven, Nala's group had much worse odds, and now Quain was more powerful than before. Sariel knew that even his ability to shimmy through thoughts, find his enemies, and bind them tightly would probably be useless against Quain with two *plaques.*

Someone—all of them—might die. And for a second Sariel felt a regret that went beyond leaving behind his mother and brothers. He would leave behind something, someone else. A warm and light thought flickered in his mind for a moment and then took flight, leaving him empty.

"Tell us what happened," Rufus said.

Phaedrus took a long sip of wine and set his goblet on the table. "The first *plaque* had just been captured. Everyone and everything was in chaos. We knew that Quain would immediately set out for the second *plaque,* but he had managed to block our ability to communicate with each other or anyone."

"He blocked your minds? All of you?" Nala set down her glass. "At once?"

Phaedrus sighed. "Yes. And he did it completely. We had to travel through matter to actually speak with Adalbert and the Council, who immediately put us at the site of the second *plaque.* The first thought, of course, was to guard it and guard it well. But too much time had passed. Quain had grown in power, gathered strength from the two *plaques.*"

"Why didn't you transport the *plaque*? Hide it elsewhere?" Sariel asked.

"We did," Phaedrus said. "We moved it three times. All our magic plus the Council's protecting it. But each time, a group of Quain's followers found us. We fought, and fought hard. Quain gave them powers, though. I hadn't fought like that before. And in each battle, we lost people. Good people. Strong, talented people."

Phaedrus fell silent, the only sounds in the room the *swish swish* of the barkeep sweeping in the kitchen, the whirl of water in the dishwasher. Sariel glanced at the people sitting around the table. One *sorcière* glanced at him, shook her head slightly, and looked down into her glass.

"Did you ever see Quain?" Nala asked.

"Never. Just his followers. We managed to overcome many, but we couldn't get to him. He's managed to be at least three steps ahead of us. The night before he took the second *plaque,* we were only able to discover where he'd been staying the week before."

"And then he got that one, too," Rufus said in disbelief. "How did he do it?"

Phaedrus raised his hands and let them fall back to the table. "We all had protection spells, our charms, our strength. Fifty of us. Fifty *Croyant* against Quain. And we were ready. We thought that together, all of us, we could weave enough spells to keep it safe."

Sariel shook his head. "He worked his way through all of you? All that magic?"

"As if it and we didn't exist at all," Phaedrus said slowly. "I have to warn you, he has magic I've never seen before in my life. Magic none of us understood and still don't. I haven't been able to explain it to Adalbert and the Council yet."

"Tell us," Nala said, her face intense. "We need to know."

"It was like this," Phaedrus began. "No warning. One minute Quain was there before us, breaking through all of our protections. We fought back as hard as we could, throwing everything we had at him. For a moment, it looked like he was overcome, even with Kallisto beside him."

Sariel sucked in air, the sound of her name slick in

his mind. His heart beat against his ribs, and he swallowed down hard. Phaedrus glanced at him, nodding, and Sariel realized that the man knew the story.

"Go on," Rufus said.

"And then," Phaedrus said, "and then it was as if the entire room broke up into a thousand pieces, all the pieces—including us—shaking and heaving. Our bodies, our hearts, all our organs, our minds all scattered and thrown. The room turned upon itself, flipped upside down."

"What form of blasted magic is that?" Rufus said, slapping his hand on the table.

Phaedrus almost laughed, rubbed his forehead, and then closed his eyes for a moment. He composed himself, exhaling. "Nothing we knew. Nothing we could stop. And by the time the few of us who made it through the blast had awakened, Quain and the *plaque* were gone. He—"

"Quain's mad. Entirely," a *sorcière* interrupted. "He's mad, and he's more powerful than any *sorcier* I've ever known. There was that terrible spell at the end, but everything leading up to it was just as dangerous. And his magic is so strong that there isn't time to call for healers. It's over, just like that. He thinks *sword*, and it's in your heart. He thinks *pain*, and you can't move. He imagines the gray, and you're trapped in it. We think—we think some of our people are lost in matter. Lost and alive."

Sariel looked up. "In matter?" For an instant, he saw Phaedrus's people hanging in the gray, still, scared, unable to move. He bit his the inside of his cheek, trying to calm himself, thinking, *You're not stuck. It's not you.*

Phaedrus turned for a moment to look at Sariel and then nodded. "This new power of his is what also gave him the ability to shake us almost to death. Somehow, he can energize matter and also harness it, still it, the wave and particle in constant, but at the same time, motionless flux. His own private prison no one else can find. That's where he has put our people. We intend to find them."

"How many are trapped there?" Rufus asked gruffly.

"Maybe five," the woman said, the others nodding. "There still might be hope for them."

"If he gets the third *plaque* . . ." Nala began, stopping, her fingers tight around her goblet.

"If he gets the third *plaque,*" Phaedrus said, "we won't be able to do anything."

"So what in the blazes can we do?" Rufus leaned back in his chair and crossed his arms.

The group was silent for a moment. Finally, Phaedrus cleared his throat.

"We know more now, that's certain. So we are going to report to the Council. I would assume that we will regroup and gather together more *Croyant* and guard the third *plaque.* I'm going to Adalbert tonight. And you are going to try to find Quain and Kallisto before they find us."

"Nice work if you can get it," Rufus said, his sarcasm heavy. "But how do you suppose we'll achieve that kind of wee magic?"

"You are a talented group," Phaedrus said. "And you have Sariel. From what Adalbert has told me, if anyone can find Quain, it's you." He looked at Sariel, his gaze slow and serious. "You have the connection."

"And if anyone can find Kallisto," the woman added, "it's you as well."

Kallisto spun into Sariel's thoughts, her eyes wide, bitter, beautiful. He blinked, feeling his anger rise up, fuming in his chest. She had never cared for him, never loved him, used him and his family. Sariel could feel the way her mind would crack apart when he trapped her as clearly as he could still feel her body in his hands.

"Who's our contact?" Nala asked. Her face was tense, but she'd found her bearing, her back straight, her eyes narrowed. She seemed taller again, regal. "We need to get started. I feel—I feel there isn't much time."

Phaedrus nodded. "You're right. Even though the Council has likely worked magic to protect the third *plaque* already, it won't be long before Quain has a plan. It could be a couple of days, maybe a week if we're lucky. We found a contact for you, but I assure you, the meeting will not be at all pleasant. He claims he has a message directly from Quain."

"We need to go now," Rufus said. "There's no time to waste."

"I know it's hard to trust in these times, but could you open your mind for a moment and let me give you the information?" Phaedrus asked Nala.

Nala looked at Sariel and Rufus, and they nodded. She and Phaedrus stood up and left the table, walking to the far end of the room. Sariel watched as she and Phaedrus stood facing each other, their eyes closed, their hands touching.

"If we aren't successful . . ." the *sorcière* began saying. Then she stopped and sighed.

Sariel looked at her, her eyes blue and tired and glossy, pale gray shadows under them like bruises.

"I know," he said. "We all do."

After Phaedrus had supplied Nala with the contact information, Sariel and Rufus stood up from the round table, unsure of what to say. Sariel knew that these people had been through what they were likely to face. What words would help either way? Finally, one of the *sorciers* raised a glass, and Sariel nodded, and both he and Rufus followed Nala to the door.

Back at the house, edgy and irritable, they waited in

the kitchen for Mazi, Baris, Lutalo, and Sayblee to return from collecting what information they could about Quain's location. Sariel paced back and forth in the kitchen, while Rufus slumped in a chair, his arms crossed. Nala sat at the table, drumming her fingers on the wood, her mouth grimly set. Outside, a steady rain began to fall, light taps bouncing off the windows.

"We shouldn't just be waiting here," Rufus said. "Phaedrus said we don't have a lot of time. We need to find this contact."

"They'll be here," Nala said quietly, her fingers keeping rhythm to the rain.

Rufus stood up suddenly, his hands on his hips. "Where in the hell are they? We need to get them back here now. Or do we really even need them for this?"

"We all need to hear what the contact has to say," Nala said. "And Mazi especially needs to listen. Maybe he'll have a vision."

Sariel sighed. "Ru, a few minutes, an hour. It's not going to make a difference. They'll be back soon enough. And then we can go on this fool's mission."

"If you keep those thoughts," Nala said, her voice tight and filled with disappointment at his words, "we have no chance."

Sariel uncrossed his arms and lifted his hands. "It's the truth. Out of fifty, they had twelve left. Did you see how they looked? Did you see their robes? Their eyes? Their faces? They looked exactly like people who'd been beaten and beaten soundly. Like people who'd lost what was most important to them. We're not going on a picnic, Nala. No matter what our friends discover today. No matter what this so-called informant says, you don't know Kallisto like I do, and you certainly don't know Quain like my father did. No one knows him like my father did."

Sariel stopped talking, wishing he could find the right feeling in his body. He wanted to trap both Quain and Kallisto, stop the killing, the pain, the poison leaking into the world. He knew the anger that would flow through him and wondered how he'd ever be able to contain it. But he also wanted to go home, leaving this current struggle and all the past struggles behind. He felt as tired and beaten as the people around the table had. Inside, he felt the same: worn out and empty, filled only with the fear of seeing Kallisto. Maybe it wasn't just seeing her. It was feeling her twisted thoughts, and maybe being swept up in them again, her sticky, sweet, evil current of desire. Two years ago, Kallisto had been like a candy he couldn't get enough of, a honeyed liqueur he'd wanted to sip all night.

But that was how he felt two years ago. Not now. And if they were to be successful, Nala was right. They needed to let go of thoughts like this. They needed to go in and take back what was theirs, what belonged to all *Croyant.*

But there was something else, too, and he'd reminded himself of it when he'd said, *Like people who'd lost what was most important to them.* Looking at Phaedrus and his team reminded him of losing his father and of losing something else. But he wasn't sure what.

In a twirl of almost imperceptible movement, Mazi, Lutalo, Baris, and Sayblee were back, standing in front of them, pushing back their hoods. Nala stood up, and Sariel felt her excitement and fear and hope, but the energy coming from the returnees was quiet and bitter and lifeless. Rufus and Sariel walked toward them, standing with the group in the center of the room.

"Nothing?" Nala said.

Lutalo shrugged. "Not nothing. But little. We followed the information Adalbert gave us, but if Quain was there, he's gone now. There was a vortex still in place, but nothing within it. So we missed him by hours, maybe half a day at most."

Sayblee shook her head. "We picked up a stream of thought in Regent's Park, and that's our biggest lead. He's cleaned up behind himself, that one, but not completely. As if he knows that even if we find him, it won't matter. It will be too late."

Baris shook his head, his orange hair wet, drops spraying to the floor. "We need to keep trying. We can go back out."

"There are other things to do," Nala said, taking a deep breath.

"You found the survivors," Mazi said. "They are forlorn. They've been decimated. They don't have any good news."

Nala came from around the table, standing in front of them all. "Your vision is right, Mazi, but we have one more piece of business."

"The contact," Mazi said.

"Yes," Nala said, and they stood in a circle staring at each other. Then they closed their eyes, and followed Nala once again into the gray.

The man was sickly, broken from a disease he hadn't bothered to have cured. The first thing Sariel heard when they appeared in the dim, dirty flat was the man's cough, a seal bark into the gloom. Sariel could have helped in minutes, but he was glad not to, the man's clothes dirty, his face gray with pallor and grit. His scant brown hair was plastered to his head, his eyes bloodshot and rheumy with fever.

"So you've come," the man said. "I was told to expect you. That you'd be desperate, and it's true!" He started to laugh, but his glee turned into a paroxysm of rasps and choked gasps.

Sariel tried to get into the man's mind, but unfortunately, it was blocked. Even from the perimeter, Sariel could feel the corruption in the man's thoughts, feel the twists Quain had kinked into his personality. While he knew the man's mind could give them more information than his tongue, Sariel was glad that he didn't have to clamber through the twists of the man's ideas.

"We were told you had information for us," Nala said.

"In-for-mation," the man said slowly, standing up from his bed, shuffling toward them. Reflexively, they all backed up, and Sariel saw Sayblee lift her palm, ready to fight back with fire.

"Put your fire away," the man said. "Fire doesn't touch Labaan. I've been blessed by the new king, and he's protected me. None of your fancy tricks can break through his magic."

"King!" Rufus spat. "We have no king."

"But we will," Labaan said. "We almost have him now."

"So why did he leave you here?" Sariel said. "If you are so important to him, why are you in this hovel? Unhealed. Dying."

As Sariel said the last word, he knew it was true, feeling that man's slow, blocked blood, sensing the tears and scars in his lungs.

"Dying!" Labaan said. "I'm not dying. I'll be by his side, next to him and his queen."

Sariel felt Mazi's prophetic mind spin out images, and he tried to stay away from them, knowing that the images would haunt him. But there they were, Quain and Kallisto sitting on thrones, *Croyant* doing their bidding, the rest of the world in thrall.

"It is no concern of ours why you are here," Nala said, nudging Sariel to silence with her mind as she spoke the words. "We need the information we were told you had. That you promised to give us."

"Of course, of course," Labaan said. He wheezed out

the last words and then was caught in a seizure of deep, phlegmy coughing.

They waited as Labaan found his breath and then sat back down on his unkempt bed and sank onto the filthy pillows. In a wave, Sariel found the man's despair through a crack in the mind block. Labaan had indeed been left behind. He knew that he was dying. He wanted to lash out, to take back a tiny piece of his health, his life, and his soul that he'd given Quain during the thirty years he'd been by his side.

"He has her," Labaan said, wiping his mouth with a dirty handkerchief. "She somehow came through matter, and the queen found her. Just like that! We found her without even looking. And she knows things, this one. Very useful things indeed. That's why you couldn't find him today. He knew you were coming. The silly woman's thoughts told him that. And he wants you all. The queen wants you, too, especially this one."

Labaan pointed a skinny finger at Sariel.

"Who is she?" Sayblee asked. "Who are you talking about?"

Labaan went on as if he didn't hear Sayblee's question. "So the woman is still alive. How else can you explain getting so close to him? You thought you were so tricky missing him by just hours. Our new king knew what he was doing. Oh, yes. He knew."

"God, man," Rufus said, moving forward, his hand on Sariel's arm. "Who are you talking about? Who has whom? Who is *she*?"

Labaan laughed briefly, and then stopped, catching himself before he had another fit of coughing. "The woman." He looked at Sariel, his pale, faded eyes full of delight. "We know all about your little love affair. Oh, yes. He has her. Your *Moyenne* woman. Miranda."

Chapter Ten

In the far distance, somewhere at the edge of the gray matter swirling around her, Miranda heard Sariel's voice. She wanted to open her eyes, but she was afraid that if she did, she'd lose the tiny bit of concentration she'd mustered. Sariel had said he concentrated on where he wanted to go, so she knew she had to as well. *Sariel,* she thought. *I want to go to Sariel.*

"I'm here," his voice said. "Keep coming."

Relaxing, she let herself focus on clear, happy thoughts of him, his smile, the way his eyes had looked at her over his glass that first night, the way his body felt under her hands. She saw him in her bed, at the coffee shop, in Hilo, looking out toward dawn as they stood on Felix's lanai. She thought of his smell, how he reminded her of oranges and cinnamon. She tasted him on her tongue, sweet and salty.

"Yes, that's right. Keep coming. Keep thinking," his voice continued. "Don't stop. Don't look. Just a little farther."

Miranda took a deep breath and bore down on more images of Sariel—his long soft hair, his laugh, his hands as they skimmed up her leg from her injured ankle—and then, she felt the matter lighten, lift off her skin. Without opening her eyes, she knew she was in a dark room, could feel the hard cold floor beneath her feet. Maybe he'd been waiting for her. Maybe he would be happy to see her, she thought, amazed at what she'd been able to do just to find him. Miranda opened her eyes, blinking into the darkness and breathing in the closed, stuffy air.

"Sariel?"

There was movement in the corner of the room, a tall dark shape seeming to adjust clothing—a robe! It was him!—and then he began to move forward. Miranda felt her heart beat faster, her mouth dry, her skin tenting with gooseflesh.

Swallowing, she said again, "Sariel?" His name cracked brittlely in the room, her tongue barely able to get out the word.

The shape moved even closer, but now Miranda's eyes were adjusting to the darkness, and there was something off. Wrong. The person coming to her was tall but not tall enough; imposing but not big enough. Miranda grasped her purse and backed away, too soon feeling the wall hard and cool against her back. *Find the gray*, she thought, *find it now.* Desperate, she closed her eyes, flicking them back and forth behind her lids, but the image of Sariel she'd held in her mind as she'd traveled through the matter was gone. But that's not what she needed to do! That was backward. She thought of Sariel in order to get here; to get home, she should conjure forth San Francisco, her apartment, her desk, her words on the computer screen.

Quick, Miranda thought. *Think. Think hard!*

"A little mistake," the voice said. A woman's voice, sudden and clearly not Sariel's. "Happens to the inept often enough."

Miranda opened her eyes and stared at the woman only a few feet in front of her. Something the woman was wearing had found the only available light in the room and glimmered gold. A necklace or earrings.

"Where am I?" Miranda asked, blinking into the darkness. "Who are you?"

"Where you are doesn't matter now. I think the more important question would be, Who are you?" The woman seemed to be staring at her and then began walking back and forth in front of Miranda, the cape of her long hair hanging down her back.

"I'm looking for Sariel. Sariel Valasay. I—I got here . . ." Miranda stopped, not knowing who she was speaking to and what she could say. She'd promised Sariel she wouldn't tell a soul about his abilities and his people, and this woman could be an angry hermit who lived in this dark basement, just barely able to contain her fear at Miranda's strange appearance. A story like Miranda's might throw the woman over the edge. After all, hadn't Miranda herself been full of disbelief? Just days ago, she would have laughed at the insanity of a traveling through matter story. She would have laughed and then been afraid, knowing that whoever was telling her was clearly and totally insane.

"I'm lost," Miranda said quickly. "I got . . . confused."

"Did you really? How interesting. And you found yourself here in this basement," the woman said. "But a common mistake. Sariel Valasay is often in my basement, of course. A constant visitor."

"Do you have a light we could just flick on?" Miranda asked. "It might be easier to talk if we could see each other." *And then maybe I could find a way to get the hell out of here,* she thought.

The woman laughed. "No, neither a quick escape nor a light are available at the moment." The woman moved closer, and Miranda felt her whole body flex instinctively, as if the woman were a blow she needed to deflect.

"So, I guess you are *Croyant*," Miranda asked.

"Yes. Brilliant of you to figure it out," the woman said. "More evolved than you, obviously. You can't seem to travel very well and your mind is wide open, a pool for me to jump into. I'm just beginning to see . . ."

"So why I'm here is because," Miranda said quickly, trying to keep the woman out of her mind, "I was thinking about Sariel and I heard him, too. That's how he taught me—"

"He taught you? This is getting more and more interesting." The woman was pacing again, something metal clinking as she walked. "Why did he teach you? You should have learned at home or at school."

"This might sound a little weird. But, well, I'm not *Croyant*. I didn't learn to travel through matter before because *Moyenne* are raised with cars and airplanes. You know, the normal ways to move around."

"*Moyenne* can't travel through matter, not ever." The woman came closer, closer, and Miranda smelled her dark, rich scent, jasmine and musk. "You're lying."

"No, I swear. Look, don't you have a light in here? I'd really like to explain, and maybe you can help me get out of here."

There was a moment of silence followed by a slight crack, and the room filled with sallow yellow light. For a second, Miranda closed her eyes against the sudden change, and then opened them slowly, bringing her gaze to the woman before her. She was—even in the horrid, almost dressing room light—beautiful. As Miranda had noted even in the darkness, the woman's hair hung down her back, but now she could see its amazing thickness and its rich, dark brindle sheen. The woman's eyes were brown but filled with a glow that seemed to come from within her, reflecting embers from a fire deep inside. Without meaning to, Miranda felt herself move closer, staring at the woman's flawless skin, her small, tight, rounded body, her full breasts.

"You like what you see," the woman said slowly, smiling. "Alas, I'm a little too busy for that."

Miranda jerked back. "I'm not—that's not what I want. I just think you're—"

The woman held up a hand. "Don't bother. I'm quite used to it. But now you need to tell me why you've come searching for Sariel. Sit."

Miranda pulled her eyes from the woman and looked around the room, which was large and, she realized, cold. Hugging herself, she breathed in the stale, musty air. The walls and the floor were stone, unpainted, and the room was mostly filled with old leather-bound books. In one corner were two chairs and a round table. The woman walked over to it and motioned for Miranda to follow.

The table was covered with books and scrolls; a pot of ink and an old-style ink pen lay next to a pad of paper. Miranda sat down and then looked at the pad in front of her and tried—out of old, nosy habit—to read it. The writing was fluid and large, but then the woman seemed to read her thoughts and in a flash, the pad of paper sailed off the table and landed neatly on a bookcase. Her lips in a condescending, tight smile, the woman shook her head at Miranda and sat down in the other chair, smoothing her flowing robe.

"So, about Sariel. Tell me your sad story about him. Or, I can go in and find it myself?"

Miranda frowned and crossed her arms, wanting to laugh or cry or both. How had this happened, again? Why was it that every time she got mixed up with *Croyant*, she was trapped in some room, desperate to escape? At least this time she didn't have a broken ankle.

"Look, he's—he's a friend. The last time I saw him,

well, it was interrupted, and I wanted to find him. It's not like he has a cell phone or anything. Anyway, who are you? What's your name?"

"You are *Moyenne*."

"I told you I was."

"It's hard to believe. It rarely happens that *Moyenne* manage to become *penseurs de mouvement*. It's more likely they can start fires accidentally or levitate during nightmares or bend spoons. Circus acts. Carnival shows. Freak occurrences. But this?"

"Surprises the hell out of me," Miranda said, keeping the conversation going as she tried to remember what she'd brought with her. Lipstick, Tic Tacs, Swiss Army knife. *That's right,* she thought, *I'll smear her with lipstick, choke her with mints, and cut her up with my nail file.*

The woman bit her lip, nodding. "So on a whim, you thought you could just conjure up matter and go find him."

Miranda shrugged. "Yeah, stupid, huh? Ridiculous notion. So here's the thing. Maybe you could let me leave your little subterranean nest here, and I can take a train or plane or whatever home. Where am I?"

Not saying anything, the woman stared at her, and Miranda felt something light and prying dip into her mind. She breathed in deeply and tried to look at the woman, but everything seemed fuzzy, darker, the woman's features distorted. Sariel never taught her how to block a thought, and she tried to think about one thing, something innocuous like an object in her purse.

Miranda clung to her old leather wallet in her thoughts for about half a second, and then without her wanting it, she saw the layers of memory from the past few days flick before her like a newsreel. There she was running down the street. Next, she saw Sariel's hands on her ankle. Then he was in front of her, kissing her, his hands on the sides of her face, his breath warm and orangey. Hawaii. The hospital and his abrupt departure. The poetry conference. Sariel on the bed, taking in the message. Sariel with his hands on her forehead, trying to take away his very existence. And as the woman strolled around Miranda's mind, it seemed she was reaching into Sariel from Miranda's memory because Miranda was flooded with ideas and thoughts that weren't hers: *First the first and now the second* plaque. *You're needed here at once. Quain. Kallisto. Rabley Heath. Adalbert. I have to leave Miranda. Now. Take away the evidence. No choice.*

The woman left Sariel and then turned over some memories that Miranda tried to yank away, but the woman was too strong. Almost in slow motion, the woman took them both to Miranda's bed and stood them by the foot, holding out an arm and laughing at the vision in front of them: Miranda on top of Sariel, his hands on her breasts as she moved slowly, slowly. Sariel's face as he came. Miranda's sounds as she followed him. The woman replayed it, found another, watched Sariel between Miranda's legs, focusing closer, closer.

The woman's laugh echoed in the room, and Miranda felt her face flush and then grow pale with anger.

Stop it! Get out of my head, Miranda thought. *These are mine.*

They were mine first, the woman thought back.

A few other scenes flittered past, and then Miranda felt the woman leave her mind, the memories falling back together like playing cards. After a moment, Miranda blinked into the light of the room, which was clear again. Breathing out, she looked up at the woman, knowing, now, who must be in front of her. Sariel's former girlfriend.

The woman was nodding, her chin in her hand, her eyes on the table. Miranda could see the rise and fall of her breath under her robes. Miranda stared hard at the woman, and then one of her thoughts came to her, as if

Miranda had ordered it, willed it. It wasn't sent. Miranda caught it out of the air like an annoying fly.

I'm going to kill her.

Miranda felt breath rip up her windpipe, her heart lurching. She froze, hoping the woman wasn't paying attention to what Miranda was thinking.

What else was the woman thinking? Keeping her mind as opaque as possible, Miranda extended herself, reaching out with a tentative tendril of thought, and doing so, she found a dark hard core of vicious ideas swirling just away from her reach. The woman's eyes were slits, unfocused, angry. Stilling and barely daring to breathe, Miranda was able to catch threads of thought that spun from the woman's mind like thin wisps breaking off from a cloud bank: *Go to Quain. Back to* l'enclos. *Find this worthless group. And once you have Sariel, finish it forever.*

For a second, Miranda saw a medieval fortress, a castle really, solid and completely enclosed. It was built high with thick white stone, with arched windows, turrets, and even a moat. Then she wafted inside with the woman's thoughts to a room inside the castle. A slim, wiry man sat at a table and looked up at the woman with dark soot eyes. His hair was thin, slicked to his head, and even from here, Miranda swore he radiated hate. People in robes stood in front of him, listening carefully as he spoke. But so much of what they said was in French, words Miranda didn't recognize except for a few she knew meant spell or charm. But the man behind the table spoke of colors: Gold. Red. Purple. Red again. His hands moved, his eyes lit up; he was enraptured, he was ecstatic. He was, Miranda could see, nuts.

The woman seemed to sense Miranda, and her thoughts pulled back to the dark center except for one. *I'm going to kill her. And enjoy it.*

Gasping, Miranda yanked herself back into her own

thoughts and brought forth her wallet one more time. Brown, old. Viv gave it to her for what? Her twenty-third birthday. The pictures of the kids. She would need one of the new baby. Colin. Colin, Hazel, Jordie, and Summer. Her nieces and nephews. Would she ever see them again? She shouldn't have gotten so angry. Viv meant well, even though she was hysterical. Hormonal. Maybe it wasn't true anyway.

"You think too much," the woman said. She was looking up, her face set.

"Kind of an occupational hazard of being human. Maybe you've forgotten that. Look, I guess at some point you were Sariel's girlfriend—"

"Girlfriend!" the woman exclaimed. "What an insipid word. In any case, he's not worth a word at all. Look how he treated you, my dear. He didn't even want to leave a trace of himself in your mind. He tried to take everything you had of him."

"Well, whatever." Miranda pushed out a forced, light tone, even though her insides felt saggy with sobs. "Listen, I made a mistake. I ended up here. Let me go, and I'll find my way home. You don't have to enact some kind of vengeance. I just met Sariel. We aren't a couple or anything. He obviously doesn't have trouble leaving me, so I bet you could get him back."

"That's what you think I want? To have him back? Let me show you something about your precious *friend*."

Miranda was pushed back into her chair, her eyes forced closed, and she realized she was getting a message, the same thing that must have happened to Sariel at the hospital and that last night in her bed. In front of her a scene was coming into view. There was a room—Sariel's living room. But it didn't feel warm and comforting as it had the night he'd healed Miranda's ankle. The air felt tight, taut, clenched, full of hate, the lights and the heat off. The woman was facing the window that looked out onto darkness, and, in the middle of the room, levitating off the floor, was Sariel. He was unconscious, pale, his face weary even in unconsciousness. Red welts ribboned his chest and back, and his hair was unloosed, hanging lankly. Miranda could hear her own thoughts beating into the scene, and it seemed the woman in the memory heard her, too, for she turned and looked around about the room for a moment.

"Who's there?" the woman hissed. "What do you want?"

The woman scanned the room, her hands on her hips. After a moment, she shook her head and walked over to Sariel's limp body.

"You are so weak," she said to him. "So driven by your cock. You don't deserve to come with me. But you know too much."

Sariel was roused for a moment, murmuring, "Kallisto. Don't go. Don't leave me. I love you."

The woman, Kallisto, laughed, looked at him, spinning him slowly in the air. "See what I mean? You want me still, even after this."

"Yes," he said so softly, Miranda had to strain to hear. "Please."

Kallisto flicked her hand, and another welt bloomed on his chest. She moved her hand again, and Sariel spun, his face toward the floor. Kallisto flicked both hands and welts appeared from his hips to his thighs.

"You still want me? More pain? I bet you never want it to stop."

"I want you," he mumbled.

Kallisto laughed, spun him around, flicked her hands some more.

Stop! Miranda thought. *That's enough!*

That's what he should have said back then, but he was so weak. Watch. There's even more. Kallisto thought back, pressing Miranda closer and closer to the scene.

Sariel cried out, but never changed what he was saying. Miranda listened to him beg for Kallisto to take him with her even as welts flared on his body.

After some time, Kallisto looked toward the window again, her eyes full of disgust. As Miranda watched her in the scene, she saw that Kallisto, despite her lovely skin, her long, beautiful hair, her amazing eyes, was horrid to look at. Ugly. *Bad meat*, Miranda thought. Just like Brennus said.

The memory faded, and Miranda opened her eyes, shaken by what she'd just seen. Sariel seemed so lost, so desperate, bewitched. In such intense pain. And yet, strangely, in love.

Kallisto smiled down at her, nodding. "So you still think I want him back? Such a weak man? Such a pathetic creature? Why would I want a man who couldn't even manage to take your memories as he was supposed to? And if I wanted him, I could have him now, this instant, at my feet."

"Actually," Miranda said, trying to keep her lips from trembling, "I haven't a clue of what you want. Why you would keep me here and riffle through my sex memories is beyond me. But, hey, if you want them, have them. And why you would want to show me your bondage experiences with Sariel is just too much for me to contemplate. But I watched, I saw. I just want to go home now."

Kallisto pushed back from the table, staring down at Miranda, that smug smile on her face again. "Because of his sloppy, inept job, you've been very helpful. Gave me so much useful information. Sariel is on his way or is here already. I think I might need you eventually. Sort of, as you *Moyenne* say, my ace in the hole. I can always kill you later."

"Kind of a backup plan. A handy plan B?" Miranda felt frozen, her mouth moving anyway. All she'd wanted was to see Sariel once more, and this? This was way beyond a jealous girlfriend. This was . . . this was?

"This is about the world being made right. Balanced," Kallisto said. "This is about *Moyenne* being put in their place, once and for all. After all their years of suppressing us, ordering *us* around, their time has come. Too bad you showed up here, or your *Croyant* abilities might have guaranteed your survival."

"Our world?" Miranda asked. "What do you mean?"

"I mean the world as it will be when we make it true. I mean the world as it will be with Quain as king."

"Quain!" Miranda said, remembering how Brennus looked as he spoke that name, the fear in his face even as he tried to scare Miranda. And she thought of how Sariel couldn't even say the man's name. Was that the man at the table? "Who is he? What is he going to do?"

"Yes, our new world king." Kallisto pushed her hair away from her face and stared hard at Miranda with her intense black eyes. "Maybe before you die, you can meet him."

And then, without warning, Kallisto was gone.

Exhaling, Miranda sank back against her chair, her body soaked with exhaustion. Thank God Kallisto had left the light on, but just as the thought left her mind, the yellow light flickered and went out.

"Shit," Miranda said, pressing her hands against her thighs, as if making sure she was still there. But she could barely move her hands. She tried to move her feet, but they were stuck together. In fact, she could hardly turn her neck. Miranda pulled and yanked her arms and then tried to kick herself free with her legs, but she was bound tight to the chair. She could almost feel the rough circles of clenched rope on her body.

Miranda breathed in, glad that at least Kallisto had left her lungs and other organs alone. Maybe her heart beat a bit too quickly and she could feel her stomach twinge from anxiety, but she was still alive. However, Miranda could tell that if she were left alone in this musty dark basement for a while, she would wish she weren't.

Closing her eyes because there was no point keeping them open, Miranda thought of Sariel floating in the middle of his living room. But had it really been Sariel? The limp, pleading man wasn't anything like the man she'd first seen in the corner of the bar, his gold eyes glinting at her. As she'd stood in Kallisto's memory, Miranda had felt his longing and his need, his willingness to do anything, everything, for Kallisto.

He hadn't wanted to do anything for her, Miranda thought, biting the inside of her mouth. All he'd done was show her a wonderful, amazing time, and then chickened out, trying to take her memories and disappearing, which was the exact same thing any *Moyenne* man would do if he could. And had. Like Jack. So she'd built Sariel up into something great, but why? Because he could take her to Hawaii by thinking? Because he could heal her ankle by his warm, magic touch? Because he showed up in the middle of the night and held her body like no one had done before?

Miranda tried to shake her head, but then was stopped by the invisible bonds. She had to get out of here. *Moyenne. Moyenne.* Maybe she wasn't ordinary after all. She'd gotten herself to this room by imagining it—so maybe she'd screwed up, but she knew she should be able to think her way out.

Trying to get comfortable, she started to invoke the image of matter, the roiling gray coming toward her. At first, Miranda thought she saw it, but it was only the difference in darkness between open and then closed eyes. Concentrating, she tried again, willing the matter to appear as it had before. But after a couple of minutes, she knew it wasn't going to work. It was as if there were a wall in front of her mind, a barrier keeping her—keeping her here. Clearly, Kallisto had imprisoned her in the basement in more ways than one.

"Damn it, Sariel," she shouted, her words bouncing off the stone walls and then evaporating. "Why did you leave me?" The sound echoed in the cold box of the room until it died and fell flat on the cold floor. "Why didn't you want me to remember?"

Without meaning to, she started to cry, wanting to go home, wanting to go back to Viv's, even if Viv would go on and on about the adoption story. Listening to another one of June's lectures would be better than this blasted, stinking basement where she was tied up like a turkey, waiting for the oven to preheat. Right now, Miranda even wanted Dan.

"Okay, okay. It's going to be fine," she whispered. All she had to do was think. There had to be a way to escape. Sariel had gotten her out of messes—attacking bar patrons, broken ankles, commute traffic. Miranda would have to find a way to use powers she didn't even have. Sariel could talk to her with his mind, and if she could move through space like he did, couldn't she do that, too?

Again, she closed her eyes and tried to relax, focusing on Sariel. She brought forth his face, his smooth tan skin, his long black hair, a smile on his full lips. In her image, he was looking at her, waiting for her to speak, his eyes wide with anticipation.

Sariel? Sariel? It's me, Miranda. I know I shouldn't be calling—I mean thinking—you, but I made a mistake. I'm here in some woman's house. Not some woman—Kallisto's house, you know, the one who almost killed you. I don't know where the house is. I got really upset tonight, and I wanted you, even though you wanted me to forget everything. I've been able lately to conjure the gray. I don't know why. But I was so crazy mad at my mom, my sister, Dan, that I decided to go find you. I know it was stupid. But I did it, and I'm here. She has me all tied up but with nothing I can see, and I can't seem to bring back the matter. You have to find me. Look at my thoughts—see the room. I know I'm in a basement because there are no windows. Nothing. Find me. Sariel, please.

Miranda opened her eyes and took a deep breath, feeling her tears about ready to start again. For a few moments, she waited for a message back, but there was nothing but her own thoughts, her fear racing back and forth in her head like a top.

There had to be someone else she could call. Maybe there was a way to put out a telepathic all-points bulletin, a memory 911. But that would mean Kallisto and Quain would hear it, too. Who else? Brennus? He wouldn't come find her because he probably still thought she was a spy. But then she thought of the soft air of Hilo, the sweet tang of piña colada. Felix.

She closed her eyes. *Felix, it's me, Miranda. I did something stupid, and I can't find Sariel. Not that he wants me to find him. He tried to take away all my memories, but it didn't work. Anyway, his horrible ex has me trapped. Kallisto has me. I'm in this basement. If you get this message, please try to find me. I don't know where I am. Please!*

Letting the message out into the air, Miranda began to cry for real, her sobs echoing as her words had. The basement seemed to grow colder, the air thicker, the walls pressing closer.

She should have known better. What had she imagined? That because she saw a tiny bit of Sariel's life and world she could merge into it? Miranda had never fit in, not with her family, not with anyone. Hadn't Jack taught her that she was ordinary, average, not worth the effort?

"You're so pedestrian," Jack had said a week before he'd left. "All this feeling in your poems, when the focus should be on language. The image. Not the body. What kind of poet do you think you are, anyway?"

He had taken a hit off his joint. "It's embarrassing. You're embarrassing."

So he'd left, taking her pedestrian poems with him. Jack had left, as Sariel had.

And now, she was locked in a basement. No one was coming to rescue her, just like always.

Miranda cried for a long time, liking the way her sobs felt, her insides active even if her body couldn't move. She cried for herself all alone and unsaved in this room, but also for herself in Viv's bedroom, listening to the story she still couldn't believe. She cried for the parents she would never know. She cried for the image of Sariel hanging like a rag doll in the air, pathetic and hopeless. She wept as she remembered the feeling of Sariel's fingers on her forehead. She cried for whatever terrible thing Quain was going to do to the world. She cried for Dan loving her when she couldn't love him back. She cried until there was nothing left inside her but fear, and somehow, she managed to fall asleep.

When she woke up, the room was light again, the same sick yellow it had been before. Licking her dry lips, Miranda looked around, her eyes watering from the sudden vision.

Kallisto stood before her, smiling her terrible smile.

"Nice rest?"

Miranda swallowed, not knowing what to say. She'd cried out all her tears, but now her nose was running, and she couldn't move her hand to wipe it.

"Nothing to say? No last words? Just a little snotty sniveling?" Kallisto stared at her and then turned away, shaking her head. "Pathetic."

"I'm not pathetic," Miranda croaked, her throat raw from sobbing.

"Oh, no? You give me the information that keeps us about five steps ahead of Adalbert's pathetic 'army,' and then I get to get rid of you. How is that not pathetic?"

"At least I haven't betrayed anyone," Miranda said quietly. "I saw how much Sariel loved you and then what you did to him. And I know that you are going to do something that will hurt us all. The entire world. That's pathetic. If I'm going to die, at least I'm dying honorably."

Kallisto stared at her, her lush mouth pressed tight, her eyes sharp. But then, like magic, she lightened, let out a little laugh, her eyes shining. "Nice try. But no, it won't work. And truth? You don't even know who you are. Yes, I know—the adoption. I saw it all. You're going to die a mystery. You won't have a moment to even write about it, little Miss Pathetic Poet."

More tears gathered in Miranda's throat. Kallisto was right. She would never know who she was or how she was able to travel through matter. She would never get to know Viv's new baby, Colin. She would never find out how Sariel really felt about her or why he thought he needed to erase everything.

"Oh, he's smitten," Kallisto said. "I can tell. You don't know Sariel like I do, but I can see how much he truly loves you. What a life you could have had together. But, alas. A war interrupted your little love affair. Say good-bye, Miranda."

"No!"

"No good-byes? Well, think good-bye anyway."

As Miranda watched, Kallisto raised her arm and held her hand toward Miranda, palm out. "Quain says thank you for the information and wants you to know your death helped bring him to kingship."

As Kallisto stood before her, palm raised, Miranda closed her eyes. *Good-bye, Viv,* she thought. *Good-bye, Mom. Sariel, I'm sorry. I didn't mean to make trouble.*

"Good-bye, Miranda," Kallisto said, her voice smooth, almost soothing. "See you in the next life."

Miranda clenched her teeth, waiting, the air between her and Kallisto still and thick and sharp.

But then there was a sound like a tear, the room slashed jagged with sound. Miranda opened her eyes, her vision full of people in swirling robes.

There! someone yelled, or at least Miranda thought someone yelled, the sound ringing in her head. The people turned, moving around, looking up into flashes of light. One person was pounded against a wall, another thrown down on the floor. Miranda heard the sounds of blows to bodies, soft flesh thuds, cracks of bone and skull. She smelled a flash of fire, heat, something scorched.

"*Cesser,*" someone cried out, arms flung wide, a flash of harsh quick light in the room. "*Geler!*"

Miranda turned her head as far as she could, looking for Kallisto, breathing in when she found the woman's thoughts but not her body. *What a waste,* Kallisto thought. *Look at him. Look at how marvelous he is, still. What a pitiful waste.*

Was Sariel here? Did he hear her call? Miranda wanted to shout for him, but she knew her voice would drown in the explosions of sound in the room.

Then Miranda heard another voice crawling in her head, a low murmur as a man whispered with Kallisto. As he spoke, Miranda felt the room vibrate, heat up, and she realized that she could barely breathe. The people began to crowd around her, and she noticed that they were looking upward, so she did as well. There was Kallisto hovering over them, a reddish gold light around her. From the ground, one of the people shot out a ball of what looked like fire, but Kallisto deflected it with a wall of black energy. Someone else shot out something silver, but it bounced off the energy, too. Another person was chanting something in French.

But nothing they did seemed to matter. Kallisto laughed behind her black energy and then, in a brief electric blast, disappeared.

"Follow her, Lutalo. Baris!" a woman's voice cried, and in a whoosh, two of the robed people disappeared.

The room was suddenly silent, everyone, including Miranda, staring up at the ceiling where Kallisto had hung just seconds before. But then the robed people looked down, taking off their hoods, and stared at her. In front of her, just as she had hoped, was Sariel. And Felix, both of them flushed from exertion, their eyes dark and on her.

"Sariel!" Miranda cried. "Oh, my God. I can't believe you got here. I've been calling and calling. And Felix. Oh, I can't believe it." She swallowed, trying to keep herself from crying. Finally, this was going to end. She smiled at Sariel and then looked at the other people with relief. But no one said a word. A man standing next to Sariel and Felix was glaring at her with eyes the same shape as Sariel's. The rest of the group was quiet, too quiet, and Miranda couldn't find her breath, suddenly feeling like she was in as bad a predicament as she had been minutes before with Kallisto.

Sariel pushed away a cautioning hand and walked forward, staring down at her. She wished she weren't trapped in the chair. All she wanted was to have him pick her up and take her home.

"I'm stuck. Can't move a thing. She put some kind of, like, rope spell on me. Can you get me out?" Miranda asked.

"Don't touch that spell, lad," the big man next to Felix said. "You don't know what Kallisto did to it."

A woman in yellow robes walked closer, standing next to Sariel. She was dark and imperious and almost as frightening as Kallisto. "Do you know her? Was Labaan correct?"

Miranda looked from the woman's face to Sariel's. Did he know her? Did he know her? "Holy cow! Of course *he* knows me! Sariel, tell her!"

Sariel was silent, a strange look on his face, confused and tense. He crossed his arms, his lips pressed tight. Miranda needed her hands, her arms, her legs. She needed to stand up and shake him. Turning to Felix, she almost yelled, "Felix, tell her! I went to your house. In Hilo. You made your special drinks. Why don't you tell her?"

Startled, Felix looked at the big man and then joined Sariel in front of Miranda. Another, younger woman walked closer, as did a man with wild gray hair and slightly spacey eyes. She felt their minds working their way toward hers and she tried to close down, shut off her mind from their questions about her. How dare they do this to her! It was Sariel's fault she was here.

But no one said a thing, and they moved even closer to her, their robes forming a curtain around Miranda.

The room fell silent. All of them stared down at her and then, finally, Sariel said something.

"I've never seen her before in my life."

Chapter Eleven

The woman—Miranda—stared up at him, puffy-eyed, amazed, and on the verge of anger. In contrast to her pale, lightly freckled face, her red curls were vibrant and almost uncontrolled. She was shivering, unable to warm herself, bound by an *esclavage* spell Kallisto must have put on her.

"Why are you lying?" she said, trying, he could see, to avoid tears. "Of course you've seen me. You've—you've done more than that."

Rufus almost snorted, and Sariel heard Nala think, *This isn't funny.*

"Listen," Sariel said, "I don't know who you are, except that your name is supposedly Miranda and you called out to me and to my brother Felix, your thoughts making it through Kallisto's protections. But whoever you are or whatever your name is, you were quite clearly important to Kallisto—or maybe you are part of Kallisto's plan."

Nala pushed past him a bit and stood directly in front of Miranda. "What did Kallisto want with you?"

Miranda bowed her head, her shoulders shaking.

For a moment, Sariel felt a wave of overwhelming sadness pulse from her, and he wanted to reach out and touch her shoulder, free her of the magic that kept her on the chair. But then, as quickly as the feeling came, it passed, and he felt Felix grabbing his arm.

Tears on her face and dripping down her neck, Miranda took in a deep breath and raised her eyes to his. "I was trying to find you," she said, looking at Sariel. "So I did what you taught me. I know I shouldn't be able to do it because I'm *Moyenne*—"

"*Moyenne?*" Nala said. "It can't be."

Miranda nodded. "Yeah, it's been a big surprise to everyone lately. Talk of the town."

Sariel almost smiled, liking how even in this cold, ugly room where she was bound, exhausted, frightened and surrounded by strangers, this woman, Miranda, had been able to joke.

"Go on," Nala said.

"So I thought about the gray just like you told me. And I tried to find you, keeping your face in my mind. I heard a voice I thought was yours calling me, and I went toward it. But it wasn't you, obviously. It was Kallisto." She paused, shaking her head. "You never told me about her. She wasn't so shy. She showed me what she did to you before she left. How she—how she tortured you."

"Where do I know you from?" Sariel said harshly, backing away slightly. "How do you know so much about me? How do you know Felix?"

She stared up at him, her eyes full. "Are you serious?"

"Never more so."

Shaking her head, Miranda lowered her eyes. "Just read my mind. I know you can do it. You tried to take away my memories, but it didn't work for some reason. I woke up the next morning, and they were all still there. Go on, read them."

Nala pushed Sariel closer, eager, he could tell, to find out more about Miranda. But Rufus put a hand on his arm.

"Be careful, lad," Rufus said. "You don't know what's she's got in there. She's probably as safe as a land mine."

"What do you see, Mazi?" Sariel asked.

Mazi closed his eyes and then seemed to squint, as if his vision was slipping just out of sight.

"I don't know," he said, opening his eyes. "I can't see much. A definite block from Kallisto, but it's not dangerous, just solid. But I don't see a spell that can hurt you. I don't feel anything about this one, either, that connects her to Quain."

Sariel nodded and kneeled in front of Miranda. Her knees were shaking, and he had that same desire to touch her again, and his mind burst with brief memory of—what? Wings? Flight? A dark enclosed space? A tiny voice?

"Lad," Rufus said. "Just read her mind."

"I need to touch your head," Sariel said to Miranda. "Usually I don't have to, but I'm not sure what little surprise Kallisto might have left behind."

Biting her lip, Miranda looked at him, anger and fear strung through the lines of fatigue on her face. He could tell she wanted to look fierce, but there were tears in her eyes and her bottom lip quivered.

"I don't know why you are pretending, Sariel," she whispered. "Even if you thought it was safest for me not to know about you, about the *Croyant*, I thought—I thought . . ."

"Shhh," he said, more gently than he wanted to. He lifted a hand and placed it on the side of her head, her soft curls under his fingertips. Closing his eyes, he tried to discover a path into her memory. But all he could find were the moments that had just transpired. Kallisto in the air, the *Croyant* fighting back, the group hovering around her, staring down. He felt the way her body felt trapped in the chair, her discomfort, the throbbing skin at her ankles and wrists. And then there were her feelings. Regret, anger, fear, resentment, grief, and—and love. For him. But he was walled off from the rest, as if Kallisto had shut down the woman's mind with steel.

He opened his eyes and then slowly took his hand away from her head. Standing slowly, he breathed out.

"There's a block. A big one. I can't get to anything past the time we got here."

Nala shook her head. "That is unfortunate."

"Great," Miranda said, almost yelling. "What now? Are you going to kill me, too? You shouldn't do that because Kallisto said some things before she disappeared. You need me. And I can tell you what she took from me. She went into my mind and took a lot of information. Things you couldn't take away, Sariel. She's going to use them against you all. Everyone. All of us. God! Why can't you believe me?"

"Lassie," Rufus said, his voice calmer now. "We don't know you. None of us has ever seen you before in our lives. Not only that, you say you're *Moyenne* and that's not possible if you traveled through the matter. As far as I know, you'd be the first *Moyenne* ever in history to figure it out. So how would you feel in our position? Would you be keen to free us and let us go about our business?"

Miranda stared at Rufus as he spoke, cocking her head. "Are you Sariel's brother Rufus?"

Rufus nodded. "Exactly my point. How, by God, could you possibly know that?"

"What did Kallisto say?" Nala said, ignoring Rufus's question. "You must tell us."

"Can you let me out of this chair?" Miranda asked. "Or at least take off this rope spell? I have no powers. I barely got myself here. I can't make fire come out of my hand. And I'm not a land mine."

Sariel bent down again and looked at Miranda. Even cold and shivering and angry as hell, she was beautiful. He couldn't read her mind and he didn't know her at all, but he was sure she wouldn't hurt him, other than to give him a slap or two. Maybe he deserved the punishment, but he didn't know that either.

"I think we can let you go," Sariel said. "But please don't try any magic you don't know how to do."

She nodded, and Sariel closed his eyes, found the spell and cracked it open. He heard Miranda sigh. He opened his eyes and saw her rubbing her tender wrists, which were red and slightly swollen. Even with simple spells, Kallisto was mean-spirited.

"So who are you?" Sariel stood up and crossed his arms.

"God, that question. With your magic, all you people ever do is ask me who I am. Why don't you just do some kind of magic and figure it out for yourselves?"

"You've been around a group of us before?"

Closing her eyes, Miranda shook her head and sighed, still rubbing her wrists.

Sariel looked at Nala and thought, *Can I heal her?*

Nala nodded, and Sariel said, "Here, give me your hands."

Miranda almost jumped and pulled her hands back. "No. No healing this time. Stay away from me. I don't want you to touch me ever again. Just let me tell you what I know, and I'll take the bus home."

"You're from London?" Rufus asked. He turned to Sariel. "Have you been to the U.K. lately without coming to visit Fabia and me?"

"No." Sariel felt something in his head trying to break free—an idea or a memory or a dream—but then it swirled away in his confusion. He'd healed her before? What had happened to her?

"London!" Miranda said. "I live in the city. You know, San Francisco."

"Well, you are a more talented *penseur de mouvement* than you ever imagined," Nala said. "You're in London now, and it would take one very magic bus to get you home."

Miranda stopped moving, her eyes wide. "I'm in London?"

"Yes," Nala said. "And we don't have much time. As you can see, we have some work to do. Now, can you tell me what you know?"

"And then I can go?" Miranda stared at Nala, her eyes dark and angry.

No, thought Nala, loud enough for Sariel to hear, and then she said, "Of course you can go."

"Okay," Miranda said, rubbing her arms. Felix took off his dark blue robe and handed it to her, and she gave him a flick of a smile and put it over her body. "All right. So when I was in the gray Kallisto must have been thinking about you so hard, Sariel, that I got confused. And she must have been thinking about you for a couple of days because I saw this house and this room before. Yesterday. Anyway, when I was finally in the gray, I heard your voice, so I just followed. When I got here, she went into my mind and took what I knew about the night you were at my house and got that message. It was like she was inside my memory and could go into your memory at the same time."

"I was at your house and got a message? Tell me what you know." Sariel asked.

"It was the second message you'd gotten that day. The first seemed worse to me. We were at the hospital."

"Hospital?" Sariel asked, knowing that he never set foot in those places.

"My sister was having a baby."

Sariel blinked, uncrossed and crossed his arms.

What in the blazes is going on? Rufus thought.

Shut up and listen, Felix thought back.

"So, what then?" Nala coaxed.

"Well, you were acting like a total jerk that day, anyway, and you left after the first message. You wouldn't tell me anything. Later, you came to my apartment. I mean, you just showed up, like always. We were talking and you hit the mattress and stared up at the ceiling, your eyes flicking back and forth," she said, almost irritably. "I had no idea what was going on at the time. And then you tried to take my memories and then you must have left. Just like that."

Sariel stared at Miranda, thinking back to the message he'd received about Quain and the second *plaque.* He'd been at home, hadn't he? Brennus had been there? Or was it Rufus? Why would Rufus have been in Marin and not in Edinburgh? And what about the message about the first *plaque*? Wasn't he with Philomel and Brennus in a restaurant on Geary? They'd been talking about—about vortexes?

Pay attention, Nala thought. *We don't have much time.*

"All right," Sariel said. "Then what?"

Miranda licked her lips and then rubbed them with the back of her hand. "Do you have any water?"

Honestly, Nala thought, but then there was a whoosh of air and Lutalo and Baris were back, both of them wild-eyed and agitated.

"What is it?" Sayblee asked them.

"We have to go. I think it might be a trap. Now. Let's get out of here."

Grab her, Nala thought, and Sariel pulled Miranda up by her elbows, careful with her wrists, and pressed her shivering body to him, and they all twirled back into the gray.

* * *

Something about holding her like this reminded him—reminded him of what? As they traveled back to the house on Victoria Street, she had her arms wrapped around him as if she knew his body, her hands pressed on his back, her cheek laid against his chest. Sariel wanted to stop somewhere else, just for a minute, and ask her questions. Not questions about Kallisto, but about how she knew him. It seemed impossible, as if she'd come out of some other world where she and Sariel were lovers. While that scenario was possible, what was becoming increasingly clear to him was that a piece of his memory was gone, the piece that held her. Someone had taken her away from him.

They all arrived in the house, and the minute they touched the floor, Miranda pulled away from him, her body a warm but quickly fading imprint on his.

"What happened?" Nala asked Lutalo and Baris.

Baris shook his head. "We don't know. It seemed as though they'd decided to come back for Miranda here."

"Quain was on his way, and I picked up an image of a trap. We just barely made it ahead of him. I think I know where he is." Lutalo pushed his hair back and sighed. "But he's too strong. I don't know—"

Don't say any more. We don't want Miranda to know any more than she does. She has a block on her mind, and we might not be able to take away what she hears, Nala thought.

"We were questioning Miranda, here," Nala pretended to interrupt. "Let's finish. Miranda?"

Miranda sighed. "And then I can go, right? A normal way. Virgin Airlines. British Airways. The cargo hold of FedEx."

"Of course," Nala lied again. "Please, continue."

"Okay." Miranda studied Nala for a moment, seeming, it appeared to Sariel, to try to read her mind. Then

Miranda shrugged. "In my memory, she went into Sariel's thoughts—not that I thought *that* was possible. He was thinking things I didn't know about. Something about the stolen second *plaque* and that Sariel needed to go to Rabley Heath. Is that in Scotland?"

She looked at them, but no one said a word. Sariel touched her arm.

"And then what?" he asked.

"I could tell she knew you were all here, ready to do something. But after she was done with my memories, something really weird happened to me. I got into her head. I didn't mean to. She was thinking about someplace she called *l'enclos*. And she was going back to this fortress. It's called something 'kent.' No, not kent. Kend something. Kendall?"

"Fortress Kendall," Baris said, turning to Lutalo, who nodded.

Nala nodded back. "Go on, Miranda."

Miranda bit her lip, and then said, "She was worried about someone named Adalbert. There was also an image. I don't know." She paused rubbing her forehead.

"What was it?" Nala said softly. "Anything will help."

"Okay, but it probably doesn't make any sense. It was of three colors. Gold, red, purple, kind of . . ." Miranda moved her hands, as if she held the three colors between her palms and was spinning them. "Spinning, flashing one at a time. And from the top of it was this, well, flume of energy or something. It was powerful, I know that much. And Kallisto was so attracted to this image, so pulled toward it, I think that's why she didn't notice I was there. Just before she disappeared, I heard her talking to someone. Maybe it was Quain."

Rufus cleared his throat. "This is most interesting, I must say. You, a *Moyenne,* managed to travel through matter across the flipping Atlantic and now you tell us you pushed inside the mind of the most terrible, powerful *sorcière.* And then you heard Quain himself? What next?"

Sayblee muttered something under her breath, and the rest of the group looked at Rufus and then Sariel.

"Ru," Sariel said. "I know this sounds crazy, but I—I believe her."

Everyone looked at him, and Sariel felt heat and blood rise in his face. It was crazy. Why did he believe her? It wasn't just that she seemed to know everything about him and his family, which was strange. There was something else, a shadow of a memory, a feeling—or was it her face looking up at him, her eyes glassy with fatigue and frustration, her skin pale and glowing? But Sariel knew it went deeper somehow, as if he could see that there was no lie lodged in her center. Everything about her was whole and true.

Nala looked at him and thought, *I hope you're right.*

I am right. And I think we should keep her around, Sariel thought back. *She might be useful to us later.*

Nodding, Nala turned back to Sayblee. "Take her upstairs. She needs to get cleaned up. And then we can eat."

Sariel then heard what Nala didn't say aloud. *Don't let her out of your sight. I've put a* bloqué *spell on her, so she won't be disappearing.*

"If you're done speaking about me in the third person," Miranda interrupted, "I'd just as soon leave now, *bloqué* spell or not. You promised me I could go if I told you what I know."

Sariel, Nala, and Sayblee spun back toward Miranda.

"You heard that?" Sariel asked.

Miranda seemed to not understand, her eyes weepy. She nodded, though it seemed like the movement was an effort. "I may be crazy, but I'm not deaf."

"You're tired," Nala said. "You've been through a great deal and are in no condition to wander over to

Heathrow. Have a shower and some food and maybe a rest. It's not everyone who lives through an encounter with Kallisto."

Miranda swallowed, and Sariel noticed that her sore red hands were shaking. She looked at him for a second, saw him watching her, and looked away.

"Fine. I'll take a shower and eat. But then I'm going. I'll take a cab to the airport, and if I can't get a flight, I'll sleep at an airport hotel. At least Kallisto isn't a purse snatcher," Miranda said, holding up her bag. "I can take care of myself."

"I know you can, but it's a wise decision to stay for a while," Nala said. "Sayblee will show you where everything is."

Slowly, Miranda walked toward Sayblee, and then the two women walked down the hall and up the stairs to the second floor.

"We've got to get busy," Nala said. "Lutalo and Baris, I need your memories of what happened after you left us."

She turned to Sariel, Rufus, and Felix. Sariel just stared at her, wondering what to do with Miranda.

"Between the three of you, you should be able to figure it out," Nala said. "But where she came from and who she was to you is of little importance compared to what she can do for us now. Think about it, Sariel. She got into Kallisto's mind, farther than you have."

Nala turned and walked into the lounge, Lutalo and Baris behind her. Mazi shook his head, said, "I didn't see any of that coming," and walked into the kitchen to start the meal. Sariel shook his head and looked at his brothers.

"What in the hell is going on?" he asked. "How does she know Felix and me? And she even figured out who you were, Ru."

"We need to get to Adalbert," Rufus said. "I know

Nala said it was too risky to contact him now, but he would know what was going on."

Felix sat down on the couch, rubbing his eyes. "If we send a message, Kallisto and Quain will intercept. They almost found us just now. It's too dangerous. You told me what they did to Phaedrus's people."

"But who is she?" Sariel asked.

"A spy," Rufus said flatly.

"No, she's not a spy," Felix said. "I feel—I feel like there's some kind of, well, hole in my memory. When she was talking, I would almost remember . . . something. And the only reason I'm here with you now is that I heard her in Hilo. She was crying out for help. You heard her, too."

Sariel sat down by Felix and sighed. "I did. She was so desperate. If she's not a spy or a wonderful actress, she meant it. But about that hole—"

Rufus began to pace. "You're right. I felt it, too, even before we met her. Do you think someone's been tampering a wee bit with our minds?"

"Why would they? What's the point?" Felix asked. "We didn't have anything to erase, and Sariel's memories of Kallisto are what make him so important to the mission."

"No," Rufus said. "Memories about this woman. Miranda."

"So all three of us have memories of this woman? How far back does she go in our lives? Sariel, you never bring anyone around, and you're suggesting that we all had something to erase?" Felix asked.

"I don't know." Sariel crossed his arms, tapping his foot on the floor. What was he forgetting? He got the call at his house, came to Rabley Heath for the meeting, and then went to Adalbert's house for the night. He and Adalbert had a talk, Zosime showed up, and he went to bed. Was there something else?

"Okay. What if," Felix began. "What if what she says is true? You and she were involved. And then you got the message, took her memories, and left. What if for some reason someone thought your memories of Miranda would get us or her in trouble? What if you were told you had to take them?"

"A miserable plan, that," Rufus said. "We're all in trouble, her most of all."

"But what if," Felix continued, "whoever thought up the plan didn't know she was *Croyant* and would travel through matter to find our dear brother here? What if she were strong enough to resist your taking her thoughts? Maybe they thought she would stay home like a good *Moyenne* girl and behave."

"She does have spirit," Rufus said. "Kind of a wildcat. Reminds me of Fabia. Strong. You know I wouldn't be here today without her."

Sariel nodded, thinking of how destroyed Rufus had been after his encounter with Kallisto, Sariel too drained himself to help. Even Zosime and Adalbert hadn't been able to find Rufus, his mind completely closed, and if it hadn't been for Fabia finding him that night in Edinburgh . . . Sariel couldn't think about it.

Sariel looked at Rufus for a moment, both of them holding that horrible night with Kallisto in their thoughts. *Don't let Kallisto scare you,* Rufus thought. *I'm not.*

Nodding, Sariel rubbed his forehead, an ache radiating from the center of his brain.

"So," Sariel said. "You think I've been—"

"I think you've been sleeping with her," Felix said. "And not only that, I think you were totally into her. Who wouldn't be? Did you see how she looked at you after Kallisto disappeared and the dust settled? A woman doesn't look at you like that unless she, well, loves you. She, clearly, is completely into you, even if now she wants to rip your throat out. Not that I blame her."

Sariel leaned over and put his head in his hands, mumbling from behind them. "So she thinks I'm pretending to not know her."

The brothers were silent. Rufus stopped pacing and sat down on Felix's other side. Sariel sat up straight and closed his eyes, feeling his brothers' thoughts with his, all of their minds humming together, the strains of their melded thoughts familiar and comforting. Relaxing into their combined memories, Sariel tried to find a leftover, a fragment, a clue, something the mind thief left behind. What was there? He'd had momentary glimpses of something ineffable and transient for the past couple of days, something about wings or flying. Angels? No, no. There it was. An image of a girl in a backyard, lifting off the ground, hovering in the afternoon sunlight, her sister looking up at her and believing what she saw. Then there were words, a piece of paper, pictures lifting off a page.

"She's a poet," Felix said suddenly, bringing them all out of the backyard flight.

Sariel gasped. A poet. He could almost feel his hand on the page, her words in front of his eyes. There he was, with the girl in the poem, hovering, laughing, taking off.

"I don't know who took all our memories away, though I'm having my suspicions now," Rufus said. "But Sariel, whatever those memories were, you gave them up willingly, as did Felix and I. I know that. These memories weren't dragged from us. We weren't kicking and screaming and carrying on. Otherwise, we'd have scars, rips we'd feel for days, pounding headaches, insomnia. I know from experience. Aside from this Quain business, I've been sleeping like a baby."

Rufus was right; memories stolen by force could often hurt the mind, sometimes break it. But how would

Sariel be able to explain to Miranda that he'd given her up easily, just like that?

"You might not be able to," Felix said, hearing his thought. "It might be too late."

"Aye, lad," Rufus said. "But even though the taking might have been easy, the decision might not have been. You can tell her that, when there's time."

Sariel nodded, pulling his mind away from his brothers'. He really shouldn't be concerned about making up with Miranda at a time like this. There was much more at stake right now, and from the other room, he heard Nala giving out orders to Lutalo, Baris, and Mazi. After some rest and a meal, they would be back to plotting their strategy against Kallisto and Quain. But as he listened to the shower water trickling down the old pipes, he knew he wanted nothing more than to go upstairs to Miranda, beg her forgiveness, and try, if he could, to remember what had happened between them. He wanted to talk with her before Kallisto and Quain made any happiness as impossible to remember as whatever it was Sariel and Miranda once had together.

Chapter Twelve

Letting the hot water hit her, Miranda stood under the showerhead, the stream beating down on her face. The water had calmed her a bit, helped her ignore the nerves that had made it almost impossible for her to walk up the stairs.

Sayblee, her new bodyguard, sat right outside the shower door, her figure bumpy and out of focus behind the opaque glass.

Miranda had already washed her hair twice and soaped and rinsed five times. But the cold and fear of Kallisto's dark room seemed stuck on her no matter how much she washed. And even though she'd always found a shower restorative—a cure for bad dates, terrible writing sessions, and fights with her mother—she couldn't get Sariel's face out of her mind.

He'd stared at her as if she were a total stranger. As if she were crazy. As if he didn't know her at all. As if he would never be able to remember his theft of their story. The theft of part of her life! Who had given him permission to do that!

Jerk! she thought. Typical man. Worse. Worse than a

typical man. Sariel didn't care, didn't ask, just took and left. But no man she'd ever met, not even Jack, had pretended she didn't exist. Maybe Jack stole everything from her, but at least he'd looked her in the eye and known who she was. At least he hadn't taken her existence away, too.

"Are you almost done in there?" Sayblee asked. "I'm sure the food is ready."

Miranda decided to try out her bizarre new skill. *I'll be done when I'm done,* she thought, aiming it hard at Sayblee. *Leave me alone.*

Fine, Sayblee thought back, surprising Miranda with how amusement in a thought was as loud as actual laughter. *But you might not have any skin left if you stay in there much longer. And I don't have the talent to cure damaged skin. Sariel would have to heal you, and I don't think that's what you want right now.*

No, that's wasn't what she wanted. She didn't want to get close to him for one second. Miranda sighed, rinsed off once more, and then turned off the water. She opened the shower door and grabbed the towel off the hook and stood in the shower as she dried herself. She felt like she was in summer camp or in jail, observed at everything.

"I'm a better keeper than Kallisto," Sayblee said. "You've got to admit that."

"I guess." Miranda wrapped the towel around her body and stepped out of the shower. "But can I at least call my family? My sister? I know they'll be worrying about me."

Sayblee shook her head. "In this house, you're protected by spells. But your energy out in the air, in the phone? Kallisto would find us all. She's still in your mind, Miranda. Part of her energy is in you. For some reason, you two have a very strong connection."

Miranda bit her lip and then looked at Sayblee. "But

none of this makes sense. I don't see why I can't just go home. I can't help you with Kallisto, and it's clear Sariel doesn't want to or can't remember me. There's not one damn reason for me to be here. I'm *Moyenne*."

Sayblee handed her another towel. Miranda looked in the mirror as she patted her hair, pushing her curls back off her face. If she'd hoped to stun Sariel with her beauty and charm and amazing new talents, her appearance now wasn't going to win her any points. Her skin was pale, her freckles prominent, and her eyes were still glassy, the skin under them darkened. She needed about ten hours of sleep and a bucket of Estée Lauder products to salvage any of her looks.

"You've had quite a day," Sayblee said. Miranda looked away from the mirror and at Sayblee, who despite her fight with Kallisto earlier was composed, her skin pink and pale in the right places, her blonde hair neat and pulled back in a long thick ponytail.

"It isn't every day that you find yourself able to travel through matter, for one thing," Sayblee went on. "You say you never had any skills before? You've never done anything like this before?"

Miranda wrapped up her hair in the towel and picked up a bottle of body lotion on the sink top and began to rub it on her arms and legs. "I think I flew once. Sort of like Kallisto did in the basement. Hovering really. That's it. And I was really little, so it could have been a dream. That's how my mother explained it to me."

"Your mother—your parents," Sayblee asked. "They aren't magic—a *sorcière* or *sorcier*?"

"Sorcerers? That's what you call yourselves? Sounds so medieval."

"Well, welcome to the thirteenth century, then. A *sorcière* is what you seem to be, too," Sayblee said, averting her eyes as Miranda took off the towel and began putting on her clothes.

Miranda sat on the toilet and pulled on her tights. "Can't I just be an easily trained *Moyenne*? Some kind of genetic misfit?"

Sayblee shrugged. "It's happened. Maybe every hundred years or so, a *Moyenne* comes along who can do things. There are people in your history who rose to astounding power or performed legendary miracles, that kind of thing. But often, their magic was fleeting or temporary and enormous. Look at Isaac Newton."

"The apple Newton?" Miranda stood up, tugging her tights up over her thighs, the nylon sticking on her damp skin.

"The apple led to his one magic moment, and then for the rest of his life, he tried to recapture it. Some of his experiments after that were, well, ludicrous. Once he stuck a needle into his eye and sort of rubbed it around to see what would happen. Then he stared at the sun until he was almost blind. It's kind of sad. It doesn't stick. Like with Alexander the Great, Genghis Khan, Queen Elizabeth, Ben Franklin—"

"Ben Franklin!" Miranda stared at Sayblee, who shrugged.

"Maybe. Who knows? But think about his antics with electricity. Then there's Charles Darwin."

"What do you know about him?" Miranda picked up her skirt and slid it up over her legs and hips.

"He had his great trip on the *HMS Beagle*, and then went home and had ten children. He never even coined the term 'evolution.'"

Miranda buttoned her skirt and stared at Sayblee. "How do you know all this stuff?"

Lifting her hands, Sayblee smiled. "When I'm not making fire, I read."

Miranda smiled back, thinking that Sayblee would have been great to have on camping trips.

"I hate camping. Too many bugs. I spend all my time making spells to keep them away," Sayblee said. "My brother . . ." And then she stopped, looking down and adjusting her robe. "Anyway, other than your hovering, nothing else?"

Miranda put on her sweater, adjusting the sleeves, her fingers still jittery. "Well, I haven't done anything great. I won a poetry contest recently, but that's about it."

Pulling open some drawers until she found a comb, Miranda began to slowly pull it through her hair, her drying curls making progress slow.

"So what do you think it all means?" she asked Sayblee. "My parents aren't magic—"

My parents, she thought to herself, her head suddenly feeling filled with air. *Who are they?*

Miranda looked at Sayblee through the mirror and let the comb fall into the sink.

"My parents," she said softly, blinking into the fluorescent light over the mirror. "They—"

"What about them?" Sayblee asked.

"I don't know," Miranda said after a pause. "Just before I decided to go find Sariel, I found out I was adopted. My sister told me two days ago."

Sayblee stared back at her through the mirror and then leaned forward and picked up the comb, bringing it up to Miranda's hair and slowly pulling through the tangles.

Miranda closed her eyes, realizing that Sayblee had left her mind, and she was thankful, letting herself feel another wave of sadness. All this time she'd thought June and Steve were her parents, but now she had no idea who her parents were. Maybe she never would.

Even if she were to discover who they were, they obviously weren't around to provide her with information about her background. And the questions she wanted to ask them now weren't the typical ones from adopted-out children. Upon finding their parents, most wanted to know about histories of cancer or diabetes or mental illness. How was she supposed to approach these two people who had given her away and say, "Oh, and for the record, are you a sorcerer? Any past history of flight? Success with charms and spells? Telepathy? Just thought I'd ask."

Yet all of what had happened tonight was some kind of legacy from them, these invisible people. And the only way she would be able to find out anything about them and herself would be to stay here. She couldn't just run back home to San Francisco, go back to her computer, and forget about traveling through matter, reading minds, and matching wills with Kallisto.

Sayblee continued to comb her hair, and Miranda breathed out, willing her tears to stay under her lids. Of course she felt terrible about whatever evil plan Kallisto and Quain were about to enact, but she didn't really understand any of it. And Nala didn't seem ready to reveal all to her. This wasn't her fight, even if she would hate for anything to happen to the group, the world, *Moyenne*, *Croyant*, or otherwise.

Miranda wasn't sure why they thought they needed her help, but if she stayed, she would be able to find out about her parents. Maybe when this Kallisto thing was over and if any of them survived, she would be able to ask questions, go to whatever *Croyant* library or records room there was and discover who her real parents were. Maybe there was a person with all this information stuck in his head and all you had to do was whirl around in his thoughts to come up with what you needed.

Made about as much sense as everything she'd seen today. Miranda didn't know, but she knew she couldn't go back home without the truth.

But no matter what, she was done with Sariel, even if he found his memories. Despite the time they'd had together, he'd decided she wasn't worth being with. And then, he'd either forgotten her or let someone else take her away from his mind, just like that. What mattered was that she, obviously, didn't matter to him at all.

"You love him, don't you?" Sayblee asked quietly.

Miranda thought to speak, but couldn't, her throat too thick with sadness. But because she could, she sent Sayblee a thought. *Yes. At least, I thought I did.*

When Miranda and Sayblee came downstairs, Mazi had managed to pull together a meal, chicken in a bubbling tomato and olive sauce, crusty bread, and a salad. Miranda breathed in the savory air, vaguely wondering if there was magic to help with cooking, knowing that of all skills, that was one she could really use. If she couldn't find her parents, at least she could come home with this skill.

She turned to Sayblee, confused though, wondering why there was time to create a culinary delight and then eat it when Quain and his minions were about to take over the world.

Hearing her thoughts, Sayblee smiled wearily. "He knows we're close by and that put off his plans for a bit. And your presence has put them off a bit, too. So we have some time, and no one works well on an empty stomach."

Miranda and Sayblee walked into the dining room. The rest of the group murmured their appreciation of the meal on the table, and Miranda tried to feel enthused, but her head felt full of stars, lights flickering at the corners of her eyes. It was the worst jet lag she'd ever had.

"Sit," Nala said to her, indicating a seat on the long bench. "You must be hungry."

Miranda nodded, keeping her eyes down. She didn't want to look again at Sariel or his brothers, who were still sitting on the couch together, a row of beautiful dark-haired men. Men who had no idea who she was; specifically, one man who had let her go.

Sayblee grabbed her elbow and gently led her over to the far bench, and Miranda busied herself with her napkin and cutlery as she felt the rest of the group settle themselves on the benches.

"To the cook," Lutalo said, in an attempt to lift spirits, and everyone raised a glass to Mazi and then began eating. Miranda was surprised at how hungry she was, but then, as she chewed, she realized that it had been hours if not a full day since she'd eaten. She hadn't had anything since grabbing a scone at the coffee shop, and she hadn't been able to finish that, her stomach roiling from Viv's news.

Swallowing, she tried not to think of her sister crying in her bed, leaking milk and tears. Miranda bent low over her plate and ate quickly, hoping she could go up to a soft bed somewhere and pass out before making a fool of herself, weeping wildly in front of this amnesiatic bunch. From the corner of her eye, she knew that Sariel, Rufus, and Felix were staring at her. From the outer edges of her mind, she knew that someone was tracing the waves of her thoughts. They probably all were. This was a group of the most talented *Croyant* put together to capture Quain, so all of them were most likely able to read her thoughts, pass plates of chicken with their minds, light the candles on the table with a tiny exhale. Maybe the cook hadn't even cooked, whipping up the meal with a wave of his slender hands.

But as she looked up at them between bites, Miranda realized that if she didn't know better, she would assume this was any typical dinner party. Nala talked intensely with the cook, Mazi, about the difference in piquancy of California bay leaf and Greek. Baris, his orange hair the exact color of an autumn pumpkin, was telling Felix about a pub in Surrey run by triplets. Deciding to keep her eyes down, Miranda listened to the rest of the group chat amiably, and from under her lids, watched them pass each other bread and salt, nothing magic about it at all.

After a few minutes of eating, Nala hit her glass with a fork. "I'm sorry to interrupt this lovely meal, but I have to tell you of our plans."

Miranda wiped her mouth and looked up, hoping Nala would excuse her, saying something like, "Since you aren't involved, Miranda, why don't you go to bed."

Miranda expected that she would be allowed to stay behind in this house while they went off to fight Quain and Kallisto. Because she was so new to magic and unclear about the fight for the *plaques*, she assumed she'd be dismissed, sent upstairs, sent to her room as she often was as a child when she broke plates or pulled Viv's hair. As she left the room, the group would tamp down their thoughts, keeping her out, determined to prevent the spreading of crucial information.

But Nala didn't even look at Miranda. Instead, she put down her fork and began.

"I've had an emergency message from Phaedrus and with his information and what Lutalo and Baris were able to obtain today and what Miranda saw," she paused, nodding at Lutalo, Baris, and then Miranda appreciatively, "we are certain of Quain's location. As you might imagine, it's not far from the third *plaque*."

"But what of the forces protecting the *plaque*?" Rufus said. "Have they managed to strengthen those? Adalbert said that the magic was tight. We can't do everything from our end."

"Yes," Nala said. "But look at what Kallisto was able to do today. We all used our skills and gifts, and she deflected everything. It will take what we can muster, what Phaedrus and his fortified forces can provide, and Miranda."

Miranda started, looked at Nala for a confused second, and then stared down at her plate, her stomach teeming with nerves and too-quickly-eaten food. She felt Sayblee put a hand on her knee. Breathing in deeply, Miranda looked back up at Nala.

"What do you mean, me?" she asked, keeping her eyes away from Sariel. "I can't help you. I can't even control the magic I have."

Nala seemed to grow in size, her yellow robe buffeting her. "Miranda, in all the time Kallisto has been with Quain, no one—and I mean no one." Nala's mind flicked briefly to Sariel and then clamped down, keeping Miranda from seeing more. "No one has gotten into her mind beyond a few minor images. And there have been many attempts. What happened with you today was beyond amazing."

Nala glanced at Sariel and then resumed. "Somehow, you were able to get into her thoughts and determine Quain's location. You saw her plan. If we can get you back into her proximity, you have the potential to stall her, to keep her from aiding Quain. He is not a young man. Kallisto energizes him. He needs her power, and maybe you can keep her talents otherwise occupied."

Her mouth open, Miranda looked at Nala. How could Nala even begin to imagine that Miranda could do one thing to stop Kallisto? Hadn't that woman tied her up to a chair, placed a wall around her memories that no one could get through even now, and tried to kill her? So what that she'd seen some fortress and the three *plaques* together? What this group needed was the *sorcier* equivalent of a neutron bomb to do anything to Kallisto.

"Yes. You're right," Nala said. "It will be difficult. But you can create a diversion. Without training, without knowing your abilities, you got in, Miranda. And we need you."

"But I don't know what I'm doing. The only thing I meant to do was find Sariel," she said, feeling her face flush. "And I couldn't even do that right. I don't know how I found myself in Kallisto's thoughts without her knowing, but it was an accident. Even if you have the best plan in the world, how can you be sure that I can follow through?"

The group stared at her. Miranda swallowed, took strength from the constant warming pressure from Sayblee's hand, and looked up at Sariel.

"I know you think I'm lying about you and me, but all I wanted to do was find you. Kallisto was right about one thing. She told me I was pathetic. And she was right because look what happened. Now that you don't, can't, or won't remember me, I probably should leave. This isn't my fight. I don't belong here." Miranda felt her lips quiver, but she kept looking at Sariel. She wanted to find out about her parents, but as she watched his face, his gold eyes steady and calm, she knew she needed to leave more than anything else.

Mazi shook his head, his wild gray hair sparkling in the light. "If you didn't belong, you wouldn't be here. It doesn't matter the intent, it's the action that is true."

Rufus rolled his eyes, and then slammed a hand down on the table. "It will bloody well be your fight if we fail. But then, it won't be a fight at all. Quain will destroy us all in an instant, and we won't even be able to mourn the destruction he inflicts. You won't have time to watch your cozy life disappear, lass."

Sariel hadn't taken his eyes from hers, but he didn't say a word.

Felix looked at Sariel and then said, "You were brave enough to come find my brother here, even though you didn't know how to. You should be brave enough to join us."

"But what is the plan? What's going to happen?" Miranda asked. "I'll need a lot of time to prepare, and you don't have a lot of time. It's ridiculous."

"We have enough time to work you through the steps, and tonight, we are going to discuss everything. Lay it all out," Lutalo said, Nala nodding at his words.

"And," Nala said, "through Phaedrus I had a quick message from Adalbert. I've already spoken to Sariel about it. In an attempt to protect you, Miranda, as well as Sariel, he took away all Sariel's memories of you. Same with Felix and Rufus and even Brennus Broussard. When this is over, he intends to restore them to everyone. He apologizes, but however mistaken the act, it was only to protect the mission."

"But why do I still remember? Why was I the only one left with them?"

"Because," Sariel said, "you were using magic when I tried to take them. You were stronger than I was. You hung on."

Miranda shook her head, thinking about her dream of clinging, pulling, holding on.

"I made a mistake. But if I hadn't, we would never have learned about your skill. We wouldn't be able to have an edge over Kallisto," Sariel said.

Stunned, Miranda looked at each of the people at the table. These magic people, *sorciers* and *sorcières*, managed to screw up just as thoroughly as the *Moyenne* they liked to look down on. Who gave any of them the right to go into people's heads and take away what meant most? And then, how come she had the magic to keep her memories hers? How could this Adalbert possibly restore the words and feelings and sounds she and Sariel had exchanged? How could stolen memories contain the color and vibrancy of what remained behind after they loved?

Miranda closed her eyes and stopped thinking, knowing that they were all listening in, silenced by her anger and despair. She pulled away from Sayblee's touch, stood up from the bench, and stared at them all. Tired and tentative, these people didn't look like the salvation of the planet. They may have concocted the greatest plan in the world, but if they needed her help, the destruction of the world as they all knew it was a forgone conclusion.

"I'm going to bed," she said. "And in the morning, I'm going home."

"Miranda," he said, and for an instant, Miranda thought she was back in San Francisco, awakened in her own bed from one of Sariel's late night visitations. But then she felt the strange pillow under her head, the soft blanket on her arm. Sitting up, she saw Sariel's silhouette against the window.

"What?" she asked, pulling the blanket up to her neck. "What do you want?"

"I need to talk with you."

Miranda leaned against the wall, her eyes adjusting to the bright moonlight casting its blue sheen into the room. Sariel walked over to the chair by the bed, and she saw that he was wearing a T-shirt and some soft-looking pants, his hair down and falling behind his shoulders. He looked exactly like a man whom she would walk through matter for, invoking all those principles of physics she'd never understand, even if she ever managed to travel where she wanted to. He was a man she'd sail around the world for, even if he handed over all his thoughts, feelings, and desires for her. He leaned toward her, his eyes so open, so wide, so needful. No matter his gaze, she knew he didn't have one memory of her. Not one.

"I do have one," he said. "Flying."

"Flying?"

"You in your backyard. Hovering in the afternoon."

"From my poem. The terrible poem."

Sariel leaned forward. "It wasn't terrible."

Miranda pulled the blanket up higher, feeling the cold wall beneath her back. "What do you want, Sariel?"

He paused, running a hand through his hair. In the dark, she couldn't see him well, but she could smell him, orange and musk and soap. She wanted to weep from the memory of his skin so close to hers that his smell became her only air, but she'd cried more in the past couple of days than she had in all the months since Jack left.

"What do you want from me?" she asked again, harshly.

"Tell me," he said, "what happened with Kallisto."

Miranda watched him, his firm dark form against the moonlight. "I already told you everything."

"No. What did she show you?"

"Oh," Miranda said, wondering how to get her tongue around those horrible images in his house, his body dangling, bloodied, limp, his face as Kallisto left him. "That."

"That," he said, his voice quiet and sad.

She sighed. Why was loss such a compelling story that everyone needed to hear it over and over again, grief a poem Miranda wrote constantly, the subject changing but not the song. This was Sariel's story, the one he couldn't let go of, probably not until Kallisto was gone, dead, or his again.

"No," he said. "Not that. Never again."

"But it was awful," Miranda said. "I didn't want to watch, but she forced me to."

"I want to see how she saw it. How I looked. I need to remember again."

"Are you sure?"

"Yes," he said. "Completely."

"All right," she said. "I'll tell you."

So Miranda told him what Kallisto had revealed to her, described his body hanging in the room, explained the evil look on Kallisto's face as she taunted him. She slowed, letting him see his expression of love and pain as Kallisto prepared to leave him for Quain.

After she was done speaking, the room was silent except for the ping and hiss of the radiator. Then he breathed out and leaned back heavily in the chair, his hair falling forward over his shoulders.

"She enchanted me."

"I can see why. She's very beautiful," Miranda said quietly. In her mind, she saw Kallisto's dark hair wild around her as she hovered over them, casting out her black energy.

"No, I mean she really enchanted me. With magic," Sariel said. "It had been going on for months, maybe a year. When I finally was no longer of use to her and had given her all the information I could, she left me. That scene you saw wasn't even the worst. She began to torture me for one last piece of information."

"Did she get it?"

Sariel nodded. "Yes, she did, and then Rufus came and saved me, at great cost to himself. Kallisto wasn't as strong then. But she'd gotten what she needed."

"What was the information?" she asked.

He sighed and leaned his head on the back of the chair. "She waited just long enough. I'd just come back from capturing a *sorcier* named Duman in Cairo. He'd been working with Quain, and had come across the location of the first *plaque.* As I brought him back to Rabley Heath, he began to babble, throwing out names and places, one of them the Castle of Gaerwen. The Castle of Gaerwen was the location of the first *plaque.* And Kallisto dug it out of my mind. She got what she wanted."

"Why is she like this?" Miranda asked. "What made her go to Quain?"

Sariel rubbed his forehead. "She wasn't always so greedy. When we first met—she wanted to bring the *Croyant* and *Moyenne* worlds together. She thought the world would be more integrated, more whole. Safer, happier, healthier. There's a whole group of people working toward this goal. Rufus and his wife Fabia. Fabia's parents and brother. Adalbert, our armiger. Cadeyrn Macara. Lots of us. Kallisto was one of them. But somewhere along the line, Quain got to her. Convinced her, turned her against us. Used her as she later used me. Made her do what he wanted until she thought she wanted it herself. Until she became someone I didn't understand or even know. Until she took from me what would hurt us all the most."

Miranda listened and then sat forward, bringing her knees to her chest. It was no wonder he wanted to be here. It was his information that started the whole plot in motion. It was no wonder that he gave up his memories of Miranda to fight this fight. He had no choice.

"That's right," Sariel said. "And I know, Miranda, if I had a woman like you in front of me, it would have been a hard choice to leave. I wouldn't have given up memories of you for nothing. It would have had to be important, crucial. The only way out."

She felt a wave of sadness in him, his mind full of confusion. Shaking her head and breathing in, she said, "What are these *plaques*, anyway? What do they do?"

"You know those colors you saw? The gold and red and purple in your thoughts? Well, the *plaques* are full of the spectrum of energy of those colors. The first *plaque* is purple, the second red, the last gold. They were made by ancient *sorciers* and *sorcières* to contain an infinity of thought and energy. They represent earth, air, water. They exist as repositories for all of our abilities, but they have always been kept apart."

"Why?" she asked.

"Together, they are too strong. That flume of energy you saw? Once the *plaques* are put together in a triangle, that energy, that ultimate power, can transfer to the person who arranged them. And then that person has the power—has the ability—to change everything."

"Quain wants that power."

Sariel nodded. "And when he gets it, he will harness all the power, all the energy, all our collective thoughts from hundreds and thousands of years and make the world the way he wants it."

The moon was full in the window now, Sariel's hair shining, his eyes intense. The blanket was suddenly too hot, and she shrugged it off her shoulders.

"So what's the plan?" she asked. "I mean, besides me distracting Kallisto?"

"We have to get to him before he gets to the *plaque.* Without Kallisto, he won't be as powerful, and maybe all our combined forces can stop him. We plan to attack him where he is staying now, at the Fortress Kendall, according to the information that you gave us, which was later verified."

"He's there now with Kallisto?"

"And others. We're not sure if the *plaques* are there with him, but I'm sure they aren't. He would have hidden them elsewhere."

"Where's the third *plaque*?"

"It's being guarded now by Adalbert Baird himself

and all our most powerful magic. But with two *plaques*, who knows what Quain will be able to do? We do have some time, now. He's been put off by our arrival and by the new forces surrounding the third *plaque*. There's time to teach you some things."

"What things?"

"Magic. Ways of getting farther into Kallisto's mind."

His voice was tired now, and he let his hands fall into his lap. Miranda stared at his fingers, remembering the heat from them on her ankle, the way he could make her blood move under her skin.

Neither of them said anything for a while, the moon arcing into the top windowpane, the room warm with radiator heat. Finally, Sariel cleared his throat.

"I can't make you stay for me. I know I don't have that right. You must think I threw you away, betrayed you, gave you up for something greater. I can understand how you must feel about me. I can understand why you want to leave. But for some reason, you can do what we can't. I was only able to get random words from Kallisto's mind, images flung out that I was able to pick up periodically. That was more than most who tried, so I was thought to be our way in. But you," he said, "you are special. And we all need you here, with us."

The blanket clutched in her hands, Miranda stared at him, breathing in his smell, tasting his skin even from here. "How can I?" she asked finally. "Why am I suddenly able to read Kallisto's mind—everyone's mind—and travel through matter?"

She waited for his answer, seeing his eyes on her, still and constant.

"It's not suddenly, Miranda," he said. "I've been thinking about your poetry. In a way, all the empathy and thought and energy you put into words is the same as concentrating on matter. It's the same as listening to someone's thoughts. Of course, most *Moyenne* poets don't make magic other than on paper, but it's really the same process."

"But why now?" she asked.

Sariel shrugged. "Sayblee said something to me after you left the table about your parents and the adoption, so it could be you were born *Croyant.* Maybe meeting me brought out something that you already had. Maybe my leaving made you find something in yourself that was always there just waiting. Your real life has been waiting for you all along."

He leaned forward abruptly, taking her wrists in his hands. "Please," he began, his eyes intent on her and full of regret and longing. "Forgive me for what I've forgotten. I wouldn't have let it happen unless I knew it was absolutely necessary. I might not remember the details, but somehow, I remember this, you, your skin."

As he had done the night he healed her ankle, he let the heat from his touch penetrate into her skin, her flesh, her bones. She felt her sore, aching wrists and hands heal, the skin knitting together, the muscles relaxing. Miranda closed her eyes, tears behind her lids now, knowing that he wasn't lying or pretending. Letting herself slip into his mind, she saw his amazement earlier at her cries of recognition, his bewilderment, and later, his appreciative gaze on her hair, her body, her face. She saw how he enjoyed her words, her anger, her humor, her questions.

She held his laughter in her mind, and then she felt him let her in further, past dinner, past the fight with Kallisto, back through the past three days. Circling his memory, she saw the places she should have been, a patch ripped out of a quilt, the strands repaired but the tear clear.

Miranda circled and circled around the tear in his thoughts, testing it like she would a sore tooth with her tongue. There was the meeting where she'd first met him, Brennus and the others at the bar, but she never flew in, falling to the floor, causing uproar and anger. There was no argument. No ankle. No healing. No late night visits to Miranda's apartment.

The next days were ordinary until he received first one message and then another, but in this memory, he received one at home and another at a meeting, Brennus standing close beside him. In all of Sariel's memories of the past weeks, there was nothing of her at all, but she felt where she had been, a lingering hope and happiness, a shadow of joy, an image of flight. And something else she herself couldn't remember, an older memory, something dark and safe and comforting. He felt her when she was somewhere dark and fluid, and she stayed there for a moment, wondering what this memory was. Probably a dream he'd had when they held each other in her bed, the room dark, their bodies warm.

Miranda began to pull away from his thoughts. Sariel hadn't been lying, not at all, and she let herself relax in his thoughts, in his kind, warm self. Miranda had never been this close to anyone.

Slowly, Miranda left his memories and felt the heat of his hand, his heart beating all the way to the tips of his fingers. He moved from the chair onto the bed, slipping a hand behind her neck and bringing her face to his.

"Miranda means miracle," he said, his voice near her ear.

She tried to smile, but her lip was trembling. "I know."

"That you wouldn't let your memories of me be taken is a miracle. That you needed to find me is a miracle. That you moved through matter alone to do so is a miracle. You, Miranda. You are a miracle, and I'm so sorry." He kissed her once, twice, again, his lips soft and warm.

Without knowing if she should—what if he disappeared again? What if he decided to pull her ideas from her mind? What if he forgot tonight? This minute? Now?—she pulled her hand from his and wrapped her arms around his neck, relieved and frightened at the same time. Here's what she traveled through matter for. Here's what she'd wanted. His tongue was on hers, his mouth warm and slightly sweet with toothpaste. *Just like always,* she thought. *But he forgot always.*

I'll remember later, I promise. Show me how it was, he thought.

It was good, she thought back. *It was wonderful. Except for how you liked to disappear and threaten me with mind vacuuming.*

I'm not going anywhere, he thought, and pulled her down on the bed, his hands on the sides of her face as he kissed her mouth, her cheeks, her neck.

Miranda kissed him back, pressing her body against his, letting the tears fall, but not stopping, moving her hands under his shirt. He was so lean, so tight, and she wanted their skins together without clothes. Hearing her, he sat up and took off his shirt and pants and then pulled the nightgown that Sayblee had lent her up and off. The clothes on the floor, Sariel lay next to her, pulling the blanket over them.

"You are so beautiful," he said. "I know I already know that. But you should hear it again."

"Don't forget it this time," she said, kissing his chest, running her fingers over his tiny taut nipples. And then she let her hand travel down his smooth stomach to his erection, so hard and ready for her, all his warmth concentrated in that one wonderful part. She squeezed him tightly in her hand. "Or else."

She slowly moved her hand up and down, watching him react. *Memory isn't only in the mind,* she thought. *The body remembers, too.*

He breathed in, swallowed hard, and looked at her, his eyes deep flicks of fire in the darkness.

"I know that. But I won't forget you again. I promise." Sariel moved on top of her, his body between her legs. He entered her easily, and he moaned, dipping his head to her shoulder, thinking, *I do remember this. I do.*

Closing her eyes, wrapping her arms around him, she moved with him, letting herself forget her anger, her fear, her confusion. Miranda heard his thoughts, his gratitude for her forgiveness, his need to know more of what they'd had together. And then she was riding his passion, his desire. Both of them moved together in thought and body. All that mattered in this room, in this house, in this city was their two bodies, the way the heat built up between them, his breath, her breath, the most magic thing in the world the way they moved together.

Chapter Thirteen

Miranda stood in front of Sariel, her eyes closed, her hands pressed to her sides. The two of them were in the backyard of the house, the afternoon air chill and full of mist. The rest of the group had trained in the morning, and now Nala, Lutalo, Baris, Mazi, and Sayblee were following up on the information Phaedrus had passed to them the night before. Without a doubt, Rufus and Felix weren't studying the schematics of the Fortress Kendall but watching Sariel and Miranda from an upstairs window instead. Sariel couldn't see them, but he could feel them lurking just on the fringes of his thoughts. If he weren't busy trying to teach Miranda, he'd think up something that would scare them away. Or he'd just go inside and shame them into leaving him alone. But he had to focus on Miranda. As it was, he wasn't making much headway with her.

"You're not in," Sariel said, feeling her mind trying to find an entrance into his, tendrils of her irritated thought poking around the barrier he'd put up.

She opened her eyes and frowned. "Well, it's not like I've taken classes on this before. I didn't have the advantage of learning all this stuff at school. I was busy dissecting frogs and correcting dangling modifiers."

"What?" Sariel said, loving how she looked when she was angry, her eyes full of fire. "What are you talking about?"

"Oh, something Felix said to me in Hilo," she said, shaking her head. "Never mind. Let me try one more time."

Sariel closed his eyes and centered on his image, a thick stone wall, reaching from the top to the bottom of his imagination. "You know what they say. Thirteen times is a charm. Just relax."

"I am relaxed!" she said. "Stop bugging me."

Sariel opened his eyes and smiled. Miranda's eyes were still hot, her curls wild loops from the moisture in the air. Without wanting to, he let his eyes drift down her neck to her breasts, her nipples erect from the cold or from anger, he couldn't tell.

"Do you mind?" She put her hands on her hips. "That, I could hear."

"Well, you see?" Sariel ignored the flush on his face. "You got in. That's the kind of opening you have to find. The kind you must have found with Kallisto. What was she thinking about? What was she feeling when you got into her mind?"

Miranda paused and bit her lip. Sariel sighed. "Me?"

"She was jealous. And she wanted to kill me. Anger. Lots of it."

"The combination then of just you being you and her anger created a fissure you slid into, without even trying. Imagine if you were able to do that on purpose. So let's try again," Sariel said. He closed his eyes and brought forth the image that had worked for him since school, the stone wall.

He heard Miranda breathe out deeply, and then she was silent. For a time, he felt nothing, no intrusion, no attempt to breach the stone. But then, there! He slammed down another stone, keeping her back. She tried it again, and he stopped her, just as her mind crept through the mortar. She tried again and again, and he began to tamp her down over and over, his mind moving quickly.

But then he heard her thoughts, little jibes about being *so tough, so strong, so clever. A stone wall? What a metaphor. Let me teach you about metaphor. Couldn't you find material a bit sturdier? Lead? Iron? Steel? Titanium?*

Round and round her mind went, and then, without him wanting it, she shot a sliver of pointed thought through the wall, into his mind, right into the memory of last night, the two of them in Miranda's bed.

That's better, she thought, watching them hold each other in the darkness, feeling his quick breaths as he moved inside her. Together, hovering in Sariel's thoughts, they listened to the sounds in the dark room, the breathing, the moans, and finally, the cries.

There, she thought. *That was worth the price of admission.*

Opening his eyes, Sariel walked to Miranda and kissed her, the memory of last night still strong between them. She kissed him back, happy now.

"Thirteen has always been my lucky number," she said. "No amount of patriarchy could ruin it for me."

"Don't even begin to explain that," Sariel said, brushing the back of his hand on her cheek. "I don't want to know. But we really should try it again. You went for my weakest point."

She ran her hand through his hair, clenching a fistful. "What's your weakest point?"

"You."

"But you don't even remember me. Try my mind again first. See if Kallisto's block is still there." She pushed him back, but he leaned in, kissing her on the forehead, the nose, her lips.

"It's still there, but it won't last for long. She can't maintain it from such a distance," he said.

Miranda leaned back into him, putting her arms around his chest. "You're scared to try."

Sariel was silent, listening to the thrum of her body, the hard beat of her heart. Maybe he was scared to find out what he'd forgotten about her, even though he knew it would be wonderful, just like her. But he wanted his memories back from his point of view, the way he'd experienced them. Seeing her reactions and feeling her emotions when he kept disappearing wouldn't be fun.

"Maybe I am," he said, bringing his lips to her hair, tipping her face to his.

"Try again!" She backed away before he could kiss her again, wagging her finger. "There's time for more kissing later. Unless, of course, someone steals our memories, and we have to start over from square one."

"No one's taking those ever again," Sariel said, meaning it.

"Well, there's the end of the world as we know it to deal with. That just might get in our way."

Sariel put his hands on his hips, shaking his head. For a second, he thought he should sit her down and show her the images that Mazi gave the entire group before they left on the mission. Then Miranda would see what they were truly up against. She could only joke because she didn't know what Quain was capable of. But she would soon enough. She'd have no choice.

Miranda watched him, smiling. He couldn't ruin this moment. So he went along with her. "It certainly could."

"So we're running out of time."

"Perhaps we are."

"So go ahead. Try it again." Miranda closed her eyes, standing still.

Sariel looked up and saw someone moving away from the window, and then he heard Rufus.

More training, less fooling around, lad.

Miranda opened her eyes and turned back to the house. Looking back at Sariel, her face was contrite. "He's right. Come on. Back to work."

Sariel nodded and closed his eyes, waiting for a lull in her thoughts. She wasn't blocking him, and he ignored her images of the night before, moving back through the two days since she'd left San Francisco on her own. He still couldn't believe that she'd done it. Untrained, untried, theoretically *Moyenne.* But she wasn't. Not with the magic she could do.

Moving toward Kallisto's block, he swirled through memory and sensation, searching out, trying to find the barrier, a restriction, an impasse, a pause. But all he could find was sort of a shadow. He stopped in front of it, looking at the dark swirl, wondering if he could get past without hurting her or himself. Knowing Kallisto, it could be a trap. So tentatively, he sent forth a bit of energy, which passed right through, the shadow evaporating at the touch of his mind. *Finally*, he thought.

Miranda. I'm here.

And he was. She was looking at him as she leaned against the bar, her ankle throbbing. Next, she was breathing in sage and citrus, sitting on his couch. Then he was in a room—her apartment—and they were on a bed, tangled together naked. Next they were getting dressed, laughing. Another scene: a street, both of them holding cups of coffee. Then they were holding each other, traveling through the gray. Next they were at Felix's on his lanai, drinking out of large, frosty glasses, listening to Felix talk about school. There were moments of confusion: she didn't know how to contact him. She missed him. There were times when she thought she was totally insane, hallucinating the entire thing. But mostly, he felt her acceptance of him, her attraction, her—her love. The past that he couldn't remember surrounded him, and he felt relief and loss.

Sariel circled around her memories again and saw himself on her bed, taking in a message. Then he leaned over her, pressing his fingertips on her smooth forehead. She woke up alone, nervous, her heart pounding, and then she was pacing the room, angry, upset. Then there was another memory. Miranda was sitting on her sister's bed, listening to a story. But this wasn't a good story. Miranda was confused, angry, amazed. Her sister was telling her—what? She was adopted?

Sariel was flooded with so much anger and sadness, and then, quickly, there was a last memory. Miranda was stepping into the gray, calling his name.

Sariel, she thought. *I wanted to find you.*

I know, he thought back, pulling slowly out of her mind and into his own. He opened his eyes and looked at her, her eyes still closed. Out of all the women in the world, *Moyenne* or *Croyant,* he had found her—they had found each other. He never wanted to lose her again, either in body or in mind.

Opening her eyes, she smiled and tried to smooth her hair, but the minute she took her palm away, her curls bounced back into a fiery halo.

"You believe me now, right?" she said. "I'm real at last."

Ignoring whoever was at the window and the concern he felt buzzing from the house, Sariel walked to her, grabbed her shoulders, and kissed her again, Rufus be damned.

Sariel, Felix, Rufus, and Nala stood on a hill in the falling darkness, all of them encased in an invisibility spell, their thoughts and words muffled in a *cône de si-*

lence, their ideas safely contained. The sky was pewter, the sun finally emerging from the mist only to set, leaving behind a slim slit of orange on the horizon. Sariel could smell the salt from the ocean, feel the tang of ocean in his nose. Somewhere closer to shore, a seagull called out, its cry echoing in the darkening air.

Invisible and protected by spells, the four of them surveyed the fortress, which was built in the shape of the Tudor rose, a round keep in the middle surrounded by six round bastions. The arched windows were placed few and far between in the stone walls, and there was only one large entrance. The fortress was built as a garrison, complete with a moat and a drawbridge, which managed to keep out invaders to English shores until the sixteenth century when it was finally conquered during civil unrest. Now it was a tourist attraction—an English Heritage site—and usually open to tourists who were bused in five times a day for a medieval tour complete with knights, nobility, and serfs, and a luncheon of bangers, bread, and beer. There was a large parking lot a few hundred feet away and a careful flagstone walkway that led to the main gate.

But Lutalo and Mazi had discovered that it had been closed for repairs for months. Quain had created a vortex that hadn't diminished, so workers had been led astray, driving around the Kentish countryside for miles looking for the fortress. Suddenly, the local pub patrons and farmers and gas station owners had no idea what fortress the distressed masons and carpenters and plumbers were speaking of. Around and around they all went, calling back to the registry offices in the late afternoon with nothing but confusion.

Nala pulled her robe close around herself and put on her hood. "There," she said, pointing at the Fortress Kendall. "You can see the vortex, too."

Sariel nodded, spotting the flicker of unevenness in

the air around the fortress. But he knew that there would be more than a vortex impeding them. Quain had probably enforced the fortress with spells and traps, so that just getting inside would be work enough. Sariel had tried to pick out Quain's or Kallisto's thoughts, but nothing came back to him but a dead blankness, as if there were nothing in the fortress but ancient rock and wood.

"The keep," Felix said. "In the middle there. That's the obvious place to set up. Not only would he be safe from *Moyenne* interference but he would be farther from our reach."

"Might be the exact thing he wants us to think. He's probably out in that thatched hut," Rufus said. "Eating a hog over a spit, laughing."

"It doesn't matter where he is," Sariel said. "Don't you feel his strength? His resistance? His magic? We'll be lucky to get ourselves through his barriers."

Sariel stopped speaking, thinking about Miranda. Suddenly, he didn't want her to come with them. How could she, so new to magic, crack through Quain's protections? She barely managed to get herself through matter and only today had she learned to move through someone's thoughts. There wasn't enough time to teach her what she needed to know to teach a first-level class of *Croyant*, much less battle Quain.

"We're strong," Nala said. "We'll carry her through. Lutalo has been working on actually changing certain protections and spells into others that are more easily breached. Don't ask me how, but that's what he can do. We will temporarily shift Quain's magic so that we can break into the fortress."

"And then we battle him down," Rufus said firmly. "Using Miranda to weaken Kallisto as we do."

Nala nodded, her gaze on the fortress below. "And Lutalo will hold his magic in place, while Sayblee and

Baris create distractions. Baris will take in as much information as he can, too, using whatever he can find to aid us. And when they know we are in, Phaedrus and his group will press with magic from the outside. The rest of us will push toward Quain until he is finished."

"Easy as pie," Felix said.

Sariel shook his head, crossed his arms. "We put this plan in motion when?"

"Tomorrow," Nala said. "We have to do this tomorrow. Phaedrus said they've felt Quain trying to slip through all their defenses around the third *plaque*. It's only a matter of hours, now. They won't be able to hold him off much longer."

"We have no choice, then," Sariel said.

Nala turned to him. "Is Miranda ready?"

Sariel breathed in, his chest heavy with—what? Regret? Guilt? Worry? Or was it fear? "As ready as she can be, I suppose, given that she only knew of her powers days ago."

Nala put a hand on his arm. "This is why Adalbert took your memories, Sariel. He knew how much you felt for her."

"But we'd have no plan if she weren't here," Rufus said. "No one else has gotten through to Kallisto like that. Pure images those. We have no choice."

"But maybe she should have had more of a choice," Sariel said. "She doesn't really know what we are asking of her."

"It's her world, too," Felix said. "It's what we've always wanted, *Moyenne* and *Croyant* fighting together, living together without secrecy. She's a living example of what we've always hoped for."

"If she even is *Moyenne*," Nala said. "I'm not so sure about that. But magic or not, Miranda has a skill none of us has. She may not understand what she's fighting for, but without her help, we will not be successful and she will know, soon enough, what we were trying to save."

Sariel felt his wall falling, stone by stone. He agreed with everything they said. There was no other choice but to have Miranda work her way into Kallisto's mind. But after finding Miranda's memories and making some new ones together, he didn't want her to face Kallisto again. And he didn't want the others to hear that. He slammed down his wall, keeping his mind to himself, and turned back to the fortress.

"Kallisto has a weakness," Felix said. "If she has a weakness, so does Quain. No matter how evil and corrupt he is, there's something inside that will turn him. He's still human, so there's hope if we can find our way into the fortress and find our way to him. We can end this."

The sky was dark now, the sun only a trace of umber. Below them, the fortress was a black hole in the landscape. What were Kallisto and Quain doing in there? Sariel wondered. What kind of evil magic did they practice together?

"Tomorrow morning," Nala said. "We will do it then."

She looked at them all, her face vibrant even in the misty darkness. Sariel could feel her power pulsing around them, and he knew that they had a chance with her in command and with Miranda as their surprise weapon. Maybe then Sariel could find his way into Quain and subdue him. Maybe then the world would be safe.

Nala nodded, and they all turned into the matter, whirling back to the house for one last night.

When they arrived back at the house, there was another training session going on, but this one was full of laughter. They'd arrived in the lounge, and the first sound Sariel heard was Miranda's giggling coming from the kitchen. Then Sayblee said, "That's it. Right. Perfect. Keep going. Oh, don't tilt!" There was more laughter, and Sariel walked into the kitchen to see Miranda hovering about four feet off the ground, her arms outstretched.

When she saw him, her mouth opened in surprise, and then her expression changed to confusion as she began to fall. Sariel ran to her, catching her in his arms just as she was about to hit the tile.

"Great timing," Sayblee said. "We almost had takeoff."

Sariel looked at Miranda, who clutched at his shoulders. "So you can fly."

"That's debatable," she said, looking up at him, smiling. "I think I'm a hovercraft only. One with very little fuel. It's a long time until I move up to rocket or space-shuttle status."

Sariel let her down, but kept an arm around her waist. "So what else can you do? What other tricks do you have?"

When Miranda looked at him, her face open and full of a love he could remember, in that instant, Sariel imagined that he was falling, too.

"I have a few tricks up my sleeve." She put her head against his chest, and he heard her think, *I'll show you later.*

Sayblee shook her head. "Okay, that's it. I'm leaving. Miranda, we can practice again after dinner." She left the kitchen, stopping in the lounge to talk with the others. Sariel squeezed Miranda and leaned down to kiss her.

"Did you find the fortress?" she asked when he pulled away. "Did you find where Quain is?"

"Yes," he said, the rounded image of the fortress

pressed against his lids. "I need to talk with you about this. Let's go for a walk."

"Okay. Let me see if I can borrow a parka and an Arctic weather kit, complete with emergency gear. No wonder Felix never leaves the Big Island."

Sariel let her go and leaned against the counter as she walked out of the kitchen. He heard her easy laughter and talk with the others, could almost see her happiness trail from her in a gold stream. All that good energy. All that feeling and love. All that ability and strength. How could he take her back into Kallisto's and Quain's evil tomorrow? But how, he thought as he turned to the window and caught his own reflection, could he not?

Sariel went to the sink and turned on the tap, filling himself a glass of water. He'd have to tell her the truth about what had happened to Phaedrus and his group. He'd have to tell her how someone can get lost in another's mind, putting both the seer and the seen at risk. And he would have to tell her what happened to his father. How Hadrian and Quain were once colleagues, allies, close friends. How Quain had betrayed him, killed Hadrian. Killed him dead.

Bundled in a borrowed jacket, scarf, and hat, Miranda held onto Sariel's arm. He was silent for a while, watching the mist swirl around the buildings and houses on Victoria Road, listening to snatches of thought from passersby. *If he didn't get the loo fixed, he bloody well can't expect me to stay the night,* and *Brilliant, just brilliant* and *Wicked cold, this.*

Sariel thought of Rufus listening to thoughts like this all day in Edinburgh, and smiled, seeing his brother's bored face in his mind.

"What aren't you thinking about? Something about

Rufus?" Miranda asked. Sariel almost jumped, stuck in minutiae.

He turned to her, watching her smooth pale face, the smattering of freckles on her nose and cheeks, her eyes ocean blue in the lamplight.

"Rufus, and a little bit of everything," he said. "There's just so much I need to tell you."

"So tell me. Obviously, I can take any story now," she said. "Not like before when you first told me about vortexes."

She smiled and then seeing his blank look, shrugged. "You'll remember. It was a long explanation because I kept asking so many questions. But let's just put it this way, I believed you even back then."

They walked in silence for a while, nothing but the sounds of the street and the gravel underfoot. Finally, Sariel breathed out deeply.

"You have to know this. There's only so far you can go into someone's mind before that person's mind and yours become joined," he said, imagining the way it felt to be inside another person's head. It wasn't like being in matter, which was vast and forever. A mind was closed and rich and thick and almost claustrophobic. And as you got closer and closer to the beginning of that person's thoughts, it was even denser, sticky with the past, dangerous to stay in.

"Joined?" Miranda said. "You mean like stuck?"

He nodded. "It's happened. And it makes both people crazy. They can't pull apart, no matter who tries to intervene. They become mental and emotional—"

"Conjoined twins?" Miranda said, shivering and holding his arm tighter. "That's horrible. Can you ever separate them?"

"No," he said. "As long as they live, they live in both minds. When one dies, so does the other."

A police van peeled by, siren blaring. On the corner

of a street, three teenagers grouped together, laughing. Sariel and Miranda continued walking, and when it was quiet again, he went on.

"So tomorrow," he said. "You can't go too far into Kallisto's mind, no matter how tempting. She might be so distracted you will have the chance. But we don't need you to go too far. Just enough so that we can stop her. Nothing more. If you start to feel slow, sluggish, trapped by thought, pull back. Force yourself to stop."

As he spoke, he felt her fear, heard her repeating his own words in her mind. *Stop. Nothing more. Pull back.*

Miranda nodded. "Okay. I will. I promise. But what is it really, Sariel? There's something else you want to tell me, but you're hiding it behind that wall of yours. This time, I can't get past it."

They turned onto Kensington Road, Palace Avenue, and then made their way toward Kensington Palace, walking for a while in silence. Lights shone from a top floor of the palace, and tourists stood at the black gate even now, wanting a glimpse of the place Princess Diana once lived.

"You're right," he said finally. "I don't know how to show you."

"So tell me. My God, Sariel, I can take anything now."

He squeezed her arm, wishing that they could both go back to her memory, the one of their first lovemaking. How much easier it would be to live in that time than in this one!

"Don't do that," Miranda said. "You know you can't live in the past. Even I know that. And after what my sister Viv told me before I left, I don't even know my past anymore."

"You're right," he said. "It's about my father."

He didn't say another word for a moment, not knowing how to continue.

"Tell me," she said softly.

A couple walked by, the woman walking a Yorkshire terrier on a thin leather leash. Miranda nodded at them, and then turned back to him.

"You can tell me."

"I know," he said, sighing. How much more personal could this fight with Quain be for him, he wondered? A father dead, a former lover wanting revenge and seemingly furious over his new lover. All of that as well as the destruction of everyone's way of life. Where were the words to explain? But then he felt her mind so softly in his, and he closed his eyes for a moment, letting her lead them both through the confusion of his ideas. After a moment, Sariel heard her gasp.

"He killed your father," Miranda said. "Oh, Sariel."

He nodded. "They were friends and partners for a long time. They worked together, doing what I do." Sariel looked at her, feeling her question. "Catching people who practice wrong magic. They were a team."

Turning away from the palace and back into the park, they walked on, their thoughts together. Just thinking about Quain and his father exhausted him, so Sariel let Miranda see what he knew, opening up the scene as he had been given it, giving her what his father had passed along before he died.

First there were stairs, echoes from others running away in fear, *Moyenne* and *Croyant* alike. Then the scene widened, opened up in a Paris métro station, *Châtelet*, across the Seine from Notre Dame. Mysteriously, a vortex had dissolved and now commuters and tourists looked around in confusion, finding themselves at the wrong station, on the wrong line, on the wrong bank of the Seine altogether.

While other *Croyant* collected themselves and began to enchant the *Moyenne*, moving them carefully out of the métro onto the Boulevard de Sébastopol, Hadrian and Quain circled down upon their quarry, Felipe Zimbardo, a thief, a murderer, a *sorcier* using his power for his own gain.

Over here, Quain thought out, looking at Hadrian. "*He has a* sortilege du`déguisement. *He's blending himself into the tile.*

Hadrian nodded, moved closer, waited for Quain to make a move. But then something went wrong. And even Sariel's memory flickered, faded, came back half strength. Hadrian's actual memory didn't survive past this point in the story, so all of what Sariel could give Miranda was a secondhand memory, stories from a *sorcière* named Laelia, who often worked with Hadrian and Quain.

As they circled closer to Zimbardo, Quain suddenly struck out, a blaze of energy taking Hadrian by surprise, throwing him down, flat on the tracks. And then—and then the train pulled through into the station at top speed from Les Halles. Despite Laelia's and other *Croyants'* attempts to stop the train, Quain froze all movement save for the train barreling down with its awful wheels. No one could do anything until it was too late for a spell, too late for a healer. Too late for anything.

On the tracks, Laelia held Hadrian's head in her lap, cried, called out with her thoughts, not understanding what had just happened. And then the scene faded, the light in the métro station growing dim, Laelia's cries fading into weakened echoes.

Sariel opened his eyes and stood in front of Miranda, who was pale, her eyes squeezed shut. For a moment, they stood still in the cold air.

"No," she whispered.

Sariel nodded, thought, *I wish it were no.*

"Oh, my God," Miranda said, blinking. "Why?"

Sariel swallowed, trying to find the answer he'd never been able to find. Miranda looked up at him, wiping his face with her mittened hand.

"I'm not sure why completely. But my father had found out what he was planning. Quain had gone to the Council a few months before, asking for more powers. Wanting to create a new system. My father and mother had voted against him," Sariel said. He breathed in, his lungs full of the cool air. "Quain took his revenge, and after that moment, he was lost to his own plan. For years, I blamed Adalbert and the Council for my father's death, and even though I did my job, I turned down assignments that might have led me closer to Quain. I was scared about what I might do if I ever found him. How I would feel."

Miranda nodded. "I think Brennus said something about that the first night I met you. What did he say? Something like, 'You've chosen to ignore the signs.'"

Sariel felt himself laugh, despite his sadness. "I'm really looking forward to remembering that whole conversation. Let's just put it this way: we are not in each other's fan club."

They started walking again, heading back to the house. "I don't think Brennus has a fan club," Miranda said. "But you do."

Grabbing her, he turned her to him, taking her shoulders in his hands, leaning down to kiss her. Her nose and face were cold, but her lips were warm, her mouth hot, her tongue against his. Here. Sariel wanted to stay right here, in Hyde Park on a freezing fall night before anything could happen to ruin everything.

He put his arms around Miranda tightly, holding her body against his, his mouth against her smooth neck, wishing it wasn't so cold so he could rip off her bulky parka and make love to her behind one of the giant plane trees, putting a vortex around the whole dammed park.

Without knowing it, he'd been waiting for her, as if her story had been connected to his long ago. Nothing

Sariel had ever felt for another woman—not even Kallisto—matched what he felt for Miranda.

He was thinking too loudly, he knew that. Hadn't he learned to keep his thoughts a secret? Look what had happened with Kallisto.

"I'm not Kallisto," Miranda whispered against his face. "I'm much better looking, with my frizzy hair and red nose."

Sariel had no words or thoughts for hers, just feeling. Holding her even closer, he let loose the energy in his body, the kind he used when he'd healed her ankle. Feeling Miranda's shivers and cold face, he touched her with his hands, with all of his body.

"Oh. Oh, my," she said, her voice trailing off.

He warmed her, through her parka, through her clothes, all the way to her skin and up to her most amazing, adorable red nose.

The house was quiet, everyone asleep or trying to sleep. Every so often, Sariel caught a strong thought or image from one of the bedrooms: the Fortress Kendall at dawn, Quain's pale face, sneering, a whirl of people fighting as magic flashed in a cavernous room.

Miranda was asleep, her body curled against his, her breath light and untroubled because she really didn't know what was going to happen tomorrow. She was too new to their world, too untried. Even though she had done well, today's training had been a game, a lark. How could she really know what she was going to face, even with the story he'd told her about Hadrian?

Sariel kissed her shoulder, tracing the line of her arm, and then dipping down to her waist and up to her hip, her skin smooth and pale. He let his hand slide onto her belly and then moved up to her breasts, letting the weight of one rest in his palm. He'd only known her for a couple of weeks and then—without his memories—for only a couple of days, and he didn't know what he would do if something happened to her. How could that be? How could you meet someone and feel like this?

Miranda stirred, turned, and held onto his shoulder. "It happens," she mumbled, yawning. "Haven't you read any poetry? Any Shakespeare? Browning?"

"You're awake?" He kissed her forehead.

"How could I let a petting session go by?" she said. "I'm still not convinced that you won't disappear."

He pulled away, looking her in the eye. "Miranda, this is serious. This isn't a dream. Everything that's going to happen tomorrow is real."

They stilled, staring at each other, the room warm around them. Finally, Miranda took in a deep breath and turned onto her back.

"I never told you about Jack. Have you heard me think about him? Or was he floating around there in my brain?"

Sariel leaned up on his elbow. "No Jack. I think I remember a Dan somebody."

Miranda closed her eyes and shook her head. "God, Dan. Always Dan. No, he's my editor. But at one point, I thought Jack Gellner was my ultimate true love. The thing was, loving him was so hard, even in the beginning when it's supposed to be easy. The falling in love part wasn't even fun, but because he was a poet and I was a poet, I thought we were going through some tormented, destined writer love. Sort of a Sylvia Plath, Ted Hughes kind of thing, and we know how happily that ended."

"What did Jack do?" Sariel asked, certain he really didn't want to know, even if the story ended with Jack gone and Miranda here. But if Miranda had watched what had gone on with him and Kallisto in his house that terrible night, he could listen to her story about Jack.

"I thought he was such a brilliant writer and a true, absolute, one hundred percent genius that I decided that his drinking and his drugs were part of his brilliance. Part of his quirky charisma and intellect," she said. "Then I thought that the way he ignored me was part of it, too. Then I lumped in the strange calls and his girls on the side. I let all his behavior slide because I believed that real love is hard and gritty and intolerable. I thought true love had to hurt. And it was real when he left me and stole my computer and a year's worth of writing I'd managed not to back up on disk. That was what felt real."

At her words, Sariel felt protective, angry, jealous, and an image of Jack—a good-looking, blond man—flicked between them. He shook his head and breathed in.

"There are only five geniuses on the planet," Sariel said, smoothing her hair. "No one knows who they are."

"Well, Jack isn't one of them." She brought a hand to her eyes. "But my point is, that was my life with Jack. For me at the time, it was real. But this? Us? You?" Miranda turned onto her side, watching him. "Even Quain. That feels more real to me than anything I've ever felt before. It may be dangerous and horrible and tragic, but I'm involved in something that's worthwhile. And somehow, I've met you. With the magic and mystery—with you, with me and my life—I feel more real than I ever have. In a weird way, I feel like I was meant to be here all along."

She sat up, looking down at him, running a hand on his chest. "For the first time, things are making sense. I always knew something was off. I never fit in, except with artists and writers. My sister was always normal and perfect. Talented with great hair. My mother never seemed to expect much of me—she still doesn't, every achievement a surprise to her. And I think I always knew my dad was holding a big secret. I'd see him watching me as if he were trying to figure me out, as if he were seeing someone else. But when I'd try to catch his gaze, he'd look away, talk about baseball or the weather. Or he'd ask me about my poems, anything but tell me the truth."

"He never said a thing to you about the adoption?" Sariel asked.

"Not once. Never. So all those years, I felt wrong. Finally, here, with you, I feel like I'm who I'm supposed to be."

Taking her in his arms, he pulled her to him, lying back on the mattress, pressing her against his chest, her breasts and belly and thighs burning into him.

"This is where you belong," he said into her ear, cupping her face in his hands. "This is where I want you."

"So we'll do what we have to, and we'll go home," she said, pushing up a bit, looking at him. "I have my theory that I invented when I was a kid and nothing seemed to be going right. I used it all the times I was feeling different and alone. It's called the 'Everything Will Work Out' theory. Things come together as they are supposed to."

"Have you written about that?" Sariel asked.

"No." She pushed up on her arms, her breasts hanging like ripe fruit in front of him. "But when we get home, I will."

He put his hands on her breasts, and she bent down to kiss him once, twice, and then before he could pull her tight, she whispered, "And after we've had a good vacation and you've taught me some more magic, I'm going to write my novel. It will be about us."

Turning her onto her back, Sariel put his mouth on her pulse, moving his mouth up to her ear. "All I ask is that it has a happy ending."

"It will," she said. "I promise. All we need to do is get through tomorrow."

Sariel whispered "Yes" against her skin, moving his mouth over her body, wanting nothing more than to live in the story they'd started, wanting a happy ending, despite everything.

Chapter Fourteen

Miranda woke up at four in the morning, shivering, even though Sariel was warm against her side. *This is it*, she thought. *This morning I go off to battle.*

She turned onto her back, wishing she had another skill, one that allowed her to pull Sariel, herself, everyone back into the past, back to the place where they could fix this horrible mess. Where would they have to go? All the way back to the scene Sariel had shown her the night before? Would they have to make sure Hadrian didn't end up on the tracks, dying in Laelia's arms? Maybe then Quain wouldn't have escaped. Maybe none of what was planned for today would be necessary. Maybe no one would be hurt. Maybe no one would die.

Moving into Sariel's side, she closed her eyes, hoping for sleep. Sariel breathed in and out, reaching out a hand for her, mumbling. She went into his mind and saw images of movement, fire streaking through a closed room. She felt sorrow and worry and fear.

Pulling away from his dreams, Miranda sighed. She would never be able to fall back to sleep. Her body was awake with nerves, jangling with energy. Not even a Xanax would help.

Two more hours until they awoke, prepared to leave, and thought themselves into a room where they all might be killed. She had paid attention to Sariel's memory of Hadrian. Death came so fast to *Croyant*, trains whipped down the tracks at hundreds of miles per hour, spells keeping away healers. At least in *Moyenne* life, the known rules of physics applied and 911 was still in operation.

Okay, she thought. *Plan. Plan as if you know this is your final chance to live.*

Miranda put a hand on Sariel's shoulder and closed her eyes. She imagined the fortress, the room, she pictured Kallisto, felt the steel of protection around Kallisto's mind, and then found the way in, the softness, the vulnerability. Sariel. Miranda would slide in, just like that, find a way to occupy her, let the others work their charms. It would have to be all right. It couldn't end now; the story was just getting good, perfect, the way she had always wanted it.

Focus, Miranda thought, even as she yawned, her mind growing fuzzy. *Live.*

By six in the morning, Miranda was up, dressed, and standing in the yard of the house with the others, the sky still dark but beginning to lighten. Sariel stood next to her, his hand holding hers. Rufus and Felix stood next to Sariel, all of the brothers looking serious, their long dark hair pulled back with leather ties, their eyes anxious. Lutalo, Baris, and Mazi seemed to be preparing their magic, muttering slightly under their breaths. And Sayblee stood by Miranda, her thoughts completely still, and her energy focused on her hands. Miranda could almost feel the fire growing insider her.

As they waited for Nala, the group was solemn, listening vaguely to each other's morning thoughts—half dream, half conscious. Whenever a worry fluttered up through thought, someone would think another word to push it away, a *No* met with a *Yes*, a *Pain* met with a *Triumph.* Finally, Nala walked out to the yard, closing the door of the house behind her with a flick of her hand.

"Everything is ready," she said, buttoning her yellow robe at her neck, her face calm and serious. "I'm going to pull forth matter for us all. I want us to arrive simultaneously because whatever will happen will start the moment the first arrives. Make sure you are prepared, ready to work according to plan."

Nala looked at them all, her gaze falling last on Miranda. "Are you ready?"

Miranda knew Nala said the words to the entire group, but she heard them in her ears and felt Nala gently slip into her head. *Follow the plan, and we'll be successful.*

Nodding, Miranda gripped Sariel's hand tightly. She felt Nala leave her mind, and she breathed out, hoping Nala hadn't seen the truth. When Miranda had awakened this morning for the second time, Sariel lightly shaking her shoulder, she knew that despite her attempts to rally herself to action, all she wanted to do was go home to San Francisco, taking Sariel with her, the end of the world or not. What she wanted was a nice cup of espresso, the *San Francisco Chronicle,* and Sariel sitting with her at her kitchen table, the morning light shining in, the weather warm, no fog, only a light sea breeze.

Nala raised her hands, but then dropped them. "Before we go, I want to tell you that this fight is our most important. I know that I've asked a great deal from everyone, and if we overcome Quain it will be worth it.

And if we don't, it will be worth it because we made the attempt."

Miranda closed her eyes, a hundred images flashing behind her lids like a crazy movie reel. June, Steve, Viv, Seamus, the kids, even Dan. Pages and pages of poetry. Jack. Sariel at the bar, his hand tight on her arm as they pushed out onto Fern Street. Sariel in her bed, her arms. Sariel's story about his father.

She shook her head and opened her eyes to find Sariel watching her. He brought a hand to her cheek, and at the warm touch of his fingers, Miranda knew why she was here. Because there was no other place she should be.

Raising her arms again, Nala closed her eyes as did they all. Miranda saw the gray rolling toward her, felt the air in swirling particles, and they all moved into it, the Fortress Kendall in front of them.

Before there was anything to see, there was sound, a crack, a whirl of whistling noise, the harsh splinter of wood. Then there was smoke, the flick of fire, and the acrid tang of sulfur.

They'd made it into the fortress; Lutalo's alchemy had worked.

Miranda reached for Sariel, but for some reason, he wasn't there, and she turned her head to see Nala throwing some kind of energy toward two figures in the room. Lutalo pushed Miranda back, and as she pressed against the cool wall, she tried to remember what she was supposed to do. Kallisto. Kallisto's mind.

Focusing on the two figures in the far corner of the large, cavernous room, Miranda recognized Kallisto, her robes swirling as she easily fended off Sayblee's fire. Miranda crouched down and closed her eyes, trying to move her mind through the dense waves of energy in the room. Slowly, she made her way to Kallisto's thoughts, flinching at the hatred the woman exuded. Miranda cringed at the woman's essence, something black and dark and hot, but she remembered what Nala and Sariel had told her. Only she had done this. So she focused on Kallisto's jealousy, the raw nerve she'd shown to Miranda that day in the basement. How Kallisto wanted Sariel to capitulate and follow her, despite her claims that she didn't need him, didn't want him. Miranda worked her way through this flaw, her need, and there she was. Miranda was in.

She knew her physical body was at the back of the room, behind the group that was slowly working its way toward Kallisto and the man, who must be Quain. But Miranda suddenly felt that she was not there as well, part of her inside Kallisto's thoughts and her body. And what power! What force! Miranda felt a thrum of heat and fire each time Kallisto put out energy or deflected what came from the group, and she knew that Kallisto wasn't tired or even drawing a deep breath. She was just playing with them all, juggling magic as she would rubber balls or oranges.

Do you think I'm that ridiculous? came the thought. *Do you really think you have the ability to subdue me?*

Miranda ignored the comment, but she tried to pull away, back into her own body.

Am I that stupid to allow our location out accidentally? What better way would there be to get this messy bunch here?

No, Miranda thought back, stuck in place, her mind feeling slow and tired, as if she were the one throwing out magic. *It's a trap.*

Yes, Kallisto thought, turning most of her attention to Miranda even as she fought off spells and Sayblee's thunderous fire. *How could they think this plan would work? Once we have them, there's no one in the way. Your backup won't arrive to help you. The third* plaque *is already ours. And you, you sad thing, are already gone.*

For some reason, Miranda couldn't even think her way back, finding herself trapped in Kallisto's malicious gloating. Turning out to face the room with Kallisto's vision, she saw Lutalo on the floor, the rest exhausted, trying to fight their way forward. She looked to Kallisto's side and saw the man, Quain, standing almost motionless, his arms outstretched. The only clues that he was doing any magic at all were the tiny flicks of his eyes.

And what terrible eyes: cold, dark, dead, and merciless. Even separated like this from her body, Miranda felt her nausea, the rippling pulses in her stomach.

Be still, came a thought, not Kallisto's. A man's. Quain's. *Be still before you die.*

Another threat, she tried to think. *But I'm still alive.*

Not for long, he said, his voice as hard as the stone walls around them.

Turning her vision back to the room, Miranda tried to yank herself free. She needed to get back to her body. She needed to help them. Help Sariel. But where was he? Straining against Kallisto's grasp, she scanned the room. He wasn't there.

He's gone. Kallisto laughed. *Stuck in his own nightmare.*

You were his nightmare.

Maybe, Kallisto thought, her words full of a bitter laughter, *but now he's stuck in the gray. The very thing he's feared his whole life. He's running and running, unable to find his way out, the matter pressing against his mind and body.*

Everything was getting slower and slower, Miranda feeling her mind pull like taffy from her body. Sariel was stuck in matter? What had Kallisto done to him?

But even as she thought about Sariel, she began to forget her questions. Her head seemed to be unfurling, opening up into nothingness, her synapses slowing. Sariel had told her to back off. But when? Back off from what?

From getting too close. That was it.

Miranda felt her body breathe in, and she tried to find the center of her consciousness, that tiny bead of black in the middle of this sticky confusion. Where was she? Where was her center? All around her was Kallisto's mind, her sharp, quick movements as the group attacked her, her laughter at what she saw Miranda doing now, her constant, low-hummed conversation with Quain.

Letting all of the noise slip by, Miranda pulled together what was left of herself, searching for something she could hold onto. What had given her the energy she felt coming from Kallisto? Had anything made her feel as defined as the woman whose mind she floated in?

She waited for an answer, ignoring everything around her. What was it? There was something. And then the idea pulsed in front of her. Writing. What Sariel had told her back at the house was true. When she was really writing, she felt like she did now, disconnected from flesh, pulled into the ideas and images swirling around her. She grabbed onto the idea, letting herself draw strength from it. She saw herself at her desk, leaning over the keyboard, thinking about flight. Thinking about love. Thinking and writing and imagining about God and the planet and her mother and father and Jack and Sariel. She forgot her fingers, her arms, her mind, her eyes, focusing only on the words she had imagined all these years, knowing now that magic was anything you left your body for, whether it was writing or baking cookies or tending rosebushes. Magic was nothing more than attention, and Miranda saw that her writing, her words, were like sailing through matter or hovering over a kitchen floor. Magic. She was magic, and she felt her body rise up and then, with a sound she heard in her bones but not her ears—a rip of matter and time—she was back in the corner of the room, watching Kallisto and Quain, seeing the group as it was being pushed back against the wall.

Not waiting for an instant, Miranda stood up, closed her eyes, and conjured matter, knowing exactly what she had to do.

She thought of Sariel, his face in her mind as she moved through the gray. But he wasn't there, nothing was. This gray seemed different from any she'd been in, which, she knew, wasn't saying much. Before, even the time when she ended up with Kallisto, Miranda had seen her destination, felt it in her mind, sensing an end. This matter was almost hollow, filled with nothing, a claustrophobic vacuum of space too loosely strung to become anything.

Sariel, she thought. *Where are you?*

Forcing herself to keep searching, she scanned the matter, listening, waiting for a sound, a voice, a message. She kept her eyes closed, filling her thoughts with Sariel, and then finally, from somewhere, a voice.

Here.

Catching the word and holding it in her head, Miranda moved forward, regaining the strength she'd lost while trapped in Kallisto's mind.

Where?

Here.

She felt like she was flying as she had never flown before. Rather than hovering, she was rushing through space and time, turning, twisting, honing in on Sariel's location, knowing that in an instant she'd see his straight stance, his hair hanging behind his shoulders, his strong arms crossed over his chest. Then, in another instant, they'd go back together and fight with the group until it was over.

Miranda drew closer and was about to call out to him when she was caught in flashes of panic, strong, electric currents of fear. She stopped, pulling up short, and saw that Sariel was staring at her unseeing, his face pale, his arms straight at his sides.

Sariel, she thought. *What is it?*

He didn't say anything, his message incoherent, full of random feelings and images: a closed box, deep cold, black curtains, pressure, sadness, clawing, need. Everything in his mind churned together, and Miranda knew he was more afraid than he'd ever been.

Slowly, she moved toward him, wanting to touch him, take his arm, hold him close and find a way back to the room where they were needed. But he moved away, shaking his head.

Stuck, he thought.

No, Miranda said. *We're not stuck. I know the way out.*

His gold eyes were darkened, wild, the irises huge. *We can't go back. We run and run and run, never finding an exit, an opening.*

Yes, we will. We have to.

No. We're here forever.

Your brothers need you.

Sariel blinked, breathed, and then closed his eyes. *Help.*

She moved toward him, taking the end of his sleeve in her hand, working her way slowly up his arm. If only she could heal like he did. She would be able to calm him, warm him, bring him out of panic. Lord knew she'd talked enough college dorm mates down from bad pot brownies, trips, and one too many Vodka Collins. But this seemed worse, as if he'd slipped into his worst . . .

nightmare. Nightmare? That's what Kallisto had said she'd done. Put Sariel in his greatest fear.

It's just a dream, she said, holding his shoulders. *Let me wake you up.*

Sariel nodded and leaned into her, his body shaking. Miranda flooded him with reassurance, finding it somewhere inside herself. *It's a dream. I'm here. Let's go back. I'll show you the way.*

Miranda, he thought. *Miranda.*

They stood there for a moment, until she felt him hold her back, pressing against her, his head resting on her shoulder for a minute as he breathed his fear away. She felt his quick heartbeat slowly calm to normal rhythm.

"Are you all right?" she asked. "Are you here with me?"

He nodded against her shoulder and then lifted his head, breathing in, keeping his eyes on hers the entire time.

Miranda smoothed his hair. "She did this to you on purpose. It's not real. We're not stuck."

"We're not stuck," he repeated, and she could tell he didn't believe her yet.

"I was in her thoughts. She told me she did this to you on purpose, sent you here to your worst fear."

He rubbed his forehead and then shook his head. "God, why didn't I realize what she'd done?"

"Because she put you in a place where you couldn't realize anything," Miranda said, grabbing his hands. "She knew exactly how to hurt you. But we've got to go back. It was a trap all along."

"All right," he said. "Let's get out of here. Now."

Miranda smiled and was just about to close her eyes and conjure them both back to the room when there was a shriek, a wail, and Kallisto was in front of them, her robes fluttering in the matter, her eyes slits of black fury.

"Let me go, you bitch," Kallisto said, raising her hand to release some magic.

In a reflex, Miranda held up her hand, whispered, "No," and she felt some protective energy come from inside her and surround her and Sariel.

Kallisto screamed as if she'd been cut. She banged up to the protection and then backed off.

"You're attached. What happened in the room?" Sariel asked, the color back in his face.

"Let me go!" Kallisto screamed. "I can't be here. I need to go back." She pulled at her hair, her robes, moving at them fast then hitting the protection again.

I was in her mind. Too deep. But then I managed to get out and come here, Miranda thought. *She must have followed me.*

Not on purpose, Sariel thought, staring hard at Miranda. *She had no choice. Your mind pulled her with you. You were stronger than she thought.*

Kallisto spun in the air, throwing out energy, heat, anger. "You worthless man!" she said. "Why are you with her? How did she get here?"

Putting a hand on Miranda's head, he thought, *Follow me. Do what I think.*

In a second, she felt Sariel's thoughts twist with hers and together, their connected thought pushed through the protection Miranda had created and vined toward Kallisto. Miranda felt as though she could see the deep purple and gold rope of their twined energy. Sariel moved them forward, snaking into Kallisto's thoughts, which were available because she was separated from Quain and somehow still connected to Miranda.

More, Sariel thought, and they were in, and their combined thoughts branched off, split, divided into veins of control.

Stay with me, Sariel thought. *Don't stop.*

Miranda didn't stop, even though Kallisto twisted and fought, her mind shooting them both with images of pain and torture and taunts of an infinity of gray matter. Again, Kallisto pushed out the scene of Sariel hanging in the room, his voice and face suffused with love and despair.

Sariel paused, but Miranda urged, *Go on.*

Sariel tore away from the image, leading Miranda around and through, until Kallisto began to quiet, her images slipping into the ether, her thoughts a vague beat of slight resistance.

Now the body, Sariel thought, and they wound around Kallisto, wrapped her tight, taking away her ability to move, layering control on her arms and body and legs until she was still and calm and empty of thought.

With a movement of his arm, Sariel cut the link between them and Kallisto, and Miranda breathed in quickly, feeling the woman truly leave her mind and body, the umbilicus of connection severed.

Now come back, Sariel thought, and Miranda followed him, moving into his mind and then, finally to her own. Blinking, both of them opened their eyes and stood there still, exhausted. Miranda felt the sweat trickle down her neck and her hands shook and tingled.

"We've got to go," Sariel said.

"But what about Kallisto?"

Without looking at Kallisto, who hung like a ghost in the gray, Sariel said, "We're leaving her here in my nightmare."

Turning away, he held Miranda, and together they thought of Felix and Rufus and the rest of the group and the fight that might already be over, and pushed back into the room.

Chapter Fifteen

In a moment, Sariel and Miranda were back, standing next to Sayblee, Baris, and Mazi. Sariel flung out a protection spell, ready for the fight, but then he saw that no one in the room was moving. Everything was quiet, still, even Quain, who stood at the front of the room, his arms crossed in front of his chest. Rufus and Felix and Lutalo were on the floor, and Nala was on a table, stretched out and lifeless.

"Oh, God," whispered Miranda. "What happened?"

Very good question, Quain thought. *The answer, of course, is not much, despite all your careful planning.*

Quain shook his head, looking at Sariel with his dark eyes. *So sad. What a tragedy.*

His heart beating wildly, Sariel started to move toward his brothers, but he felt Miranda hold him still. He jerked away from her grasp, but she grabbed him again.

Don't, she thought. *You can't help them if you're hurt.*

She was right. He and Miranda had come back unexpectedly, thrown up a protection spell, and were safe, for now. Sariel wouldn't be any good to Rufus or Felix or any of the group if he were dead.

"And you will be," Quain said. "Soon enough."

Sariel cringed at the voice. At one time, he'd thought the soft, smooth sounds of Quain's conversation reassuring, hearing it from his bedroom as he was trying to fall asleep. Downstairs, Quain and his father and mother would talk, the wisp of sound enough to lull Sariel to dream.

How touching, Quain thought, his sneer a hiss in Sariel's head. *Childhood memories at a time like this.*

Sariel felt Miranda try to get Sayblee's attention, but the three of them—Sayblee and the two men—were under a *rêve* spell, awake but not conscious enough to hear or speak or think. Then he felt Miranda try to work her thoughts over to Rufus and Felix, but Quain stopped her.

"I haven't quite decided what to do with them all. They may come in handy later. I've lost so many these past weeks. I had to send my other help ahead, so they could prepare for—well you know what will happen. You'll see a brief bit before I dispose of you. But you do have some talent here. And the pretty young thing with her fire arts, well, I'm quite smitten with her already," Quain said, stepping over Rufus as he walked toward Sariel. Quain's robes were singed, one hand red with burn. "And I seem to have lost my best recruit, your lovely former *petite amie.* But off with the old, on with the new, I always say."

"Why are you still here, Quain?" Sariel said, trying to keep his body from lunging out of the protection spell, needing nothing more than to squeeze the life out of Quain. "Don't you have bigger plans than this?"

Quain smiled, his teeth white, slick, and even. Next to Sariel, Miranda flinched, grabbing onto Sariel's arm.

"It was rather a surprise to see Kallisto pulled away like that," Quain said, walking the perimeter of the protection spell. "I'd had such hopes for her, but you." Quain looked at Miranda. "You were stronger than she expected. Stronger than any of us imagined. Much like your mother, I suppose. Annoying woman. Always in the way at the worst of times."

Miranda took in a quick bite of air, her mind full of confused thoughts.

Don't pay attention, Sariel thought, taking her hand. *He's trying to provoke us.*

"Leave Miranda out of this." Sariel kept his eyes on Quain's, watching the thin man's every move as he circled them.

"How noble. Such a gentleman, after all," Quain said. "And again, I see a parent's influence. How touching this all is. I'm almost beside myself."

At Quain's words, Sariel felt his mind fill with angry buzz, all his thoughts white with heat and hate. How good it would feel to grasp his scrawny neck in his hands, strangle him until there wasn't breath or beat in his body, use his feet, hands, legs, his entire body to stop the man from feeling or thinking or being able to walk the planet at all.

Sariel, Miranda thought. *Stop.*

"She's wise," Quain said. "And strong. Stronger than even Kallisto. So I'm going to have to borrow her. Probably forever, or until she's worn out, from work and perhaps pleasure. You see, what I have in mind today needs just that little bit of extra energy. Kallisto was going to help, but, sadly, she's all tied up. What do you say, Miranda? Ready for a little adventure?"

"Leave her out of this," Sariel said. "This isn't her fight. This isn't her battle. She doesn't have the training or background to help you. Take me. I'll do what you want. Just leave Miranda out of this."

Quain smiled broadly, shaking his head. "Again! The nobility! The poise. The sacrifice. What your father wouldn't give to see you now. How puffed up and proud he would be. How much you sound like him, always Zosime and the boys. The family. *Croyant.* The planet. When he could have come with me, worked with me, been by my side and changed everything."

Sariel stared at Quain, watching the man talk, pace the room, his hands moving wildly.

"But no. So virtuous. So 'normal.' So average. So *Moyenne* in thought. That little suburban ghetto you grew up in?" Quain sneered. "You should have known your father years ago, when he was a young man, before that hag Zosime. The magic in the man. He could have had anything he wanted. The world could have been just at his fingertips."

Smiling a face full of hate at Sariel, Quain stopped pacing, standing in front of Sariel again. "What a waste. What did he get out of that life? Two worthless boys." He pointed at Rufus's and Felix's still bodies. "And one who is scared of matter and had to be saved by a woman. Then there's Zosime. A wife? My God, if you could have really known Hadrian like I did. If you could have seen him then. In Rome . . ."

Quain went on, his mind lost in memory and rage, and Sariel quietly took Miranda's hand. Suddenly, he understood everything, the largest missing piece of his life puzzle finally crashing at his feet. Why hadn't he thought of it before? *Croyant* or *Moyenne*, magic or not, everything seemed to always boil down to love, and its offshoots, lust and jealousy. Despite magic and spells and charms, Sariel knew that the only way to counteract death and fear was love. With a sour, acid taste in his mouth, Sariel knew that Quain had loved his father, stayed as his partner for love, killed him for love, punished the world for a love he had never had enough of.

Because he'd been rejected by love, he embraced hate and fear and murder.

I could have ended up like him, Sariel thought, thinking of his anger after Kallisto betrayed him and the way he'd wanted to hide from everything and everyone he'd loved. If not for Miranda, he might have become as lost and hard as Quain.

But he wasn't like Quain. He had found Miranda, and Sariel knew that if Miranda were taken, she'd need clues to get to Quain, just as she had with Kallisto.

Miranda? he thought.

She didn't think back right away, her mind full of stunned amazement at Quain's rant.

Miranda, Sariel said again. *Pay attention.*

What? she thought after a moment. *Sariel, what are we going to do?*

I'm going to give you some images, he thought back. *Take them all. Use them all if you have to. Remember what you did with Kallisto.*

But she said it didn't work, Miranda thought.

She was lying. Look where she is now. Remember that. I'll come as soon as I can.

And then, as Quain told stories of the past, the past he wanted more than the future he was killing for, Sariel gave Miranda the images that might save her and them all.

Quain was sweating, his robe wet at the neck. His story over, he wiped his face with his hand, even his angry smile gone. "But that's the past. And look how far I've gone without Hadrian. In only a matter of minutes, I'll have the third *plaque.* The world will finally be the way I want it."

Sariel squeezed Miranda's hand once, and then let it

go, moving as close as he could to Quain within the protection spell.

"That's right," Sariel said. "Just the way you want it. But where are your followers, Quain? All those recruits you had all over the world? In the past week, they've fled their posts, hunted out by my colleagues. You say you've sent your people on ahead of you, but they weren't here when we arrived. No one was here but Kallisto, and she's gone for good. The only person still loyal is that tubercular Labaan. And now, when you need the rest, who is standing by your side?" Sariel pushed out the words, letting his stone wall fall in his mind. Quain couldn't see what he was doing.

Quain laughed, throwing back his head, his face pasty and yellowed, his eyes a burning black. "I have two *plaques* and soon the third. I don't need anyone but your lovely girlfriend, Miranda. My miracle. She'll be my conduit. My energy. Too bad she won't survive it."

Miranda breathed in deeply, but she didn't say a word. Sariel felt her mind close down, protecting the images he'd just given her.

Quain stopped talking, staring at Sariel, lifting a hand and then letting it fall to his side. "You are so like him."

His stomach clenched at the thought of Quain touching him, but Sariel kept his gaze even and strong, his mind shut. He said nothing, watching Quain's anger and megalomania twist across his face.

"Enough! Enough!" With one quick movement, Quain shattered the protection spell, grabbed Miranda, and then held up a hand.

Sariel felt the wall in his mind shudder, but he clamped it down, knowing that the plan that he and Miranda had was the only thing that could save her.

"Good-bye, Valasay. Give your father my regards,"

Quain said, holding up a hand, and then all Sariel felt was darkness, pain, the quiet of the empty room, and then nothing.

He floated in his mind, circling the wall he still held tight. His consciousness scurried like a rat along the stones, trying to find something. But what? He moved, sniffing in the corners, round and round and round. Sariel felt the dirt below the wall, his little feet moving in swift, flickering steps. He had a question he knew he needed to answer, but it was so easy to pad around the wall, nothing new in sight, the dirt and stone and the movement of his feet something he would get used to. But there was something. What was he looking for? What had he lost?

He knew he needed to find it, so he moved faster, a fan of dust behind him. Round he went, again and again, until he began to see something, a light, a waver of white and gold. That was it. Sariel ran toward the opening, but it was far away and receding. The faster he went, the faster it disappeared. So he pressed on, his body growing as he did, changing from rat to cat to lion to horse to gazelle. All he could feel was his blood and breath and muscles, his entire being wanting nothing more than that fractured slit of color. On and on, round the wall, toward the light. And there it was. All he had to do was jump across it, but he was in his body again, his man's body, and the jump was far and wide and long and hard. But he had to. He knew it. It was for someone he loved. Someone very important. Who was it? Who did he need to jump for? As he stared at the light, his mind slowly opened.

Miranda.

Sariel started running again, swinging his arms, and then he leaped, pushing off hard with his legs. His feet touched the edge of the light, and then he slipped and fell and then clung to the corner of brightness, his body dangling into a pit of forever darkness. As his hands slipped on the bright, smooth surface, Sariel could feel the darkness reach up tentacles that curled around his ankles, his calves, moving up to his thighs. Aching up from the bottom of the pit, he felt such an endless welling of despair and loneliness and hate. He wouldn't go there. He couldn't.

Pulling as hard as he could, his arms shaking from the effort, he kicked off the tentacles, battering them with his feet and then yanked himself up on the ledge, taking in a huge lungful of air, blinking against the brightness. Breathing out, he pulled himself up fully and let his eyes adjust. In the middle of the light was a misty window and through it, he saw the room he'd just left. There, stretched out and unconscious on the table, was Nala. Sayblee, Baris, and Mazi still stood like zombies, their shoulders touching. Lutalo, Rufus, and Felix were on the floor, barely breathing.

Some other form he didn't quite recognize lay right before him, cold and motionless.

He knew he had to get back to the room. Three more steps. That's all he needed to take. But his body felt heavy and stuck. Each tiny movement felt like he was lifting mountains. But he did it. One foot down, the next up and before it. One. The next foot moved, the other moving. Two. He was breathing hard, his lungs empty, his head pounding, his hair slick with sweat. Only one more. He pulled his foot up, set it down and then he leaned forward, grabbing the edges of the light, and fell through, hearing his own scream as he plummeted down, falling so fast and with such speed, he slipped out of consciousness.

Sariel jerked up, panting. He was sitting on the floor of the room, shivering in a cold sweat, his body weak.

Everything was as he'd seen it from the light, just the same. Miranda was still gone.

He wiped his face and grabbed onto a chair, pulling himself up and leaning against it for a moment. As he stood, his heart slowly began to beat in a normal rhythm, his breathing slowed, and he went back to his mind and lifted the stone wall, letting all his thoughts out.

Turning toward Mazi, Baris, and Sayblee, who moved slightly to imaginary waves in a nonexistent ocean, Sariel closed his eyes, held up a hand and said, "*Réveiller.*"

Sariel opened his eyes and watched them carefully, but they didn't startle, blink, turn to him. They were blank, empty, seaweed swaying in tidal currents. Nothing. Sariel was too weak, his powers drained from escaping the darkness.

He sat in the chair, leaned over, and rested his head in his hands. Miranda was with Quain. Even now, she could have already been used up, cast aside. Quain might be changing everything at this moment, the world in chaos. And Miranda? Miranda!

Sariel breathed in and stood up, holding out his hand, and closing his eyes. Again, he said, "*Réveiller.*"

Without opening his eyes, he slumped back into the chair, his legs unable to carry his weight, all his muscles in revolt. But at a murmur, a sigh, he looked up. The three of them were looking at him, rubbing their faces, turning to look for the others.

"What happened?" Sayblee asked. "Where's Quain? Where's Miranda?"

When Sariel heard Miranda's name come from Sayblee, the name of his beloved in the room like a song, he stood up, shaking off fatigue.

"Quain has her," Sariel said quickly. "We need to wake the others. I don't know what spell he used. But he put me somewhere—it took all my energy to wake you up."

Mazi and Baris nodded and hurried over to Nala. Sayblee came to Sariel, put a hand on his shoulder, letting her hot, fiery energy course between them. For a minute, they were joined by her heat, and Sariel felt life come back to him, his blood and heart beating stronger, filling his brain with oxygen.

Slowly, Sayblee took away her hand and looked at him. "Are you better?"

Sariel breathed out, his lungs no longer heavy from exertion. "Thank you."

"Let's go tend to your brothers and Lutalo." She grabbed Sariel's arm and they walked together toward the unconscious men. "We need to—"

"We need to find Miranda. Quain is going to use her up and toss her away," Sariel said. "He's going to kill her to get what he wants."

Nala awakened on the table, holding her arm against her body. "We must go," she said, as Mazi healed her wound. "Leave them for later."

Sariel ignored her, putting a hand on Rufus and Felix, as Sayblee touched Lutalo. He wasn't going to fight Quain without his brothers. Now that Sariel knew what hurt Quain, the three Valasay brothers were the weapon of choice. They were from Hadrian, of Hadrian, and, like Hadrian, didn't want Quain. Hated him. With the images he'd given Miranda, Sariel knew that he and his brothers could do the rest.

Cold to the touch, his brothers seemed almost frozen, stiff and still and barely breathing.

"Sariel!" Nala said, but he ignored her, busy determining what Quain had done to the three men.

"It's a *paralysie* spell," Sariel said. "Counteract it with *survenir.*"

Sayblee nodded, closing her eyes and putting both hands on Lutalo.

Breathing in, Sariel closed his eyes, feeling the warmth inside him expand and pour from his hands to his brothers. "*Survenir,*" he said, letting the word into his body and pass from his skin to theirs.

For a moment nothing happened. Sariel opened his eyes and wondered if he was still weak from escaping the pit, but then, Rufus stirred, and then Felix.

"Bloody hell," Rufus said, sitting up, blinking. "What am I doing on the flipping floor?"

Felix rubbed his forehead and then pushed back his hair, wincing as he touched a knot on his head.

"Check me for a concussion later, bro," he said as Sariel extended them both a hand, pulling up his brothers.

"We don't have much time. But I have to show you something."

Standing close, their arms entwined, Sariel let his brothers see and hear the memory of his conversation with Quain and then showed Rufus and Felix the images he'd given Miranda.

"He's mad," Rufus said, opening his eyes.

"He's deadly," Sariel said.

"Let's go," Felix said, and the three of them separated and turned to the rest of the group. Lutalo was awake but limping slightly, Sayblee holding him by the elbow. Baris, Mazi, and Nala watched Sariel, waiting for a word.

"Nala," Sariel said, and she held up a hand.

"I listened in. You are right. It's the only plan we have. We need to get to the third *plaque.* We need to finish this."

Limping and groaning and moving slower than they had earlier, the group came together, conjured matter, and disappeared.

Chapter Sixteen

Jerked away from Sariel and then jolted into a room warm with yellow light, Miranda gasped. She'd seen no gray and come to the room faster than any of the times she'd traveled matter.

"You're used to horse and buggy, my dear," Quain said. "You just traveled at the speed of light."

"Where are we?" Miranda said, trying to distract him while she pulled down the wall in her mind as Sariel had taught her. As her eyes adjusted to the light, she saw the comfortable room, the upholstered wingback chairs, the dying embers in the stone fireplace, the thick plaster walls. On a rug, a shaggy dog slept, deaf to the sounds of the intruders.

"You are in my home," said a voice from a dark corner.

Miranda felt Quain's surprise and then anger fill the room. Slowly, she let a tendril of thought rest near his mind, waiting for the moment when she would have to go in and let loose the images Sariel had given her. A flash of grief and worry surged through her mind, and she clamped it down behind the wall. She couldn't think of Sariel. Couldn't remember her last vision of him on the floor, pale and still, his dark hair splayed around him.

"Adalbert," Quain said, his voice slick with power.

"Yes, and I see you've brought a visitor. You're both welcome, if uninvited," Adalbert said, coming out from the corner. He was old, his hair white, his face covered in a wispy beard. "What can I do for you?"

Quain moved forward. "Where is it?"

"Where is what, Quain?" Adalbert said. "Do sit down."

Ignoring him, Quain moved even closer. "You don't have the *plaque* here. And how stupid of you to divert me. Never mind. I have time now that I've managed to dispose of your second team, no better than the first you sent after me. Quite practically, I'll kill you and move to the *plaque*'s true location."

"Oh, my boy. You've arrived at the correct place. It most certainly is here," Adalbert said.

Quain laughed, the sound strained and hoarse. "Don't think me a fool! If it were, where are all the spells? The guards? All your loyal people? How could I have come without cracking through a hundred curses?"

Miranda hugged herself, watching Quain closely. His mind was whirring, ideas flowing in his head, thoughts hissing like steam even at the edges where she hovered.

"You are being rather rude," Adalbert said. "Do you want to introduce your guest?"

"Silence, old man!" Quain roared, moving closer, his arms wide. "Don't condescend to me. Where is the *plaque*?"

Adalbert held open his palms and shook his head, a small smile on his lips. "Alas, I'm afraid I can't quite divulge that information."

With a shudder, Quain released a sound, a movement that Miranda could only liken to a sonic boom.

She felt it in her feet first, the waves moving up her body, into her chest, throat, head. She felt all her organs, her blood, her bones seem to split apart atom by atom. Miranda could feel herself pulling away from herself, the only thing holding her together something thick in the middle of her, something elastic, and she closed her eyes, focused on that. And there was something else, something giving her strength from outside, something holding her skin together like a gentle hand.

As the entire house shook, frames and pictures dropped to the floor, glass in the kitchen cracked and splintered on the tile, and the thick, ancient walls rumbled and groaned. On the floor, the dog howled.

Shaken and tossed at the same time, Miranda was thrown back hard against the wall and then thudded to the wood floor, her tendril of thought near Quain's mind tearing away. Adalbert fell with a moan, and she breathed in, wanting to help him.

Quain leaned over Adalbert and then roared, shaking the room again. Again, Miranda felt as though her body were being pummeled from the inside out, her heart and stomach ready to punch out of her body. But then the room stilled, and she tried to find her breath.

"You may be old," he said to Adalbert. "But your mind is strong. I'll tear into you and get what I need."

But instead of hurting Adalbert, Quain paced, talking to himself. Exhausted, Miranda stayed sitting on the floor, but brought her tendril of thought back to his mind, resting on the edges, cringing at the hate and anger inside the man. If he was still a man. Something about him seemed metallic, hard, cold, as if his soul had been converted to lead by the alchemy of revenge.

Slowly, she moved the tendril in, letting it slip through his thoughts. But she was scared, knowing what had happened when she'd gone too far into Kallisto.

The last thing she wanted was to be trapped in Quain's mind, following him around forever, swirling in his hate and fear and ugliness.

But she had to. For Sariel. For her fallen angel on the floor of the Fortress Kendall. For him, she would do all that she hadn't been able to do in her life. Here, with her new magic, she would create something good before she died. Something that would last longer than words.

You are brave, came Adalbert's thought. *And you will succeed. Keep going, and I will help you.*

Not wanting to attract Quain's attention, Miranda didn't answer Adalbert, but moved on, past Quain's wild diatribes, searching for the place to unload the pictures and thoughts and feelings about Hadrian.

Adalbert struggled to his feet, smoothing his robe. "The truth is, Quain, that I will never tell you where the *plaque* is. You could shake this whole house down to stone and mortar and dust, but I wouldn't tell."

Miranda gasped, Quain's hate flushing red and black in his mind. She lost her place in his thoughts, almost pulled out, but then felt something strong guiding her, holding her firm.

"You will tell me!" Quain yelled. "Now!"

"Now is a good time," Adalbert said, and Miranda heard it from Quain's ear.

Breathing in, she opened her mind, flooded Quain's with all that Sariel had given her. First there was a portrait of Hadrian, so exactly like Sariel, his long black hair tied behind his neck, his dark eyes full of love for the person who took the photo. Zosime. Then there was Hadrian with his three boys, teaching them how to conjure matter, the four of them laughing as they moved through the gray. There was Hadrian kissing Zosime, holding her close, telling her that he loved her as Quain stood in the next room.

"Does he have to stay?" Zosime was saying, her voice an irritated whisper.

Hadrian shrugged. "I can't just send him home. But I'll figure a way to get rid of him. Don't worry. He's not going to be my partner for that much longer. Adalbert's promised."

Quick flashes of story pressed through Miranda into Quain: Hadrian's irritation over the way Quain dealt with a prisoner. A secret meeting with the Council about Quain's methods of punishment. A dinner party, where no one wanted to listen to his stories. Zosime and Hadrian leaving a meeting early to avoid Quain altogether.

No, Quain thought.

Yes, Miranda thought back, giving him more. Retold stories of Hadrian's youth, the girls he kept secret from Quain so Quain wouldn't scare them away. Meeting Zosime and disappearing, wanting to avoid Quain. Miranda left him the feelings: guilt, annoyance, irritation, anger, despair, and finally boredom.

Quain howled, twisting his head. *You lie!*

No, she said, and she began to pull out, away, but then she knew something was wrong. The firm guidance she'd felt from Adalbert disappeared. She felt heavy, stuck, the same way she'd felt in Kallisto's mind. All around her, Quain's reactions and thoughts swirled, pressing her closer and closer to his center, his dark, nasty center, black and full of greed and fear and violence.

Say you lie!

No, she thought weakly. She couldn't leave, and she wouldn't. Miranda knew that everything that had been important to Sariel was dependent on her staying, giving Quain these thoughts. So she repeated them, and even though they now came from her slowly, she felt Quain's renewed anger.

With her last bit of energy, she thought some more, letting out the final images, the last words Hadrian said, retold to Zosime by Laelia.

"I love her," Hadrian had said, gripping Laelia's arm as she knelt over him on the métro track. "Tell her that. Tell the boys. I love nothing as I love them all."

Quain moaned, his *No* the sound of a train whistle in a long dark tunnel. But Miranda held on, thinking. She thought through the sound of something coming into the room, a whack and whir of magic. She thought through the sound of three strong male voices crying out together, *"Cesser!"*

Miranda thought as she imagined that Quain's mind was drifting away from her, his anger lighter, lessened, gone. She thought until she couldn't think, until her thoughts were filled with static darkness. And her last thought, when she could feel the electricity from her body flickering and fading away, was of Sariel. Sariel on the floor of the room, Sariel holding her in his arms in the dark, warm room of the house. Sariel's face above hers, his arms around her shoulders. As her mind shut down, she breathed in oranges, musk, the salt of his lovely skin.

She was floating in pure light, comforted by arms that weren't there. Miranda couldn't open her eyes, but she saw the brightness from behind her eyelids, felt the warmth of the space on her skin.

Where was she? This wasn't like the near-death scenarios on *Oprah.* There wasn't a pinprick of light at the end of a dark tunnel. Her father, Steve, wasn't waving from the opening, beckoning her, calling for her. No Jesus or Buddha or Mohammed in white robes, welcoming her back to the source. No chorus of angels. No soul mate waiting with anticipation for her return. No view of herself on the floor of Adalbert's house, sprawled out dead.

This was like cotton. Like being asleep and awake at the same time. She was alone here, but not lonely. Her body was so free and lithe, and she twisted and twirled, flying high as she'd always imagined she could, the warm buoyant air holding her like . . . holding her like . . .

"Miranda?" a woman said in her ear.

Turning to the strangely familiar voice, Miranda tried to pull open her eyes. But she couldn't. She remembered dreams where she tried to read, her lids stuck together as if with glue, the images of words fuzzy and dark when she managed to lift a lid for a second. She was dreaming. This white cotton world was a dream, as was the voice she recognized but couldn't remember.

"Yes?" Miranda said to the voice.

"How are you?"

"I'm fine. I'm dreaming." Miranda spun in the white, breathing in the pure air. "I'm dreaming and spinning."

Miranda felt the woman move closer, resting a cool, smooth hand on her shoulder. "This isn't a dream."

She stopped moving, feeling the woman's hand on her body, light and weightless. "Am I dead? This isn't how it's supposed to be. I've read a lot, and this is not what I'm supposed to get."

"No, you aren't dead. But you have to make a choice. And it's an important one." The woman sat next to her, and Miranda could feel her heat and energy, a current known and unknown at the same time.

"Who are you?" Miranda asked.

"My name's Laelia," the woman said.

Resting back on the air, Miranda thought she knew that name, something in her mind registering it. But all her memories seemed to be leaving her, nothing as important as the next moment of air and movement.

"Oh. Hello," Miranda said. "Why are you here?"

"I needed to talk with you," Laelia said. "Before you go on."

"Go on where?" Miranda asked. "Go to what?"

But as soon as she asked the questions, she didn't care, knowing that she could stay here in this warm protection forever. She wouldn't have to do anything here but float and think her thoughts that were so light and unconcerned. Maybe she couldn't open her eyes. But did she need to? She could feel everything with her body, spin unclothed and unconcerned, all of this like a warm bath that never gets cold. All of this feeling, the light twists and turns her body made in the air, was like sailing through the best poem she'd ever written. Better.

"Miranda!" Laelia shouted.

"What? God, what? You sound like my mother." As she said the word mother, the idea of mother, the idea of June, began to fade as well.

Laelia grabbed her by the shoulders and leaned close. Her breath smelled like spring.

"Were you ready to leave? Were you ready to say good-bye to Sariel?"

At the sound of his name, Miranda suddenly felt heavier, fuller of body and blood. Breathing in, she smelled oranges.

"Sariel," Miranda said. "No. No, I wasn't ready to leave him."

Laelia gripped her harder. "He's trying to save you right now. Can't you feel him? Can't you hear him?"

Trying to find a strand of thought, Miranda concentrated, worked against the pull of her body to the smooth air all around her. Sariel. Was he there? Could she feel him? What was he saying? Was he hiding somewhere in the brightness? Wait. She felt something, but it was so light it took all her concentration. At first, it felt as tiny as a dust mote flitting across her cheek, but the pressure grew, and she recognized a feeling. Warmth. Not like here with its white buoyancy. But rich and warm like melted butter, like caramel, like the color of Sariel's amber eyes.

The heat radiated up her body, filled her with dense flesh, with blood that moved through all her veins and arteries, with harsh air she pulled into her lungs. His hands were on her, his voice at the edges of her mind. *Wake up,* he said, his voice full of sound and feeling. *Come back to me.*

"You can hear him now," Laelia said, shaking Miranda's shoulders harder. "You must go to him. Wake up, Miranda. Wake up."

Miranda pulled open her eyes and looked up at the woman, her figure framed by the fading light. She breathed in, stunned. Looking back at Miranda was herself, capacious red hair, freckles, light blue eyes.

"Who are you?" she asked, but Laelia said nothing, bending down to kiss Miranda's forehead.

"Do as I did not. Go into life," Laelia said, and she faded away with the light, leaving Miranda heavy and sad and limp as unfolded laundry.

Sariel's voice was louder now, telling her to stay with him.

"I'm here," she said, reaching up and feeling his long, smooth hair under her hand. "I've come back."

When she opened her eyes again, Miranda was in a bedroom drawn dim with thick velvet curtains, and her body did not feel light and buoyant and free as it had in the buoyant light world. She felt sore and stiff and achy, as if she'd had the flu for weeks. On the table beside the bed was the same tray of healing herbs and the strange triangle she'd seen at Sariel's house when he'd healed her ankle. Obviously, she was in need of healing again.

This wasn't just the flu or a terrible fever she was recovering from. In fact, she felt like she'd been beaten with a chair or maybe a couch, her neck and back so painful, she dropped her head back on the pillow.

"How are you, my dear?" Adalbert said, looking down at her kindly. He was smiling, but she could see that he was tired, too, and a large purple welt gleamed on his cheek.

Miranda turned gingerly, her neck aching as she did. "I'm not sure," she said.

"Quite understandable." Adalbert smiled. "Though we already met under the most trying of circumstances, I'm afraid we've not been properly introduced. I'm Adalbert Baird."

"Miranda Stead." She tried to move her hand from underneath the blanket, but Adalbert waved her off.

"No, no. Don't move. You need to rest."

"I feel like I was run over by a lorry, or whatever it is you call them here."

"Worse," Adalbert said. "You were hit with a *dérangement du matière* spell, as was I. Never felt such a thing in my life."

"You mean when Quain made that—that sonic boom thing?" she asked. "He messed up matter?"

Adalbert nodded. "And as we are created of matter, we were, as you say, messed up, too. All the atoms in the room pulled away from each other for an infinitesimal amount of time. And then slammed back together. Then Quain did it again. Bodies don't take kindly to that."

"But I saw you stand up afterward," Miranda said. "I couldn't get off the floor."

He patted her knee gently. "I was trained to protect myself, and fortunately, I was given information quite recently on how to protect myself from just such a powerful spell. And if I recall correctly, you were busy working on Quain. You did a wonderful job, my dear."

She looked at his cheek again and noticed that he was favoring one hand over the other.

"Minor injuries. Doesn't hurt at all. Sariel will tend to me later," he said. "I learned to fall in Aikido classes during a six-week class in the village with five-year-olds. I can somersault with the best of them, even though they laugh at me and call me 'Grandpa.'"

His voice was soothing, deep, and calm, the voice she always imagined Santa Claus or God would have. For a moment as she listened to him speak, she drifted away into a light sleep, but then awoke minutes later, her body prickling with adrenaline.

"He didn't get the *plaque*?" Miranda asked, opening her eyes.

"No, he didn't. And while you were delivering Quain the message from Sariel, Phaedrus and his group were able to retrieve the other two *plaques* and save the remaining members of their group. They also found Kallisto and took her to a place even she will not escape from."

Miranda nodded. "Are you sure?"

"As sure as I can be, though Kallisto has proven an interesting case. But one thing at a time. We need to focus on healing and mending this rift in our world."

"But how did you manage to get to Quain?" Miranda asked.

"Quain's protective spells were weakened when you enraged him with the memories." Adalbert sighed. "Unfortunately, Quain was still strong enough to elude us."

"He's out there still?" Miranda asked, feeling her body tense and ache.

Adalbert nodded. "But much less powerful."

"Are we safe?"

Adalbert breathed in, bringing a finger briefly to his mouth. "For now, yes. It will take quite a while for him to recover, much less to return to power. And now we know his secrets."

Closing her eyes for a minute, Miranda thought about all the time before the moment she met Sariel. She'd felt safe in the world, even though there were toxic agents held in dark caves by terrorists, earthquakes just under the skin of the earth, diseases growing in petri dishes in clandestine labs in the Ukraine, flash floods held in the clouds overhead. Quain was like these horrors now, devastating, but something she could ignore, at least for the time being.

Maybe later she and Sariel would do something about Quain, but not now. Not for a while.

Miranda opened her eyes and nodded slightly, trying not to move her body too much. "Sariel told me about the *plaques.* How they hold all the power. But are they religious? What do they mean?"

Adalbert fumbled in his pocket, and then glanced at Miranda as he held up his pipe. "Do you mind?"

She shrugged and said, "No." Pipe tobacco always reminded her of her father. Even now, she could hear the *tap tap* of Steve's pipe on the mantel in the family room as he dislodged tobacco, the silence that followed as he tamped fresh smoke into the bowl of the pipe with his thumb.

Adalbert lit his pipe, sucking down on the stem. "Three is an ancient number."

"Like the Trinity."

"Older. Much older. It represents the cycle of life. The ancients worshipped a woman's body because it moves through three cycles, the maiden, the mother, and the crone."

Miranda smiled. "I've always thought there needs to

be something between mother and crone. Maybe badass woman?"

"That sounds like a poem you could write," Adalbert said, taking in a draft of smoke and then blowing a forked plume out through his nostrils. "But to the ancients, *Moyenne* and *Croyant* alike, a woman moved through these stages, bleeding, giving life, dying so new life could begin. *Moyenne* beliefs moved away from recognizing this pattern, turning to gods and then one god, the One. However, the ancient *Croyant* respected that cycle, worshipped the rhythms in the earth and in humans, and made the *plaques*, forging them with power, to represent the cycle as well as the elements of earth, water, and sky. Each plaque is a part of the three."

"*Les Croyant de Trois*," Miranda said, as if repeating the words by rote. "The believers of three."

"Yes," Adalbert said.

"The three cycles. Not three gods."

"Quite correct. And if Quain had been able to put them together, he would have been able to create. Creation is not specific. It's not good or bad. It just is, but he would have been in control of it. And as you saw, what Quain wanted was control, power, and most importantly, revenge. He wanted all of us to pay because he'd lost his best friend, his love, his connection to life."

Leaning back on her pillow, Miranda realized she could still feel Quain, taste his despair at the memories she'd flooded him with. For thirty years, he'd held his vision of Hadrian tightly, blaming the loss of him on Zosime or the children or the job. Quain's mind had been bitter and hateful and full of sharp spikes of rage, but under it all was loss and grief, nothing more sinister but sinister it became.

"So where was the third *plaque*? Why did we end up at your house?"

Adalbert laughed. "It was on my dining room table. Quain couldn't see it there because it looked so ordinary amongst the plates and cups and half-eaten pudding."

Miranda closed her eyes, laughing in her throat, too tired to move the sound into her mouth. Because she knew he could hear her, she thought, *If the* plaque *is so important, why did you have it on your dining room table?*

"It seemed the safest place for the moment. This house," he paused, and Miranda opened her eyes, watching his hands move in a circle, "is well protected. It withstood the shock of Quain's assault, and I know its secrets."

Miranda moved slightly, tweaking her neck in the process. She closed her eyes at the pain. She was so tired. How long had she been sleeping?

Adalbert waved his hand. "You've been sleeping for two days, Sariel with you most of the time."

"Where is he now?" she said.

"He had," Adalbert said, "a little errand to run and asked me to stay here with you for a while."

Two days. Two days with Sariel that she forgot. Now they were even.

"Yes, the memories. You'll be glad to know," Adalbert said, "that Sariel is in full possession of his time with you."

Miranda smiled and then flushed, wondering what Adalbert must think of her, falling into bed with Sariel when she thought he wasn't real.

Adalbert pulled gently on his beard. "Love is an amazing thing. I try to not judge it, whatever its form."

They were silent for a while, Miranda closing her eyes and letting this information sink in. Sariel remembered. They could put the past and the present together and start right. Now, she knew who and what he was and could live in his world. The question was, could he live in hers, with June and Viv and her poetry and her past that she knew and the past that she didn't? Miranda slipped back into sleep, into her dream, the light, the buoyant air, the woman holding her, kissing her forehead.

She opened her eyes and turned slowly to Adalbert. "Who was she?" And then, before he could answer, she asked, "Who am I?"

For a moment, Adalbert didn't say anything. The antique wooden clock on the bureau ticked out seconds and then minutes. She felt Adalbert searching her mind, finding her memory of the woman in the white world. Resting back on the pillow, she let him see the dream time she'd floated through, the moments after she let loose the last of Sariel's memories.

Clearing his throat, Adalbert nodded. "When I heard from Nala and Phaedrus about you, I realized that something that had happened long ago was coming back to haunt me. Because the world works in circles, I wasn't surprised to find you with us, but I felt responsible that you'd had no training. That you'd had to face Kallisto without knowing your true powers."

Outside, the light was beginning to fade, starlings *whooeeing* in the branches of the birch tree just outside the bedroom window. Miranda waited, stayed outside of Adalbert's thoughts, wanting her story the old-fashioned way.

"The woman who came to you was named Laelia Barton—"

"Yes," Miranda said, remembering now where she'd heard the name before. "Hadrian's friend. The one who gave Sariel the memories of the train."

Adalbert nodded, pulling on his beard. "Correct. Laelia worked occasionally with Hadrian and Quain, doing the same work Sariel does now. She was with Hadrian when he died, and the experience of his death, the manner of Quain's betrayal, destroyed her. What we didn't know then was that she was pregnant. She was distraught, upset, and stopped working and stayed at home. Rather than intervene, the Council and I decided to let her have her time to herself to heal herself. For months, we didn't hear from her and then one day, we learned that she'd walked onto the train tracks and was killed. Like Hadrian."

Suddenly, Miranda's stomach started to ache, tears pricking her eyes. Here it was. Finally, she'd found the love of her life, and in just one second, Adalbert was going to tell her Sariel was her half-brother. It was too Greek tragedy, too ironic, too awful, and she looked at the ceiling, shaking her head, wishing she could disappear right now.

"Oh, no. No!" Adalbert interrupted her thoughts. "No, my dear. She didn't love Hadrian that way. Certainly, she loved him, but as a friend, a colleague, and partner. His death destroyed her, but so did love. And she wasn't in love with Hadrian. She was in love with your father."

Breath left Miranda's body, and Viv's weepy words came back to her. *Dad was gone again on one of his trips and then he came home. A trip somewhere. Far away. And then he walked into our room and put you in the crib.*

"Yes," Adalbert said. "Your father loved Laelia, but because of your mother and sister and because he could not be a part of the *Croyant* world, he chose his life in the U.S. over her. Laelia took her life when he was here on business, and he brought you back with him."

Miranda tried to say something, but she had no words. Her entire life was clicking into place. June's distance and periodic disappointment and disapproval, Miranda's flight in the backyard, her red hair in a family of blondes, her inability to fit in. *Click, click, click.* All her strangeness and awkward moments and feelings of being just on the outside of what was real for everyone else slid into a pattern she could understand. Nothing had ever made as much sense as what Adalbert was telling her.

Adalbert continued. "It wasn't until much later that we found out about you, and by then, you were in your life in San Francisco. We thought it best to let you live in ignorance, never thinking that you'd find yourself in a room full of *Croyant.* Never imagining that you'd fall in love with Sariel. Never thinking you'd be as talented as you are." Adalbert patted her knee again. "I've tired you out. I should have waited until you were stronger."

"What was she like?" Miranda asked, bringing her hand out from under the blankets and putting it on Adalbert's. "My mother. Am I like her?"

"She . . ." Adalbert thought and then nodded. "She was intuitive and gifted and fragile. She could identify a person in a crowded city by a single sigh. She was beautiful and sensitive, too sensitive, I fear, and she was a poet. That you were able to finish what she could not would have given her so much happiness. It must have, actually, if she appeared to you."

Stunned, Miranda imagined Laelia's face over hers. *Go into life,* she'd said, even though she'd ended her own. She must have figured it out somewhere in that brightness, learned that life was worth it despite pain.

"Love," Adalbert continued, "is the magic we can't always understand, regardless of skill or gifts or powers. Here I sit, the armiger of the *Croyant* Council, and yet"—he waved his hand—"alone in this large house. Childless. Look how love twisted Quain and Kallisto. Even Laelia couldn't bear its weight. If you have found love with Sariel, regardless of how quickly it appeared or how startling your initial meeting was, you owe it to yourself to feel it. To stay with it, to try it out even if there's hurt at times. Both of you chose each other over death, using your feelings to reunite. It would have been so much easier to stay in that dream world, Miranda, to float with no burden. Life is much harder than death. But you heard his voice and came back. Don't forget his call."

For a moment, Miranda felt the future like a gaping hole. She felt like her brain was full of those atoms Sariel told her about in one of his discussions about matter—free radicals—the kind that ricochet wildly and damage other cells as they bound hopelessly. There were too many things to worry about: Quain, Laelia, June, Sariel.

"Will we be okay?" she asked. "What will happen?"

Adalbert took another suck on his pipe and then blew a smoke ring. Both of them watched as it moved in the air, sagged, and drifted apart. "My dear girl, because we can't measure now, later is impossible to determine."

He leaned over her. He smelled of wood smoke and tobacco, his blue eyes filled with the light she'd seen in her dream. As he touched her shoulder, her body filled with warmth that swirled into her soreness, her aches, her longing for Sariel. His touch lifted the pain away, and Miranda breathed in, feeling lighter.

"Sleep now," Adalbert said.

Miranda tried to smile, to nod, but she was already asleep, hearing in her deepest mind Sariel's voice say *Come back to me.*

Chapter Seventeen

It was late when Sariel returned to Adalbert's house, the sky black and starless, the house cleared of dinner dishes. Sariel stood outside the door of Miranda's bedroom, carrying the things he'd brought back from his place and hers. Before going upstairs, he'd checked in on Felix, who had a concussion, and Rufus, who'd managed to break three fingers when he'd fallen to the floor at the fortress. Both were healed, but resting, watching football on Adalbert's television, Fabia sitting between them on the couch.

"Why doesn't he just make a forward pass?" Felix was saying. "Rugby is a completely ridiculous game."

Rufus laughed. "Don't say that outside this house. Or else you'll be thrown into the middle of a scrum."

"Both of you need to turn the bloody telly off and go to bed," Fabia said. "Or the scrum you'll face will be me."

Sariel smiled at Fabia's firm tone and adjusted the packages under his arm. As he was about to knock on the door, he heard Sayblee's voice and Miranda's laughter. He thought about seeping into both their minds, but didn't, liking this woman-talk, the girl sounds he was never privy to as a child and still found mysterious.

"Oh, he's hot," Sayblee said, her voice clear through the door. "I could have told you that. When we were at school—"

"School? You went to school with Sariel?"

"A lot of us did. We've known each other for ages," Sayblee said. "But anyway, he was the guy all the girls wanted. Except he was shy."

"Shy?"

There was a pause, some laughter, a whisper, the sound of the creaking bedsprings.

"Oh, my. Well, maybe he's changed," Sayblee said. "But Felix. Now there was one confident boy."

"He's single," Miranda said. "An absolute doll. Lives in Hilo. You could do a lot worse."

"Too much of a flirt. A real ladies' man. I could tell you a few stories I've heard about Felix. I wouldn't go near him with a ten-foot pole," Sayblee said, and then there was a gasp and some loud giggles. Sariel shook his head and knocked on the door, opened it, and looked in.

Miranda turned toward him, her eyes liquid with laughter and surprise, and he almost dropped all of his packages and bags, her face was so open to him. Without even meaning to, he was in her thoughts and body, feeling her heart rate increase, seeing the words in her mind. *Finally! You're back. Where in the hell were you?*

Sayblee sat up off the bed and kissed Miranda on the forehead. "I'll come by and see you tomorrow before I leave." She walked past Sariel, thinking, *You're one lucky guy. Don't screw it up this time,* and left, closing the door behind her.

Sariel stood in front of the bed, watching Miranda, feeling her creep into his thoughts. *Are you going to stand there all night? Don't you want to check up on your patient? Give her a physical?*

He put down his things on the bureau and walked over to the bed, taking up Sayblee's warmed place. Miranda leaned into him, her head on his chest.

"Where did you go?" she asked.

"There was a sale at Nordstrom I couldn't miss," he said. "Lingerie."

Miranda looked up at him, her eyes so blue, her face pale, her freckles a swirl of stars. "No, really."

Lying down next to her, he pulled her tight. "I needed some things from home. And I knew you did, too. I don't want you to travel for a day or two. I also checked your messages."

Miranda pulled free and sat up. "My God! I should have called home hours ago. I bet they all think—"

"They do," Sariel said, pulling her back, wrapping his arms around her. "Kidnapped, murdered, trussed, and tossed into the bay. The prime suspect was Jack. They've had the police out in force, detectives, the works."

She gasped and then laughed. "Don't kid. He'll think I did it all to show him up at the Holitzer ceremony."

Sariel kissed her head. "For the first couple of days, Dan called every half hour. He even picked up some of your dry cleaning and watered your plants. Your machine was lit up like Times Square. So I called Viv, told them we were in London, a quick getaway. I think she believed me. Did you tell her about me? I mean, the magic?"

"When I thought you were a dream, she went all Jungian on me. You were my repressed anima," Miranda said. "But I should call."

"Later."

He bent his face to her hair, breathing in her clean

smell, the shampoo and soap and lavender lotion Saybleee had brought her. She kissed his chin, moving her lips slowly until she pressed her mouth hard and warm on the dent at the bottom of his neck.

"Suprasternal notch," she whispered.

"What?" He closed his eyes, letting her warmth flow into him.

"Here." She licked him, her tongue running along his collarbone. "I learned the name of it from a movie. A very romantic movie."

Sariel felt himself grow hard, wanting that warm tongue everywhere on his skin. He needed to take them both back to the memories Adalbert had returned two days ago. That first time! The way she'd opened herself to him, even though she thought she was delusional. He wanted her taste, her smell, the way he felt inside her.

"It was amazing," she said, her mouth on his shoulder. "I still thought you were a fantasy."

Sariel pulled himself over her, kissing her mouth, pushing away the blankets. He found his way under her nightgown and ran his hand along her side, curving over her hip, dipping along her waist, moving up to her breasts.

"You seem all better. How do you feel?" he asked her.

"How *do* I feel?" she said, sitting up and pulling off her nightgown. He swallowed, not wanting to ever stop seeing her body, her smooth, pale flesh. She'd lost weight in the past week, and the rub of her ribs under her skin made him want to kiss her just under her breasts, tracing his lips down the flight of her bones.

Miranda reached out a hand and tugged on his shirt. "Well?"

Sariel stood up, took off his clothes, watching her watch him, seeing her eyes rest on his erection. He looked down and shuffled off his jeans, imagining that even her glance could make him come.

"You're not getting off that easy," she said, lifting the blankets as he got into the bed and pressing him to her. "I need to feel you inside me."

He took her face in his palms, kissed her lips lightly, and then harder, wanting to taste everything he remembered. She opened up to him, her tongue on his, her hands in his hair, behind his neck, running along the muscles in his back. Slipping his hands under her, he raised her hips to him and slid inside her, gasping at how warm and wet she was.

Oh, my God, he thought, leaning down to her neck, biting her lightly.

Not God, she thought, *us. Us, us, us.*

They moved together, long, slow movements, and Sariel felt their minds meet in the same warm way their bodies were.

Yes, she thought. *Always.*

Yes, Sariel agreed. *And now. And later.*

Then their thoughts became images, skin and heat and fire and breath. Slick wetness, sound, blood, bone. He felt her muscles underneath her skin, her legs wrapped around his body, her breath in his ear.

Miranda pulled his lips to hers, kissing him hard, and then took his shoulders in her hands and turned him, pushing him to the mattress, keeping him inside her as they rolled. She brought his hands to her breasts and closed her eyes, riding him.

Sariel didn't close his eyes. He watched as her breathing changed, her face grew slack, her mouth opened slightly. He watched, feeling himself swell and pulse, all of him wanting to be inside her. He watched until he couldn't watch any more, closing his eyes until there was nothing but her tight flesh around him contracting, his own release inside her, their cries in the dark room.

"The woman in the white was my mother," she said later, the house silent around them, nothing but the soft *shif shif* of blankets and their own breaths in the darkness. "Her name was Laelia Barton."

For a moment, Sariel couldn't breathe, only feeling the memory that had floated in his head the past weeks, the small voice in the tiny warm space, a memory that came from the time he knew Laelia Barton.

"Laelia? My father's friend?" Sariel turned to her, his body humming with memory. "I knew her."

Miranda nodded, her eyes full. "She knew you, too. She told me to follow you. To go to you, as if she trusted you. As if she'd been waiting for you to find me."

She pressed her face on his chest, absently running her fingers through the hair on his chest, circling a nipple, and then letting her hand rest on his tight, firm stomach.

"After I gave Quain all the messages, I was twirling in the white, and she came to me. I didn't remember who she was, even though some of the memories I'd passed to Quain were hers," she said. "And then today, I realized I'd known her before that time in the light. Recognized her body. Knew her from the memories in my head."

Sariel breathed in, watching the ceiling. He knew Laelia's touch, the way she'd passed a bubble of memory to him when he was only four years old, a memory that didn't open until he was sixteen and could understand what had happened to his father.

"What do you remember about her?" Miranda asked, pushing herself up.

Stroking her hair, he nodded. "Now I can see how much you look like her. In a weird way, when I first saw you fall into the bar, I thought of her. Connected you two together. The face. The hair."

"But you were so little." Miranda stared down at him.

Sariel pulled her back down to his body, wrapping his arm around her shoulder. "Just before my father died, she came to the house. After that visit, I only saw her once more, at my father's funeral. I can still see her sitting in this big green chair we used to have, laughing. I didn't know about my gifts then or much about magic except for what my parents had taught me. My life was playing with my brothers outside, doing little tiny bits of magic with toy soldiers, making them move on their own. Creating little funnel clouds in the dust and pretending they were tornadoes the soldiers had to survive. That kind of thing. But when she came to visit that time, I felt something when I saw Laelia. As I walked up to her, I heard her voice and then her thoughts and I heard something else. A beating from inside her. A small river of thoughts coming from a warm, wet, dark place. Something like, *Life. Life. Move. Warm.*"

Closing his eyes, he let his memory seep into Miranda's mind, brought her to the living room, let her see Laelia's surprised face as she felt Sariel find what she had hidden. There was Laelia's hand on his head, her quick thought, *It's my secret. Please don't tell.* The way she turned back to Zosime and Hadrian as if nothing were amiss. And because Sariel had been four, nothing was amiss, Laelia's secret disappeared into the next moment of play and food and rough-and-tumble with Rufus and Felix.

Miranda gasped, holding him close. "You knew me? You heard me?"

Sariel nodded because he could barely speak, knowing now what he had felt before, that Miranda's and his story was older than two weeks—that it had begun long before. He couldn't believe how connected he and Miranda were even before the night she fell into the meeting. It was as if what the ancients said was true: There are no accidents. No coincidences.

At the bar that night, when he'd heard Miranda's thoughts before she had fallen through the door and onto the floor, he'd recognized her. Known her. Remembered the way she wanted to live even when she was too tiny to even be noticed.

"I didn't really know that I did, but I remembered you," he said, his body alive again with nerves and warmth, his hands moving on her body. "That first night, it was like I was searching for a clue, an answer for why you seemed so familiar. Otherwise, I don't think I would have been so . . ."

Miranda lifted her head, smiling even though there were tears on her cheeks. "Fresh? I felt you rubbing my leg, you dog."

"And I remember you liking it," Sariel said. He pulled her to him, taking her face in his hands, looking at her.

"We're connected, Miranda. Our stories are connected." He brought her to him, kissing her forehead, her cheeks, her nose, her lips, her chin. Then she kissed him back, lying down on him, her hand reaching for him, bringing him into her body.

"Now we're connected even more," she said, laughing for a moment, stopping as the laugh turned to breath and feeling as she moved on top of him.

Sariel watched her, her wild red hair, the curls falling around her shoulders, her breasts swaying over him. And again, like before, he could hear her thoughts. *Life. Life. Move. Warm.*

When Sariel woke up in the morning, he felt for Miranda, but she wasn't in bed. He sat up, alert and almost panicked. Still partly asleep, his thoughts flew to Quain and Kallisto, even though Kallisto was now imprisoned and Quain had vanished. In a partial panic, he imagined that they'd taken her again. He'd never be able to find her this time.

He sat up, rubbing his face with his hands, ready to tear the blankets off himself and search for her, but there she was, sitting in the stuffed chair by the fireplace dressed in the nightgown she'd thrown off last night, looking through the box he'd brought back from her apartment.

Hearing his movements, she looked at him, her face wet. She held up a photograph, gently shaking it. "He saved this for me."

Sariel got out of bed and put on his jeans, walking over to her and sitting down on the armrest. Miranda handed him the photo, and he held it carefully. There was Laelia just as Sariel remembered her, her hair the same cranberry as Miranda's, her eyes as blue, but darker, less air and more ocean. Laelia was holding a man around the neck, the man Sariel had first seen in the photograph in Miranda's bedroom. Steve. Miranda's father.

Letting his hand slide onto the image and then into it, Sariel could still pick up the feelings: Laelia's great love and total fear; Steve's desire and lust and affection and guilt. His thoughts about his family back home, his split, his feelings of responsibility, his amazement that someone as lovely as Laelia would want him. But at that moment, at the tiny sliver of time that—yes, his father had taken the photo—Hadrian had seen through the camera's lense, they were happy. In love. A couple completely in love.

"They loved each other very much," Sariel said, handing the photograph back to Miranda, who took it, staring a moment longer at her parents' faces before carefully moving her hands through the box. She pulled out another piece of paper, read it, and then shook her head, sighing, and handed it to Sariel. He took it and read the poem.

When I think of you, tiny and curled in water,
It's hard to imagine that you will come to land
one day, breathe air, look at me with human eyes.
So I'll have to name you, give you permission to change
from sea creature to mammal, name you for the world.
When you rest, bloody and stark on my stomach, I'll name
you Mirabelle, give you the name that tells you what you must
do, always. Look at Beauty.

Miranda was crying, her face in her hands. Sariel put the poem on the table and got down on his knees, moving the box from her lap and taking her hands away from her face so he could see her eyes.

Miranda shook her head, tears hitting his hands and face. "She couldn't."

"What, love? What, my Mirabelle? What couldn't she do?"

"She couldn't look at beauty. She saw only the pain," Miranda said, her voice filled with sorrow.

Sariel thought to argue, to tell her that Laelia saw the beauty in her daughter's eyes, in Steve's occasional visits, in Hadrian's friendship, in magic. But Miranda was right. At the end, Laelia had turned from the light, stayed in the same dark swirl of darkness Sariel had run around as a rat, sniffing the wall, finding only dust.

He bent his head to her thighs, kissing the exposed flesh, feeling her pulse under his lips. Looking up, he nodded. "Sometimes darkness is comfortable. Easier.

After Kallisto left, I could have stayed there. I almost did. But I had my brothers and mother. And now I have you. Laelia turned away from everyone who could have helped her. Her despair took over her life. It wasn't about you or how much you were worth. It was how much she imagined she didn't matter."

Bending down over him, hugging his neck, her hands on his back, Miranda cried. She was shivering, so he put his arms under hers, began to stand, and picked her up, carrying her to the bed. He put her on the mattress, lay down with her, and covered them up, holding her tightly until she stopped crying and her shivering stopped.

Finally, she exhaled and kissed his forehead. "I feel like I had that saved up for a long time."

"Probably," Sariel said, "since you felt her absence. You had her for three months. She was your whole world, and then she was gone."

Miranda leaned up on an elbow and wiped her eyes. Then she looked at him. "I might have to cry a lot for a while. Are you prepared?"

Laughing, Sariel reached over to the nightstand and picked up the box of tissues, placing them in front of her. "Like a Boy Scout."

She sat up and blew her nose. They were quiet for a while, listening to finches *chet-chet-chet* outside the window. He slid his hand up and down her leg, memorizing the landscape of ankle, shin, knee, thigh. Slowly, she smoothed his hair, her fingernails zigging lightly over his scalp.

"What did Adalbert mean?" she said finally.

"Hmm?" he murmured, pressing a shot of heat into a sore spot he found under her knee. "About what?"

"About us. Choosing each other over death."

At her words, Sariel was back again at the wall, feeling his rat body scrabbling around and around and then turning to face the light, running toward it, changing as he went, his only thought saving Miranda.

He sat up, pulling her to his side. "Just as Quain took you, he slammed me with an *être tombé* curse. It's like being in, well, limbo. Not dead, not alive. But I couldn't be dead. I knew I had to find you, so I managed to pull myself out of it. It's not something I want to try again."

She put a hand on his chest, pressing her fingers on his skin like a starfish. "And the light I was in? With Laelia?"

"That wasn't a curse," Sariel said. "You'd been hit with two *dérangement du matière* spells and then pushed all your energy into Quain. You were—"

"Dying?" she asked, her voice low.

He nodded slightly, trying not to relive his feelings when he'd found her on the floor of Adalbert's house, so still, so pale, her breath the slightest of movements. As he'd bent over her, trying to assess her injuries, he'd felt insane, not caring about anything but filling her body with quick, hot energy, needing her back, alive, with him. It wasn't until Miranda was conscious and in his arms that he realized he hadn't heard a thing Felix or Rufus had said. He hadn't noticed Adalbert, Zosime, and the rest of the group standing around him, sending out all their energy to help bring her back.

"Laelia told me to listen to you. To go back to you. To choose as she hadn't," Miranda said.

Sariel couldn't speak. If he'd come a moment later, if Quain hadn't disappeared, Sariel might have been too late. He'd almost lost her before even having the chance to know her completely.

"Laelia chose life," he said, catching his breath. "She gave you what she couldn't give herself."

Again, they were silent. The house was waking, sounds of laughter and the clanking of pots whirling up the stairs. Sariel heard his mother's voice, a light tease directed toward one of his brothers.

"Well," Miranda said. "Today is the day I get to really talk to your mother about your childhood. Hopefully, there will be a lot of embarrassing photos to show me. Maybe you wearing her high heels and a wig or something? And she can tell me about all your boyhood crushes. She can just funnel me a load of memories that I can savor for years to come."

Sariel pulled her down on the bed, leaning over her. "You play your cards right, missy. Soon enough, we'll be at Viv's house. I know your sister could give me an earful."

He kissed her to keep her from saying anything else, her smile of protest under his mouth. But then she was kissing him back, her arms around his neck. He slid his hands under her nightgown, her nipples hard under his fingertips.

"If you touch me the way you did the night you healed my ankle," she said in his ear, "I'll tell you anything you want."

Sariel remembered her moan in the air that night, the way she'd sat bolt upright, assuring him she was fine, just fine, her face flushed. Smiling, he took off her nightgown, and his own jeans, and then slid to her feet, holding both in his hands.

"You mean like this?" He pushed energy through his palms and fingers into her skin, finding her veins, slowly stroking upward. They were connected now in their minds, and he could sense her growing excitement, feel the way his energy already pulsed at her thighs.

"Yes. Yes," she said. She threw her arms out beside her, breathing hard. "Please don't stop this time."

Sariel sent more energy through his hands, slowly gliding up her shins, her soft skin radiant to the touch.

He stopped moving, feeling his energy lapping just far enough away from her center.

"Oh, God, Sariel," she said, breathless. "You're killing me."

She moved a hand to his, urging him upward. So he focused his energy and moved on, almost to her knee.

Miranda began to pant, her back arching at the energy inside her, and Sariel closed his eyes, thought of nothing else but heat and motion and Miranda, sending up a streak of light directly inside her.

Her hands dropped away from his, and he couldn't hear her thoughts as much as he could feel her body, a strong shimmer of nerves and blood and energy radiating from her center in wave upon wave, expanding into her body, rushing underneath him as he lay on top of her legs.

"Oh," she whispered, her eyes closed, her body limp. "Sariel."

He kept climbing, kissing her on his way, up, pressing his mouth on her wetness, parting her legs with his knee as he lowered himself on top of her, slipping inside her, holding her tight and rocking into her, this woman he loved.

At breakfast, Sariel sat next to Miranda and across from Fabia at Adalbert's table. Zosime helped serve up eggs, toast, and ham, while Adalbert fussed at the hob over his oatmeal again. Baris, Lutalo, and Mazi—healed from exhaustion and minor injuries—had departed the day before to meet with the Council and form another plan. Sayblee had just left, kissing Miranda on the cheek and promising to see her soon. From the corner of her eye, Miranda noticed Felix following Sayblee with his eyes, blushing when he saw Miranda's smile.

As soon as she disappeared into matter, Sariel put an

arm around Miranda. "She means that literally. Sayblee has a habit of just appearing when you least expect her."

His blush almost gone, Felix said, "Yeah, like that time in the boys' bathroom. She got a great loo—"

"Exactly my point," Sariel said, shooting Felix a look and a sharp, one-word thought. "But I don't think I was the Valasay brother she was really looking for."

"Really?" Fabia said, smiling. "Do tell."

"Sayblee says—" Miranda began.

"Adalbert," Felix interrupted, fiddling with his napkin and looking at Adalbert hovering over the steaming pot. "I think he's a bit crazy about oats," he whispered. "Wonder what spell he's invented for them now."

"I'll have you know," Adalbert said, "that it's a secret I'll never share with you!"

They laughed, and then Rufus sat down next to Fabia, squeezing her hard and kissing her on the cheek.

"So you two will be off tomorrow," Rufus said. "Can't Fabia and I tempt you to Edinburgh for a day or two? With Quain on the run, we'll have some time off."

"I would love to," Miranda said. "I've never been to Scotland, and I have a secret addiction to reading romance novels at night about magic Highland men. But even though I've talked with my mother, I know she still thinks I've been kidnapped. It was a miracle that my family called off the search."

Felix nodded. "You'll just have to claim you were swept off your feet by my brother here, and you forgot about everything else. That explanation just might work if he weren't so ugly."

"Felix," Zosime said. "I'm going to have to send you to your room."

Zosime put down the platters of food in front of them. "I tell you, Miranda, they haven't changed. They still seem like they're ten, eight, and six, no matter what magic they can do."

Everyone began to eat, but Sariel found himself unable to lift his hand or even do more than stare at Miranda as she spooned eggs onto her plate and laughed at something Rufus said. How had this happened? How had he gone from being alone and lonely and angry to sitting with his entire family at this safe table at Adalbert's house? How had he managed to forget about Kallisto and her betrayal? Why did he feel so full in his body, so content? Nothing was bothering him, and it was as if nothing ever would. Not even Felix's teasing. Not even Brennus's dictatorial commands. Not even Quain.

Sariel wanted nothing more than to sit here forever, listening to the words and laughter, feeling nothing but the slim, strong weight of Miranda's leg against his. If he never went out searching for a *sorcier* gone bad again he wouldn't care. How had this come to be?

Amid the clatter of plate noise and the whistle of the teakettle on the range, he felt Zosime thinking to him.

Don't ask how, she thought to him. *Just be.*

She smiled and then asked Adalbert the secret to his delicious oatmeal.

"If you think you're going to get something better than this at my house," Miranda said, indicating Zosime's fluffy scrambled eggs, "think again. I'm a poet, not a chef. Eat up now."

Sariel turned to her, lifting a finger to her cheek, all of his feeling just on his tongue, but he couldn't find the words to express them, no sentence or phrase big enough to hold them all.

He nodded and slowly turned to his plate, feeling his heart fill up his entire body, his love for Miranda and his family taking him over.

"Okay," he said. "I'll eat. But I'm already full. Completely."

Chapter Eighteen

Late in the afternoon on the following day, Miranda and Sariel packed up their things, taking little breaks to kiss and touch and then mess up the bed Miranda kept making.

"Okay, that's three times," she said, adjusting the comforter. "I can barely change my sheets once a week."

She frowned at him, but then smiled, seeing his worry that she was really upset. "Just teach me those tricks you do. Like the quick change routine you did the first night? A robe and then no robe? Can you do it with sheets?"

Sariel put down his bag and walked to her, hugging her tightly. "Housecleaning will be a breeze," he said. "More time for love."

Leaning on his chest and breathing in the clean cotton of his shirt, Miranda wished they could stay at Adalbert's. It would be so much easier than going home and having to face June and Viv. And Dan. In a way, fighting Quain had been nothing compared to the sad, confused look that would shrink June's face when Miranda brought up Laelia. But Miranda knew she had no choice. In the two brief phone calls she'd had with June since recovering, Miranda knew she had to go home and face them all, with everyone still convinced that something terrible had happened to her. And the story that Miranda was so glad to have now, the story of her life and her connection with the *Croyant* world, was a story that pained June, reminded her of years of troubles in her marriage. Talking about it—if they ever managed to—wouldn't be easy.

"I'll be there." Sariel kissed her forehead.

"I know," Miranda said. "It's just that my mother and I have never really talked. It was like she needed an interpreter to understand me, going through either my dad or Viv. Now I'll have to do it by myself."

Sariel squeezed with his arms, and then pushed her away, looking into her eyes. "It'll be okay."

She smiled, rubbing her forehead. "So you can see into the future, too?"

"No, I just know you. You're brave and strong and can handle anything. I saw you with Kallisto and Quain. And even with *my* mother!"

"What? You mean her assault with the thirty years of photo albums? That was nothing! Bring it on," Miranda said, turning back to her bag.

"No, it was her memory of my musical that was the worst torture, I'm sure." Sariel shook his head. "She's never shown that to anyone else."

"You were an adorable Don Quixote," she said. "The best production I ever saw, replete with a working windmill that turned into an actual fire-breathing dragon."

He smiled and began to pack up his tray of healing herbs. Miranda watched him, his hair tied behind his neck, his arms strong, his body perfect in his jeans. How had this happened? Not the magic and the fight that saved creation but Sariel himself, here with her in this room?

Lucky, I guess, he thought, still busy with the tray.

Very, she thought back.

She sighed and then picked up her nightgown, feeling the flannel between her hands, the same kind of nightgown Viv wore that day she was so upset, weeping about the big secret. If Viv only knew how big the secret was.

Are you going to tell her?

Miranda looked at him. "I can?"

Sariel zipped the tray into a case and turned to her. "Of course. *Moyenne* all over the world know about us, but we make sure they are sympathetic. And we always have the option of taking their memories."

"What about the things Brennus said to you about me?" Miranda asked.

"That," Sariel said as he picked up another bag and put it in the middle of the room, "was about war. About fear. About pulling in the troops. I don't think Quain is likely to convert Viv to his side."

Miranda tied her bag and set it down next to Sariel's. "What if she freaks out? Or thinks I'm crazy? Or runs around the neighborhood shouting, 'My sister is magic!'?"

"Love," Sariel said, bringing his hands to her face. "Sweetheart. We'll take their memories and become an ordinary couple. We'll show up in a car on Sunday afternoons for family get-togethers. We'll board airplanes and travel with them on family vacations. I'll pretend to get a normal job and wear a suit when Viv and Seamus come into the city to meet us for dinner and a play. If we're sick, we'll talk about going to the hospital. Either way, we'll be together in a way your family can understand."

Miranda stared at him, looking up into his eyes, which in the light of the afternoon room were almost bronze. She felt her heart pounding in her chest, imagining what would have happened if the three men hadn't chased her up the street that night. She would have never found Sariel at all.

"You did find me, and I'm not going anywhere except home," he said, bringing his lips to her forehead. "Let's finish up and get out of here before my mom comes in with memories of my potty-training experiences."

Miranda nodded, watching Sariel as he folded up an extra blanket. They would go home, together, and she would go to Viv's first, by herself, and talk with her sister.

Miranda still wasn't perfect at moving through matter, but this time, she didn't end up in a strange basement with a dangerous woman. Instead, she appeared in Viv's bedroom, standing by the dresser, watching as Viv leaned over the bed, changing baby Colin's diaper.

Miranda had intended to appear in the bathroom because she didn't want to scare Viv, but somehow she couldn't wangle the door and, sighing, she let herself fall out of matter, knowing she would have to quiet Viv immediately.

But instead, Viv looked up, blinked, and stood straight, her hands on her hips. Viv looked much better since the last time Miranda saw her, her blonde hair washed and styled, her face not full of despair. In fact, even with Miranda standing suddenly in front of her, Viv didn't seem surprised or panicked. She didn't say anything, staring at Miranda, hard, her anger a flower that burst into bloom in her mind.

That's great, Viv thought. *Because you can't see her, you're imagining her here. Stop it. Okay, vision, go away. God, what an idiot. Because you miss her so much, you're turning into her, imagining people coming and going. Because you think you ruined your relationship, you're inventing this out of thin air.*

"It's really me," Miranda said quietly. "I'm not a vision."

Viv brought her hand to her mouth, her face pale, her dark eyes wide. "How? Miranda? How did you get here?"

So many responses ran through Miranda's mind, and because she was with Viv and not June and Seamus and Dan, she said what was true. "I came . . . through matter. It was magic."

Colin kicked his legs on the bed, but Viv didn't look down at him, her face huge with the confusion that Miranda could read in her mind. Instead, she laid a gentle palm on Colin's chest, blinking at Miranda.

"Matter? Magic?" Viv said quietly.

Miranda waved an arm. "Air. But Viv, don't think about it now."

She walked toward her sister and put an arm on Viv's shoulder. "It's me. I'm back."

For a second, Viv held her breath, and then she reached up, exhaling, and put her arms around Miranda's neck. "Oh, my God! I can't believe it. It is you."

"It is. I'm here."

Viv clung more tightly, squeezing Miranda hard. "What happened? When that guy called, I was sure he'd kidnapped you. I didn't think I'd ever see you again. And it was because of what I told you. About the adoption. It was all my fault."

In Miranda's arms, Viv began to cry. "I should have never told you. I was selfish and stupid, and I'm so sorry. I hurt you too much. I thought you ran away. I thought maybe you were going to do something worse. Something . . ."

Closing her eyes, Miranda pressed Viv against her, listening to her sister's sorrow, the words in her mind: *Careless, bossy, out of control, mean. Baby sister. Love. Love.*

"It's okay, Viv. I'm fine." Miranda pushed Viv back, looking into her sister's watery eyes. "I'm way better than fine."

Together, they sat on the bed, and Miranda picked up Colin, holding him in her arms, smiling into his brand new face. "That's a boy," she said, jiggling him a bit. "That's my baby."

Viv wiped her eyes. "Were you really in London?"

Miranda nodded. "Yeah. And then in Kent."

"With that guy."

"Sariel." Miranda said his name, a flush of energy electric in her body. In the corner of her thoughts, she could feel him, could see him smiling as he looked out the window of his house. *Can I come over yet?* he thought.

Soon, she thought back. *In a bit.*

Hurry up, he thought. *I miss you.*

"Is he—is he what you said that day after your 'dream'? Magic and all? Fighting evildoers?" Viv wiped a milky swirl of drool off Colin's chin. "Oh, how can I even be asking that? That would be crazy, right?"

"It would be crazy but also true," Miranda said.

Viv shrugged. "I should have known from the poems on your computer."

Miranda turned to Viv. "You read them?"

"Well, the police told me to read through all your files," Viv said. "Everything was evidence. We were desperate to find out where you were. We needed to know what happened."

"Well, those poems were just evidence that I haven't been able to write a thing lately." Miranda laughed, gently rocking Colin.

"Evidence that you were in love. I think your next book should be called *Magic Man* or *Learning to Fly.*"

"Snoop," Miranda said. Colin pursed his baby rosebud mouth, then squeezed tight, his face turning red. "He's either having a little movement in there or hungry."

Viv sighed, taking the baby from Miranda. "He's hungry. I was changing his diaper in between, well, breasts. Dan's out in the living room, so I came in here to nurse."

Miranda shook her head and laughed. "Dan will be with me until the end of time. I can't seem to escape him."

Viv raised an eyebrow. "I think you finally have." She leaned against the headboard, lifted her shirt, and put Colin to her breast. "He's found another love."

Confused, Miranda crossed her arms. "He what?"

"During all the nightmare of your 'kidnapping,' he was here at the house every day. He started driving me crazy with his flyers and the 'Find Miranda' group, so I pawned him off on Robin. The next thing I knew, they were, well, together."

"Dan and Robin?" Miranda felt her mouth open.

You're jealous, Sariel thought. *Don't even try to deny it.*

Don't say that, or I'll slam down the metal door, dude, Miranda thought. *I'm relieved.*

"What are you thinking?" Viv said. "You aren't upset, are you? I thought you'd be happy."

"Oh, I am. Believe me. Now Dan and I can just talk about my books."

"Which," Viv said, "are selling like hotcakes. You even got on the front page of *The San Francisco Chronicle.* Nothing like an abduction to rev up sales."

Miranda and Viv laughed, and they settled into silence, nothing but the sound of Colin's tiny sucking noises in the room.

Finally, Viv sighed. "You are what? Magic? I knew

something—I mean, ever since that time you flew in the backyard. That was so amazing. Mom convinced me we both had sunstroke."

"You remember that?" Miranda asked.

"Of course I remember," Viv said, lightly running her finger over the soft fuzz on Colin's head. "It's not something you forget, your sister flying around the backyard. I'll never forget your face, how you said, 'Vivie, look at me!' I actually tried to do it myself a few times, but I discovered that I couldn't fly. I'm just a good jumper. Came in handy for cheerleading later."

"I'm more of a hoverer than a flyer."

Viv turned to Miranda and giggled. "Like hovering is normal? This is so wild."

"I know." Miranda sighed, leaning into Viv's shoulder.

"So why, Miranda? How?"

"I found out about my birth mother. She was one of Sariel's people," Miranda said slowly, wondering how much she could tell Viv.

Viv looked down at Colin, who seemed to be slowing, his eyes fluttering with sleep. Her mind rang with the word *people.* "She wasn't Dad's reason for business trips, was she?"

Surprised, Miranda looked over at Viv. "How did you know?"

Viv gently removed Colin from her breast and put him on her shoulder, patting his smooth baby back. "You know when I said I hadn't looked in the box?"

Miranda nodded.

"I kind of lied. I mean, I didn't really look through it, but as I was putting it away into the trunk, a photograph fell out. Dad and a woman. A woman who looked just like you."

"Her name was Laelia Barton," Miranda said. "She killed herself."

Viv pulled in a quick intake of air, and though she didn't start to cry, Miranda could feel the tears in her thoughts. "Randa," she said, her voice full of soft sadness. "That's terrible."

"Dad brought me home. There weren't any adoption papers in the box because he didn't need any. I was his."

"You're ours," Viv said. "I knew it."

Colin pushed out a tiny burp, and Viv brought him off her shoulder, stood up, and placed him in the bassinet by the bed, covering him with a blanket. Turning to Miranda, she breathed in.

"You know, I don't understand any of this, really, except that you love him. And that you're back. That's all that really matters to me," Viv said. "No more secrets. I promise I'll keep it to myself, but I don't want anything between us, not ever again. Tell me everything, even if you think I'll go mad at the very idea."

"There's still Mom," Miranda said. "I'm going to have to tell her something."

Viv smiled, putting a hand to her mouth to cover a laugh. "She's been out of her mind. After you called her from England, she went to her bed for a full day. She wants to talk with you about everything. Let her, Randa. Let her tell you her story. The way she knows it."

"Did she ever tell you anything?" Miranda stood up and walked to Viv, both of them looking down into the bassinet.

"I don't think she knows about the magic part, but she definitely knew about your mother," Viv said. "She'll be over later. You two can talk after dinner, after she's calmed down. Or if she calms down."

"Viv," Miranda said. "For now, don't tell anyone about me. The magic, okay? I don't really understand it yet, and I need to figure it out first. Then maybe you can tell Seamus."

Viv put her arm around Miranda. "Personally, I don't want to talk about it with anyone because I've always hated the idea of a nuthouse. So I won't tell, but you better find a better way to travel unless you want people to start asking questions."

Miranda pushed a loose strand of gold hair away from Viv's face. "I know. I'll go back home and arrive the regular way."

Meet me at my apartment, Miranda thought. *We need to drive.*

I'll beat you, Sariel thought, flashing into matter.

Moving away from Viv, Miranda said, "And you know what else?"

"What?" Viv said, her hands on her hips again, her smile wide.

Miranda lifted her arms, smiled, and began to lift off the floor.

"I still fly!" And with that, she rose higher in the room, looking down at Viv's amazed face, and then pushed into matter, hoping she'd beat Sariel to her apartment.

The most incredible piece of magic was that Miranda sat at Viv's large oak dining room table with Sariel. His leg was pressed against hers, but he was talking with Seamus about rhododendrons and azaleas, acid soil, and mulch. Another miracle was that Dan wasn't even looking at her, turned almost sideways to stare full-on at Robin, who was enrapt by his conversation about sales distribution and advertising.

And June, who had begun crying once Miranda walked in the door and had just finally stopped, was holding Hazel on her lap and smiling at Miranda. Aunt Bell sat next to her sister, patting June on the arm. Summer and Jordie played under the table with Legos, their laughs and giggles muffled by the long tablecloth and adult legs. Now and then, Miranda felt Summer touch her shin, as if reassuring herself that her aunt was really home.

How could this happen? Miranda wondered. *How could I be here in this house in this way with this man?*

Lucky, I guess, Sariel thought, not missing a beat in his conversation with Seamus.

Stop saying that! she thought, smiling.

You know it's true.

Luck had nothing to do with it, she thought back. *It was magic.*

Viv held Colin on her shoulder and leaned against Miranda so that Colin's light breath was in her ear.

"It's not magic," Viv whispered, unaware that she'd caught one of Miranda's thoughts. "But it's absolutely unbelievable."

Sariel put his hand on Miranda's thigh, squeezing lightly. She felt a poem burst open in her mind, but she didn't want to put it into language, put it in writing, needing the act of creating it to go on and on, nothing but the promise of perfect words on a clean page for the rest of her life.

The next two volumes in Jessica Inclán's trilogy are now available in trade paperback from Zebra Books.

REASON TO BELIEVE will be a Zebra mass-market release in July 2008.

BELIEVE IN ME will be a Zebra mass-market release in 2009.

Please turn the page for a preview.

REASON TO BELIEVE

Fabia opened her door, quickly running down the hall and stairs and then pushing out onto the street. The temperature had dropped even more than the report had predicted, Fabia's cheeks flushed from the slick slap of cold air. Rubbing her gloved hands together, she walked toward the man, slowing as she neared him.

"Hello," she said softly, blinking against the streetlight.

He stared at her—no, past her—his face expressionless. His face was smudged with dirt, a deep, dark red scratch running from temple to jaw, one eye blackened. Blood swelled the skin under his eye and hung in a painful purple moon over his cheek. As Fabia moved closer, she realized that his hair wasn't so much matted from the wet, dank air as from dried blood. There was a clear, perfect circle of reddish broken skin around his neck, and she noticed now that the dirt she'd seen under his nails this morning was actually blood.

Whatever had happened, he'd fought back. Whoever he'd fought with probably looked as bad as he did.

"Are you all right?"

The man turned to her, tried to look up, and then took a deep breath, his mouth trying to move. He was trembling, his arms tight against his body now, his black eyes filled with fog and sadness. Again, she tried to reach for his mind, but the iron wall was still there, planted solidly.

What do you think? Fabia asked Niall without even meaning to.

All that blood, Niall thought. *Maybe it's not his.* Moyenne *are messy murderers.*

He hardly looks capable of a right killing, Fabia thought.

True. He didn't do his level best, there. So he might be on the lam. Injured from the barbed wire he crawled under, Niall thought. *Just call the police.*

Fabia stared at the man, ignoring Niall for a moment. Maybe she couldn't read the man's mind, but there was something about him. Something kind even in his quiet, painful desperation.

Bloody bleeding heart, Niall thought. *But just be ready to escape. Be prepared to step into the gray, okay? Hop back to your flat.*

Yes, sir, Fabia thought, shaking her head. But Niall was right. It was easier to extend this kindness knowing that if the man grew strange or crazy or even dangerous, she could disappear in an instant, traveling through matter to the police station, where she could report the crime she'd just escaped. The *Moyenne* she worked with at the clinic were always amazed that Fabia would go to flophouses and tenements and dark alleys looking for clients. What she couldn't tell them was that she was protecting them by doing so, keeping them away from danger from which they might not be able to escape.

Fabia bent down, trying to attract his gaze. But he

wouldn't look at her, and she could feel the tension radiating from inside him.

"Hi, there," she said. "My name's Fabia Fair. I live at the flat just down a bit."

He didn't move his eyes, but he blinked, once, twice.

"Would you like to come with me?" Fabia said, crouching down farther and looking into the man's desperate, searching eyes. "How about a wee bit to eat?"

He licked his lips, breathing in, scanning the ground as if he'd dropped some change. *Not drunk,* Fabia thought. *Schizophrenic.*

Perfect, Niall thought. *Go from Cadeyrn to just another crazy. Get yourself into another fankle.*

Haver on, man! Would you mind affording me some space here? she thought back. *Go watch your bleeding telly.*

Fabia closed her mind to her brother and moved closer to the man. He was shaking, his knees hitting together. Again, he moved his mouth, but then shook his head, tears streaming from the corners of his eyes.

Fabia watched him, trying everything she knew to get inside his mind, but there was no opening, as if the block was put there on purpose. And not by the man, who clearly was in no shape to create or even maintain a block, even if he were *Croyant,* magic, like her. And there was something about him, even with his quaking gaze and his long, thin, dirty body. Fabia couldn't read his mind, but she could feel . . . kindness.

"All right," Fabia said. "That's it. Please, come with me."

She stood up straight and held out her hand. The man breathed in, looking at her hand and then her face, her hand, her face again, and then slowly, he lifted his dirty palm from his knee, studying his movements with surprise as if he'd never moved before. His fingers quivered, shook, and Fabia took them in her small gloved hand, feeling how cold he was even through the leather and wool.

Shit, she thought to herself, hating how *Moyenne* treated their castaways, knowing that in her world, the world of *Les Croyants des Trois,* this man would have food and a bath and a bed, no matter what was wrong with him. Adalbert Baird made sure of that, finding places for the damaged and weak. The only people who escaped his care were the ones who disdained it. Like Caderyn Macara. Like Quain Dalzeil. *And what will happen if Quain wins?* she thought.

We'll end up like this poor sod, Niall thought.

Shut it, thought Fabia, and clutched the man's hand more tightly.

"Come on," she said. "Don't be scared."

But the man was scared. More than scared. She felt his fear in the energy coming off his body, in the sizzling whites of his distracted eyes, in his stiff, hesitant walk. Who had done this to him? What had happened?

"It's all right," Fabia said, her hand holding his as they walked slowly to the door of her building. "You'll be fine."

He turned to look at her, his black eyes so dark she couldn't see the irises. His forehead was creased with worry, his face gray with cold and hunger and fear. Despite the filth on his clothing, the blood on his head and body, and his clearly distressed mind, Fabia wanted to stop, pull him to her, and comfort him.

BELIEVE IN ME

An unbuttoned white linen shirt lay on the floor by the hallway. As she stared at it, she heard a soft giggle float under the bedroom door and then a smooth, seductive laugh followed it, the sound of which somehow reminded her of caramel.

Pig, she thought. *No, that's too harsh. Dog. Goat, maybe. No, a goat is too cute. Skunk then. Or just pig.*

Sayblee walked to the bookcase, picked up photo frames full of happy people she knew well, his brothers and sisters-in-law, his mother Zosime. She stared into their eyes, and soon she felt the impressions of their warm feelings for him as she held the images in her hands. Funny guy, she heard or, really, pulled into her mind, as she moved her fingers over the photos. *Why doesn't he settle down? So handsome. All he needs is a good woman. If he wasn't so adorable, I'd kill him. Can he ever be serious? What a charmer. Those eyes would do anyone in. That smile!*

Sayblee's shoulders dropped. She breathed in and took her hands away from his photos.

When she'd accepted this mission, she'd agreed to

work with him, and work with Felix Valasay she would, even if it killed her. But it was hard to deal with someone who could live like this, who probably did a seduction scene like this every night of the week in this so-called post. Who could he possibly find here, that would lead any member of *Les Croyant des Trois* to Quain Dalzeil, the *sorcier* who was determined to destroy the *Croyant* way of life? The *sorcier* who had managed in recent years to affect all of *Croyant* life—creating fear, enchanting the best and brightest, leaving people to live in fear. Sure, Felix managed to come to the aid of people needing him now and again. He'd been there with her just a year ago when a group of *Croyant* had fought Quain and Kallisto in the English countryside. But the Big Island? This house that smelled like tacky perfume and was filled with enough sexual energy to make the very floor vibrate?

Sayblee shook her head and turned toward the hallway. Why did Adalbert Baird, the Armiger of the *Croyant* Council, insist that Sayblee was the only *sorcière* who could go on this mission? So what that she had her particular skill of being able to burn anything she wanted: steel, concrete, quartz, titanium? But from what Adalbert had said, there would be no magic for a while as they blended in with the *Moyenne,* setting up the trap so slowly and ordinarily that they would attract no attention from Quain or his followers. Her special powers weren't needed at all, or at least until the very end of the mission. So why did she have to end up with this particular *sorcier?*

Another annoying giggle and then a lazy laugh slipped into the living room. The very air seemed to pulse with gardenia and hyacinth and rum. This was horrible! Intolerable. How was she supposed to interrupt that? She sat down on a beautifully carved wooden chair and sighed, staring at the rows and rows of hardback books, most of them probably uncracked since Felix graduated from the Bampton Academy. What to do? She'd never known how to engage Felix, to move smoothly into conversation with him. Since their days together at Bampton, she'd steered clear of him, even though Sayblee was very fond of his older brothers, Sariel and Rufus, boys who had turned into solid, reliable men. Married men. Committed men. Men!

But there was something about Felix that was just plain dangerous, and Sayblee had recognized that when she was twelve. She'd turned a corner one afternoon after a long class on levitation, and there stood Felix, smiling at her with that smooth, slightly crooked smile, his almost-green eyes full of a fire so unique that Sayblee didn't have a clue how to kindle it. Even then, his black hair was long, held back for classes with a leather string, strands always coming loose and falling in front of his face. Hair she'd wanted to touch, push away, tuck into place.

She'd barely managed to hold on to her textbooks and keep walking, ignoring his taunt of, "Baby, can I light your fire?"

Now, sixteen years later, Felix still had the ability to disarm her. The last time they'd been together had been at Adalbert's house at Rabley Heath, and she'd left one morning early to avoid an awkward good-bye. Her awkwardness. She hadn't wanted to see him smirk, listen to him tease her about her school pranks, rattle on about how she used to set the cafeteria cooks' hats on fire when meatloaf was on the menu. She hadn't wanted to look into his lovely eyes and see, well, so much satisfaction.

And this situation here? Well, it wasn't going to be easy to pull Felix away from Hilo and his little lifestyle. But Sayblee had no choice. What had Adalbert said to her just before she left? He'd stared at her with his kind eyes, his hand running through his long gray beard as he spoke.

"We have the chance, finally, to end this troublesome situation with Quain once and for all," he said. "I think you'd do just about anything to make that happen, Sayblee. Am I not right?" He'd looked at her from where he sat in his deep upholstered armchair. A fire crackled in the hearth. His dog, a Zeno Hungarian Kuvasz, dozed at his feet, the dog's quick breaths full of rabbit dreams. And Sayblee could see the image of her brother, Rasheed, flicker in Adalbert's mind. The Armiger was right. As always.

More than anything, Sayblee wanted to find Quain. They'd been so close to catching him last year. For a moment, he'd been right in front of her in the cavernous room of the Fortress Kendall as she fought with Felix and the rest, but, as always, he'd gotten away. Oh, how she'd wanted to push her fire at him, subdue him, flatten him to the floor. Sayblee wanted to lean over him and demand he tell her what happened to Rasheed.

She wanted the impossible, to have Quain croak out "Your brother's still alive." She wanted Quain to tell her that Rasheed hadn't left of his own free will, that he'd been enchanted, charmed, drugged, coerced. She wanted to strangle out of him the truth that Rasheed was good, that he'd never turn his back on *Croyant* life or his family. She wanted to have the perfect answer to give to her mother, Roya, so that she would burst into life again and forgive Sayblee for not saving Rasheed in the first place. She needed to obtain all the information she could from Quain, and then . . . and then. . .

Sayblee closed her eyes and sat back hard against the wooden chair, trying to ignore the further giggles that floated toward her. No. She wasn't doing this just for Rasheed and for her mother, who had never recovered from Rasheed's betrayal of all that the Safipour family believed in and his alliance with Quain. Sayblee was on the mission for all *Croyant,* and what she had to do was get Felix Valasay out of his bedroom, preferably dressed, hopefully alone, and she couldn't sit here one moment longer.

She stood up and in her mind she moved down the hallway, into the bedroom, and heard the noise of two people moving together—their bodies warm, their minds full of anticipation—could hear Felix whisper into the woman's ear, "You smell so good. I just can't breathe in enough of you."

Sayblee opened her mind and shot out a thought. *Yeah, she smells like your house. In about a minute, I myself will be smelling like a cheap drink from Chevy's.*

She heard his intake of air, his body moving away slightly from the woman's. Sayblee?

Yeah, it's me. I'm in your living room. I managed to figure out you had a special guest when I was in the air. You and I need to talk. It's Council business.

Right now? Couldn't you go hit the bars for a couple of hours and come back later? Maybe take a nice long night walk on the beach?

Sayblee checked her irritation, biting her lip before thinking tersely, *Adalbert sent me.*

She waited for a reply, but there was no thought, no sound but the rustle of bedclothes and then the soft murmur of the woman asking a question. Felix's low voice rumbled an answer. More rustling. Then there was silence. Sayblee sighed and turned her mind away from Felix and what was going on in the bedroom and sat down on the couch. She tried to get comfortable, crossing her legs, uncrossing them, smoothing the sleeves of her blouse, the fabric of her skirt on her thighs. She pushed her hair away from her face and then pulled it forward, finally sighing and tying it back with a band she pulled from her pocket.

She looked toward the bedroom door, leaned forward, sat back. Then she stood up, realizing she didn't want to be lower than Felix when he came into the room, giving him the advantage of looking down at her. She walked to the window, stared out at the ocean which was flat and strangely calm, the moon a pan of white on its surface.

"Could you have knocked?" Felix said, walking into the room shirtless and barely wearing the Levi's he was slowly buttoning up. "I could have arranged a later date with the fair maiden, Roxanne. You know I always say business and *then* pleasure." He paused as he spotted the shirt on the floor, bent down, and picked it up with a crooked finger, smiling to himself.

Sayblee breathed in, kept her mind closed tight because, *God!*— she couldn't let him know how she was seeing him at this very moment in the living room's soft light. Impossibly, he looked even better than he had the year before, his tall, lean body golden tan from all his important *Croyant* visits to the beach and the pool and hot tub. He must also have crucial *Moyenne* contacts at the gym—his shoulders, arms, and abs tight and firm, each muscle clear under the tight gold of his skin. Clearly, he worked out for hours every day. His black hair was lit gold at the ends by days on Hawaiian waves and fell down his back like a silk curtain. He smiled, watching her with his almost-green eyes, his expression full of good humor, even though she'd interrupted him in his pleasure. She swallowed and lifted her chin, her mind clamped so tight that she knew she'd have a throbbing migraine by morning.